ALISON WEIR is the top-selling female historian (and the fifth-bestselling historian overall) in the United Kingdom, and has sold over 3 million books worldwide. She has published eighteen history books, including her most recent non-fiction book, *Queens of the Conquest*, the first in her England's Medieval Queens quartet. Alison has also published several historical novels, including *Innocent Traitor* and *The Lady Elizabeth*.

Katheryn Howard: The Tainted Queen is Alison Weir's tenth published novel and the fifth in the Six Tudor Queens series about the wives of Henry VIII, which was launched in 2016 to great critical acclaim. All four previous books in the series were *Sunday Times* bestsellers.

Alison is a fellow of the Royal Society of Arts and an honorary life patron of Historic Royal Palaces.

Also by Alison Weir

The Six Tudor Queens series
Katherine of Aragon: The True Queen
Anne Boleyn: A King's Obsession
Jane Seymour: The Haunted Queen
Anna of Kleve: Queen of Secrets

Six Tudor Queens Digital Shorts
Writing a New Story
Arthur: Prince of the Roses
The Blackened Heart
The Tower is Full of Ghosts Today
The Chateau of Briis: A Lesson in Love
The Grandmother's Tale
The Unhappiest Lady in Christendom
The Curse of the Hungerfords
The King's Painter
The Princess of Scotland

Fiction
Innocent Traitor
The Lady Elizabeth
The Captive Queen
A Dangerous Inheritance
The Marriage Game

Quick Reads
Traitors of the Tower

Non-fiction
Britain's Royal Families: The Complete Genealogy
The Six Wives of Henry VIII
The Princes in the Tower
Lancaster and York: The Wars of the Roses
Children of England: The Heirs of King Henry VIII 1547–1558
Elizabeth the Queen
Eleanor of Aquitaine
Henry VIII: King and Court
Mary Queen of Scots and the Murder of Lord Darnley
Isabella: She-Wolf of France, Queen of England
Katherine Swynford: The Story of John of Gaunt and His Scandalous Duchess
The Lady in the Tower: The Fall of Anne Boleyn
Mary Boleyn: 'The Great and Infamous Whore'
Elizabeth of York: The First Tudor Queen
The Lost Tudor Princess
Queens of the Conquest

As co-author
The Ring and the Crown: A History of Royal Weddings, 1066–2011
A Tudor Christmas

ALISON WEIR

SIX TUDOR QUEENS

KATHERYN HOWARD
THE TAINTED QUEEN

REVIEW

First published in Great Britain in 2020
by HEADLINE REVIEW
An imprint of HEADLINE PUBLISHING GROUP

1

Cataloguing in Publication Data is available from the British Library

ISBN 978 1 4722 2777 5 (Hardback)
ISBN 978 1 4722 2778 2 (Trade paperback)

Typeset in Garamond MT by Avon DataSet Ltd, Bidford-on-Avon, Warwickshire

Printed and bound in Great Britain by Clays Ltd, Elcograf S.p.A.

HEADLINE PUBLISHING GROUP
An Hachette UK Company
Carmelite House
50 Victoria Embankment
London EC4Y 0DZ

www.headline.co.uk
www.hachette.co.uk

SIX TUDOR QUEENS

KATHERYN HOWARD
THE TAINTED QUEEN

1538

THE HOUSE OF TUDOR

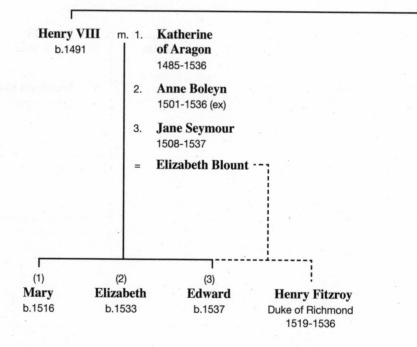

Henry VIII   m. 1.   **Katherine**
b.1491   **of Aragon**
                          1485-1536

              2.   **Anne Boleyn**
                   1501-1536 (ex)

              3.   **Jane Seymour**
                   1508-1537

              =   **Elizabeth Blount**

(1)   (2)   (3)
Mary   **Elizabeth**   **Edward**   **Henry Fitzroy**
b.1516   b.1533   b.1537   Duke of Richmond
                                                   1519-1536

Henry VII m. **Elizabeth of York**

Margaret m. 1. **James IV**
b.1489   King of Scots

2. **Archibald Douglas**
Earl of Angus

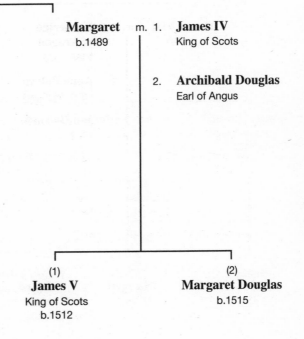

(1)
James V
King of Scots
b.1512

(2)
Margaret Douglas
b.1515

THE HOWARDS
AND THE TILNEYS

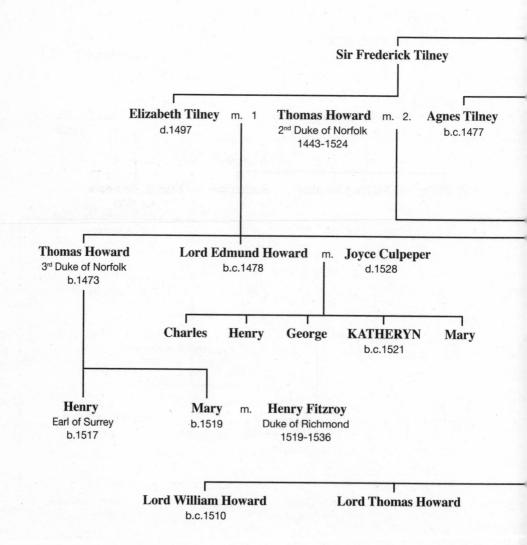

Sir Frederick Tilney

Elizabeth Tilney   m.   1   Thomas Howard   m.   2.   Agnes Tilney
d.1497   2ⁿᵈ Duke of Norfolk   b.c.1477
1443-1524

Thomas Howard   Lord Edmund Howard   m.   Joyce Culpeper
3ʳᵈ Duke of Norfolk   b.c.1478   d.1528
b.1473

Charles   Henry   George   KATHERYN   Mary
b.c.1521

Henry   Mary   m.   Henry Fitzroy
Earl of Surrey   b.1519   Duke of Richmond
b.1517   1519-1536

Lord William Howard   Lord Thomas Howard
b.c.1510

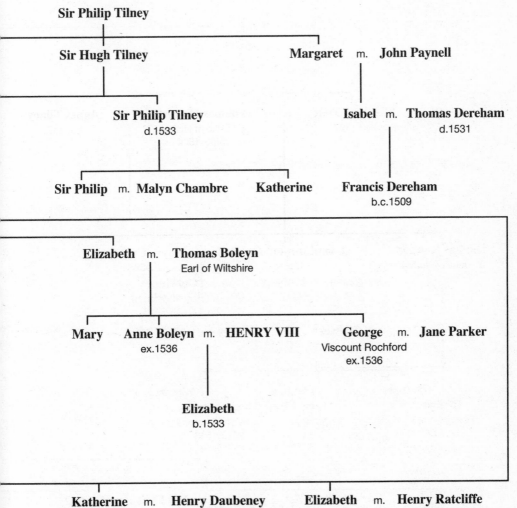

Sir Philip Tilney

Sir Hugh Tilney

Margaret m. John Paynell

Sir Philip Tilney
d.1533

Isabel m. Thomas Dereham
d.1531

Sir Philip m. Malyn Chambre   Katherine

Francis Dereham
b.c.1509

Elizabeth m. Thomas Boleyn
Earl of Wiltshire

Mary   Anne Boleyn m. HENRY VIII
ex.1536

George m. Jane Parker
Viscount Rochford
ex.1536

Elizabeth
b.1533

Katherine m. Henry Daubeney
Earl of Bridgewater

Elizabeth m. Henry Ratcliffe
Earl of Sussex

THE CULPEPERS AND THE LEIGHS

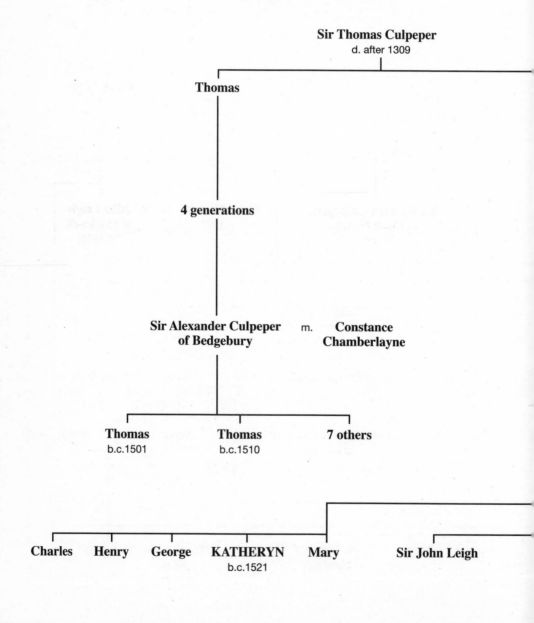

Sir Thomas Culpeper
d. after 1309

Thomas

4 generations

Sir Alexander Culpeper   m.   Constance
of Bedgebury   Chamberlayne

Thomas   Thomas   7 others
b.c.1501   b.c.1510

Charles   Henry   George   KATHERYN   Mary   Sir John Leigh
                              b.c.1521

Walter   **Ralph Leigh**

3 generations

Sir Richard Culpeper   m.   1.   **Isabel Worsley**   m.   2.   **John Leigh**
of Oxon Hoath   d.1527   **of Stockwell**
d.1484   d.1523

Thomas   **Margaret**   m.   **William Cotton**
1484-1492

Lord Edmund Howard   m.   2.   **Joyce**   m.   1.   **Ralph Leigh**
b.c.1478   c.1470-1528

Ralph   **Isabel**   m.   **Sir Edward**   **Joyce**   **Thomas**   m.   **Margaret**
        b.c.1495   **Baynton**   **Arundell**

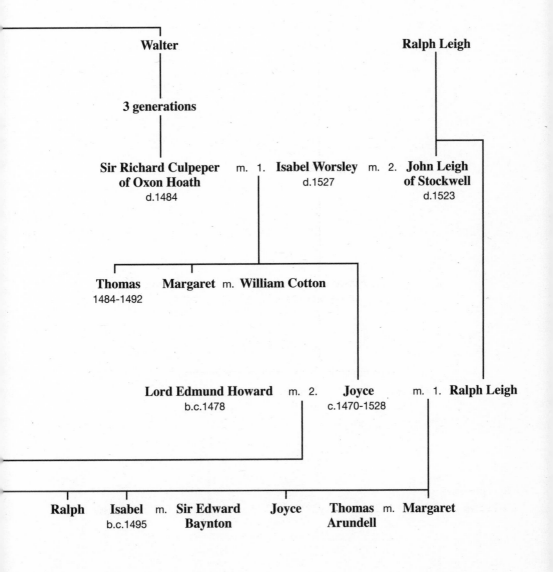

To our lovely neighbours, with thanks for so many good times: Shelley, Burnell, Caroline and David.

Thus, as I sat, the tears within my eyen,
Of her the wreck whiles I did debate,
Before my face me thought I saw this Queen,
No whit as I her left, God wot, of late
But all bewept, in black and poor estate,
Which prayed me that I would ne forget
The fall of her within my book to set.

George Cavendish, *Metrical Visions*

Part One

'Flourishing in youth with beauty fresh and pure'

Chapter 1

1528

Katheryn was seven when her mother died. She would never forget being led by her nurse into the dim, musty bedchamber where Father was kneeling beside the bed, his head in his hands and his shoulders heaving, and the chaplain was saying prayers. It was shocking having to kiss the cold forehead of the still figure lying in the bed, which looked so unlike the mother she knew.

Why had she died? She had been up and about only yesterday. Yet she had heard her mother screaming in the night, and somehow knew that the little stranger lying in the next room had something to do with it.

'You must be brave,' her half-sister Isabel murmured. 'Our lady mother is now in Heaven, watching over you.' It was hard to understand that when Mother was clearly lying here.

When Katheryn started wailing, Isabel took her hand and led her out.

'Hush, sweeting,' she said, sounding choked herself. 'Let us go and see our new sister.'

Katheryn stared down at the snuffling infant lying in the cradle. Mary had plump pink cheeks and a pouting mouth. She was tightly swaddled and wore a close-fitting bonnet. It would be ages before she was old enough to play with Katheryn.

'You must be a mother to her now,' Isabel said. Katheryn wasn't sure about that. Babies held little appeal for her; they didn't *do* anything. She would far rather be romping with her brothers, Charles, Henry and George, even though they were much older and did not always want to be encumbered by a needy little girl.

3

She had even older brothers and sisters too, Mother's children by her first husband. In the days after Mother died, they came down from Stockwell to pay their respects, headed by John Leigh, Katheryn's eldest half-brother, whom she adored. All the Leighs doted on her, especially Isabel. Isabel was lovely: tall, very fair and still pretty, even though she was thirty-two, which seemed ancient. She was being very kind to Katheryn and had offered to stay on to help Father. It was a mercy that Isabel had been at Lady Hall when Mother died, for Father had now disappeared behind his chamber door, being too sunk in his own grief to heed his children's misery. It was Isabel who clutched Katheryn to her flat velvet bosom, dried her tears and came hastening when she woke screaming from a nightmare. Isabel had come to help with the new baby. Katheryn thought Isabel should have babies of her own, since she loved them so much, but Isabel was not yet married.

Katheryn was not now interested in practicalities. All she knew was that Mother was gone and that her world had been shattered. She understood what death was, for the household chaplain had explained that it was like going to sleep, although you never woke up because you had gone to Heaven to be with God, and that was something to rejoice over. But no one seemed to be rejoicing at all, and Katheryn thought that God was very selfish, taking her mother away when she loved her so much.

There came the day when Katheryn was kneeling on the floor of the hall, playing shovelboard with Isabel as her nurse looked on, and Father summoned her to his private closet with its dark panelled walls. To the child, Lord Edmund looked wild-eyed and haggard in the candlelight.

'Come here, Kitty,' he said. It was his pet name for her. 'I have something for you.' He held out his hand and there in his palm lay a glittering ruby ring. 'Your mother left it to you,' he went on. 'She wanted you to have it. You must take great care of it.'

Katheryn picked it up, gazing at it in wonderment. She had never owned such a beautiful object; indeed, she owned barely anything at all, save for her clothes and a few playthings. They were poor; she had grown up knowing it, just as it had been drummed into her that, despite their poverty, she was a Howard and a member of one of the greatest and most noble families in England. The Duke of Norfolk himself was her uncle.

The ring gleamed at her, then its image blurred as tears welled at the memory of her mother wearing it. She would treasure it; it was all she had left of her.

'Give it to Isabel to keep safely for you until you are older,' Father said. 'You will be going away soon; this house is no place for children.'

'Going away? Where, Father?' Katheryn asked, alarmed. She did not want to leave Lady Hall.

'Your Aunt Margaret Cotton has gladly agreed to take you. Your brothers will go to the Duke to be trained for knighthood, and Mary will live with her wet nurse in the village. You will leave for Oxon Hoath on Monday.' Monday was just three days hence.

The tears spilled over. 'Are you coming too?' Katheryn whispered.

Lord Edmund laid his hand on her head and sighed. 'No, Kitty. Isabel will go with you. I have to stay here and attend to my affairs. God only knows what the future holds, for there is no money left. Be grateful that your aunt is a woman of true Christian charity and is willing to look after you.'

Katheryn did not think she had ever met Aunt Margaret Cotton, and did not wish to do so now. 'I want to stay here with you,' she said.

'Alas, Kitty, I am not fitted to rearing children,' Father said. 'It is better you grow up in comfort than starve with me.'

'Are you going to starve?' Katheryn asked.

'Well, probably not,' her father said. 'But I cannot give you the life you deserve, and Aunt Margaret can.'

Katheryn cried again at that. She had not dreamed that losing Mother would mean losing Father as well. He had never loomed large in her life, yet he was part of that familiar world that was now crumbling. He patted her head again and called for Isabel. It was she who comforted the child, shaking her head in sorrow at the nurse.

Katheryn sat in the litter, wrapped in blankets against the November chill, with Isabel beside her. She was sunk in misery as she watched her father waving farewell and Lady Hall vanishing in the distance, and craned her head through the window for a last glimpse of it, until Isabel told her to sit back and pulled down the blind.

'It's freezing, sweeting,' she said.

Katheryn sat there trying to remember her mother's face. It was horrible knowing that she would never see it again. She might never again play with her boisterous brothers in the field that lay between Lady Hall and the church at Moreton. Her head was full of memories: the Christmas gatherings at Lambeth, receiving a cloth doll made by Mother at New Year, getting her brothers to carry her pig-a-back and Father reprimanding them for being too rough with her, and her nurse grumbling because there was no money for new clothes. But her most cherished memories were those of her mother. Mother sewing by the fire, or making cordial in the still room, Mother teaching her how to make daisy chains, Mother kissing her good night, her gentle hand stroking her hair. Tears welled.

'You've not met your Culpeper kinsfolk, have you, sweeting?' Isabel said. 'They are my family too. Our mother was a Culpeper before she married. Aunt Margaret is her sister. You will come to love her, I am sure.'

They jolted through Epping Forest, passing through the villages of Chipping Ongar and Kelvedon Hatch. Presently, Katheryn fell asleep, and only woke up when Isabel shook her shoulder at Tilbury. Here they were to catch the ferry across the Thames to Gravesend. Down by the jetty there was a man selling hot pies, and Isabel bought three, one each for her and Katheryn and one for the groom, and some hot spiced ale.

It was a short journey by boat to the Kent coast. Isabel folded Katheryn in her cloak as they stood on deck and watched Gravesend looming near.

'Is it far to Oxon Hoath?' Katheryn asked as the vessel rocked on the tide.

'About sixteen miles. We'll break our journey and stay overnight at Meopham. That's about five miles from Gravesend.'

But they found nowhere suitable to stay at Meopham and had to ride on a further six miles until they arrived, exhausted, at the Bull Inn at Wrotham, which looked inviting. Isabel paid for a private chamber and asked for food to be brought up to them. They had the daily ordinary, a bowl of rich beef stew and slices of apple pie. Then Isabel put Katheryn to bed and sat sewing in a chair by the fire. It all seemed so strange, after the known and the familiar, and Katheryn started crying into her pillow. Instantly, Isabel was there, holding her in her arms.

'I know, I know, sweeting. She was my mother too and I miss her dreadfully.' Clutching each other, they wept together until Katheryn fell asleep.

Aunt Margaret Cotton was waiting for them at the door of a big old house with uneven walls and stout timbers. She was a plump matron in her forties with ruddy cheeks and a brisk manner, but Katheryn could see warmth and sympathy in her eyes.

'Oh, the poor mite!' she pronounced. 'I'm glad you brought her to me, Isabel.'

'So am I, dear aunt,' said Isabel, and the women embraced each other.

'William!' Aunt Margaret called, and a kindly-looking man appeared. He greeted Isabel with a kiss and patted Katheryn's head.

'You're a pretty little thing,' he told her. 'I hope we're going to be friends.' Katheryn ventured a tentative smile.

'Come in the warm, child,' Aunt Margaret instructed. 'Let's get some decent food into you.' In the hall, she stood back and appraised Katheryn. 'I can see you're my sister Joyce's child; you look just like her, dear, apart from your hair. That auburn hair comes from the Howards. Joyce was fair, like me.' She dabbed her eyes with a kerchief. 'I can't believe she's gone. I hope he had her buried decently!'

Katheryn saw Isabel frown at Aunt Margaret. 'Of course he did,' she said. 'She's at Lambeth, in the Howard chapel.'

That seemed to satisfy Aunt Margaret. 'Now, Katheryn,' she said, 'you shall meet your cousins.' She led them into a parlour where four children in her very image were sitting at a table. They all rose and bowed or curtseyed as their mother introduced them. 'This is Thomas;

he's eight, and John, who is seven. Joan's our eldest; she's fourteen, and Anne is twelve. Joan and Anne are both to be wed soon. We shall miss them when they leave the manor.'

The children all seemed friendly. Thomas was a mite shy at first, but Katheryn thought he might be interesting and kind when you got to know him, whereas John had a mischievous look about him, and would not sit still, to his parents' exasperation. The girls were sweet things and made much of Katheryn, who was eager to point out that she had brothers too and loved to play games with them.

'Do you play catch and ninepins?' John asked.

'I can play anything!' Katheryn boasted.

'So can I!' he countered.

The adults left them to it and went off to unpack Katheryn's things. Anne suggested a game of hide-and-seek and pulled Katheryn along with her to show her the many hiding places the old house afforded.

'It's an ancient place,' she told her. 'It's two hundred years old!'

There were lots of corners and crannies within the numerous stairs and chambers, and cupboards and closets galore; soon Katheryn was racing about and shrieking with the rest. By the time they were called to dinner in the parlour, she was feeling a lot happier.

Within a week, she felt quite at home at Oxon Hoath, where everyone was so kind to her. She could see in Aunt Margaret comforting resemblances to her mother, and Uncle William was a very merry fellow who had an endless store of jokes. There was a litter of kittens in the barn, and a host of dogs about the place. Above all, she was struck by how well the Cottons lived, what good food they had, and their fine clothes. She had never known such plenty at Lady Hall or at her father's town house in Lambeth. She felt drawn into the bosom of the Cotton family, who treated her as one of their own. Only at night did she weep for her mother.

The young Cottons enjoyed a lot of freedom and the run of the house and its surrounds. It stood in the middle of a great deer park and had been in the Culpeper family for generations. There were lots of Culpeper relations living nearby, at places called Bedgebury, Wakehurst and Preston Hall, many of whom came visiting while Katheryn was at Oxon Hoath. Later, she learned that her grandfather had been the last of his particular line, and that his estates had been divided between his two daughters, her mother Joyce and Aunt Margaret. How different life might have been if Mother had inherited Oxon Hoath!

One day, as Margaret and Isabel were overseeing the boiling of plum puddings for Christmas, Katheryn was sitting under the kitchen table, playing with a kitten and listening to her elders conversing. Much of what they said went over her head, but her ears pricked up at one point.

'You did better for yourself than Mother,' Isabel said. 'She married the son of a duke, but you've had the happier life.'

'Aye,' Aunt Margaret agreed. 'I still have the house and much of the property left me by your grandfather. Edmund squandered all Joyce's inheritance on his extravagances and gambled the rest away at cards. Now there is nothing left but what the Howards have given him. I daresay he'd wager the very roof over his head if he thought it could bring him a fortune. And him an educated man, who has learned Latin, French and logic and God knows what else. He ought to know better!'

'It cannot be easy being a younger son with no inheritance to look for,' Isabel said, ever the pacifist. 'Edmund is one of nine, you know.'

'All the more reason not to be such a spendthrift with Joyce's money!' Aunt Margaret retorted. 'He told me last Christmas that he's deeply in debt. I didn't sympathise, for he had only himself to blame. Those poor children have nothing; the girls will have no marriage portions. What is to become of them, I don't know! Think how well your father provided for you and your brothers and sisters. I know you haven't been found a suitable husband yet, but the dowry is there. It gets my goat, how those Howards are so stuck-up and high-and-mighty, and yet so wanting where it matters. We Culpepers are descended from King Edward the First too, you know!'

Katheryn was surprised to hear the glorious Howards, and her father, spoken of so unkindly. Clearly her aunt had got it wrong. Father had always been nice, if distant, although he was prone to disappearing mysteriously for weeks on end and people often seemed to get angry with him. Perhaps, when he was away, he was playing cards. Katheryn had not known there was anything wrong with playing cards, or that she did not have a marriage portion, whatever that was. She was more worried about her finger, which the kitten, fed up with being pulled about and bedecked with ribbons, had just scratched. She crawled out from under the table with the protesting animal in her arms.

'Mercy me!' exclaimed Aunt Margaret, and Isabel said something about little pitchers.

'My finger hurts,' said Katheryn, holding it up. Isabel fetched a damp cloth and dabbed at it. 'It's nothing,' she said, smiling. 'Be brave.'

'Culpeper's a funny name,' Katheryn observed.

'I'm told our ancestors were spice merchants,' Aunt Margaret said. 'They were called pepperers.' Katheryn giggled. She had forgotten about what she had just heard. But that night, lying in her comfortable feather bed in the beamed chamber she shared with Isabel, she remembered and was glad that she didn't have to be poor any more. Father had been right. Coming to Aunt Margaret's was the best thing that could have happened to her.

Of all the Culpeper relations who came to stay, Katheryn liked her distant cousin Tom best. He was one of the Bedgebury Culpepers, the senior branch of the family. He came that winter with his parents and six siblings. At eighteen, Tom was eleven years older than Katheryn, but so debonair with his dark good looks, and so kind to a motherless little girl. He took the time to sit with her and admire the kittens, winning her heart completely.

'We have lots of animals at Bedgebury,' he told her.

'I wish I could see them,' she said.

'I hope you will visit us soon,' he smiled. 'Alas, I am hardly ever there. I serve the King and am mostly at court.'

Katheryn's eyes widened. The King had been a constant, dominating, unseen presence at Lambeth and Lady Hall, for Father had often spoken of him, wishing he could do something to earn his favour and, more often than not, complaining that he hadn't. The King was powerful. He ruled everyone in the land. To Katheryn, he was a vague and distant figure, mighty and menacing.

'What's the King like?' she asked.

'He is very kind to me, sweeting, and treats me well.'

'Are you scared of him?'

Tom chuckled. 'No. He is a good fellow, and a considerate master.'

Katheryn frowned. This didn't sound like the King of whom her father had sometimes spoken. That King was mean and nasty.

'I know his Grace well,' Tom told her. 'I've been at court since I was a child. I was his page at first; now I am a groom of his Privy Chamber, and I hope to rise further in time.'

'Can I come and see you at court?' Katheryn asked.

'Oh, no, sweeting. The Privy Chamber is no place for fair young maids like you,' Tom said, giving her a hug. 'When I am next home, I will ask Cousin Margaret to bring you to Bedgebury.'

Katheryn thrilled at the prospect. She did so like Tom. She felt very lucky to have all these kind Culpeper relations.

Chapter 2

1529

In February, Katheryn's eighth birthday was celebrated with a gathering of Culpeper children, and she received, to her delight, a set of skittles from Aunt Margaret and Uncle William, and a beautiful pink dress from Isabel, in which she felt like a queen in a fable. There was nothing from Father, but, with such riches, Katheryn didn't mind.

A week later, Aunt Margaret dished out Katheryn's dinner and placed the plate before her. 'I have some news for you, child,' she said. 'Your father has taken another wife. You have a new mother.'

Everyone else at table remained silent, and Katheryn sensed that they did not approve of this. An alarming thought occurred to her. 'Do I have to go home?'

'I should hope not,' Aunt Margaret retorted. 'This is your home now.'

It was good news, although Katheryn wondered if it meant that Father no longer wanted her to live with him, even if she did have a stepmother who could look after her now. It didn't trouble her greatly, for she much preferred being at Oxon Hoath.

Father visited in the spring, bringing his bride. He kissed Katheryn, marvelled at how much she had grown, and thanked Aunt Margaret for her good care of her. Katheryn found herself looking at him with new eyes, after having heard about his failings, and it worried her that he seemed somehow diminished and no longer the father she had known and revered. Yet she did not fail in her courtesy to him.

The new Lady Edmund was a tall brunette called Dorothy, very talkative in a whimsical way.

'You know, my child, you are as beautiful as Helen of Troy,' she said

12

to Katheryn. No one had ever said that Katheryn was beautiful before, and she had no idea who Helen of Troy was. Perplexed, but pleased, she just smiled at her new stepmother.

'I am sure we will get on very well,' that lady said.

Dorothy had been a widow, Father told them over dinner, and had been left comfortably off, so he trusted his financial problems would soon be resolved. He had rented out Lady Hall, and they were on their way to Hampshire, where Dorothy owned an estate called Place House.

'My dear wife tells me it's a pretty part of the world,' he said, squeezing Dorothy's hand. For an awful moment, Katheryn was worried that he would say she must go with them, but he did not, to her relief. Instead, he was intent on regaling his bride and everyone else with stories of his past exploits.

'Dorothy doesn't know that I organised the jousts for the King's coronation,' he boasted. 'And, my dear, I took part in those held at Westminster to celebrate the birth of Prince Henry, God rest his soul.' He crossed himself. 'I was Marshal of the Horse at the Battle of Flodden, where my father won a great victory over the Scots. I too distinguished myself, and he knighted me on the field. It was after that that the King restored my father to the dukedom of Norfolk.'

Dorothy was smiling admiringly at him, but Katheryn – and probably everyone else – had heard all this before. She was growing bored and her cousins were fidgeting. But Father was in full flight. 'I went to France in the train of the Princess Mary when she married King Louis. King Henry himself gave me silks and cloth of gold to wear when I attended him at the Field of the Cloth of Gold, and I was one of the challengers in the tournaments.'

'What an interesting life you have led, husband,' Dorothy said.

'I have had my moments,' he observed, beaming at her.

'How are the children?' Aunt Margaret enquired.

Father smiled. 'The boys are doing well in their knightly training under the Duke's sergeant-at-arms. Mary is still living with her wet nurse near Lady Hall.'

'Have you any news of the King, my lord?' Uncle William asked.

Edmund frowned. 'The legatine court has been revoked to Rome, on the Queen's plea. His Majesty is not pleased, as you can imagine.'

Katheryn had no idea what he was talking about. 'What's a legatine court?' she whispered to Thomas, who was sitting next to her.

Father heard her and spoke before Thomas could reply. 'It's a special court set up to decide whether the King is truly married to Queen Katherine.'

'He wants to marry someone else,' Thomas said. Katheryn was shocked. She had been named for Queen Katherine, who was kind and good and charitable, and loved by everyone.

'Thomas!' reproved his mother. 'That's enough!'

'But it's true,' Father said. 'It's no secret that he means to wed my niece Anne Boleyn.' Katheryn had heard that name mentioned before, several times, in the past year, but had not taken much notice. 'If he does, we Howards will be riding high. My niece thinks very well of me.'

'Some of us would prefer it if the King cleaved to his lawful wife!' Aunt Margaret said tartly.

'But she is too old to give him a son to succeed him,' Dorothy ventured.

Aunt Margaret bridled. 'They have a daughter. If I am capable of administering my estates, there is no reason why the Princess Mary should not rule England.' Dorothy subsided, looking embarrassed.

She and Father left soon after dinner, saying they must be at Tonbridge by nightfall. Father gave Katheryn his blessing as she knelt before him and bade her be a good girl.

'I hope to see you before too long,' he said, as he mounted his horse. Waving his hand in a final farewell to his hosts, he rode off, with Dorothy sitting side-saddle on her palfrey beside him.

When they returned indoors, Katheryn saw Aunt Margaret shaking her head at Uncle William. 'He's the most incorrigible rogue I've ever known,' her aunt declared. Katheryn followed them through to the parlour, where she sat on the floor playing skittles with Thomas and John, while her elders sat around the hearth. She listened as they chatted, for they were talking about her father. It was as if they thought she couldn't hear or understand them.

'All that bragging!' Aunt Margaret exclaimed in a low voice that, unfortunately, carried.

'I thought he would never stop,' Anne said.

'It's amazing how he sees himself,' her mother went on. 'At Flodden, his contingent was the only one to be defeated. He didn't mention that! And he managed to lose their baggage.'

'It's easy to see why he gets no preferment,' Uncle William added. 'He fell foul of Cardinal Wolsey, do you remember? And the King!'

'Yes,' said Aunt Margaret. 'I've not forgotten how he undermined the good rule of justice in Surrey when he was Justice of the Peace – and got hauled before the Court of Star Chamber.'

'And then, to show that he did take his duties seriously, he was extremely cruel to those poor younglings who were executed after the Evil May Day riots,' Uncle William recalled. Katheryn's ears pricked up at this. Her father, cruel? She could not believe it. They had got it wrong, surely.

'He was probably doing his best to impress the King!' Aunt Margaret observed.

'If he was, my love, he couldn't sustain the effort. He was back in the Star Chamber a year or so later, to be judged by his Grace himself for inciting riots. He had to kneel and beg for mercy. It was thanks to his father that he got a royal pardon; the others accused with him weren't so lucky.'

'He's a turbulent, reckless man, and thinks himself above the law.'

'My Grandfather Leigh had his measure,' Isabel said, head bent over her sewing. 'He ensured that Lord Edmund could not contest his will.'

'Your Grandmother Leigh was unhappy about Joyce marrying him,' Aunt Margaret revealed. 'She tried to protect Joyce's inheritance, but he squandered it all and ended up in hiding to avoid being sent to debtors' prison. There was scarcely any meat and drink for the children! Do you remember him sending poor Joyce to seek the Cardinal's help? She was a saint, my sister, to put up with him.'

Katheryn listened, dumbstruck. Bending over the skittles, praying her cousins would not see her cheeks flaming in shame, she realised why her father had once mysteriously gone away for a long time.

The adults fell silent, and the only sound in the room was the wooden ball hitting the skittles.

'Well, I must get the servants to clear the table,' Aunt Margaret said, rising to her feet. Katheryn watched her go, in some distress at what she had heard. She had not understood it all, but had gathered enough to know that her kind relatives thought her father a wastrel, and stupid into the bargain. Worse still, perhaps they were right.

Chapter 3

1530

Katheryn was nine when her cousins, Joan and Anne, married. She was a bridesmaid at both their weddings and wore her beautiful pink dress.

Afterwards, Aunt Margaret said she found the house empty without them, and went about with a sad face, pining visibly.

'It's like having an arm cut off,' she said. 'You think you have them for ever and then, suddenly, they're gone.' She cuddled Katheryn to her. 'Thank goodness you're here, sweeting, and Thomas and John.' She wiped away a tear. She was definitely not herself.

Katheryn missed her aunt's laughter and her brisk confidence. It was left to the indomitable Isabel to try to raise Margaret's spirits, but in vain, for she was behaving like someone bereft. The sad atmosphere in the house grew heavier when news came that Katheryn's stepmother had died in childbed, leaving Father her estate in Hampshire. Katheryn did not mourn Dorothy, for she had hardly known her and had not seen her or Lord Edmund since their visit; yet she felt sorry for her, and for Father, although she was rather relieved when he did not come to Oxon Hoath, as he would surely have guessed that her feelings towards him had changed. Since hearing about his shortcomings, she could not feel the same about him, try as she might. Already, Aunt Margaret and Isabel were wondering how he was coping, and how soon it would be before he mortgaged Place House.

By July, Aunt Margaret was a shadow of her former self, all her vigour and ebullience diminished. Everyone put it down to missing her girls, but soon they began to realise that she was ill. In September, she took to her bed, leaving Isabel in charge of the household.

Katheryn was in terror lest God take Aunt Margaret too. That would be one loss she could not bear. Margaret was the centre of her world, loving, reassuring and all-powerful. Every day, she went to the family chapel and prayed with all her might that God would make her beloved aunt better. But He was not listening.

One evening, Isabel gently shook Katheryn awake and bade her rise. Holding a candle, she led her to Aunt Margaret's bedchamber, where everyone was kneeling around the bed, and the chaplain was intoning the last rites. Uncle William and the boys were weeping, and from the pillows came the rasping sound of laboured breathing. Aunt Margaret's face was grey and sunken; she seemed unaware of anyone being there. Katheryn knelt next to Isabel and prayed as hard as she had ever done in her life. 'Spare her! Spare her!' she whispered urgently.

The breathing grew weaker and fainter. It was some moments before Katheryn realised that it had ceased. There was a terrible silence as the priest crossed himself. 'Of your charity, pray for the soul of our sister Margaret,' he enjoined them all.

'No!' Katheryn wailed, and Isabel quickly scooped her up in her arms and carried her out. 'It is God's will,' she whispered, sounding choked.

Katheryn lay on her bed, worn out with crying. If only Aunt Margaret could walk through that door and comfort her! She willed it to happen, but it was no use, of course. Aunt Margaret was gone to that Heaven where Mother and all their departed loved ones awaited her. She was in bliss, as the priest had said, but her family here on earth was devastated.

The pink gown had been laid away in Katheryn's chest, and she had been given the mourning clothes Joan had worn as a child when an infant sibling had died. The black worsted gown scratched a bit, but she was too sunk in misery to care.

As she lay there, she wondered what would happen now. If Isabel stayed on to care for Uncle William, the boys and herself, all would be well – or as well as it could ever be, for Uncle William had taken his loss hard. Just six months ago, this had been a happy, bustling household; now it was a silent, brooding place where you felt you had to tiptoe around in case you intruded on someone's grief. If it were not for

Isabel doing her best to cheer them all, Oxon Hoath would be a very dismal place indeed.

The next day, Uncle William came into the kitchen as Katheryn was seated on a stool at the big table, watching Isabel and the cook make quince tarts.

'I have heard from your father, Kitty,' he said, holding a letter. 'It seems you have a new stepmother.'

'Already?' Isabel raised her eyebrows.

'Yes, Edmund wasted no time. Probably it's another rich widow.' He showed Isabel the loosely written page. 'Anyway, he writes that he is at Lambeth and that Katheryn is to return to him there. He asks that you escort her; he will send a groom with a litter next week.'

Katheryn did not know whether to be happy or sad. A few weeks ago, it would have grieved her inconsolably to leave Oxon Hoath, but now she was not so sure. She liked her father's house at Lambeth well enough, and maybe she would be happier there – if she could ever be truly happy again. But that would depend on what this new stepmother was like. At least Isabel would be there, in case she proved a dragon. Katheryn had been told fairy tales involving stepmothers, most of whom had been evil.

But what of poor Uncle William? How would he fare without Isabel to look after the house and his sons?

'These changes are not good for the child,' Isabel said, crimping the pastry cases, 'but when the Howards beckon, there's nothing to be done about it.' She sounded resentful. 'Can you manage without me for a few days? I'll stay long enough to ensure that all is well, then return.'

'Aren't you staying with me?' Katheryn cried.

'I think Uncle William needs me here,' Isabel told her, looking to him for affirmation. 'I'm not even sure if I'm supposed to be staying on at Lambeth. Oh, Katheryn, don't cry, sweeting.' She wiped her hands on a cloth and hugged her. 'I will come and visit you. And I promise that I will make sure you are happily settled with your new stepmother before I leave.'

Katheryn nodded, feeling numb.

'We ladies all have to go where we are told,' Isabel went on. 'My brother has so far failed to find me a husband, so I have to live as a dependant. I could have gone to Stockwell with our sisters Margaret and Joyce to live with John, but I prefer it here, and I'm fortunate that I have been made welcome.' She smiled at Uncle William. 'You, Katheryn, are lucky. You have a father to look after you. Be grateful for that.'

Uncle William took Katheryn's hand. 'Run along now and find Thomas and John. I'm sure you can find something to do with them.'

She found the boys playing chess in the parlour, and they readily stopped their game and fetched the spillikins so that they could play together. Concentrating on removing each stick carefully from the pile so as not to move the others helped to calm Katheryn down, but inwardly she was resolved. If the latest Lady Edmund was an ogress, she would escape from Lambeth by whatever means she could and come back here with Isabel.

It took them three days to travel up to Lambeth. They went via Otford and Bromley, where they stayed at good inns. Soon they were travelling along Church Street towards the Thames, and Father's house, the house in which Katheryn had been born, was ahead of them, opposite Lambeth Palace, the town house of the Archbishop of Canterbury. It was a modest residence compared to the palatial Norfolk House, which lay behind it between Church Street and Paradise Street: that was a magnificent building of brick, timber and whitewash, surrounded by beautiful gardens and orchards that extended right down to the riverbank. Katheryn's uncle, the mighty Duke of Norfolk, her father's older brother, lived there whenever he needed to be in town. He could take the Archbishop's horse ferry across the broad Thames to the court at York Place, a stone's throw upriver, or to Parliament at Westminster, or further north to London itself.

St Mary's Church stood in front of Lambeth Palace. As they neared it, Katheryn felt a pang. There lay her mother, cold in her grave among her husband's Howard ancestors. Isabel had said that a ledger stone had just been laid to mark the place, and that they would go and pray for her soul before she left. Katheryn did not want to think of her mother lying buried under the ground; she wanted to remember her as she was in life, warm and kind and comforting.

But there was no time to dwell on sad things because they had arrived at Lord Edmund's house. Father's steward was at the door, ready to help them alight, ordering the grooms to see to the horses and store the litter by the stables. Katheryn stepped into the familiar screens passage, as, from the hall on her right, her father emerged. On his arm was a pretty, smiling lady with kind eyes and a face like that of the Virgin in the chapel at Oxon Hoath.

'Katheryn, Isabel, welcome!' Father greeted them. 'This is Margaret, my wife. Katheryn, curtsey to your stepmother.'

Katheryn did so, but Margaret raised her and kissed her on both cheeks.

'What a delightful child, Edmund! You did not tell me you had such a treasure.'

Katheryn looked up at Isabel, who nodded encouragingly as if to say that it was going to be all right. Then she slipped her hand into her stepmother's proffered one.

'Let me take you upstairs, child,' Margaret said. 'I'll help Isabel to unpack.'

She preceded Katheryn up the spiral stair in the corner and along the gallery to the nursery chamber.

'You'll need to be quiet,' she told her. 'Your sister Mary is having her afternoon nap.'

Mary! Katheryn had not realised that she would be here. She had thought her miles away in Epping Forest – when she thought of her at all. She was not best pleased. Yet, when Margaret opened the door and she saw what lay on her bed, her resentment turned to delight. For awaiting her was the most beautiful green velvet gown, edged with biliments of gold embroidery. The pink gown had had its day: it had been let out twice and had a band of contrasting material added to the hem to make it longer, but soon it would be too small. But this – this was magnificent! Wearing such a gown, she would feel like a true daughter of the Howards and not a poor relation. Immediately, she warmed to her new stepmother.

Margaret's touch was everywhere, from the polished surfaces of the furniture and the snowy linen on the beds to the summer flowers in vases on the hearths and the good fare served at table. Had Lambeth been like this in her mother's time? Katheryn could not remember.

'You are lucky that God has sent you such a stepmother,' Isabel told her when she came upstairs to kiss Katheryn good night. 'I am satisfied that I will be leaving you in good hands.'

Katheryn thought herself even luckier when she found that the kitchen cat, a redoubtable tabby mouser, was expecting kittens. She began to believe that she could be happy here. She still missed Aunt Margaret, but the memory of her was dimmed by this new world. She found herself captivated by her little sister, Mary, now two years old, and the most winning child. She enjoyed playing with her and helping the nurse to look after her. Margaret and Isabel looked on approvingly.

Isabel did not return to Oxon Hoath as planned because Uncle William went away to visit some Culpeper relatives and the house was closed up. Katheryn was grateful for each day that her half-sister was spared to her. Then, one day in the autumn, Father returned from the court at Whitehall in an ebullient mood. At supper, to Katheryn's surprise and dismay, he revealed that Sir Edward Baynton, a courtier high in the King's favour, was eager to marry Isabel. Sir Edward had mentioned that he was looking for a wife, and Father had offered him his stepdaughter's hand, hoping thereby to commend himself to the King.

'You will be a great lady,' he said, getting up and embracing Isabel. 'Sir Edward has vast lands in Wiltshire and a big house there and is expected to rise high in the King's service.'

Isabel was thrilled. 'This is wonderful news!' she cried.

'I don't want you to leave us,' Katheryn said, her lip trembling.

Isabel took her hands. 'Sweeting, I was going to leave anyway. Be happy for me, please! I am thirty-four and may never have another chance to wed, and this is a brilliant match for me, the best I could ever have hoped for. I will be at court a lot of the time, just over the river, and can visit you often.'

Katheryn was unwilling to be mollified. 'What about poor Uncle William?'

'Our sister Joyce has said she will stay with him for a while if I marry Sir Edward, so he will be looked after. And you can be my bridesmaid!'

Katheryn cheered up at that. 'Can I wear my green dress?'

Isabel was not the only one to be married that winter. In November, Margaret Leigh, Katheryn's half-sister, married Thomas Arundell, an upcoming courtier, and Katheryn and Isabel joined the whole Leigh family for the wedding, which was hosted by John Leigh at his house at Stockwell, not far from Lambeth. Isabel told Katheryn that John had made friends with Thomas Arundell when they served together in Cardinal Wolsey's household, but, lowering her voice, explained that it was best not to mention the Cardinal as he had angered the King by failing to help him put away the Queen. Katheryn felt sorry for the Cardinal, who must have hated his task; but she liked John Leigh, who was a big, cheery fellow with a black beard and a booming voice, and very hearty in his welcome.

It was the third time she had been to a wedding, and, at nearly ten, she was old enough to thrill to the romance of it all: the bride in her rich crimson gown, the groom in his swaggering finery, the solemn vows at the church door, the beauty of the orisons offered up by the choir as everyone followed the newly-wed couple inside, and the fabulous feast that followed. Lord and Lady Edmund were among the throng of guests, and Katheryn's brothers, looking much older and more self-assured, and everyone was very merry. One day, she hoped, she too would have a fairy-tale wedding like this.

Chapter 4

In January, Isabel married Sir Edward Baynton at Stockwell. Again there was a large gathering and Katheryn was able to see her brothers once more. She drew many admiring glances in her wondrous green gown. She knew she looked pretty with her dark auburn hair loose about her shoulders and an emerald pendant her stepmother had given her around her neck. Isabel was radiant, clearly happy with her new husband. He was a dignified, serious man of muscular build with greying hair, yet pleasant in manner with all the courtesy of a seasoned courtier, and he was clearly smitten with Isabel, with whom he was much of an age. Katheryn was surprised to find that he had brought with him seven children. Father, resplendent in his one good velvet gown, explained that they were the offspring of his late wife.

'Isabel will have her hands full!' he added. Katheryn could not help feeling a pang of jealousy at the thought of those children receiving more of Isabel's attention than she herself would in the future. But Margaret was looking after her now and she liked her stepmother very much.

'I have some excellent news,' Father said, as they sat at supper in the parlour one evening in April. The boys were home from Norfolk House, and were wrapped up in their own affairs, but now they turned to Father with new interest. He beamed at them all. 'My good niece, the Lady Anne Boleyn, has been looking out for me, as has Master Cromwell, who is set to replace the Cardinal as the King's chief minister. I account him a friend, you know.'

'Edmund, do get to the point,' Margaret said.

'Oh, yes, the good news!' He beamed again. 'I have been appointed comptroller of Calais on a good salary. Well, a reasonable salary, out of which I must fund my clerks and horses, but it is timely, for my creditors are pressing me.'

'I am pleased for you, Father,' Charles said. He was fifteen now and seemed taller and broader every time Katheryn saw him.

'Are we going with you, Sir?' asked George. Charles and Henry looked hopeful, but Katheryn feared that this news would mean another unwelcome change for her.

'No,' said Father. 'None of you are going with us. It is better that you stay here, where Uncle Norfolk can befit you for court and get you preferment. You boys will return to Norfolk House on Sunday. Isabel is taking Mary to her house at Wiltshire. You, Katheryn, will go to my stepmother, the Dowager Duchess.'

This was terrible news indeed. The one thing Katheryn remembered about the Dowager Duchess, widow of her grandfather, the old Duke of Norfolk, was her supreme indifference to the overtures of a small girl trying to make friends with her at a Christmas gathering at Norfolk House long years ago. She was very old and grand, and lived in a fine house called an inn, which was attached to Norfolk House at its river end.

'She is not only your grandam, but also your cousin,' Father told Katheryn. 'My mother was her aunt; they were both Tilneys. The Tilneys are a great East Anglian family and have long been close to the Howards.'

Katheryn didn't care about the Tilneys' credentials. She was too horrified at the prospect of being banished to the Dowager's inn, and having to say farewell to Margaret, who was going with Father to Calais. Then they would be across the sea and so far away . . . The thought brought tears to her eyes. It seemed that all those she loved best were taken from her: Mother, Aunt Margaret, Isabel and now her stepmother. Was she to be spared no one who cared for her and looked to her needs? She burned with jealousy to think of Mary going to live with Isabel.

'There is no need to look so glum, Kitty,' Father reproved her.

'But I don't want to go and live with my Grandam Norfolk,' she blurted out.

'Nonsense!' Father barked.

'I want to live with Isabel!' she cried.

'It's out of the question,' Father retorted. 'Isabel is the wife of a knight; your grandam is a duchess and has far greater influence.'

'It will be to your benefit,' Margaret soothed, laying a hand on Katheryn's. 'It is quite usual for noble children to be reared in great households, and you are now of an age for that. Under the Duchess's rule, you will learn the skills and graces that will help you to make a good marriage or even obtain a place at court.'

Her father and the boys were nodding their agreement, but Katheryn didn't care if she never got married or went to court. She felt bereft and abandoned.

'I don't want any arguments.' Father wagged a finger. 'The Duke himself decided that you shall go to the Dowager, and he will not be gainsaid. Over the next few days, Margaret will help you to pack your chest, for we must take ship for Calais as soon as possible. I have pressing duties awaiting me there.' In his mind, it was clear, Father had already departed. He was not interested in assuaging the hurt feelings of his daughter.

Katheryn sat on the window seat that faced Norfolk House. Her gear was all packed, and she was just waiting for Father to come and escort her to the Dowager's residence. Her brothers were with her, hopping from foot to foot, anxious to be gone themselves and return to the masculine pleasures of the Duke's service.

Katheryn had only seen her uncle of Norfolk at those rare, long-ago Christmastides, and could barely remember him, but his presence loomed large in her life for his word was law to all his Howard relations – and to a great many other people. As the foremost nobleman in the realm, he was as respected and obeyed as if he were royalty, which he almost was, by marriage at any rate, for his first wife had been Anne of York, the King's aunt, and his second was a Stafford with the Plantagenet blood of the old royal house in her veins. Katheryn had long known this, for it was the stuff of family lore, as was the Howards' descent from King Edward I.

'You will like living at Norfolk House,' Charles said.

'But I won't be living at Norfolk House,' Katheryn retorted. 'I'll be living there.' She pointed to its far end.

'It's all the same building,' he replied. 'They just have separate households. There's another inn at the other end, which is lived in by our uncle Lord William Howard, the Dowager's son. When our grandsire built Norfolk House, he made provision for his widow and his children.' Katheryn knew that her grandfather, the old Duke, had sired twenty children on his two wives. There were Howards everywhere, it seemed: at Lambeth, at court and all over the kingdom, intermarried with the finest families in the land.

'Tell me how he got his title back!' she demanded. It was a story she loved to hear, and she desperately needed something to divert her.

'Not again!' jeered George.

Charles sat down, a resigned look on his face. He always indulged her. 'The first Duke was killed at Bosworth Field, fighting for King Richard.'

'On the wrong side,' Henry pointed out.

'Indeed, because Richard was also slain and Henry Tudor won and was crowned king on the battlefield. Grandfather was Earl of Surrey then, and when the new King asked him why he had fought for Richard, he told him that he had been his anointed monarch, and, if they had put the crown on a stock, he would have fought for that. The King was impressed by his loyalty and restored the earldom of Surrey to him, but he would not let him have the dukedom of Norfolk. That was given him by our King Henry after Flodden, where Grandfather won his great victory and saved the kingdom from being invaded by the Scots. When he got the title back, he built Norfolk House. He also built the Howard chapel in St Mary's Church over the road. That's where we'll all end up buried one day, like Mother.'

Katheryn was so miserable that she dared not think of Mother. If she did, she would burst out wailing. She had been, just the once, with Isabel, to the church and knelt at the graveside; she had felt strangely comforted to be near her mother again, but the sight of the cold ledger stone had brought home to her the finality of her death. She had no desire to go back.

'The Duke entertains a lot at Norfolk House,' Charles was saying. 'He has many visitors, courtiers and foreign envoys. I've met John Skelton, whom our family made poet laureate, and we all get on well with our cousin Surrey and Lady Mary.' Surrey was the Duke's son and heir, but Katheryn had no recollection of him, although her brothers had told her he wrote verses and had a quick temper. Mary was his sister.

She knew there was some mystery concerning their mother. The Duchess of Norfolk did not live with the Duke. Katheryn had overheard the boys sniggering about a certain Bess Holland making the beast with two backs with their uncle, whatever that meant, and they had said it was because of her that their aunt was a captive. But when Katheryn had asked them about it, they'd told her to mind her own business.

Father was calling them from below. It was time to leave. Reluctantly, Katheryn walked down the stairs, her brothers following. In the hall, the great travelling chests stood ready, awaiting transportation to Calais. Servants were bustling about cleaning, making the house ready for its new tenants. In a day or so, Father and Margaret would be gone, and Katheryn had no idea when she would ever see them again. She stood stiff as stone as Margaret put on her cloak and smoothed down her hair, then took her by the hand and followed Father out of the front door.

They dropped off the boys at Norfolk House first, and waited until they had walked through the archway at the entrance and disappeared into the courtyard beyond. Then they walked along by the diapered brick wall to a gateway near the river. A porter admitted them and led them through a timber-framed arch that opened onto a paved courtyard. They followed him to a door at the far side and found themselves standing in a vast hall where liveried servants, officers and ladies were all hurrying hither and thither. An usher stepped forward and invited them to accompany him upstairs to the great chamber.

The Dowager Duchess must have been apprised of their coming, for she was regally seated on a richly upholstered chair beneath a canopy of estate bearing the Howard arms. Edmund and Margaret made obeisances to her and Katheryn dropped a careful curtsey.

'Welcome, Lord and Lady Edmund,' the Dowager said in a dry, reedy voice.

'Greetings, Madam,' Edmund replied. 'I trust you are in health. We have brought Mistress Katheryn to you.'

'Let me look at her.'

Margaret gave Katheryn a little push, and she stepped forward. When she dared raise her eyes, she saw that the Dowager was much older than she remembered, but refined in her appearance and dress. Her face was thin and hawk-like, her eyes sharp, her manner serene and assured. She was dressed in black silk, but glittered with jewels.

'Well, child, what have you to say for yourself?'

Katheryn knew her manners, and Margaret had told her what to say. 'Greetings, my lady. You do me much honour in welcoming me to your household. I am very grateful.'

The Dowager smiled. 'Prettily said, child. I hope you will be happy here. Now, Mother Emmet will take you to your chamber. She is mistress of the maids here.' A plump, dark-haired woman who reminded Katheryn of a docile cow stepped forward and took her hand.

'Say goodbye to your parents,' the Dowager commanded.

'Farewell, daughter,' Father said, and kissed her heartily. 'Be a good girl and do as you are bid. God willing, we will see each other again before long.'

'Take care of yourself, child. You will be well looked after here.' Margaret smiled as she kissed her.

Katheryn was too overcome to say much. 'Goodbye,' she said in a small voice. Then Mother Emmet was leading her away, away from everything she knew, and taking her through a door in a corner and up lots of stairs to a gallery hung with many pictures. At the far end, she opened a door and Katheryn stepped into the loveliest room she had ever seen. It was better than the cosy chamber she had slept in at Oxon Hoath, better even than Father's grand bedchamber. There was a carved oak tester bed set against a wall hung with a tapestry covered in flowers. There were white walls, crimson velvet curtains at the latticed window, through which Katheryn could see the gardens below, a dainty table and stool, and a blue chest, cunningly gilded, for clothes. Her own chest was standing beside it.

'You like it, I can tell,' smiled Mother Emmet, and proceeded to inspect Katheryn's few items of clothing, pausing to admire the green gown. 'You should wear this when the Duke comes,' she said, laying the cloth doll on the pillow. 'Haven't you got any other possessions, child?'

'Only these.' Katheryn showed her the little bag she had brought with her and took out her skittles and her sewing pouch, which she had made from old scraps of velvet.

'Mercy me!' exclaimed Mother Emmet. 'I'd heard your father was poor, and now I believe it. Well, I dare say we'll find some toys in the attic for you. The other young ladies here are all quite a bit older than you.'

'Other young ladies?' Katheryn echoed. She had seen herself living all alone here with the Dowager.

'Yes, quite a lot of them. My lady keeps a grand household and supports many relatives and dependants. Married ladies of rank have their own rooms. Chamberers sleep with the unmarried gentlewomen in the dorter next door. The young ladies attend the Duchess as waiting women and look to her to find them good husbands, as she will do for you one day. You are fortunate in having been so well placed.'

For all the kind welcome and the beautiful bedchamber, it still did not feel like it. Yet Katheryn had heard laughter as she passed along the gallery, which gave her hope that her older companions might be a merry bunch who would be kind to her and help her to get to know this bewildering new world.

That evening, at six o'clock, Mother Emmet washed Katheryn's face and hands, combed her hair, brushed her dress and took her down to the great hall for supper. There, overwhelmed by the sheer number of chattering people seated at the long trestles, she looked in vain for the Duchess at the high table.

'Her Grace dines in her parlour,' Mother Emmet explained. 'Her chamberlain and chief household officers preside at the board. I have arranged for two of the married ladies to take care of you.' She led the way to a seat on one of the side tables, which was occupied by a lively group of women and girls, all much older than Katheryn. 'Lady Tilney and Mistress Bulmer, this is Mistress Katheryn Howard, my lady's granddaughter by marriage,' she said. 'She knows you will be looking after her.'

The two women rose and made quick curtseys. 'Of course,' one said. She seemed nice, with her sweet voice, pretty face and brown hair. 'Welcome, Mistress Katheryn.'

'Lady Tilney is the wife of the Duchess's nephew, Sir Philip Tilney,' Mother Emmet told Katheryn, who hurriedly curtseyed. 'We have many Tilneys here!'

'You may call me Malyn, child,' Lady Tilney said. 'My husband is an usher of the King's Privy Chamber, and I came here earlier this year to bear my son. He is out at nurse now, in Stangate.'

'How old are you, Katheryn?' asked Mistress Bulmer, her plump companion, as Mother Emmet moved away to her own seat at the top of the table and they all sat down, making room for Katheryn. There was something Katheryn did not like about Mistress Bulmer; the woman smelt musty and had a whispery voice, so she had to strain to hear her.

'I'm ten,' she said. 'My father is Lord Edmund Howard.' The women exchanged glances, like most people did when Father was mentioned. 'The King has sent him to Calais. He's a very important man.'

Another girl sitting by giggled. Malyn nudged her. 'This is my lady's granddaughter, so show some respect. Katheryn, would you like some rabbit pie?'

The food was not as nice as Margaret had served at Lambeth, and definitely not up to Aunt Margaret's standards, but it was edible, and plentiful. Katheryn could not eat much, though. She wanted nothing more than to go home. But, after tomorrow, someone else would be living there, and Father and Margaret would be on a ship bound for Calais. There was no home any more. Suddenly, she was crying great gulping tears.

The young ladies hastened to comfort her. Malyn cuddled her and stroked her hair, and Mother Emmet came running. 'It's been a long day for her,' she said. 'Come, my lamb, let's put you to bed. A good night's sleep, and you'll be right as rain.' She lifted Katheryn up and carried her past the staring company and out of the hall. Soon, Katheryn was in bed, with a candle left burning on the table. She lay there quivering, racked with the occasional sob, and at length dropped off.

Mother Emmet was right. In the morning, she did feel a little better. She was called early, for Mass in the chapel and breakfast. Everyone was kind to her, and a group of the young ladies took her into the gardens to play tag. Most of them were older than her – she judged them to be between fifteen and their mid-twenties – but they were willing to indulge a ten-year-old.

'Mind you don't get untidy,' Mother Emmet called after her. 'The Duchess wants to see you after dinner.'

'I wonder what Old Agnes wants with you,' a girl called Dorothy Berwick said, as they walked along the path that led down to the Thames. Katheryn was startled to hear her stately grandam referred to in such a way.

'She probably wants to find out if Mistress Katheryn is feeling better now,' Dotty Baskerville, one of the chamberers, speculated. She was a dark-haired beauty, buxom and chatty.

'Is the Duchess nice?' Katheryn asked.

'Old Agnes?' Kat, one of the pretty Tilney cousins, a slender girl with flawless skin, chimed in. 'Some call her hard and malicious; at least, her children do. She's always quarrelling with them over one thing or another. But she's too preoccupied with her own affairs to pay much attention to us. She leaves us to our own devices, which suits us very well. Mother Emmet's in charge, but she's soft; she'd let us get away with murder.'

'Not that we're neglected,' Dorothy said. 'We have our board and keep, we get new clothes every Easter, and our duties are light. Old Agnes isn't one to sit with her maids in a sewing circle from dawn to dusk, thank God! One day, maybe she will bestir herself to find us husbands. In the meantime, we make our own pleasures.' The girls started laughing. Katheryn wondered what they found so funny.

Soon, she was running about with them, dashing behind hedges, hiding in arbours or shrieking at the top of her voice with the hunters.

No one came to tell them off for making a noise or summoned them to some task. Katheryn was beginning to think that, if life was always going to be like this in the Duchess's establishment, she might just learn to like it here.

Later, she stood before the Duchess, trying not to think of her as Old Agnes, although she feared the name might be stuck for ever in her mind.

'Well, Katheryn,' the Duchess said, 'I hope you are feeling better today. I was sorry to hear that you were so upset last night.'

'Yes, I am, thank you, my lady,' Katheryn replied, not sure if it was true. She still felt abandoned and unloved, and she was wary of her daunting grandam.

'I'm glad to hear it,' the Duchess replied, sitting straight-backed in her great chair. 'We will keep you occupied and banish your sadness. From tomorrow morning, you will spend two hours taking lessons. I have engaged a tutor who will teach you your letters and some French, and a dancing master, so that you can learn the accomplishments befitting a daughter of the Howards.' Dancing! Katheryn's spirits began to rise, although she was not too keen on learning French. 'These are the things that will increase your chances of making a good marriage, which is a necessity, seeing you have no dowry,' the Dowager was saying. 'But, with your pretty face and noble blood and connections, that can be overcome.' That was encouraging, and praise indeed from the formidable old woman. 'Anyway, we won't have to worry about it for some years yet. Now, child, make sure you are in the chapel closet tomorrow at ten o'clock.'

Katheryn made her way there the following morning in some trepidation, frightened that the lessons would be too hard for her to master. She was dismayed to discover that Master Chamber, the tutor, was a young clerk with a distant manner and no empathy with a child, especially a female one. Under his vigilant eye, she laboured monotonously, yet made little progress. She knew some of the alphabet, but the letters, when put together, made very little sense.

'C-A-T,' Master Chamber repeated for the umpteenth time. 'Write cat!'

'T-A-C,' Katheryn wrote. It looked untidy, even to her.

The tutor sighed irritably. 'We'll leave it for today and have more practice tomorrow.'

She did much better with her dancing master. He told her she had a natural grace, and she had no difficulty learning the steps of the pavane, the *basse* dance and the *passemezzo*. She loved these lessons, loved the music of lute and shawm that the Duchess's consort of musicians played for her, and the evident admiration of those who came to watch.

When she was not at her lessons or joining in the rough-and-tumble in the gardens, though, she felt miserable. Malyn Tilney remained friendly, and Joan Bulmer was amiable enough, although there was some mystery about her, for Katheryn had heard one of the other girls saying that she had left her husband to serve the Duchess, and no one knew why. But, although the young ladies played with Katheryn sometimes, and asked how she was getting on, they had their own concerns and interests, which were not those of a child. Most of the gentlewomen took little notice of her. She often heard much merriment from behind the door of their chamber, but was never invited in to share the fun.

She was lonely, an outsider. Mother Emmet was kind, but she was busy with her many duties, which seemed to consist of acting as maid to all the young ladies, who treated her as if she was purely there to be always at their beck and call. She did not neglect Katheryn – she saw that she had clean linen, minded her manners and was tucked up in bed at a reasonable time each evening – but she was often preoccupied.

At mealtimes, much of the conversation at the gentlewomen's table went over Katheryn's head, but she did hear a lot about the Lady Anne Boleyn, who was still riding high at court and in the King's affections. There was much comment about Queen Katherine being banished from court in the summer, and the young ladies spoke of placing wagers that the King would marry Anne soon. Only a few looked disapproving. Katheryn knew she should be pleased that her cousin was to be queen, for it would be a triumph for the Howards, but she felt sorry for poor

Queen Katherine, and one day she heard things about the Lady Anne that troubled her.

They were at dinner in the hall, eating roast beef and avidly discussing the King's Great Matter of his marriage, when Joan Bulmer mentioned that Anne was of the new religion.

New religion? Katheryn had no idea what that meant. She had been brought up to say her prayers, go to Mass, know her catechism, confess her sins, revere the Pope in Rome and, above all, love God.

'What's the new religion?' she asked.

'It means she is a follower of Martin Luther,' Joan Bulmer said disapprovingly, which enlightened Katheryn not at all, for she had never heard of Martin Luther. 'They reject most of the sacraments of the Church and place great reliance on preaching.'

Malyn came to Katheryn's rescue. 'The sacraments are baptism, confirmation, Mass, penance, anointing the sick, Holy Orders and marriage. Martin Luther rejects all but baptism and the Mass. He has also spoken out against wrongdoing within the Church and, though he be a monk, he has taken a nun to wife. That's why the Church is very angry with him.'

'He sounds quite wicked!' Katheryn cried, shocked. She turned to Joan. 'Does the Lady Anne reject the sacraments?'

'We don't really know,' Malyn said quickly, spearing more meat on her knife. 'It's said that she is hot for reform of the Church.'

Katheryn was puzzled. The churches she knew and the priests she had met were perfectly all right and had no need of reform. 'Why?' she asked.

'You are a one for questions,' observed Joan.

Malyn was patient with her. 'There are some bad priests who sell forgiveness for money, and many clergy are very rich, even though Our Lord was but a humble carpenter. Some think they should follow His example.' That sounded very fitting, and Katheryn nodded, feeling reassured about her cousin Anne.

'I hope the Lady Anne becomes queen,' she said, and several pairs of eyes swivelled in her direction, not all of them friendly. She felt wrong-footed, when she hadn't meant to offend anyone. Yet she was entitled to her opinion! Anne was her cousin, after all. She'd bet no one else here was so closely related to her.

She was ignored for the rest of the meal and, as often happened, began to feel so unhappy and bereft that she ended up weeping. Already she had the reputation of being a cry-baby.

'For Heaven's sake, Mistress Katheryn, cheer up!' Dorothy reproved her. 'All of us have left our families to come here, but you won't see *us* sobbing and moping. We know it's for our own good.'

'Some of us weren't as young as Katheryn when we arrived,' Margaret Bennet, one of the Duchess's married gentlewomen, reminded her. Her husband was my lady's groom of the chamber and they were happy together. Margaret was so fair that she had no eyebrows, but she had a quiet, unassuming, kindly manner. 'You ladies ought to remember that the child is missing her father and mother. Katheryn, the homesickness will pass, I promise you.'

The way Katheryn felt just then, this was hard to believe. She was glad when Malyn and another young lady, Meg Morton, offered to teach her chess.

Chapter 5

1533

In February, Katheryn turned twelve. She had been at Norfolk House for almost two years now, and Margaret Bennet had been right: the homesickness had worn off. Gradually, she had become accustomed to the bustle and routine of the Duchess's household, and memories of her earlier childhood had dimmed. Father and Margaret were still in Calais, but Charles, Henry and George sometimes came to see her. She no longer missed Isabel so much these days. Her half-sister was living in Wiltshire, immersed in the affairs of her stepchildren. She still wrote regularly and took an interest in Katheryn, yet it seemed now that she belonged to another world.

Katheryn had come to enjoy her life here. The young ladies had grown friendlier, and she had become the special pet of her grandam's male officers, who ran her household and could be quite frosty towards the young ladies in it, and even of the crusty old porter. She was a favourite with the Dowager's gentlemen and grooms of the chamber, relatives and dependants who, like her, relied on the old lady for a roof over their heads and preferment. The Duchess summoned her from time to time and asked how she was faring and if she was saying her prayers and being diligent at her lessons. The answer, quite simply, was no, but she always said truthfully that she was doing well at her dancing and trying her best with her letters and her French. Then it was as if her grandam forgot about her till the next time.

On her birthday, though, she sent for her.

'I have a gift for you, she said, sitting straight-backed in her high chair and handing Katheryn a little velvet pouch. Inside was a small gold crucifix on a chain.

'When you wear it, think on the suffering of our Lord,' her grandam admonished. 'I am told that you are wilful, and frivolous and pleasure-loving, and that you are wanting in piety.'

Katheryn blenched. What harm was there in having high spirits, enjoying a laugh with the other girls and loving fine clothes? So what if she baulked at doing tasks she didn't like, such as mending hems, making tarts and helping in the still room, the kind of things Mother Emmet deemed suitable occupations for a young lady? And did God really mind so much that she was not always in chapel when she should be?

'These tendencies must be checked,' the Duchess continued. 'We cannot do just what we want in this life. You must look to your improvement.'

'Yes, my lady,' Katheryn murmured, her cheeks hot with embarrassment.

'But you have a kind heart,' the old lady said, and smiled. 'That is more important than most things.'

Katheryn cheered up immensely when Dorothy Berwick bounced into her room later that morning.

'Mistress Katheryn, we've been talking about you and we think that, now you are of marriageable age, you are quite grown up enough to join us in the gentlewomen's chamber, if you wish,' she said. 'In fact, we think you are becoming very pretty and will attract many suitors.'

Katheryn blushed at such unexpected praise. She knew, without conceit, that she was pleasing to look at: her mirror told her that every day. She had the Howard nose, but her face was round and pretty, her eyes heavy-lidded and blue, her lips full and rosy red, and her hair hung down her back like a rippling auburn cape. And it was true, she was growing up. Beneath the laced velvet bodice there were budding breasts and, two months ago, she had begun to have what Mother Emmet called her flowers, the show of blood she would experience each month until she ceased to be of childbearing age. She had worked hard at her dancing and deportment, and was as poised as a grown lady. If only she were taller!

She was thrilled that she was to be admitted to the sisterhood of the gentlewomen's dorter, for she had long yearned to be one of that merry crowd and to join in the laughter she had so often heard behind the closed door. And she was pleased when Mother Emmet told her that she could still keep her own chamber and have privacy when she wanted it, as was only fitting for a daughter of the Howards.

But she would sleep in the dorter tonight and join in the fun! Gathering up her night-rail and robe, she followed Dorothy along the gallery, excited at the prospect.

She walked into a long, high-ceilinged chamber with wooden beams, whitewashed walls and latticed windows. It contained about ten large tester beds, all with their curtains looped back, and a long trestle table in the middle of the room. Some beds were untidily strewn with discarded clothing and some were still unmade. There was one other young woman there, who was wearing only a thin shift and rummaging through a chest.

'Hurry up, Margery, you'll be late for dinner,' Dorothy chivvied her.

Katheryn wrinkled her nose. The dorter smelt stuffy, redolent of sweat, feet and unemptied chamber pots.

'I know, it stinks,' Dorothy sighed. 'The maids are late as usual. They're supposed to keep the room clean and aired. Don't worry, they'll be in later, and they'll put fresh sheets on a bed for you. I'll open a window. You might have to share,' she went on, indicating a bed in the corner. 'It depends on who is sleeping where. We often share with each other. There are more of us than there are beds.' Margery looked up at her and laughed.

That evening, after Mother Emmet had locked them into the dorter, Katheryn was made to feel very welcome by the young gentlewomen. There were about fourteen of them, all relations and dependants of the Duchess, some hoping to attract husbands, some just glad of a noble roof over their heads. The Dowager's married ladies, like Malyn Tilney, shared chambers with their husbands, but Margaret Bennet preferred to sleep in the dorter as it was more comfortable than the cupboard in which she claimed hers slept. Already, Katheryn was friends with several of the gentlewomen, and she sensed that they were a little in awe of her because she was so closely related to the Duchess; always, she was

'Mistress Katheryn' to them, although, to each other, they just used Christian names.

The chatter and laughter went on until very late, far later than her usual bedtime. No one told her to go to bed, so she stayed seated at the table with the others. She was surprised when, towards midnight, some of the gentlewomen got up and began replacing the burnt-out candles, and a petite, moon-faced girl called Alice Wilkes opened a cupboard and took out a covered platter, removing the cloth to reveal a joint of ham.

'Purloined from the kitchens!' she announced, and everyone giggled. Someone else spread a cloth on the table, while others took more items from the cupboard: plates, knives, beakers, a raised pie and a bowl of fruit. Then Dorothy produced a ewer of wine and the feast was complete.

'Tuck in, ladies!' Alice cried. 'You too, Mistress Katheryn.' They all helped themselves. It was delicious, all the more so for being illicit.

That was not the only surprise in store for Katheryn.

'Has someone got the keys?' Meg Morton asked.

'Here!' Alice said triumphantly, holding them up. She turned to Katheryn. 'Old Agnes has the keys brought into her own chamber at night, but she has spare ones on a hook in her stool room, and it's easy for those of us who attend her to bed to borrow them. We always return them before morning, and she never notices they've gone. Snores like an ox!'

Katheryn could not help laughing. 'But why do you want to leave the dorter?'

'We don't want to leave,' Kat Tilney chuckled. 'We have visitors!'

'They're here now,' Dorothy spluttered, as a soft knock was heard on the door.

Katheryn stared as a group of young men entered. She knew them all – the ever-humorous Mr Waldegrave, the diminutive and merry Mr Damport, Mr Ashby, Mr Faver and Margaret's husband, Mr Bennet; they were all gentlemen or grooms of the Duchess's chamber. Bringing up the rear was Mr Maunsay, a brawny, handsome usher.

'They have come to share the feast,' Mary Lascelles explained. Of all the women in the dorter, Katheryn liked her the least, for she was opinionated and put on airs. She had been nursemaid to the Duchess's granddaughter, one of Lord William's children, but the child was now older, so Mary had been found a place in the Duchess's household.

'Mistress Katheryn!' smiled Damport. 'It is good to see you here. You are quite the young lady now. Will you have an apple?' He handed her one with a flourish.

'Thank you, Sir!' she said, and bobbed a curtsey, entering into the spirit of the occasion. Soon, everyone was sitting on the beds, eating, drinking and laughing, their banter punctuated by loud whispers of 'Shh! Someone will hear.'

Winking at Katheryn, Mr Waldegrave produced another flagon of wine. The drink went straight to her head. When she stood up to cut another slice of ham, she felt the world tilt, and Dorothy, in fits of laughter, helped her to her bed, where she lay down, fully dressed, and closed her eyes.

'We'll let her sleep alone tonight,' she heard her say.

'It won't be for long,' someone else giggled. Vaguely, Katheryn was aware of a lot of scuffing and sniggering, and later, when she came to and opened her eyes, she could dimly make out, in the moonlight that streamed through a window, the shapes of people huddled together on some of the beds – people who had not troubled to draw the curtains. Some were sighing or moaning, as if in pain; others were snickering. By now, she knew, in theory, what the beast with two backs was, but she did not immediately connect it with what was going on in the dorter. Then a man got up and walked quite casually past her towards the stool chamber, naked as the day he was born, and the truth dawned on her.

She turned towards the wall and lay there, her face flaming, her heart juddering. How could they be so shameful?

Mother Emmet and the Duchess could not know what was going on, for surely they would have put a stop to it? It was impossible to believe that Malyn Tilney knew either. But – her eyes roved around the moonlit room – Dorothy, Kat, Alice, Meg, Joan and Dotty . . . They were all doing it, seemingly oblivious to each other or to Katheryn herself. And Margaret too, judging by the sounds coming from behind her bed curtains. Only Mary was lying alone, her curtains open. But what of the others, who had gone to bed alone and drawn their curtains? Had they not ears to hear what was going on? Surely they must know.

She told herself that they were just having fun, that what they were doing hurt no one. She would stay quiet and say nothing. She had had the time of her life this evening; she had felt included and accepted. Why upset the cart? Mother Emmet had told her more than once that well-born young ladies did not compromise their virtue if they hoped to make a good marriage. Let others ignore that good lady's precepts; she, Katheryn, would not join in the bedtime romps – but she could partake of the good cheer and companionship. Who was she to betray her friends? Having found Paradise, she was not about to leave it.

'You saw us,' Dorothy said in the morning, dimpling. 'I hope we can rely on your discretion.'

'Of course,' Katheryn assured her. 'I had a wonderful time. Do you have feasts very often?'

'As often as we can,' Alice smiled. 'At least once or twice a week, if we can smuggle in enough food and drink. They're very lax in the kitchens. They don't miss it. We get word to each other when we're ready. The young gentlemen are willing to come whenever they can. But this must remain a secret.'

'I won't tell anybody,' Katheryn said.

'Good girl,' Alice beamed. 'One day, you will have admirers of your own.'

After that, Katheryn slept in the dorter most nights and joined in the feasting and frolics with zest, ensuring that she always went to bed before the others fell to less innocent pastimes. Sometimes, she could not resist watching them, for the noise they made kept her awake, and she was curious. Before long, lovemaking held few secrets for her. She had seen it all.

On a bright April day when all the trees were in blossom, the Duchess's chamberlain summoned everyone into the hall and announced that the Lady Anne Boleyn had been proclaimed queen. There was much applause and very few glum faces, because the Duchess's close kinship to the Lady Anne was well known.

As soon as they had been dismissed, the gentlewomen burst into excited chatter. Pert Meg Morton turned envious eyes on Katheryn. 'I'll wager you'll be a maid-of-honour before long!'

'Really?' That had not occurred to Katheryn, although she had known that good things would befall the Howards if Anne became queen. Not that they were befalling Father. In his infrequent letters, which Katheryn had to ask others to read aloud for her, he complained that he was still in debt and want. He had asked Master Cromwell to beg the King for help, but the King had declined. 'I am unable to repay Master Cromwell's kindness,' he had written. 'Though I have many kinsfolk, I am as poorly befriended as a man may be, and I have been so beaten in the world that I know what a treasure a faithful friend is.' His troubles were well known at Lambeth, much to Katheryn's embarrassment. She did not want people pitying her because she had such a wastrel of a father.

When Katheryn learned that the Duchess was to bear Queen Anne's train at her coronation, she began to hope that she too might be invited, until Mr Waldegrave explained to her that only the Queen's attendants and the wives of peers were permitted to attend. At their last meeting, the Duchess had also voiced the hope that Katheryn might join Queen Anne's household. Katheryn was praying that her grandam would ask for a place for her, but time went by and the word was that the Queen's attendants would have been chosen by now.

She was consoled by the news of a great river pageant when Anne came upriver from Greenwich Palace to the Tower of London prior to making her state entry into the capital before being crowned. Katheryn was going to watch with a crowd of the young ladies and gentlewomen.

That day, the late May sunshine was blazing. Mounted on the most docile palfrey in the stables, Katheryn rode between Malyn and Dorothy through Southwark and past London Bridge to Bermondsey. Escorted by their gentlemen friends, they joined the throng on the crowded riverbank facing the Tower. They managed to weave their way to the very edge of the water and let Katheryn stand at the front, where she could see; it was muddy and her good leather shoes were soon mucky, but she was too excited to care.

They waited for ages, not knowing exactly when the Queen was due at the Tower. Street sellers were making their way through the press of people, and Mr Waldegrave and Mr Damport bought hot pasties and ale for them all, as they would likely miss supper. At last, towards five o'clock, the great procession appeared at the bend in the river. What a sight it was! There were so many gaily decorated barges, many of them carrying minstrels playing the most beautiful music, and amazing water pageants with terrible monsters and wild men casting fire, which made Katheryn and some of the other young ladies scream. Now the Queen's barge was in view, making its stately way along the Thames, hung with cloth of gold and heraldic banners. They caught a glimpse of Queen Anne herself, dark-haired and gorgeous in a shimmering gown. As her barge approached the Tower, there was a fanfare of trumpets and a deafening peal of guns. Katheryn could just make out the Queen disembarking and being greeted by some important gentlemen before disappearing into the fortress.

The crowds dispersed after that. Katheryn and her friends were hoarse from cheering, but it had not escaped her notice that a lot of people had remained silent and disapproving. It was the only blot on an otherwise wonderful afternoon, and the day was crowned when they got back to Lambeth and found a banquet waiting for them in honour of the occasion. Katheryn wolfed down lots of sweetmeats and sugary confections, and Mr Damport brought her a goblet of wine to sip. She went to bed in her own chamber with her head spinning.

Three days later, she was among the throng assembled in the hall to watch the Duchess depart for the coronation. Her grandam made a magnificent entrance wearing her golden coronet and rich robes of crimson velvet furred with ermine. She swept past, followed by a horde of attendants and the many lords and ladies who had been accommodated at Lambeth, and Katheryn, slipping behind people's backs, was able to see her climb into her gilded carriage and ride away.

When the Duchess returned late that evening, after the coronation banquet, she sat in her great chair in the hall and told her avid household how the Queen had processed to Westminster Abbey in her royal robes with her hair loose beneath a rich coronet and a caul of pearls and stones. Her train had been so long that the Duchess had been unable to bear the weight herself, so Sir Edward Baynton, Isabel's husband, who was the Queen's new chamberlain, had had to support it in the middle. Katheryn was thrilled to hear about Sir Edward's promotion, for Isabel's sake. Her half-sister must be a very great lady now!

The Duchess related how Queen Anne had been attended by a great train of lords and ladies in robes of scarlet. She had sat in a rich chair set up on a scaffold before the high altar, and Archbishop Cranmer had placed the crown of St Edward upon her head, a sceptre of gold in her right hand and a rod of ivory with a dove in her left.

'Some of you may understand the significance of this,' my lady said. 'For the benefit of those who do not, the use of St Edward's crown signified that the Lady Anne was crowned as a reigning queen, not just as a consort. It is a high honour for one of Howard blood, and an expression of how much the King loves and honours his Queen.'

'God grant she bears him a son,' a man behind Katheryn muttered.

'It's quite obvious why he had to marry her,' a woman murmured in reply. 'Fancy going to your coronation with a high belly and your hair loose like a virgin!'

Katheryn turned around and frowned at Dolly Dawby, a sour-faced chamberer, and Mr Dunn, the yeoman of the cellar. 'Pray God the child is a prince,' she said reprovingly.

It was exciting to think of a king with Howard blood sitting on the throne. Wagers were now being laid on the sex of the coming royal baby, and the young ladies were hiding away a store of wine to celebrate its birth. It would be a prince, it must!

It was a girl. Everyone seemed to slump with disappointment when the news arrived in September. Katheryn could imagine the King's frustration. Every man wanted a son, and he had none.

'It's imperative that he gets an heir,' Mr Waldegrave said at the next midnight gathering. 'There are so many rival claimants to the throne that, if his Majesty died, there might be civil war.'

'Hush!' hissed Dorothy. 'You should not speak of the King's death!'

'No one's going to tell on me,' he retorted, grinning around the room.

'Can't the Princess succeed?' Katheryn asked.

'No, she's a girl. It's unnatural for a woman to rule men,' Damport said, then ducked as Alice Wilkes boxed his ears.

'Women are just as capable as men!' she hissed.

'I'd like to see you lead an army,' he baited her.

'Ever heard of Joan of Arc?' she snorted, making a face.

'If only the Queen had borne a prince,' sighed Kat Tilney. 'We'd be celebrating now.'

'Who needs an excuse?' Mr Ashby asked. 'Robert, fetch the wine. We can drown our sorrows.'

The only consolation was that the Duchess was chosen as godmother to the Princess.

There were to have been tournaments, but these had been cancelled. Nevertheless, on the King's orders, the *Te Deum* was sung in churches – including the chapel at Lambeth – in thanks for the Queen's deliverance, and there was a splendid christening. When she returned to Lambeth afterwards, the Duchess told her assembled staff that she personally had carried the Princess Elizabeth in her arms to the chapel of the Observant Friars at Greenwich.

'She was wrapped in a purple mantle with a long train furred with ermine, and a canopy was held over us, with the heralds preceding and my lords of Norfolk and Suffolk walking on either side. She is a goodly child, very serene for one so young, with red hair, like his Majesty, and a good pair of lungs on her when she pleases. She certainly bawled lustily when the Archbishop baptised her at the font. I saw the King afterwards; he hides his disappointment well. He was saying it would be a son next time. One can only admire his stoicism. He's been waiting for a son since he married the Lady Katherine in 1509. We must all hope that Queen Anne will be with child again soon.'

Chapter 6

1536

The Duchess's attempts to secure Katheryn a place as maid-of-honour to the Queen or the Princess had all ended in failure. Katheryn was sure it was because of the King's exasperation with her father. Lord Edmund's letters were full of complaints. He had not received a New Year's gift from the King this year; his Grace had sent inspectors to Calais to make sure that goods were not being smuggled out, which was really Father's job. Clearly, Father had been remiss. He was always involved in one petty lawsuit or another and was still deeply in debt.

When her brothers came to see her, they told her that Father had again sought Master Cromwell's help in retrieving his credit with the King.

'He seems to think that Master Secretary will solve all his problems at a stroke,' Charles said. The others laughed mirthlessly. Katheryn wondered how her stepmother was faring, and what Isabel would make of all this. She sighed. It seemed that Father would never become solvent and that he courted trouble after trouble.

But then something happened that made all this look trivial.

Early one evening in May, the young ladies and gentlemen were enjoying a cold repast at a table they had set up in the shade of a tree in the gardens. They were quite private here, well away from the Duchess's windows and prying eyes and ears – not that there were many people taking the air, Katheryn noticed. There was fowl and salad, and Robert Damport – he was Robert to her now – was filling her goblet with wine when they heard a distant boom from downriver.

'What was that?' Kat Tilney wondered.

'It sounded like cannonfire,' Edward Waldegrave said.

'Are we being invaded?' asked Meg Morton, in mock alarm.

'No,' replied William Ashby, a young man who liked to hide his serious side behind a clownish exterior. 'It was some kind of explosion.'

'I think it's coming from the Tower,' Edward opined. He was knowledgeable about military matters. 'They always fire the cannons there when something momentous takes place, like a royal visit.'

They continued their meal, chattering away happily, and some young men snatched kisses from their willing paramours. Katheryn watched them wistfully, strangely moved. She was happy enough, but restless. She had kept her resolve not to entertain gentlemen in the dorter at night, but her awareness of what was going on around her in the dark, and her occasional glimpses of sexual activity, always aroused her, and she was beginning to feel left out. She was fifteen, and still the Duchess had not arranged a marriage for her – or anyone else, for that matter. Her tutor had given up trying to instruct French, and told her he could make no further progress in teaching her letters – which was rather unfair, since she could read and write after a fashion, and much effort – but she was still having dancing lessons and working hard on her deportment. She had gained poise, she knew, and loveliness.

It was spring, the world looked beautiful and her blood sang in her veins. What harm would it do to indulge in a little flirtation, a few kisses and caresses? For two years now, she had seen her fellow gentle-women coupling with their lovers, and none of them had suffered for it; indeed, it enriched their otherwise monotonous lives. Must she always remain a bystander, an envious observer of the romancing and lovemaking going on around her?

Of course, she did not want to risk the disgrace of an illicit pregnancy, but she had become aware that not one of the young women had become pregnant, which puzzled her for some time. She had been wanting to ask someone, but hadn't had the courage, but sitting next to the sympathetic Dorothy emboldened her. Lowering her voice, she asked, 'Dorothy, how come none of the gentlewomen ever get with child?'

Dorothy flushed and glanced around the garden as if checking to see that no one else had come within earshot. 'Some of us don't go all the way. Some do, but there are ways to prevent conception. I don't know what they are, for such practices are forbidden by the Church. You had best ask one of the others. Joan may know, although you might not get a straight answer.'

'What?' said Joan Bulmer from across the table. 'Did I hear my name?'

'Mistress Katheryn wants to know how it is that none of you get pregnant.'

'Methinks her grandam wouldn't want her to find out.' Joan was blushing. 'And I'm not telling her.'

Alice intervened. 'I think a woman has the right to know. Mistress Katheryn, there are several ways. It's easiest if the man withdraws before he spends his seed, but some of them don't want to do that, or just can't. Taking oils of mint, rue and savin and honeysuckle juice can work, or you can insert pepper, or wool soaked in vinegar, or certain herbs, inside your honeypot. Or men can sheath their weapons with Venus gloves of lambskin or sheep's gut. Thus, you can enjoy your sport and not have to worry about conceiving a bastard.'

'And no one would be any the wiser,' Katheryn observed.

'Mistress Katheryn, don't even think about it,' Margaret Bennet urged. 'The Duchess would be horrified. You're of nobler blood than the rest of us, and you daren't risk being caught in fornication.'

'But the Duchess never comes near nor by,' Katheryn said. 'And I am not planning to bed anyone. I was just curious.'

When they carried their plates and goblets back to the kitchens, they found them empty, which was unusual.

'They're all in the hall,' said the porter, coming through the back door. 'There's news of the Queen.'

'Damn!' swore Edward. 'We didn't hear any summons.'

'They don't cry them in the gardens, remember,' Joan said.

Katheryn and her companions hastened to the hall, where the Duchess was seated in her chair of estate, clad in black and looking pale as she spoke to the rest of her household.

49

'We must await further news,' she said. 'You may go now.'

Katheryn grabbed Malyn's sleeve. 'What's happened?'

'The Queen's been arrested and taken to the Tower,' Malyn replied.

'Oh, no! Why?' Katheryn was appalled. It dawned on her why the cannon had been fired.

'No one knows for certain, but several gentlemen were taken as well. The Duke himself arrested the Queen.'

'Oh, sweet Jesus, what will happen to her?'

'I have no idea,' Malyn said.

Katheryn pushed through the throng to her grandam, who was rising to leave.

'My lady! What has the Queen done?'

The Duchess sat down, leaned forward and murmured in Katheryn's ear, 'The Duke informed me that she is accused of adultery and plotting the King's death. Tell no one.'

This was shocking news.

'What will happen to her?'

The Duchess swallowed. She looked every one of her sixty years. 'It's high treason, for adultery compromises the succession; and it's treason now even to imagine the King's death, let alone plot it. If she is found guilty, they will do with her what they always do to traitors. They will execute her.'

'That's terrible.' Katheryn could not take it in. The love between the King and Queen was famous; that she should betray him was incredible. 'She cannot be guilty!'

'The Duke thinks she is, but he would. He is the King's man and will always put his duty to his Grace before his family – and there is no love lost between him and the Queen since they quarrelled. In truth, I do not know if she is guilty. If she is, she has been unbelievably stupid.'

'Can you do anything to help her?'

'Mercy, child, I am just a poor widow; my word carries no weight at court. Now go. I have a powerful headache and must lie down.'

In the three weeks that followed, fresh news reached Lambeth intermittently. Five men accused of adultery with the Queen had been tried in Westminster Hall and condemned to death. It was Charles who came to tell Katheryn that Queen Anne herself had been put on trial in the Tower and sentenced to die.

'Her marriage to the King has been dissolved,' he revealed, looking as crestfallen as she felt. She could imagine how grim the atmosphere would be in the Duke's household.

That day, some of the young men of the household went to Tower Hill and witnessed the beheading of the Queen's lovers.

'One was her own brother,' John Bennet said, disgusted.

'They all made a good end,' Edward Waldegrave murmured, crossing himself. 'It was a hard thing to watch.' He looked sick.

Katheryn could not imagine what it was like to have your head cut off. She couldn't even begin think about it, her horror was so great. Yet, in a day or so, her own cousin, no less a personage than the Queen of England, was to suffer such a death. She could not get the thought out of her mind and spent an hour in the chapel that evening, praying that God would move the King to relent or, if that wasn't possible, that Anne be given the courage and fortitude to face her end.

Just after nine o'clock, two mornings later, Katheryn was in the dorter, mending a hole in a shift, with just Izzie, one of the chamberers, for company, when the cannon sounded again. She froze when she heard it. She and Izzie looked at each other.

'The Queen . . .' Katheryn whispered.

The shift fell to the floor as she began weeping, grieved, not only for the suffering of Queen Anne, but also because the Howards had lost their standing at court and in the world, tainted by the crimes of one of their own. For so long, Katheryn had rejoiced with her kinsfolk in having a Howard queen on the throne; now, there was only shame and horror in it.

The Duchess gave the order that no one was to wear mourning. Anne Boleyn's name was never to be spoken again. Her portrait was taken down and burned in a back yard. It was to be as if she had never existed.

* * *

Early in June, the Duchess summoned her household again.

'The King has taken a new wife,' she announced. There were gasps of disbelief.

'And his last one in her grave not three weeks,' Dorothy muttered.

'Mistress Jane Seymour was proclaimed queen on Whitsunday at Greenwich,' the Duchess told them.

Jane *who*? Katheryn wondered. She had never heard the name Seymour.

'She served the late Queen, I believe,' a chestnut-haired man standing to her left said. She had not noticed him before. 'Make of that what you will,' he muttered.

She looked up at him. He appeared to be in his late twenties or early thirties. His eyes were a true green, which struck her as very unusual – and attractive. She noticed that he had full lips too.

'I take your drift,' she said, and looked away, aware of those green eyes on her.

When the Duchess dismissed the household, Katheryn wandered into the gardens, unable to believe that the King had remarried so soon and wondering what the new Queen was like. Would she speak up for the Howards? Or would she regard them as enemies? Was it possible that she had had a hand in the late Queen's fall?

Those intense green eyes kept intruding on her thoughts. She had no idea who the man was, but he had stirred her fancy and unsettled her. Thoughts of him distracted her all day, until the time came for the dorter door to be unlocked and the young gentlemen admitted.

Edward Waldegrave had heard of Jane Seymour. When the girls began furiously speculating, he said he'd heard a ballad about her being sung in a tavern some weeks past. 'It wasn't very complimentary,' he said.

'I have a friend at court who told me she is staunch in the old faith and a friend to the Lady Mary,' said William Ashby. 'He also said she's as plain as a pikestaff and has skin so pale that it looks white.'

'How chivalrous of him!' Margaret Bennet observed.

'No doubt there'll be much competition for places in her household,' Dorothy remarked.

'Well, I'm a Howard. I won't stand a chance.' Katheryn made a face. 'I'll probably be here for ever and ever, with no preferment at court and no husband.'

'I'll marry you,' Robert cried, and flung himself dramatically down on one knee.

'Stop it, fool,' Alice reproved him. 'You haven't a penny to your name. The Howards wouldn't even consider you.'

'Well, I would,' Katheryn said, winking at Robert, 'if my grandam would let me. Now, can you pass me another comfit?'

The next day, the Duchess summoned Katheryn to her private parlour. Waiting with her there was the green-eyed man and another, older gentleman with grey hair.

'Katheryn, this is Mr Manox' – the green-eyed man bowed – 'and this is Mr Barnes,' the Duchess said. Barnes smiled guardedly. 'I have appointed them to teach you music and singing, accomplishments that will increase your chances of securing a position at court in the future.'

Katheryn was thrilled to hear that the man about whom she had been fantasising was to be her tutor. She had never owned a musical instrument, although she had sometimes tried to play those owned by the other gentlewomen, and she did love to sing. She would enjoy being taught music by Mr Manox. She wasn't so sure about the reserved Mr Barnes.

The first lesson took place the following afternoon. Mr Manox had set a virginal on the table in the little parlour, by the open window, and Katheryn spent an hour familiarising herself with the keys, while glancing at him furtively and thinking how handsome he was. After the lesson ended and he went away, Mr Barnes arrived and began teaching her how to breathe so that her singing voice came from deep within her.

'You have done well,' he said, in his reticent way. Then he nodded and bade her good day.

Katheryn found herself enjoying her lessons. Mr Barnes soon had her singing like a nightingale, or so he complimented her. He was really a nice, kind man, although she suspected he was flattering her on account of her rank. Yet she did think she sounded pleasing.

She quickly mastered the keys and learned to play simple tunes on the virginal, as Mr Manox beamed his approval. Catching his passion for music, she sensed something wild in him that answered to the restlessness in her, although he never overstepped the bounds of propriety. He was always courteous and professional.

She found her eyes drawn again and again to his face, which was becoming more attractive to her with each passing day. She was insatiably curious about him, but he never said anything about his personal life. Once, as he prepared to leave after their lesson, she asked him where his home was.

'My family lives in Streatham, two or three miles away,' he said. 'The Tilneys have connections there, which is how I came to the Duchess's attention. I consider myself very fortunate to have done so.' He smiled, and it was as if the room was infused with brilliance. Katheryn was entranced. She had thought him attractive, yet now she realised he was devastatingly handsome.

No! she admonished herself. He was not for her. He was a music master and far below her in rank. She was grateful for the arrival of Mr Barnes, which saved her from having to reply to his compliment; she hoped Mr Manox had not noticed her staring at him in adoration. Thereafter, she avoided all occasion for conversation with him and tried to focus on her music. Only at night, when she heard the muffled sounds of the couples nearby, did she think about him, and always she told herself that she would not stoop so far.

In July, when people were still gossiping about Queen Anne and Queen Jane, the household reverberated with talk of another scandal involving the Howards. Lord Thomas, one of the Duchess's younger sons, had been arrested with the King's own niece, the Lady Margaret Douglas, and both were in the Tower.

The Duchess was in grief. She had taken her barge to court to press the Duke of Norfolk to use his influence to save her son, and the gossips were having a field day.

'They precontracted themselves without the King's consent,' Charles said, as he, Henry and George sat with Katheryn and the other young ladies sunning themselves by the river.

'Isn't that treason?' Kat Tilney asked.

'Probably,' Meg replied, crunching an apple. 'It's said that Lord Thomas had designs on the throne, seeing that the King's daughters are both bastards now. The Lady Margaret is the daughter of his Grace's sister and could inherit the crown.'

Katheryn had only the vaguest recollection of Lord Thomas. If he had visited his mother at Lambeth, she had not recognised him. 'Will he too be executed?'

Charles nodded. 'The word is that both he and Lady Margaret have been attainted by Parliament and sentenced to die.'

'What do you mean, attainted?' Katheryn asked, thinking what a dreadful year this was turning out to be.

'It means that there is no trial. Parliament decides on the person's fate.'

'That doesn't seem right,' Katheryn said. 'Surely they should have the right to speak up for themselves?'

'Don't ask me,' Charles said, shaking his head. 'I didn't make the laws.'

'The King will not execute his own niece,' Meg said.

'He executed his wife!' Kat reminded her.

'But his own flesh and blood?'

'There's not much hope for Lord Thomas then,' Katheryn said.

But the King sent neither the Lady Margaret nor Lord Thomas to the scaffold. Both were left to languish in the Tower, presumably to reflect on their transgressions. In the circumstances, he had been remarkably lenient. Katheryn would always remember that.

Chapter 7

1536–7

The errant lovers were still in the Tower at Christmas, but the Duchess ordered that the season be celebrated as lavishly as usual, and there was much revelry. On Twelfth Night, there was to be the customary feast. The house was packed with merrymakers, all dressed in their finery. Along with everyone else in the household, Katheryn had received new clothes at Easter, as happened every year, but these were always serviceable, usually of good black cloth, meant to last. Fortuitously, poking around in the attics – a treasure trove for anyone who bothered to rummage among the piles of discarded items that had been deposited there over the years – she had found a chest containing some old garments. At the bottom was an old-fashioned gown of worn crimson velvet with a high waist, tight sleeves and a flowing skirt. She had hung it up, sponged it and embellished it with the gifts she had received at New Year: a pretty pink ribbon sash from Isabel and a silver pendant from Father and Dorothy. The effect was pleasing and drew compliments from the other young ladies. With her long hair rippling down her back, she felt like a queen as she entered the hall.

It was the custom for women to enter from the left side of the screens passage and men to enter from the right. A great Twelfth Night cake had been baked, and slices were being offered to guests as they arrived. Katheryn ate hers right away, for inside she might find the coveted bean or pea. The lucky finders would be king and queen for the evening. She held her breath as she chewed carefully. To her joy, her teeth met something hard. It was the pea!

'I've got it!' she cried, and the young gallants came forward and, hoisting her to their shoulders, carried her to the high table and deposited her in the Duchess's chair, which her grandam vacated, bowing and entering into the spirit of the evening. Then another group of young men set down someone in the chair next to her. It was Mr Manox, who had found the bean and was being proclaimed king. He grinned at her and her cheeks flamed.

She knew what was expected of them. Their word was law for the evening, and their orders had to be obeyed. They would lead the singing, the dancing and the disports. She could not believe her luck!

She smiled back at Mr Manox.

'Remember, Mistress Katheryn, there are no rules,' he said.

The company was waiting expectantly. They both stood up.

'What shall we ask?' Katheryn whispered.

'I command that every gentleman in this hall should demand a forfeit of the lady sitting nearest to him,' he cried, 'and that if she will not comply, she must kiss him three times in recompense!'

There was much laughter as everyone hastened to obey him. Then Mr Manox saw that the Duchess, seated at his right hand, was looking at him questioningly.

'My lady,' he said, 'I demand that, for your forfeit, you impersonate the Devil!'

The Duchess smiled. 'Some would say I do that every day!' Then she proceeded to gnash her teeth and roar damnation at those near her, which had Katheryn shaking with mirth.

'What do you command, Mistress Katheryn?' Manox cried.

She stood up and raised her hand. 'Hush! Hush! I command that every gentleman in this hall gives his chosen lady a gift. And you can't go and fetch one. It must be something you have with you.'

She watched as men began divesting themselves of rings, daggers, even caps, and then realised that Mr Manox was holding out his hand to her. In it lay a small gold crucifix on a chain.

'It was my mother's,' he said. 'I have carried it with me ever since she died, but now I want you to have it.'

'I couldn't possibly accept it,' Katheryn cried, flushing at the realisation that this was more than a game. It was a declaration of particular affection, and she was touched that he should want to give her something that was clearly precious to him.

'Tonight, you have to obey me!' he said, his green eyes warm and glittering.

'Very well, Sir, but I reserve the right to return it tomorrow,' Katheryn said. 'Even so, I appreciate the honour you do me.'

He smiled and pressed the cross into her hand. The touch of his fingers set her spine tingling. Suddenly, she wasn't as bothered about the difference in their ranks.

After the feast, she was thrilled when he rose, took her hand and escorted her out to lead the dancing. And how they danced! They began with stately pavanes, then quickly progressed to riotous *branles*. Everyone was on the floor, and the ladies were lifting their skirts and kicking high. Then, amidst the press of people, Mr Manox was pulling Katheryn through the throng and out through the screens passage, where one or two servants were already lying drunk. Up the stairs he ran with her and into the little parlour where they had their lessons. By the light of the moon shining through the mullioned window, he took her into his arms, and she went willingly. His lips closed on hers, gently at first, then insistently, his tongue probing. Startled, she drew back, but he drew her closer and she could feel a stirring beneath his codpiece. Suddenly, she wanted him. It did not matter who he was; she did not think she had ever seen such beauty in a man or felt such desire.

Yet she had not completely taken leave of her senses. 'Wait!' she murmured, freeing herself. 'You go too fast, Sir!'

'It is only because you have enchanted me,' he replied, his eyes searching hers. 'Alas, Katheryn, my case is hopeless. I love you. I have known it for weeks. I cannot help it. And I think you feel something for me too.'

A rational voice in Katheryn's head was drowning out the rushing clamour of her blood and telling her that this could not be. Even if the difference in rank did not matter, she was familiar with the romances and knew that a lady must never appear too eager to gratify her lover's demands.

'I am not sure what I feel, except that I do like you very much,' she said. 'But I am a Howard and no wench to be tumbled in secret.'

'Well I am aware of that,' Mr Manox said bitterly. 'I know I am not worthy of you. I was content to worship from afar – until tonight. You have no idea what you do to me, but, believe me, a kiss has sufficed. I count myself a lucky man indeed, that you should condescend so far.'

This was more what Katheryn expected to hear, the kind of response that suitors gave in love stories, in which the heroine was always aloof and unattainable, or might just condescend to giving a kind look or a gentle caress. Clearly, Mr Manox understood this, even if he had got carried away to begin with. And, she had to admit, so had she, until she came to her senses. Thank goodness he was a gentleman and had not taken advantage of her.

If she could grant him no further favours, she could at least be pleasant to him.

'Let us go back,' she said, smiling. 'They'll be passing the wassail bowl soon.' And she ran ahead of him, down the stairs.

The next day, Katherine paused in the hall looking at the piles of fading evergreens that lay on the floor. The men had taken them down late last night, after the feast. It was sad to think that Christmas was nearly over. Today was Epiphany, the last opportunity to make merry. Tonight, there would be revelry and disguisings; they would eat roast lamb and an Epiphany tart made in the shape of a star, and she would wear her finery again.

Margaret Bennet came over, smiling at her. 'You were enjoying yourself with Mr Manox last night!'

Katheryn felt herself blush. Had Margaret seen them disappearing? 'It was a wonderful evening,' she said.

'I'll wager he has a fancy for you,' Margaret giggled.

'Do you?' Katheryn asked, walking on towards the storeroom where they kept the dressing-up chest. She wanted a crown to wear tonight.

'It was obvious, the way he was looking at you,' Margaret replied.

'He's my music master!' Katheryn retorted.

'He's very handsome!'

'Oh, stop it!' Katheryn shut the door in Margaret's face. As she searched through the chest, she told herself she had done nothing

59

wrong, and certainly nothing to compare with what other young ladies in the household got up to. Of course, in the cold light of day, she saw that it was impossible for a daughter of the Howards to love her music master. Yet she could not forget those magical moments in the parlour.

At dinner, the other girls teased her about favouring Mr Manox.

'Will you dance with him again tonight?' Joan Bulmer asked.

'Yes, I think I will,' Katheryn smiled. 'He is a good dancer.'

'And was he good at anything else?' Alice winked at her.

'I don't know what you mean,' she retorted.

'Don't think we didn't see you disappearing with him!' Meg chortled.

'We didn't do anything,' Katheryn insisted.

'Did he kiss you?'

'I can see from your face that he did!' Joan grinned.

'It was a mere flirtation,' Katheryn said firmly. 'Nothing more.'

After dinner, Malyn Tilney took her aside. 'I could not help overhearing your conversation at table,' she said. 'Katheryn, Manox is your music tutor and employed in a position of trust. Making advances to his pupil is a serious breach of that trust. The Duchess would not approve. He could lose his place. I beg of you, take thought for your reputation.'

Katheryn tapped her foot. 'Malyn, it was just some fooling about. I don't know why you and everyone else are making such a fuss about it.'

'Very well,' Malyn said, still looking concerned. 'Just be careful.'

That evening, Katheryn found Manox and gave him back the crucifix. He protested, but she pressed it back into his hand and walked away.

After Epiphany, the music lessons resumed, but Mr Barnes was no longer teaching Katheryn. He had been ordered to tutor Kat Tilney instead.

Katheryn found herself spending long periods alone with Manox. Whether anyone was aware of that she had no idea. She had long ago realised that Mother Emmet was so lax in her supervision of her charges that they could have committed murder and she would not have noticed. All she wanted was an easy life with no confrontations.

Katheryn sat at the virginal, aware that Mr Manox was looking at her intently. Why not? she thought. It was about time she had some fun, and surely a little dalliance would do no harm. She lowered her head and looked up at him sideways, smiling invitingly.

He laid his hand on hers. 'I enjoyed Twelfth Night,' he said.

'So did I,' she told him.

'I meant what I said. I love you. Tell me I may hope.'

'Hope for what?'

'That you might return my love.' His eyes were deep green pools, pleading, admiring . . .

Katheryn laughed. 'Mr Manox, this is all very new to me. You must give me leisure to discover my feelings. It might help to spend more time together.' She was encouraging him, she knew, and was no longer sure if it was right or wrong. All she knew was that she was strongly attracted to this beautiful man and wanted to keep his interest, right or wrong be damned! She would do as she pleased. No one really cared what happened to her, and Isabel, in whom she would have liked to confide, was far away in Wiltshire, absorbed in her first baby.

'I can think of nothing better than to spend more time with you, Mistress Katheryn,' Manox said, squeezing her hand. 'You must let me know how it can be contrived.'

'You could play skittles with me in the long gallery after supper,' she smiled.

'That would be wonderful,' he told her. 'But now, I think we should get down to our music. And please, call me Harry.'

'I'll have to think about that,' Katheryn said, giving him an arch look.

When Katheryn appeared with Mr Manox in the gallery, there were several other people there. Eyes turned as they walked past, and she was aware of murmured asides. She did not care. It was not every young lady who had such a handsome man as her devoted servant.

In the days that followed, she and Harry – as she now called him – spent an increasing amount of time together. They walked in the gardens, they sat for ages on a seat by the river, talking, and the music lessons grew ever longer. Closeted in the little parlour, they would find themselves chatting when Katheryn should have been practising, but she was too conscious of Harry's physical presence to concentrate on her music. Before long, they would be in each other's arms, unable to resist the temptation to kiss – long, lingering kisses that left them breathless and wanting more. Katheryn's resolve was rapidly weakening.

'I do love you,' she said, which made Harry even more fervent. Kissing led to caressing, and his fingers would rove down Katheryn's breast to the neckline of her bodice. The sensation was so divine that she did not protest when they delved further. His touch on her nipples was unbearably exciting and gave her thrilling sensations in the pit of her stomach. She did not want him to stop. But when his hand moved to her skirt and made to lift it, she stayed him.

'No!'

'Why not? I want to see you, my love, and touch you.'

'No, please!' She did not trust herself to let him. 'Not yet.'

His hand strayed back to her breast.

They were at pains to be discreet. No one, it seemed, knew their secret. Katheryn took care to prevent the young gentlewomen from finding out. The Duchess was too absorbed in her own lofty affairs to notice what her step-granddaughter was doing, and Mrs Emmet seemed oblivious, as usual.

She had no idea where this was going, but she didn't care. The future could look after itself. All that mattered was that Harry loved her.

By Eastertide, it was hard to control her desire for him, and harder still to put him off. He was always begging for more.

'Let me feel the secret parts of your body!' he begged, his kisses hot and urgent.

'No,' Katheryn protested. 'We might get carried away.' The girls in the dorter had spoken of a point of no return, beyond which a man lost control, and she feared to provoke Harry that far.

'Then give me some token of your love!' he panted. 'Show me how much you love me.'

'What token shall I give you?' she asked. 'I assure you, I will never be naughty with you, and you are unable to marry me. It would not be allowed.'

But Harry was undaunted. 'All I want to do is touch you. What harm can that do?'

Katheryn had no arguments left. Besides, she really wanted him to touch her.

'All right.'

She watched him gaze at her in rapture. 'You will? You'll give me your promise that you will let me?'

'Yes,' she murmured, 'but not today, as it will soon be supper time. Then you will be away visiting your family for the Sabbath. But when you come back, you may do as you wish, on condition that you will desire no more of me. And we will have to find somewhere more private. This room has no key.'

'Katheryn, you are an endless joy to me,' Harry cried. 'I cannot fully express my feelings for you, or my gratitude. I love you so much, my darling!'

'I love you too,' Katheryn breathed. In that moment, she was tempted to promise him all of herself. She knew how to prevent a baby coming, after all. But she feared that, by giving much, she would lose much. She had heard it said that men lost interest in that which they obtained too easily.

Two days later, in the dark of night, Katheryn met Harry in the deserted gallery and, carrying a candle, he led her silently to the antechamber to the Duchess's chapel, locking the door behind him and drawing her down onto a wooden bench.

'Are you still willing to keep your promise?' he whispered.

'I am,' she said. 'Touch me!'

The sensation was exquisite. That night, she learned what pleasure really was. There was nothing shameful or sinful about it: it was the most natural thing in the world. And when Harry bent his head down and kissed the brown mole on the inside of her thigh, then proceeded further with his tongue, she thought she would die of bliss. The waves of rapture came again and again. It was like being in Heaven. Then he wanted her to touch him and give him the same pleasure, and she held him in her hand in wonder as he swelled with lust, spilled his seed and gasped in ecstasy. True to his word, he did not ask for more.

Wrapped up in their passion, they sought each other out whenever they could. Soon, Katheryn's friends guessed what was going on and ribbed her about her handsome suitor.

'I'll wager you make good music together!' Alice Wilkes teased her.

'I can see from your face that you are in love,' said Meg.

Katheryn took it all in good part. It thrilled her to talk about Harry; his name was forever on her tongue. It was good to have her secret out in the open. It made her feel at one with the girls who made merry in the dorter. No longer had she cause to envy them. And they would not tell on her because she knew their secrets.

The young gentlewomen were pleased that she had found a suitor at last and kept urging her to bring Harry to the dorter at night to join in their frolics, but she would not. That which she shared with him was too precious to be debased by exposure to prurient eyes.

She was in love, and the world looked rosier for it. She went about in a daze, counting down the hours until she could next be with Harry. She knew his feelings for her to be strong and true, and revelled in his adoration. Never had she felt so special!

The only sour note was struck by Malyn and Mary Lascelles, who must have heard talk about her and Harry and seemed disapproving. Mary was probably jealous, but Malyn, she knew, had her interests at heart. Clearly, she had not wanted to broach the matter.

'Mr Manox is a presentable man, but he is a servant, Katheryn, and Howards do not marry servants or dally with them,' she said. 'It is best not to become involved with him. I would hate to see you get hurt or your honour compromised. It would not take much, you know.'

'You don't need to worry about me,' Katheryn assured her, feeling her cheeks go hot.

Malyn looked doubtful, but said no more. Her words left Katheryn feeling disturbed. She must take more care in future. The last thing she wanted was the Duchess finding out. It could be the end of it for her and Harry, the end of everything that made life wonderful – and that she could not bear.

The trysts in the little parlour and the chapel closet continued. There were stolen kisses and daring caresses, and such sweet rapture that Katheryn wanted to hold back the clocks and enjoy this time for ever. All through the summer, she went about on wings, glowing with love.

On a mild August day, Katheryn found a stone bench in the garden and sat down to read a letter from Father. It was unusually cheerful, for, he wrote, he had been elected mayor of Calais. She was so pleased for him. After six years, he and Margaret had clearly entrenched themselves across the Channel and at last it seemed that things were going well for them.

She smiled when she remembered how miserable she had been when they left her at Lambeth. It seemed a long time ago now. She had made a life here, and now had a very special reason to be grateful for having been given a place in the Duchess's household. Yet she wanted something more. The world was out there beckoning, and she longed to be a part of it. If she were honest, she wanted to marry Harry. They had never discussed it – it was as if they both knew there was no hope of it being permitted – but Katheryn liked to indulge in fantasies in which she wore gorgeous finery and stood exchanging vows with him in a church porch, or of her proudly presenting him with the sweetest baby boy. She felt that time was passing her by. She knew of a lot of girls of sixteen who were already married, and mothers.

The other thing she longed for was to go to court, for she had heard that the Queen was with child, and anyone who gave her good service at such a time would probably reap the benefits, but Father's promotion had come too late. There would be no places left in the Queen's household by now, even if a Howard girl was welcome, so there was no point in Katheryn wondering if the King would now look favourably on her. Besides, going to court would mean being separated from Harry.

She got up and trudged back to the house. They would be serving dinner soon. And this afternoon, she must hasten to Norfolk House to show her brothers Father's letter.

On a crisp October morning, the church bells began pealing joyfully. Leaning out of the dorter window, Katheryn could hear other bells in the distance. The sky was ringing. She ran downstairs.

'Have you heard?' Malyn said, grabbing her as she entered the hall. 'The Queen has borne a prince! We have an heir to England! Oh, what a happy day!'

The Duchess was standing on the dais, beaming, surrounded by her daughters, the countesses of Derby, Oxford and Bridgewater, who all happened to be visiting, and her ladies.

'Lord William brought me the news this morning,' she said. 'We must feast tonight.'

Katheryn was aware of Harry standing next to her. 'Wonderful tidings!' he said. 'It means we no longer have to fear a disputed succession and civil war.'

'Do you think my lady will be asked to carry the Prince at his christening, as she did the Lady Elizabeth?'

He smiled down at her. 'I doubt it. The Queen's relations will have precedence this time.'

If the Duchess felt snubbed, no one was aware of it. When news came that the Duke of Norfolk was to be a godparent, she was all smiles. This was proof indeed that the Howards were back in favour after being out in the cold following the fall of Queen Anne.

Two weeks after Katheryn had heard them pealing, the bells of Lambeth and London sounded again. This time, they were tolling solemnly. The Queen was dead. It was a sobering reminder of the hazards of childbirth and revived painful memories of her mother. At least she had known her mother; the precious little Prince would never know his. Her heart went out to him. Suddenly, she found the idea of marriage not so appealing after all. If they let her marry Harry now, she could be dead within a year. It was a terrifying thought.

The Duchess commanded that mourning be worn until the funeral was over. Soon, she was plunged into her own grief when, having been told, to her joy, that her son Lord Thomas was to be released from the

Tower, word came that he had died there of a fever. Ramrod straight in her chair, swathed in black and looking ravaged, yet never shedding a tear, she told Katheryn that the Lady Margaret Douglas had been set at liberty and sent to Syon Abbey. 'I am told that she too is devastated,' she added. 'But God's will be done!'

For a month, Katheryn was obliged to wear an old black dress that was rather tight under the arms.

'But you look very fetching in it,' Harry said, when she complained. She peered into her mirror that night. He was right. Simplicity suited her. The black gown was low-cut, and with no jewel and her hair loose, the effect was quite striking. So striking, in fact, that she had to keep fighting Harry off.

'We're supposed to be mourning the Queen,' she chided him.

'I'm trying to forget my sorrow,' he grinned. 'Come here, you little witch!'

There was a knock on the parlour door. Katheryn sprang out of Harry's arms as Will Ashby came in.

'A letter came for you, Mistress Katheryn,' he said, handing it to her with a knowing look before departing.

It bore Father's seal. As Harry watched, she read it in mounting dismay. It seemed she would never get to court. The King himself had overturned Father's election. 'He will in no wise agree that I shall be admitted to the mayoralty,' Father had written, 'and I cannot continue in Calais without some other augmentation of my income.'

She handed it to Harry to read. 'I feel so ashamed. What could my father have done to be so slighted? He must be liked in Calais, or he would not have been elected.'

'Maybe the King has some other candidate he prefers. Don't let it upset you, sweetheart.' He pulled Katheryn onto his lap and began nuzzling her ear. 'At least he is still in post. It is no small thing to be comptroller of Calais.'

Chapter 8

1538

Father was coming home. As Katheryn sat by the warm fire in her chamber, slowly making her way through his letter, she was delighted to hear it, yet not so thrilled to learn that the King's Council had summoned him. 'They say I do not obey the King's orders,' he had written, 'and now I am to be questioned about the state of affairs in Calais.' There was a lot more, but she was too agitated to read it. Even now, she was not good with words.

Alarmed, she went running in search of Harry and met him in the long gallery.

'Look,' she urged, pressing the letter into his hand, barely containing her impatience as he perused it. 'What if Father cannot satisfy the Council? Will he be dismissed? Or could something worse happen to him?'

Harry hesitated, as if searching for the right thing to say. 'Reading between the lines, it seems he wasn't very efficient at his duties, that's all. I very much doubt it merits a spell in the Tower.'

'But he says he is being victimised.'

Harry sighed. 'Darling, it's an excuse.'

'No, he's an honest man,' she protested. 'Consider what grief it is to him to be thus slandered.'

Harry did not reply. She felt a little let down.

Father's next letter informed Katheryn that he had been dismissed. He had appealed, reminding Master Cromwell of his poverty and the expenses of maintaining his house in Calais, and was hoping that Cromwell would see that he sustained no loss.

Katheryn felt sorry for him. Everything he did seemed to end in

68

disaster. She was sorry for herself too. Why couldn't she have a father who was rich and successful and in favour with the King? She prayed that no one at Lambeth learned of Father's disgrace. That would be too humiliating.

Lord Edmund came home in April. His sister, the Countess of Wiltshire, mother of the late Queen Anne, had died, and he was in time to join the gathering of Howards and Tilneys that assembled for the funeral. Katheryn was shocked when she greeted him at Lambeth, for he looked so old and drawn. He must be sixty now, she realised, and life had not been kind to him.

When he had greeted her brothers and she knelt in turn for his blessing, he raised her and hugged her tight.

'It is good to see you, daughter. You have grown into a young lady. I hardly recognise you!'

Margaret, her stepmother, was as warm and friendly as ever, but Katheryn noticed that, as they joined their kinsfolk in the Duchess's chamber, she kept giving Father anxious glances.

'He is not well,' she murmured. 'He has trouble with kidney stones, and this latest disappointment was a heavy blow. But he is hoping that he can persuade the Council to restore him.' She sighed. 'I've tried to convince him that he should retire, but he doesn't listen to me any more. He is the toast of the ladies of Calais, and some are no better than they should be.' Katheryn laid a hand on her stepmother's. It couldn't be easy being Father's wife.

'Don't worry, we'll be all right,' Margaret said.

They curtseyed to the Duke of Norfolk, who had taken his step-mother's chair, as of right, and sat there like a basilisk, eagle-eyed and tight-lipped. A stern martinet in his sixties, he did not look like a man to be trifled with. For a moment, those steely eyes rested on Katheryn appraisingly, then the Duke nodded and gave them what passed for a smile.

'Greetings, Lady Edmund, greetings, Katheryn.' He indicated that they should sit, and they took their places beside Father. Sitting on a bench, next to her brothers, Katheryn felt small and insignificant amidst this great gathering of her kinsfolk in their black velvet and their silks and furs.

The talk was all of poor Elizabeth, the late Countess.

'She never got over Queen Anne's death,' the Duchess said.

'She was ill before that,' the Duke reminded her.

'Losing her children in such a terrible way must have hastened her end,' Lady William Howard added. She was a pretty woman, exquisitely dressed, but light-minded, Katheryn had heard.

'I wonder how the Earl is coping with his loss,' the Duchess was saying.

'Thomas Boleyn was ever a survivor,' the Duke said. 'Remember how he was prepared to testify against his own children to save his neck? I doubt my sister had much to say to him after that.'

'I wish I had been here to comfort her,' Father said.

They walked in procession to St Mary's Church. In the Howard chapel, Katheryn found herself standing near her mother's grave. She felt guilty that she had not come to pray there more often, but she still could not bear to think of Mother entombed here in the cold ground. How different her life would have been if her mother had lived.

Father did not linger after the interment.

'I am for St James's Palace,' he said, as they stood in the church porch. 'I am hoping to see Master Cromwell.'

Margaret shook her head, watching him go. 'He never gives up,' she said, as people began making their way back to Norfolk House. Katheryn sat with her stepmother as the funeral meats were served, wishing that Harry was here. He was at Streatham, visiting his family. They had been in love for over a year now, and still she counted down the hours until their next meeting.

'Your father is planning to speak to the Duchess about finding a husband for you,' Margaret said, as they lingered in the hall, where the tables were rapidly emptying. 'He thinks she has been dilatory in the matter.'

Katheryn was appalled to hear this. She did not want to be married to anyone but Harry. Dare she confide in her stepmother? If Margaret disapproved, she might take steps to prevent Katheryn from seeing Harry again. He could lose his position! No, it was better to stay silent.

'If I don't like the man chosen for me,' she said, 'do I have to marry him?'

'We women seldom have a choice,' Margaret said, helping herself to a piece of marchpane. 'But I doubt your father would consent to a marriage you found abhorrent.'

'He might be grateful to any man who would marry me,' Katheryn muttered, biting her lip. 'I have no dowry, so it may be hard to find one who is willing.'

'A dowry would not be the only consideration. Many would relish an alliance with the Howards. And you are very pretty.'

Katheryn smiled at her. 'Thank you. I just wish I could marry whom I please.'

Margaret gave her a searching look. 'Do you have someone in mind?'

'Oh, no! I just wondered if Father would be amenable.'

'I think, if the man were suitable, he would be ready to consider it.'

Hope began to burgeon in Katheryn's breast. 'What would he consider suitable?'

'There is someone, isn't there?' Margaret pressed her, looking concerned.

'No! I promise you,' Katheryn protested.

Her stepmother appeared unconvinced. 'I suppose some young lord or gentleman of means, with a good reputation, would find favour.'

Of means. Harry would inherit only his father's house and the modest land around it. He had no title or ancestry to speak of.

'Well, I hope the Duchess finds someone nice for me,' Katheryn said.

She saw little of her father in the days that followed. Lord Edmund spent his days skulking around St James's Palace, waiting for an opportunity to speak with Master Cromwell. It never arose. When he received a letter from his superior, Lord Lisle, the Lord Deputy of Calais, summoning him back, he was jubilant.

'They must have thought better of sacking me!' he declared, and began making hasty preparations to return. Katherine doubted he had even thought to discuss her marriage with the Duchess and reflected that she had had a lucky escape.

'Farewell, daughter,' Father said on the day he departed. 'God be with you. I hope I will see you soon.'

Margaret hugged her. 'Take great care,' she said, and squeezed Katheryn's hand.

A letter from Isabel came in May. They had kept in touch, even though Katheryn found writing a chore, and she enjoyed hearing Isabel's news and reports of young Henry Baynton's progress. But this letter brought bad tidings. Sitting by the window in her chamber, Katheryn learned that John Leigh, her half-brother, had safely braved all the hazards of a pilgrimage to Jerusalem, only to be arrested for treason on his return. 'He is a prisoner in the Tower,' Isabel had written. 'He is suspected of having been in contact with Cardinal Pole on his way home. Pray for him.'

Near to tears, Katheryn took the letter to Malyn Tilney's chamber and showed it to her.

'Who is Cardinal Pole?' she wanted to know.

'He is the Countess of Salisbury's son, the King's cousin on the Plantagenet side,' Malyn told her. 'He went to Italy because he did not approve of his Majesty divorcing the Lady Katherine, and wrote a treatise castigating him for marrying Anne Boleyn. It so angered the King that Mr Pole had to stay in Italy, where the Pope made him a cardinal. It would be a rash man indeed who entangled himself with so base a traitor, but, from what I hear, Master Leigh is not a rash man. Cheer up, Katheryn. All will be well. Have you heard that we are going to Chesworth for the summer?'

'To Chesworth?' It was the Duchess's country house in Sussex, and Katheryn had spent two summers there when she was younger. She flung her arms around Malyn. 'Oh, that is good news! I love Chesworth! It's the most magical place!'

She felt much better. All *would* be well. Malyn had said so, and Malyn knew about such things. And Harry would love Chesworth too.

It was good to be back in glorious Sussex, and on such a beautiful June day. The Duchess's train had passed Horsham and Katheryn was eager to reach their destination. Only another mile to go now.

She couldn't see the house from the road, for it was well secluded, but as soon as she passed through the gates she found herself in the familiar paradise of wildflower meadows and ancient hedgerows, populated by hordes of butterflies. The River Arun, which rose in St Leonard's Forest nearby, flowed through the estate and formed part of the moat. Soon, at the end of the long, tree-lined approach, Chesworth House appeared before them, its older range of oak to one side, and the newer one of mellow red brick, built by Katheryn's grandfather, the second Duke, to the other; this was known as the Earl of Surrey's Tower, because the Duke had borne that title when he began it.

The gentlewomen's chamber, with its lofty beamed ceiling, was at the top of the new wing. Katheryn staked her claim to a bed by the window and hummed as she stowed away her belongings. Then she ran downstairs to enjoy the sunshine out on the terrace. Harry was already there, waiting for her, and together they explored the enchanting formal garden before wandering into the lush green park beyond.

'Oh, it feels so good to be here!' Katheryn cried, lifting her arms heavenwards and twirling around. Harry laughed and caught her hands, then whirled her around even faster, until they collapsed, breathless and giggling, on the grass. No one was in sight, and soon they were kissing and pleasuring each other, revelling in a glorious sense of freedom. It was so heady that they both got carried away, until Harry drew Katheryn down on his lap and she felt something stabbing at her, followed by an unbearably sharp, hot pain.

'No!' she yelped, and jumped up. 'Ow, that really hurt!' She rubbed herself. 'You promised you would not go further than touching.'

Harry groaned. 'I'm sorry, sweetheart. The moment felt so right. Forgive me.' He was so contrite that she took pity on him, and soon they were back in each other's arms, as ardent as before.

'You didn't enter me properly, did you?' Katheryn asked later as they lay on the grass.

'No, darling,' Harry assured her. 'You drew back before I was inside you. There wasn't any blood, was there?'

'No. I must still be a virgin, God be thanked.'

'It won't happen again,' he promised.

The summer days at Horsham were long and leisurely. The music lessons continued, but little progress was made, for tutor and pupil had other pursuits on their minds. At night, they would creep into the old wing, through the deserted hall, and make for the Duchess's chapel chamber, which was more isolated than the one at Lambeth. There they would stay for much of the night, lost to all the world except themselves.

The other gentlewomen teased Katheryn. 'Why don't you bring him to the dorter so that he can join in our revelry?' they urged again.

But Katheryn would only smile and say nothing. She did not want to think of the precious thing she had with Harry being brought down to the level of the crude dalliance in the dorter.

She was happy, though, to join her fellows in other pleasures. One day, she begged food from the kitchens, packed it up and carried it into the park, where the young ladies were seated on the grass.

'A banquet!' Dorothy cried. 'Thank you, Katheryn!'

Later that afternoon, as she lazed on the grass watching the others play hoodman blind among the trees, Katheryn noticed Mary Lascelles, who was seated on the terrace wall, observing her with a sly smile. Mary was a conceited prig who thought herself above the others in the dorter. She never joined in their frolics, but she often watched. They usually ignored her and Katheryn took care to stay out of her way, but lately it had seemed that Mary's eyes were often on her. Irritated, she rounded on the woman.

'Has my face gone green or something? Why are you always watching me?'

'I beg your pardon,' Mary said. 'But you intrigue me, Mistress Katheryn. Methinks you should be more discreet. I know what's going on with your music master. It's plain as day.'

'It's none of your business!' Katheryn snapped.

'That's as may be, but I speak as a friend. What he is doing is doubly reprehensible because he must know he can never marry you, and you are a virgin of noble blood. He is putting your reputation in jeopardy, and your chances of making a good marriage.'

'How dare you!' Katheryn cried. 'You know nothing of my affairs. Stop poking your nose in.'

'You might one day thank me for it,' Mary said, unperturbed. 'If the Duchess were to find out . . .'

'You wouldn't dare.' Katheryn was alarmed.

'*I* wouldn't. But, in a big household like this, such things cannot be kept secret and people will talk. Already they gossip about you in the dorter, and the young men they sleep with enjoy drinking with their fellows. They can be indiscreet when they have had one mug of ale too many. Just be careful, Mistress Katheryn Howard.'

'I'm not a fool,' Katheryn retorted, riled. 'And there is nothing to gossip about.'

'I don't think you're as pure and honest as you would have us believe, Mistress Katheryn,' Mary murmured, kneeling down and starting to pack up the hamper. 'You think you're above the rest of us, but you're no better. You fornicate in secret, don't you?'

Katheryn's temper flared. 'That's a wicked lie!' she hissed.

'See how she blushes!' Mary said. 'You deny, then, that you tumble with Mr Manox? I've seen you together in this very park, when you thought no one was watching. Take care of your reputation, Mistress Katheryn, take great care.' And she got up and walked back towards the kitchens, leaving Katheryn shocked and speechless.

How many other people knew what she had been doing with Harry? She thought they had been discreet. Oh, this was terrible! They must do something to remedy the situation before her reputation was irredeemably ruined. It could not go on.

All her pleasure in the day was gone. As she walked back to the house, her mind was working furiously. She and Harry could not go to the Duchess for help; that way lay disaster. They could run away together, or flee abroad, but they would soon run out of money. Or they could go into London and find a priest to marry them. That seemed the best solution. Once they were wed, no one could put them asunder. They would just have to brave the storm of anger that would surely ensue.

'Harry,' she said that night, as he closed the chapel closet door behind them, 'I have to talk to you.' She told him what Mary had said, but he shrugged.

'She's just jealous because no man wants her,' he said. 'That sour face would curdle milk.'

'But Harry, don't you see, if she knows about us, she might tell others, and they might tell the Duchess. Other people might have guessed about us. We can't go on like this.'

He stared at her. 'You mean you want to end it?'

'No, you silly fool!' she cried. 'I want us to get married. I know how it can be accomplished . . .' She stopped, seeing the expression on his face. It was not the look of a man who has been given his heart's desire.

'Katheryn, we can't,' he said, his tone bitter. 'Don't think I haven't thought about it, for I have, many times. But it is impossible. My father is not a rich man nor of gentle blood. The Howards do not marry with such as us. They would cut you off, I would lose my place and we would have nothing to live on. I could not let that happen to you.'

Or to myself. The thought came to her, unbidden.

'Couldn't we live with your parents?'

'And bring down the wrath of the Howards on their heads too? Sweetheart, you are being unrealistic. It can never be.'

Katheryn grabbed his hands. 'But I love you, and you love me. I will not give you up. You are the one to whom I will give my maidenhead, even if it might be painful to me.' She had not forgotten the pain she had suffered the other day. 'I will belong to no other. We *will* find a means to be together.'

Harry shook his head. 'You are a fool, Katheryn. You live on day-dreams. We are as together now as we'll ever be; it can go no further. Don't delude yourself. We can never marry.'

Katheryn was stung. They had had a few squabbles, but he had never spoken so sharply to her, and she was desperate to placate him. 'Then I will be your mistress! I will give myself to you, not doubting that you will be good to me, as I know you for a true and loyal gentleman.'

'Would that I *were* a gentleman! We wouldn't be in this dilemma. Maybe we *should* become lovers, for it's all we'll ever have. Don't you think it shames me that I am not worthy of you? For God's sake, let's do it tonight!'

Katheryn recoiled. She had never envisaged losing her virginity amidst such anger and bitterness. She had not realised these feelings went so deep in Harry.

'Of course you are worthy!' she cried. 'I'll prove it to you! Come to the chapel chamber tonight.'

Harry grasped her by the shoulders. 'Do you mean that? Do you really mean that?'

'I do.' She held his eyes with hers.

She did not go to the dorter. There was to be a banquet that night, and she would not be able to get away without people asking where she was going. Instead, she crept out of the house and sat up talking to Harry in the little banqueting house on the deserted terrace, where they were shielded by wooden lattices from anyone who might venture there. She felt wound up inside, unsure whether she had made the right decision. To be truthful, she was regretting offering herself, for Harry was still in a strange mood and not his usual loving self.

She had soaked a scrap of woollen cloth in vinegar and pushed it as far inside herself as she could. It had made everything feel sordid, and she was upset that Harry had not thought to ask her about preventing a baby. Did he not care if he got her with child?

It grew late. Candles were being doused in the house; she looked up and saw Malyn drawing her curtains. Hopefully, Malyn had not noticed them. A distant bell chimed midnight. Soon, all was in darkness. Harry rose and held out his hand. 'Let's go in,' he said.

The chapel chamber was dim in the candlelight. They sat down on a bench and Katheryn wondered how they would rekindle their passion to the point where she was ready to consummate it.

'You're having second thoughts,' Harry said, laying his hand on hers. 'Don't worry, I won't hold you to what you said. I'm sorry I've not been the best company. It's devastating to know that you can't marry the woman you love because others think you are not good enough. Your mentioning marriage this afternoon really brought that home.'

Katheryn's eyes brimmed with tears. 'When we do come together, I want it to be in joy, not when we're downcast like this.'

'You're right,' Harry said, drawing her to him. After a pause, he spoke. 'I had a letter from my father today. He is urging me to marry the daughter of one of our neighbours. He says he wants to see his grandson before he dies.'

Katheryn sat up, horrified. 'Do you want to marry her?'

'Before God, no!' Harry swore. 'I want you. I just don't know what to say to him. He's put forward all sorts of good reasons for the marriage.'

Katheryn exhaled in relief. 'Tell him you love another.'

'As far as he's concerned, love doesn't come into it. He'd laugh at me.'

'Then—'

Footsteps echoed along the chapel gallery. The door flew open, and there stood the Duchess, fully dressed, her eyes blazing with wrath. 'I was told I might find you both here,' she said in an icy voice. 'What do you think you are doing?'

Katheryn jumped to her feet. Her cheeks were burning and she felt as if her knees would give way. 'Begging your ladyship's pardon, we were only talking.'

'At this time of night? What have you got to say for yourself, Manox?'

'My lady, I apologise.' Harry had also leapt up, and now bowed his head. 'I was worried about a letter from my father, and Mistress Katheryn found me dejected in the gallery and kindly offered to listen to my woes.'

'A likely tale. I can tell from your faces that you were up to no good. You, girl, have been entrusted to my care, and I am responsible for seeing that you grow up honest and virtuous. I gave you a roof over your head when that fool of a father of yours hied over to Calais, and I have played a mother's part to you – and this is how you repay me. Come here, you little strumpet!'

As Katheryn stood rooted to the spot, Harry cried, 'Madam, I beg of you—'

'Hold your peace.' The Duchess stepped forward, raised her stick and brought it down once, twice, hard on Katheryn's buttocks. It stung terribly, even through her gown and kirtle. Then her ladyship turned to Harry and beat him too, as Katheryn cried uncontrollably.

'You are never to be alone together again, do you understand me?' the Duchess barked. 'And you, Mr Manox, are dismissed. You will leave this house tomorrow morning.'

'No!' Katheryn wailed, as her grandam grabbed her arm and dragged her out of the closet.

'I'm sorry!' Harry called after them. 'Katheryn, I'm sorry!'

Bruised, and broken in spirit, Katheryn lay on her bed, lost in misery.

'We didn't do anything wrong,' she had repeatedly told the Duchess on the way back to the dorter. She had pleaded desperately for Harry to be reinstated, but to no avail.

'You will be locked in until he has gone,' the Duchess told her. In vain did Katheryn wait at the window the next morning, hoping for a last glimpse of him as he rode away.

Chesworth lost its magic. In the last weeks of their stay, she moped around, avoiding the company of the other gentlewomen, wanting only Harry's presence, his kisses and his reassurance that all was well between them. Deep inside, she was worried that his father would make him marry the neighbour's daughter, and that Harry, thinking Katheryn lost to him, would agree. He would have to placate his father in some way, for the old man would be angry that he had lost his post. Worse still, she suspected that Harry had known about the proposed marriage before and wanted to wed the girl. Certainly, he had been less than ardent on that last day, arguing against marrying Katheryn and not seizing the opportunity of making love. She had offered him her most precious gift – and he had shunned it. That was how it seemed now.

She was under-occupied, with too much leisure in which to work herself up into a passion of grief and anger and fear. Two days after Harry's departure, Dorothy and Izzie, the chamberer, came upon her as she sat weeping in a secluded corner of the gardens. They hastened to comfort her, and she poured out the whole story.

'He made no protest at his dismissal,' she sobbed. 'He just let me go.'

'He is a servant,' Dorothy said, squeezing Katheryn's hand. 'What would it have availed him?'

'He's not worth it!' Izzie said. 'A man worth his salt would have spoken out. He could have said that his intentions were honourable and that he wanted to marry you. He had nothing to lose by it.'

'Try to forget him,' Dorothy said.

But Katheryn could not. She was holding on desperately to the hope that, once they were back at Lambeth, she could contrive to see Harry; he did not live so far away, after all. Better still, she was praying that he would try to see her.

Chapter 9

1538

They returned to Lambeth late in July and, to Katheryn's joy, there was a sealed letter waiting for her in the porter's lodge. It was from Harry. He had secured a new position as music tutor to Lord Bayment's children – the same Lord Bayment whose house was only just up the road! Could he see her? He missed her so much.

Inside the letter was a small package containing a tiny gold locket in the shape of a heart. Katheryn gasped in delight and hung it around her neck at once, concealing it beneath the partlet that covered her square-necked bodice.

Izzie was willing to take a reply. 'Don't appear too eager,' she counselled.

Katheryn took her advice, and soon there was another message from Harry. He would be at the gate of Norfolk House on Thursday evening and begged that she meet him there.

She was in a fever of anticipation. Thursday would not come soon enough. It did not matter if the Duchess found out. She would brave her wrath – nay, risk all – to see him.

She wore the black dress because Harry had liked it, and the locket, which drew many admiring compliments from the other young ladies. After supper, she bathed her face in rose water and combed her hair. She had washed it that morning and it rippled in an auburn cloud around her shoulders. She felt herself beautiful, beautiful for her lover. And he would be her lover, in every sense. She was determined on it.

As she hastened through the screens passage to the front door, a man loomed up in front of her.

'Now here's a pretty sight! And where might you be going, Mistress Katheryn Howard?' It was Mr Dereham, the new gentleman usher, a close cousin of the Duchess who had joined the household on its return from Chesworth. Katheryn had encountered him daily, supervising the service at table and the work and conduct of the upper servants in the Duchess's apartments, and was a little in awe of him, for it was he who swore in new servants and kept a vigilant eye everywhere. He was intense and very attractive, and there was an aura of the dangerous about him, for he looked like a pirate with his close-cropped black hair and sardonic expression. She could imagine him holding a dagger in his teeth.

She bristled. She was not a servant, and her movements were none of Mr Dereham's business. 'That's for me to know and you to wonder, Sir,' she said, in her haughtiest tone, and swept past.

'I hope he's worth it!' he called after her.

Harry was waiting for her by the gate. To her surprise, the sight of him did not cause her heart to jolt in the old way. But she was pleased to see him and assured herself that things would soon be as they had been between them.

'Darling!' he said and enfolded her in his arms. 'Shall we sit in the churchyard?'

She looked along the street towards the Duchess's inn. There were always people coming and going in and out, and she was praying that no one noticed them. Mr Dereham, the saints be thanked, was nowhere to be seen.

'Let's walk along the river towards Lambeth Marsh,' she said. That would be safer.

They took the gravel path that led to the Thames.

'I feel dreadful about what happened that night,' Harry said. 'I was shocked speechless when the Duchess appeared. I hope you weren't too sore after that beating.'

'I recovered,' Katheryn said. 'I was very upset, but I am over that now.' She wanted to ask Harry if he was to be married, but feared provoking another black mood.

'I hope we can continue to see each other,' he said. 'I am only along the road.'

'Of course,' she agreed, wondering why she felt so differently towards him. What had happened to her?

On the riverbank, they stood and admired the sky over Westminster. It was azure blue, streaked with a golden sunset. Harry put his arms around her and turned her to face him. When he bent to kiss her, thrusting his tongue in her mouth, she put her heart and soul into it, wanting to respond in the way she had weeks ago, but the feeling eluded her. In her mind, she kept seeing Mr Dereham's swarthy face. It intrigued her; there was something about the man.

'Shouldn't we just be grateful for what we have?' Harry murmured, his hand cupping her breast.

'Yes,' she agreed, pushing it away, no longer sure that she wanted him to touch her.

'I want you,' he said huskily. 'I know you want me too. I know what a lusty girl you are.'

She recoiled, not wanting to hear him speak to her like that.

He kissed her again, with increasing purpose, his hands clasping her buttocks. She was more than grateful to hear voices approaching. She pulled away and began strolling back towards the house.

'You should go,' she said. 'I would not like you to get into trouble if someone sees you here.'

'That would not matter, for it has been wonderful to see you again, sweetheart,' Harry said. 'Can I come again tomorrow?'

'I will send to you,' she told him.

They were near the gate. Harry lifted her hand to his lips. 'I will count the hours,' he said.

Dorothy took a note telling Harry that Katheryn would meet him two days hence in the same place. Katheryn did not confide her inner turmoil to her friends. Being in love had been wonderful; she wanted the feeling back, and to admit that it just wasn't there any more would make its absence even more real. So, each time, she agreed to see Harry again, glad for Dorothy and Izzie to carry messages and love tokens

83

between them, and pretended that all was well, as she was willing it to be.

One evening, while she was waiting for Harry outside Norfolk House, she saw, through the archway, Mr Dereham strolling towards her with Joan Bulmer on his arm. The sight gave her a pang – and it troubled her. Joan seemed to have forgotten that she was married. It was one thing to take any old lover, but Mr Dereham? It was unsettling seeing them looking happy together, as she had been with Harry.

'Hello, Mistress Katheryn,' Joan said smugly. 'Waiting for Mr Manox?'

'What?' Katheryn was shocked. 'Who told you?'

'The girls in the dorter were talking about it. It's no secret. Even Francis here knows about it.'

Mr Dereham grinned.

Katheryn vowed to kill Dorothy and Izzie when next she saw them. How dare they break her confidence!

'We hear that you are soon to be wed,' Mr Dereham said.

Katheryn gaped.

'Dorothy said that you are betrothed and much in love,' Joan added.

This was too much!

'We are no such thing,' Katheryn retorted, 'and I'll thank you not to listen to idle gossip!'

'But you *are* seeing him,' Joan countered.

'That's my affair!' Katheryn said, and walked off.

'Did you tell Dorothy or Izzie that we are troth-plight?' she asked Harry when he arrived, not waiting to greet him.

'No, I did not,' he said, frowning, as she began walking past Lambeth Palace.

'Well, it seems they are telling all and sundry that we are! So I was wondering why they are under that impression.'

'Maybe they made the assumption when they saw the locket I sent you.'

The locket. It must have cost a pretty sum. Katheryn wished she had not accepted it, realising that it did look like a betrothal gift. 'And was that your intention?'

'No! I saw it in a shop in Cheapside and thought of you.'

'All right, I believe you. But I hate people drawing false conclusions about us.'

'Would that they were true,' Harry said, taking her hand. 'Why are we going this way? There are places we can be private in the gardens of my lady's house. There's that arbour by the rose bushes. Let's go back.'

Reluctantly, Katheryn agreed. Although it was painful to admit it to herself, she knew now that her love had died, but she had not the heart to tell him. She let him lead her back to the Duchess's inn, praying they would run into someone she knew, someone who could rescue her. But it was dark and the gardens were deserted. Her hand in his, she followed Harry to the arbour and let him kiss her. When he grew passionate, she tried to ward him off, wresting his hand from her breast.

'Not here,' she whispered. 'Someone might come!'

'There's no one about,' he answered, lifting her skirt. 'Relax, Katheryn. You know you want it.'

'Yes, but not here!' she snapped, and stood up.

'I'm sorry,' he said, smiling ruefully at her. 'I get carried away by your beauty.'

'I must go in,' she said.

'Is something wrong?' he asked.

'No,' she lied, desperate to be gone. 'It's . . . it's just that I can't relax out in the open here.'

Harry rose to his feet. 'Leave it with me. I will arrange something. We must be together, Katheryn. You promised, and I can't stand the waiting any more.'

Yes, she had promised. And now she bitterly regretted it. 'It grows late,' she said. 'I will be missed. Send to me.' And she picked up her skirts and hurried away.

'Don't forget that you promised, Katheryn,' he called after her, and there was an edge to his voice.

She turned. 'Sometimes, in the heat of the moment, people say things they don't mean.' Then she began walking away, as quickly as she could.

'You little bitch!' she heard him say. She ignored it and hurried into the house, intent on finding Dorothy and Izzie. They were alone in the still room, making scent, and looked up in surprise as she banged the door behind her.

'Why did you tell people that I am plighted to Mr Manox?' she cried.

'We thought you were,' Dorothy muttered.

'And what gave you that impression?' Katheryn raged. 'You just assumed it. You thought you could make me the butt of a nice little scandal.'

'We are very sorry,' Izzie said, looking tearful.

'We really thought it was true, that you were to be married,' Dorothy said.

'We weren't the only ones,' Izzie added. 'Some of the girls saw you two together in the garden.'

'We won't say anything about it again, to anyone,' Dorothy promised.

Katheryn relented and forgave them. If it had been her in their place, she would have gossiped too.

Two days later, her heart sank when Mary Lascelles followed her into the dorter. It was afternoon and the chamber was deserted. Katheryn had come only to fetch the lute she had appropriated from the parlour where Harry had tutored her. She had almost mastered it.

'Guess who I saw this morning by the porter's lodge, asking for you,' Mary said.

'I have no idea,' Katheryn replied.

'It was Mr Manox,' Mary told her, with apparent relish. Something in her manner warned Katheryn that more was to come. It was bad enough that Harry had come seeking her out again, but it was worse that Mary, of all people, knew about it.

'Was it?' she retorted, grabbing the lute and making for the door.

'You want to marry him, don't you?' Mary challenged.

Katheryn stopped. 'If I did, I wouldn't discuss it with you.'

'It's what everyone thinks,' Mary went on, 'but I know differently.' She was baiting Katheryn.

'You know nothing!'

'No? Mr Manox was quite forthcoming. I told him he had no business to be aspiring to a daughter of the Howards. I asked him what he was doing, playing the fool in this fashion. I said that if my lady of Norfolk got to hear of the love between him and you, Mistress Katheryn, she would undo him. I told him you are of a noble house and if he dared to marry you, some of your blood would kill him!'

Katheryn listened, appalled. 'You had no right!'

'Maybe not, but I have done you a favour,' Mary smiled, 'because I have exposed him as the villain he is. He bade me hold my peace and admitted quite brazenly that his designs are dishonest.'

'What?' Katheryn cried, horrified.

Mary was still smiling. 'He said he knows you very well, and bragged that, from the liberties you have allowed him, he had no doubt that he would be able to have his way with you.'

'He told you that?'

'He was adamant that you love him and he loves you, and that you have promised him he shall have your maidenhead, even though it might be painful for you, and that you believe he will be good to you afterwards. My dear, you should beware of this man!'

Katheryn was shaking with shame and indignation. Mary's malice was bad enough, but for Harry to speak of her in this way was inexcusable. The worst of it was that some of it was true. She had said those things to him. This was his revenge, she had no doubt!

'Fie!' she exclaimed. 'I care nothing for him, nothing at all!' She was pacing up and down in her fury. 'He shall not speak of me like that. I will have him explain himself. Mary, will you come with me to Lord Bayment's house and be there when I confront him? You can testify to what he said.'

Mary nodded. 'Of course.' She was clearly enjoying this; she would never have refused.

They walked up Church Road to Lord Bayment's imposing residence and asked to speak to Mr Manox. When he came into the hall where they had been asked to wait, his face flushed. He knew why they were there!

'Mistress Lascelles has told me what you said about me,' Katheryn declared, glaring at him. 'You revealed to her the most personal details of our relationship and told her that your intentions towards me were dishonest. Is this true? Did you say those things?'

Harry nodded. He would not look her in the eye. 'I can explain,' he said.

'Then do so!' Katheryn had rarely felt so angry.

'Let's sit on the window seat and be private,' Harry said, his voice hoarse. She joined him there, leaving Mary standing at the other end of the hall, and taking care to sit well apart. She could smell ale on his breath.

'I'm sorry, sweetheart,' he said, hanging his head. 'I am far in love with you, and was so desperate to see you that I knew not what I said.'

'So it was the drink talking?' she retorted.

'No, no, no. She was too nosy, and taking a prurient interest in us, so I decided to shock her. I didn't think she'd tell you. I never meant to behave dishonourably towards you or upset you.'

'You realise that your words, if repeated, could ruin my reputation. My life too would be ruined. If the Duchess heard, she could cast me out, and I'd have nowhere to go.'

'If she did that, I would marry you,' Harry said, taking her hand. She drew it away.

'You've already told me why that cannot be,' she reminded him tartly.

'Look, I know you're angry, darling, but I didn't intend to hurt you in any way. I was an idiot. Please forgive me! I'll go on my knees if you wish.'

'Don't be a fool,' Katheryn said, thawing because he looked so abject. He did sound sincere – and his excuses seemed plausible, if rash. 'Very well,' she said. 'I forgive you.'

Harry seized her hand and covered it with kisses. 'May I see you again?'

'I'll think about it,' she told him. 'I will send to you.'

'Can we not set a time now?'

Katheryn relented. 'All right. Come on Sunday after dinner.'

She walked away, not giving him the opportunity to kiss her goodbye.

On Sunday afternoon, he was there waiting for her. This time, she led him to the orchard, where they strolled among the ripening apple trees. She had decided that it must end. She did not want him any more; in fact, she despised him, and was wondering what she had ever seen in him. When he tried to kiss her, she evaded him, and after a time she said that she had to visit her brothers and bade him a hasty farewell. Surely, she told herself as she raced up the stairs to the dorter, he must realise that all was over between them.

Chapter 10

1538

That night, the young ladies all gathered in the dorter for another midnight banquet. Dorothy and Meg had purloined a leftover joint of beef and some spice cakes from the kitchens, Kat and Alice had raided the buttery when the butler wasn't looking, and now produced two flagons of very fine Rhenish wine; Joan and Izzie had been to the market at Borough and bought rabbit pasties, and Margaret Bennet and some of the chamberers had been into the pantry at separate intervals and taken out manchet bread rolls, a jam tart and some cold salmon. Katheryn's contribution was a small basket of windfall apples from the orchard. It was going to be a veritable feast!

The key had been safely stolen and, at midnight, when they heard a tap on the door, Dorothy opened it to admit the young gentlemen who were their guests this night. Robert Damport joined Alice Wilkes and John Bennet gave his wife a warm hug, as other gallants greeted their sweethearts. Katheryn was surprised to see Edward Waldegrave go straight to Joan and kiss her soundly on the mouth. She had thought Mr Dereham was courting Joan, and that Edward was sweet on Dotty Baskerville. But here Dereham was, not seeming to care at all, kissing all the girls in greeting, then advancing towards Katheryn, smiling wolfishly. She felt a frisson of excitement at the sight of him. There was something powerfully attractive about him. Had she ever thought Harry handsome? He had been an Apollo beside this Mars.

'I had hoped to see you here, Mistress Katheryn,' Mr Dereham said, opening a sack and unloading wine and more apples.

'You are welcome, Sir,' she said, smiling up at him. He helped her to lay out the food he had brought and stood beside her at the table as they filled their plates. Then he sat down next to her on her bed. She rather liked his boldness. Around them, the others were eating and chattering in the candlelight.

'I have never seen you here before,' Katheryn said.

'Oh, I have been here on several nights, although you were absent – pursuing your pleasures elsewhere, they told me.'

Katheryn flushed.

'There is good sport to be had in this chamber of nights.' He was looking at Joan, who was kissing Edward Waldegrave.

'That's as may be, but I have no part in it,' Katheryn told him, 'nor ever have had.'

'Not even with the gallant Mr Manox?' His tone was sneering.

'Never!' she said.

'That's not what I heard.'

'Then you heard wrong!' She glared at him. 'Did you come here to bait me, Mr Dereham?'

'No, Mistress Katheryn,' he replied, his dark eyes holding hers. 'I came here because I wanted to get better acquainted with you. Let's say I am captured by your beauty – if you want to play by the rules of this game of love we're all supposed to play.'

'You speak of love, Sir? I hardly know you.' Nevertheless, her heart was racing.

'Love, lust . . . call it what you will, I want you. As soon as I saw you, I knew that I wanted you.'

'Stop!' She held up her hand. 'As my lady of Norfolk would tell you, I am not for you.'

'I am her cousin. Does that make me too base? My family is an ancient one. Our line stretches back for centuries. My grandmother was a Tilney, like her. My mother was that Isabel Paynell to whom the poet Skelton addressed some very lovely verses. He called her "the freshest flower of May". She was then in attendance on the late Duchess of Norfolk and was indeed very beautiful. This was before she married my father, you understand. He's been dead these seven years.'

'I have heard that you are a gentleman of a poor house,' Katheryn said.

'Not true!' Dereham smiled. 'But I am a younger son and have no fortune and no inheritance to look forward to, so I have to make a living. I was a gentleman pensioner of the Duke of Norfolk before I came here. Our family seat is Crimplesham Hall in Norfolk; my brother, Sir Thomas Dereham, reigns there now. This is our crest.' He held out his hand, on which there was a ring with a deer's head. 'It's a pun on our surname. Do my credentials find favour with your ladyship?'

Katheryn laughed. She was enjoying his company and his wit. 'You sound grander than the Duchess! And we are cousins too, by my reckoning.'

'But not too close, I hope,' Dereham murmured, a twinkle in his eye.

'Well, I have no fortune either,' she sighed. 'I too live on my lady's bounty. So maybe we are not ill-matched after all! Maybe she would approve.'

'We don't have to have her approval to enjoy each other,' he said, downing his drink and giving her a naughty look.

'I don't know what you mean!' Katheryn giggled, flushed with wine. 'Methinks you are too old for me, Sir. I am but seventeen.'

Dereham made a face. 'I am only twenty-nine,' he told her. 'Not quite a greybeard!'

He took their empty plates to the table, then came back and reached for his sack, taking out a lute and a ballad book. Quietly, he began to play – and play well. The piece was the King's own song, 'If love now reigned', and that was followed by one called 'Adieu mes amours'. It was delightful, sitting there beside this debonair man and being entertained thus. The music was having its effect on others too. Some were kissing, others withdrawing behind curtains or lolling back on the beds.

Dereham finished playing then turned to her. 'Will you be my amour, Mistress Katheryn?' His allure was so great that she did not hesitate. She went into his arms and gave herself up to his kisses. Before she knew it, they were rolling together, fully dressed, on the bed, mad for each other.

'Be mine!' he urged.

'No! It is too soon,' Katheryn protested, against all her body's instincts. 'It would be wrong.'

'Why wait? We want each other?' His breath was hot on her ear.

'I want to know you better,' she whispered.

For answer, he took her hand and guided it inside his codpiece. 'Now you know me better,' he chuckled.

'You're a very bad man,' she told him, but she did not take her hand away, and soon it was too late for him to ask for anything more.

'What are you doing to me?' he groaned.

'What you wanted,' she laughed. 'Don't go to sleep. The other gentlemen will all be leaving soon. None of you must be here in the morning.' Already, there were sounds of people stirring around them.

He heaved himself up, then bent down and kissed her. 'May I come tomorrow night?'

She nodded. 'I would like that.'

He reached for his sack. 'I'll be here. Oh, and Katheryn – I may call you that, I trust, now that we are better acquainted?'

'Yes, of course,' she giggled.

'Please call me Francis.'

A maiden should be shamefast, she told herself, as she lay abed the next morning, thinking about the night before. Chastity is to be prized. But what was wrong with taking your pleasure where you found it? Why should she deny herself the delights she might know with Francis Dereham? No, she would not!

There was only one problem. Harry. She must end it and weather the storm. It was not fair to keep him under the false illusion that she loved him.

'I see you have a new admirer,' Mary said, as they stood together washing their faces.

Katheryn stole a glance at her. Was she going to start meddling again?

'Mr Dereham is of good family,' Mary said. 'You could do a lot worse, seeing as you have no portion.'

'I do like him,' Katheryn admitted, relieved that Mary was not going to make more trouble for her.

'He likes you. It's plain for all to see,' Mary went on.

'He wants to come again tonight.' She hesitated. Given that the Duchess's anger with her had abated, she did not want to risk arousing it again. 'Mary, will you steal the key from the Duchess's chamber and bring it to me? She would never suspect you. I'll get some food from the kitchens and we can let the others know we're having a little banquet.'

Mary gave her a complicit smile. 'All right. I've done it before.'

'Oh, thank you!' Katheryn cried and kissed her.

Mary looked startled, but then she smiled. 'Don't allow him too many favours,' she warned.

'As if I would!' Katheryn turned away, her cheeks burning at the memory of what Harry had said to Mary about her.

Katheryn spent over an hour composing a note for Mary to take to Harry. She was trying to be as kind as possible, but it was hard to find the right words. 'You have been a good friend to me,' she wrote, 'but I think it best we do not see each other again. We have no future, and that which was between us is over, on my part and I think on yours too. Farewell. I wish you well.'

She folded it, gave it to Mary and waited for the storm to break.

That afternoon, Malyn told Katheryn that Mr Manox was at the lodge, demanding to see her. 'The porter says he's in a terrible state. Oh, Katheryn, what have you been doing?'

Katheryn's heart plummeted. 'Nothing!' she cried. Bracing herself, she hurried down to the lodge and found Harry there, pacing up and down agitatedly.

'What do you mean by this?' He thrust the crumpled note at her.

'What I said. I'm sorry, Harry, but I can't see you again.'

'Has the Duchess found out about our meetings?'

'No.' She hung her head. 'It's my decision.'

'Oh, God,' he moaned. 'I love you, Katheryn! Please don't do this.'

'You'll thank me for it in the long run,' she blurted out and fled indoors, weeping, hating herself for having hurt him. But she had had to tell him the truth. She just didn't love him any more, and he would have been hurt far more deeply if she had let things continue.

* * *

At midnight, Francis arrived with Edward Waldegrave, bringing fruit and wine, which they shared among the gentlewomen. Joan being absent, visiting her mother, Edward switched his attentions back to Dotty Baskerville, while Francis, having been very free with bestowing his kisses on every other young woman present, joined Katheryn and played his lute. Vexed as she was with that, she thrilled to his banter and the touch of his arm on hers.

'I want you,' he told her again, as they lounged on her bed, drinking. 'I really want you. Say you'll be mine!'

She had been asking herself again why she should not have a lover. Some of the girls here passed from one gallant to another. She was fed up with being virtuous. There was no marriage on the horizon for her, nor ever would be if the Duchess went on forgetting to bestir herself. Why should she not enjoy the pleasures of love here and now? She would never want any man as much as she wanted Francis.

'I will,' she breathed, and slid into his arms.

'You mustn't worry,' he murmured into her ear. 'If I used a woman a hundred times, I would get no child unless I wanted to.'

'I too know how a woman might meddle with a man and yet conceive no child unless she wishes to,' Katheryn told him. 'One of the gentlewomen told me.'

'Then can we make love?' His grip on her tightened.

She did not hesitate. 'Of course! When the others have gone to bed.'

'We can draw the curtains.'

'Let me finish my wine.' She did not want him thinking her too eager.

Francis shook his head. 'Such cruelty!' He stretched out on the bed. 'You know, some believe that a woman must reach her climax before she can conceive a child.'

'That's nonsense. Why, I've never—' She stopped, realising that she was about to admit to having permitted Harry certain favours.

'You know for a fact that it's nonsense,' he said, with that sardonic smirk. 'So Mr Manox was not such a bad lover after all! Don't worry, Katheryn, I didn't expect a beautiful young woman like you to be a maid.'

95

'But I am a maid. I was resolved to wait for the right man before I surrendered my virginity. Now I have found him!'

It was just gone three o'clock, and she would have jumped into bed with him but for Meg saying she thought she'd heard someone in the gallery outside. No one dared open the door, and they all held their breath to see if the noise came again, but it did not.

'It's the ghost!' Francis grinned.

'What ghost?' Katheryn asked, wide-eyed.

'Oh, I don't know,' he laughed. 'There must be some headless phantom or ghastly ghoul that walks this house.'

'Don't!' she cried, to his amusement.

'I think we ought to leave,' Edward advised Francis. 'Just in case someone is about. We can't risk our delightful banquets being banned.'

'I'll come back tomorrow,' Francis told Katheryn, and kissed her soundly, arousing in her sensations she had never experienced. 'It will be a pleasure postponed, although it is misery to me to leave you.'

She went to bed feeling frustrated. All day she had longed for him, tonight she had resolved to give herself wholly to him – and now she would have to wait another twenty-four hours before they could be together again.

The hours did drag, but still they passed. When evening finally fell, Mary, whom she now looked upon as a friend, if not a close one, agreed to steal the keys again. Katheryn ran up to the dorter ahead of the others, pulled off all her clothes, inserted a rag soaked in vinegar and got into bed, drawing the curtains on the room side behind her. Then she lay, in fevered anticipation, waiting for Francis to arrive.

He came as the bell struck midnight.

'Katheryn?' he whispered. 'Are you asleep?'

'No, I'm in here, waiting for you,' she replied. When he opened the curtains, he stared at her in amazement as she lay there with her breasts exposed and her hair spread out like an auburn cloud on the pillow, then he threw off his gown and leapt in beside her in his doublet and hose, tugging at the latter to free his points.

'Katheryn!' he exclaimed, pulling back the covers and exposing the rest of her body, marble-like in the moonlight flooding through the latticed window. 'You are beautiful!' His fingers explored her, lightly, then more boldly and insistently, until she was desperate for him. Pulling down his hose, he entered her and rode her like a stallion, gasping and moaning, until he paused and began shuddering. It was painful at first, but not for long, for another sensation began to build inside her. Pressing herself against him, Katheryn felt her body explode. Never had she known joy like this!

They were lovers all through that enchanted winter. She let Francis use her as a man uses his wife, and rejoiced in it. Their hours together flew as they pleasured each other until it was almost day, when he would usually be the last man to leave the gentlewomen's chamber. Often, now, Katheryn stole the keys from the Duchess's chamber herself, locking the dorter door from the inside. It was not just lust that drove her. She was in love again, more than last time, and knew that Francis's feelings for her ran as true and deep as his desire.

The gentlewomen in the dorter knew what was going on. Some were tolerant. Even Mary teased her. Coming upon them sharing a passionate kiss, she laughed, 'Look at you two, hanging by your bills as if you were a pair of sparrows!'

'Hark to Dereham, broken-winded!' other girls would giggle, hearing the couple making merry between the sheets.

Sometimes, Katheryn smuggled Francis into her own chamber for greater privacy, but there was no key and she was so worried that someone might hear them and come in that she could not relax. It was safer in the dorter with the door locked on the inside.

On occasion, she made him strip completely to make love, needing to be as close to him as possible, skin on skin, but Meg, who had heard her, warned her that it was risky. 'What if the Duchess comes looking for the key and demands to be allowed in?'

'When has she ever done that?' Katheryn retorted, but, all the same, she told Francis he should keep on his doublet and hose.

Several times, when Katheryn had given up waiting for him, he arrived in the early hours, often as late as four or five o'clock, to find her sharing a bed with Kat, Alice or some other gentlewoman whose bed was occupied by another courting couple. He would unlace his hose and lewdly wiggle his erect penis or put his hand in the bed and touch Katheryn intimately, making the other girl huddle over to her side, hiding her eyes, enabling him to climb in and frisk with Katheryn, who could not stop laughing.

Kat complained only that they kept her awake.

'I pray, Mr Dereham, lie still!' she would hiss.

Alice, though, was angry when Francis invaded the bed, and jumped out. 'Such a puffing and blowing I have never heard!' she exclaimed and stalked off in search of a space next to someone else. 'For shame!'

The next morning, she cornered Katheryn. 'I will not sleep with you again.'

Margaret Bennet turned on her too. 'I won't lie with you either. You know not what matrimony is!' Katheryn shrugged. It was no loss to her; she preferred to sleep alone. And Francis, warned of others' disapproval, thumbed his nose at them, as it were. Sometimes, he did not even bother to close the curtains, indulging his passion in full view of whoever was looking – and Katheryn caught people staring several times.

Other nights, he would be tamer, bringing food and drink to make good cheer. It did not placate the likes of Alice. One night, when Katheryn was approaching the dorter, she heard Alice talking to someone about 'Mistress Katheryn's doings with Dereham'. Then Mary's voice said, 'Let her alone, for if she goes on as she has begun, she will be naught within a while. Everyone's talking about her, even the porter and the grooms of my lady's chamber. It's only a matter of time before the Duchess hears of it.'

Katheryn marched in. 'It's a pity you encouraged me then, isn't it, Mary? Oh, I would be well matched with Mr Dereham, you said.'

Mary's cheeks were pink. 'I meant marriage, Mistress Katheryn, not fornication.'

'So what did you think we would be doing when you fetched the key?' Katheryn retorted.

'I thought you would be courting!' Mary snapped.

'Who knows but that we will be married?' Katheryn said.

'He's not likely to marry you now,' Alice muttered. 'He's enjoyed all the blessings of marriage. Why would he bother?'

'He loves me for myself,' she replied, 'and I think I know more about my personal affairs than you do.'

She flounced out, burning with indignation, praying they would not betray her to the Duchess. She was safe, she thought. She knew too much about Alice's dalliances for Alice to risk telling on her, and Mary had not spilled the beans about Manox.

Malyn was another matter. Katheryn and Francis had now thrown caution to the wind and bedded together when they pleased, morning, afternoon or evening. One morning, they were lingering in bed after the others had gone down to Mass, when Malyn walked into the dorter with a velvet gown in her arms. At that moment, Katheryn was lying naked on the bed and Francis, wearing only his jerkin, had his hand on her privy place. Malyn dropped the gown and fled.

Desire extinguished, Katheryn sprang up, bade Francis help her hurriedly dress and went after her, finding her in the still room.

'Don't tell on me, please, Malyn,' she begged. 'I love him and we are doing no harm to anybody.'

'You do not care that you risk bringing shame on the Howards and the Tilneys?' Malyn's voice was cold.

'I hardly think my doings are of any importance. The Duchess seems to have forgotten that I exist. Am I to wither away here at Lambeth without some pleasure in my life?' Katheryn was weeping now.

Malyn, ever soft-hearted, took pity on her. 'Just *stop* what you are doing, sweetheart. Get Mr Dereham to approach my lady and ask for your hand. She may not object, for he is cousin to us all. You could do a lot worse. That would be the right way of going about things.'

Katheryn thought about it, but decided it was better not to take Malyn's advice. What if the Duchess said no? She would then know that there was something between her and Francis and would certainly forbid them to see each other. Francis would be sent away, like Harry. No, it wasn't worth the risk.

* * *

99

Francis seemed unbothered. He thrived on taking risks and urged Katheryn to be ever more daring. Once she would have been more cautious, but she was so avid for him that caution abandoned her. They spent long hours together in her chamber when everyone was downstairs during the day, not undressing fully lest someone come in. Francis even insisted on their making love in the Duchess's own bedchamber while she was at Mass or at table, and oft-times they would kiss and lie together on her great bed with its carved posts and crimson velvet counterpane, not caring if a servant came in from time to time.

'Shh!' Dereham would say, holding a finger to his lips and winking. 'Not a word to anyone!'

At other times, he insisted they use Mother Emmet's bed, or even the privy. Once he left the door open, and as he thrust his penis into her hand, Katheryn turned her head and noticed Margaret Bennet staring at them. She came to wonder if Margaret was spying on her to gratify her own lust, because on another occasion she saw her peeking through a door watching Francis lift Katheryn's skirt and gaze at her body.

The dorter was divided between those who disapproved of the love between Katheryn and Dereham, or were shocked by it, and those who felt the couple should be let alone to make their own choices. This was invariably the opinion of the young ladies and gentlemen who themselves consorted in the night hours.

The midnight banquets continued, despite the tensions among the participants. Food and drink would be smuggled in and Francis would play his lute. Tongues loosed by wine, the men and girls would talk of intimate matters.

'I saw you two leaving the Duchess's bedchamber,' Robert Damport said.

'Well, it's much more comfortable than here,' Francis grinned, his arm around Katheryn, 'and, anyway, there was a gaggle of women sorting out their attire. The matter was urgent. You see, my sweetheart here was suffering from the green sickness.'

Katheryn dug him in the ribs. 'I was not! *You* were in a lustful mood.'

'You'll have heard of the green sickness,' Francis went on, ignoring her. 'They call it the disease of virgins. It's caused by bad blood in the body in the days before a woman's course arrives, when she has a green pallor and feels weak and nervy. And there's only one way to relieve it.'

'Shut up, Francis,' Katheryn muttered, for others were listening in to the conversation.

'What's that?' Robert wanted to know.

'Well, green-sick maidens are dangerously prone to lust, and only fucking can dislodge the bad blood. Believe me, she was insatiable.' He flapped his hand in front of his face.

Katheryn smacked it away. 'Don't believe his nonsense. He's making it all up.'

'But I *can* believe it!' Robert grinned. 'I've heard you blowing and striving to have your will of her several times, Francis!' Katheryn smacked him too.

'No, I swear it's true about the green sickness,' Francis protested, laughing. 'Ask any of the ladies here.' But Robert declined and, chuckling, got up to fetch more food before going to sit with Kat Tilney. Francis pushed Katheryn back on the bed and began kissing her. Other couples were getting amorous too.

From the next bed, Katheryn heard Alice ask, 'You know what to do if my lady comes in suddenly?'

'Francis will go into the little gallery with the other gentlemen,' Katheryn replied, between kisses. It led off the dorter at the far end.

'But Francis wants to stay right here,' her lover murmured, flinging out an arm and drawing the curtain.

Towards Christmas, Katheryn and Francis took advantage of the Duchess's absence at a banquet at court and met in her gallery, where there was a wide cushioned window seat. They lit no candle, just in case someone should see a glow through the window or under the door, and made love there in the dark, their passion enhanced, as always, by the thrill of being on forbidden territory.

Afterwards, having straightened their clothing, they sat talking, sharing reminiscences of their past lives.

'You know, Katheryn, I knew I would love you the moment I first saw you,' Francis said, caressing her cheek. 'And I do love you. It's not just lust that drives me to you.' He bent forward and kissed her long and gently.

'And, I promise you, I do love you with all my heart,' she replied, returning his kiss with fervour.

'I want to marry you,' he said.

'No,' she replied. 'Let us stay as we are. My lady might say no, and that would be the end of everything.'

'But I want you – I want you for my wife. And I know you want me, so we will have each other, whatever anyone says!'

Katheryn was about to reply when the door opened and Joan Bulmer walked in. She gave a little shriek when she realised they were there.

'Oh, I thought I'd seen ghosts!' she gasped. 'What are you doing, sitting here alone without any light?'

'We were just talking,' Katheryn said. 'We wanted some peace and privacy.'

'What my lady would say if she knew you were here, I don't know!' Joan exclaimed, and hurried out.

Francis did not cease urging Katheryn to marry him. He asked her every time they met, and still she said no. It only made him all the more insistent. He came every night now to the dorter and began giving her gifts: a string of beads, a twist of ribbon and an exquisite silk flower.

'I was told that there was a little woman in London with a crooked back, who was skilled in making flowers of silk,' he said. 'I went to her and chose a French fennel, as I thought you would like it.'

In the morning, Katheryn showed the flower to the other girls.

'Not the wisest choice!' Joan observed. 'Doesn't he know that fennel stands for flattery and foolishness?'

'And for sorrow,' Mary added.

Katheryn did not care. She owned so few pretty things and was thrilled with her gift. The others were just jealous!

* * *

102

On Christmas Eve, when the gentlewomen were helping to sort the greenery that had been brought in to decorate the hall, Mary sidled over.

'So Mr Dereham is set on marrying you, Mistress Katheryn,' she murmured. 'I heard him bragging to his friends, only this morning, that he is in such favour with you that he could wed you if he wished. Fortunately, Mr Damport talked sense into him, and warned him to beware, for entangling himself in such matters would place him in no little jeopardy.'

Katheryn was fuming. She dropped the holly she was threading with ribbon and went looking for Francis, whom she found quaffing Christmas ale in the otherwise deserted buttery.

'How dare you go telling all and sundry that you might marry me!' she stormed.

He laughed. 'How beautiful you look when you're angry.'

'No, Francis, I mean it! You had no right.'

He stood up and pulled her into his arms. 'If your grandam was in favour, you'd marry me tomorrow.'

She struggled and beat his chest with her fists, but he held her fast. 'Admit it, my sweet lioness.' He kissed her hard on the mouth, silencing her protests, then drew back and smiled at her. 'Better?'

'Not until you promise to be more discreet! Someone might come in.'

'I'll behave if you admit that you do want to marry me.'

'Oh, you are impossible! All right, yes, I do want to marry you, but I'm frightened of what the Duchess will say.'

'Then, for now, let us just promise each other that we will marry in the future,' he urged.

'If that will satisfy you, I will promise,' Katheryn agreed, her anger abating. It was, after all, wonderful to have this man she loved begging for her hand.

'Say you promise, by your faith and troth.' His eyes were dark with intent.

'I promise! I promise, Francis, by my faith and troth, that I will marry you.'

'And you will have no other husband but me.'

'And I will have no other husband but you.'

His smile was triumphant. 'And I promise, by my faith and troth, that I will marry you, Katheryn Howard, and will take no other to wife. Now we are troth-plight and I may call you "wife"!'

'I don't know about that,' she said doubtfully, but inwardly her soul was singing. She was going to be his – she would be his for ever. They would contrive a way to wed, she knew it. 'It might be best to keep our plighting a secret for now.'

'I'll be as discreet as you wish,' Francis vowed, still with that air of jubilance.

That night, he took her with renewed joy and vigour. It was one of the few nights when they lay fully naked in each other's arms, and it was heavenly bliss.

When he came to the dorter on New Year's night, Francis gave Katheryn a gift. She had not expected it, and when he presented her with another exquisite silk flower, she was delighted.

'It's a heartsease, for remembrance,' he told her. 'I hope that when you wear it, you will think of me.'

'How could I ever forget you?' she breathed. 'It's beautiful. Thank you! I will stitch it on to my best bodice. But alas, Francis, I have nothing for you.'

'Nothing?' He looked crestfallen, but there was a smile playing about his lips. 'Don't the Howards observe the custom of New Year's gifts?'

'We do – but I have no money.' She felt mortified. Suddenly, inspiration came and she drew a thin silver bracelet from her wrist. 'But I want you to have this. It was a present from my half-sister Isabel, and is precious to me.'

Francis took the bracelet. 'Are you sure?'

'Of course!'

'Then let me show how grateful I am . . .'

Chapter 11

1539

Despite his promise, Francis would not keep quiet. There was already talk in the household that he and Katheryn would marry, although some who disliked him for his overbearing and cavalier ways were making cutting remarks, saying they could not believe that Katheryn had stooped so low, or asserting that Francis had no intention of making an honest woman of her. The gossip spread. One afternoon in early January, Harry – who had not attempted to see Katheryn since that dreadful meeting by the porter's lodge – turned up at the Duchess's house and demanded to see Francis, as Francis related to Katheryn afterwards when they lay on the bed in the deserted dorter.

'He was pretty angry and acting as if you were pledged to him!'

'I never was,' Katheryn protested.

'I know that. The fellow's a fool, and just envious. I saw him off, don't worry. I showed him these.' He made two fists. 'He won't disturb us again. But, darling, we have to still these malicious tongues. Please give me leave to call you "wife", and call me "husband". Then people will know that we truly belong to each other and that my intentions are serious – honourable, if you will.'

It could do no harm, she reasoned.

'Very well,' she agreed, 'husband!'

Her kissed her greedily, exploring her mouth with his tongue until she drew away to catch her breath. Then he kissed her again, longingly.

Dorothy walked in. 'Mr Dereham,' she declared, 'I trow you can never kiss Mistress Katheryn enough!'

'Are you going to stop me kissing my own wife?' he retorted, coming up for air.

'I can see something coming to pass very soon!' Mary chimed in.

'What is that?' he asked.

'Marry!' she laughed. 'That Mr Dereham shall marry Mistress Katheryn Howard!'

'By St John!' Francis roared. 'You may guess twice and guess worse!'

'Shush!' Katheryn cried, pressing her hand over his mouth.

'I'm just jesting!' he told her, pulling her fingers away.

She bent to his ear. 'What if they gossip about you calling me your wife and it comes to my lady's ear?'

Dereham pulled the curtain, shielding them from the others.

'Well, then we will have to tell the truth,' he whispered. 'The fact is, Katheryn, we are as good as wed and there is nothing she could do about it. Making a promise to wed and bedding together afterwards is as good as being married in church. Lots of people do it. It would take a church court to loose us now.'

She stared at him in amazement. She had never heard of such a thing. The Howards all got married in church and, for all she knew, probably waited until afterwards to consummate their unions.

'You mean, we are as good as married?'

'Yes!' He began nuzzling her neck.

'And I'm entitled to call you husband?'

'You are. And I can lawfully use you as my wife!' To prove his point, he began doing so.

Katheryn awoke to find that there had been a light fall of snow in the night. The gardens looked beautiful and, wrapping herself in her cloak, she went outdoors and crunched along the paths, admiring the white vistas around her. Francis found her down near the river. Their breath mingled in the cold air. Around them, the snow-covered world seemed an enchanted place.

'I have brought you a present,' he said. 'Betrothals should be marked by gifts.' He placed in her gloved hand a delicate neck chain of gold.

'Oh, Francis, it must have cost a lot of money! You are too generous.' She looked around to check that no one was about, then hugged and kissed him.

'Nothing is too good for my wife,' he said.

Releasing him, she pulled off her glove. There, on her finger, was her mother's ruby ring. She had worn it every day since it had first fitted her.

'This is your betrothal gift,' she said, giving it to Francis.

'I can't take this,' he said. 'I know it is very precious to you.'

'All the more reason to give it to you,' she insisted and slid it on his little finger.

'I love you,' Francis said, suddenly serious.

'And I love you!' she cried, flinging her arms about his neck and kissing him.

They exchanged gifts and love tokens frequently after that. Francis even gave Katheryn money when he had it to spare, for she had none and was entirely dependent on the Duchess's bounty. She used some of it to buy him a collar and sleeves for a shirt, which she had made up by a sewing woman in Lambeth. In return, having reproved her for spending his money on him – although he was very pleased with his gift – he gave her a length of pink sarcenet, which she had Mr Rose, her grandam's embroiderer, make up into a quilted cap. When she wore it, Francis admired the pattern of friar's knots.

'What, wife, here are friar's knots for Francis!' he grinned. 'An inspired choice.'

Katheryn smiled. In truth, she had not specified a pattern. 'Mr Rose said they are a symbol of true love,' she said.

'Aye, indeed they are,' Francis said, and took her in his arms.

Katheryn had not dared wear the silk flowers in the presence of the Duchess, but she wore them on other occasions and she had one on her bodice when my lady came unexpectedly into the parlour where the gentlewomen sat playing cards, looking for her lapdog.

'It's under the table, Madam,' Katheryn said, and bent down to re-trieve the naughty creature. When she placed it in her grandam's arms, she saw the old lady looking at the French fennel. She said nothing, but Katheryn knew she might wonder how she had come by so rare a thing.

She went seeking Lady Brereton, the friendliest of the Duchess's ladies. Katheryn felt sorry for her because her husband had been among those beheaded for committing adultery with Queen Anne. She had always taken care to be especially nice to Katheryn, who tried to perform little kindnesses for her whenever she could.

Katheryn found her in the still room, a lone soul in the black garb she always wore.

'Mistress Katheryn!' Lady Brereton smiled.

'I have a favour to ask,' Katheryn told her. 'A gentleman who admires me – a very good man – gave me this flower as a token of his esteem. I think my lady has noticed it, and if she asks, I pray you will tell her that you gave it to me.'

'I shouldn't, but I will,' Lady Brereton agreed. 'You have been good to me.'

Katheryn skipped off, much relieved, only to have her good mood shattered by a summons from her grandam. She approached the Duchess's chamber in trepidation, praying this was not to do with the French fennel.

It was.

'That flower you are wearing,' the old lady said, sitting straight-backed in her chair. 'Where did you get it?'

'Lady Brereton gave it to me,' Katheryn told her. 'She said I had been kind to her.'

The Duchess shook her head. 'I will ask you again. Who gave it to you?'

'Lady Brereton, my lady.' Katheryn felt her cheeks flaming.

'Don't lie to me, child. It was Mr Dereham, wasn't it? I'm not blind. I know what goes on in my household. People do talk.'

Katheryn could not speak.

'Tell me! Was it Mr Dereham?' the Duchess barked.

'Yes, my lady, but please don't dismiss him. He's a good man, and kind.'

'I know that. He is my cousin and I like him, and he may be a suitable match for you, but this is a most improper gift. Virtuous young ladies do not accept presents like this from gentlemen.'

'He is my cousin too, Madam,' Katheryn said. 'We have done nothing wrong.'

'I am very glad to hear it, but you will give that flower to me now and I will return it to Mr Dereham.' She handed Katheryn a small pair of scissors.

Reluctantly, Katheryn cut off the flower. 'May I see him again, my lady?'

'Is there a particular affection between you? I am told he has given you money. That too is unacceptable.'

Katheryn could only nod, her eyes brimming with tears. Was this to be the end for her and Francis?

'We are very fond of each other, and he did give me money, but only because he was concerned that I had none of my own.'

'Then I assume he did it from the affection that grows between kindred,' the Duchess persisted. 'Is there love between you? I mean, love that does not proceed from kinship?'

'Yes, Madam,' Katheryn admitted.

'You know what people are saying? That, if one would seek Mr Dereham, one would find him in Mistress Katheryn Howard's chamber or the gentlewomen's chamber. Child, he has no business being there, and you must not entertain him there. Do you understand me?'

'Yes,' Katheryn murmured miserably.

The Duchess gave her a penetrating look. 'I want your assurance that nothing improper has passed between you. I remember that you misbehaved with Mr Manox, and I'd hoped you had learned a lesson from that.'

'Oh, I have, Madam, and I have done nothing wrong with Mr Dereham.' They were all but married, weren't they, so how could their lovemaking be wrong or improper?

'I'm glad to hear it!' her grandam said, her tone severe. 'Now, you may consort with Mr Dereham, bearing in mind the proprieties, and I will seek your father's approval for a match between you. If he does not approve, then you must stop seeing each other.'

'Yes, my lady,' Katheryn said, praying that Father would consent.

Only, it would be ages before she found out, for it took days for letters to reach Calais.

She could barely wait to tell Francis the good news – it was good news, surely? She was in a fever of anxiety until night-time and, when he arrived at the dorter, she hurried him into her chamber, heedless of her grandam's injunction to observe the proprieties, and told him what the Duchess had said. He stared at her, his sardonic eyes suddenly luminous.

'By God, Katheryn, I was right! We may well achieve our hearts' desire. And, if your father refuses, we'll just have to be honest with him and say we are troth-plight.' He folded her in his arms. 'We'll be together, openly, and all will see how proud I am to have you for my wife!'

'Oh, Francis!' Katheryn cried. 'I do pray my father writes soon.'

'I'll go to Calais, if need be, and convince him what a good husband I'll be to you!' he declared.

Once more, she was in his arms, responding to his desire. She knew she was doing wrong in disobeying the Duchess, but it did not really matter. In her heart, she was certain that she and Francis would soon be wed.

The following morning, Mother Emmet knocked on Katheryn's door. Katheryn thanked God and all the saints that Francis had left in the small hours.

'May I come in?' Mother Emmet asked and Katheryn stood aside to admit her. The older woman's eyes roved over the rumpled bed and the pile of discarded clothes on the floor. Katheryn hastened to pull up the counterpane, hoping the mistress of the maids had not seen the stains on the bottom sheet.

'My lady of Norfolk has informed me of your light behaviour,' Mother Emmet said, her tone cool. 'I was reprimanded for it. I explained that I cannot be held responsible for the transgressions of every one of you gentlewomen and that I had no idea of your misconduct. You have disappointed and embarrassed me, Mistress Katheryn, and

110

I trust you will be more circumspect in the future.'

'I'm very sorry,' Katheryn said meekly. *If you hadn't been so bone idle, thanks be to God, a lot more of us would be in trouble.*

'I'll be watching you,' Mother Emmet said, wagging her finger. 'Be warned!'

The next night, Francis came to the dorter in a buoyant mood.

'You do know that your coming to see Mistress Katheryn here is common gossip?' Joan challenged him.

'Old Agnes knows about it,' Alice chimed in.

Francis grinned. 'I'm aware of that.' He turned to Katheryn. 'The Duchess had her sport with me today. She came upon me in a gallery and said she would know where to find me if she needed me, for it would be in your chamber. She said she blamed me for our keeping company together, and told me off for seeking you out, but then she said that my presumption might be to my advantage.'

'I do hope so!' Katheryn cried. It was becoming obvious that the Duchess approved of their marrying, and if she did, Father probably would too.

'She mentioned you to me today,' Edward Waldegrave said to Francis. He was sitting on the bed opposite, his arm around Joan, both of them scoffing custard tarts. 'She said she thought you would never be out of Mistress Katheryn's chamber, despite her telling you to stay away.'

'I was there,' William Ashby added. 'She told Edward she had suspected that there was love between you both, and that she mistrusted you and feared you might have been misbehaving yourselves.'

'She can't have mistrusted you that much,' Joan put in, 'else she would have bestirred herself before now to put a stop to it.'

'Old Agnes never bestirs herself if she can help it,' Meg said, pouring wine for them all. 'She thinks that, because she houses and feeds us, she's done her duty.'

'Only a lucky few, like Malyn, get marriages arranged for them,' Joan muttered. Katheryn wondered why Joan was complaining, since she had a husband already. She never spoke of William Bulmer, and Katheryn had never liked to ask why she had left him. Kat had said he'd been unfaithful, but Dorothy thought he'd ordered Joan out of his house because of *her* infidelity.

'I think that, in my case, she will bestir herself,' Katheryn said. 'She is going to write to my father and ask if Francis and I can marry.'

'Well, I hope she gets around to it,' Meg replied, tartly.

'I do hope so,' Katheryn said. 'I fervently hope so.'

'What worries me,' Meg continued, 'is that Old Agnes suspects the rest of us of misbehaving ourselves.'

'I don't think she does,' Katheryn assured her. 'She never mentioned it. But she's now set Mother Emmet to watch over me, so we'll have to be careful, Francis.'

'Oh, no!' Francis cried, lifting his hands in mock horror. 'Not that dragon!'

'She's hardly that,' Katheryn giggled.

'More like a pussycat,' Kat chuckled.

'Seriously,' Francis said, 'the Duchess said nothing to me either about the rest of you. I think you are all safe.'

'Nevertheless,' Joan replied tartly, 'you two have put us all in peril by your lack of discretion. I suggest you take greater care from now on.'

'We will, Joan, my sweet!' Francis cried, planting a kiss on her mouth. 'Do not worry.'

One evening in early February, the talk in the gentlewomen's dorter was all about Harry Manox getting married.

'He said his father was pressing him to marry a neighbour's daughter,' Katheryn said. 'I suppose he did so in the end.'

'I heard from one of Lady Bayment's maids that he has gone to live in Streatham,' said Kat.

'Good riddance!' remarked Francis, who was stretched out on the bed, twisting Katheryn's hair around his fingers. They all laughed.

'I bet you're glad he's out of the way!' Alice chortled.

Francis shrugged. 'I saw him off months ago,' he retorted. 'Katheryn loves *me* now.'

'And you haven't stopped talking about it,' Robert teased him.

'Katheryn, he brags about you the live-long day! The whole world knows about you both. It's probably the talk of the court too!'

'Shut up,' Francis countered good-naturedly.

'I wish you'd be more discreet,' Katheryn chided him. 'At least until we hear from my father.'

'Me, discreet?' he grinned. 'Why should I be discreet? I want the world to know you are mine.'

'It will soon, I'm sure,' she told him. 'In the meantime, please be circumspect. For my sake.'

'For you, I'd promise anything,' Francis declared, and kissed her hand with mock courtesy.

Katheryn thought no more of Harry until a week later, when she was sorting embroidery silks in the parlour and Mary burst in.

'You'd better come!' she cried. 'Mr Dereham is quarrelling with Mr Manox, and I fear there might be violence!'

Katheryn dropped the silks and ran after Mary. As they flew across the courtyard, she could see Harry standing by the porter's lodge, his face puce. When he caught sight of her, he turned away and stalked off towards the gate. Of Francis, there was no sign.

'Thank goodness they've stopped shouting,' Mary said breathlessly. 'I thought they'd kill each other. The porter was warning them to desist, or he'd fetch my lady.'

'What happened?' Katheryn asked.

'I was walking through the court and I heard voices raised and heard your name. I saw them through the archway. They were almost snarling at each other. Things got nasty when Mr Manox made a point of boasting that he knew of a private mark on your body.'

'The villain!' Katheryn cried. 'How dare he!' What a fool she had been to involve herself with such a knave!

'I thought Mr Dereham was going to draw his dagger,' Mary went on. 'That's when I ran to fetch you.'

'I'll go and find him,' Katheryn said, guessing that what Harry had said would have angered Francis deeply.

As she turned to go, she heard Harry's voice call, 'Mistress Lascelles!'

She looked back to see him standing just beyond the gate, and watched as Mary approached him. They spoke for a few minutes, Harry clearly agitated and Mary evidently trying to soothe him, but Katheryn could not hear what they were saying. Then Harry strode off and Mary came back.

'It seems he still loves you, and is jealous of Mr Dereham,' she said, as they walked back through the courtyard.

Katheryn was appalled. 'But he's married now!'

'On the rebound, I suspect. It's you he wants, and he's furious that Mr Dereham has supplanted him. Apparently, someone told him that Mr Dereham was flaunting his conquest. He came here to warn the Duchess about it, but Mr Dereham happened to see him arriving and the row broke out. Mr Manox insisted just now on speaking to you about your behaviour with Mr Dereham, but I told him to keep quiet and go away.'

'Thank goodness he went,' Katheryn said, hoping he'd give her up for lost and never come back.

They had returned to the parlour now. As Katheryn bent to pick up the silks, Mary lingered. 'Really, Mistress Katheryn, you should take more care in your choice of admirers. You're acting like a wanton.'

'That's not fair!' Katheryn retorted. 'Francis and I are to be married, you know that.'

'Actually, *you* don't know that for certain. And your love life has been the subject of more gossip in this house than anyone else's. As I've said to you before, in charity, take care. And don't value yourself so cheaply.'

'I'll thank you to mind your own business!' Katheryn barked, stung.

After Mary had closed the door, without another word, Katheryn's anger abated. Mary was a queer one, but, underneath the superior manner, she really did care, and she had seen Harry off, for which she, Katheryn, ought to be grateful.

It was time to look for Francis. Her cheeks burned when she thought of Harry revealing their intimate secrets to him. Francis knew that mark too, and had kissed it many times.

She found him in the stables, saddling his horse.

'Katheryn!' He picked her up, tiny as she was, and swung her around. 'Mary told me you heard of my little altercation with that scoundrel Manox this morning. The man is unspeakable, but fear not, he will not trouble us again. I told him that if he showed his face here one more time, I would run him through.'

'You didn't!'

'I did, and I meant it. He knew that. Now, I am for Southwark for the bear baiting. I will see you tonight.' He kissed her soundly. She responded with all her heart, grateful that he had not referred to the shameful thing Harry had said.

That evening, when the young gentlewomen gathered in the dorter, Katheryn joined them. There was to be another banquet that night, and the food was already hidden away in cupboards and chests, but it lacked three hours until midnight, so they lay on their beds chattering and giggling in anticipation of the pleasures ahead.

Someone must have forgotten to lock the door. When St Mary's clock had not long struck ten, it banged open and the Duchess walked in, in a furious mood, her ladies crowding behind her.

'Well,' she demanded, 'where is he?'

Katheryn froze.

'Where is who, Madam?' Mary asked. Everyone was looking terrified.

'Mr Hastings, of course!' the Duchess barked. 'I am informed that he has been coming to this dormitory at night to visit one of you hussies. I can see that Mother Emmet has again been remiss. As if we haven't had enough trouble with Mr Dereham!' She glared at Katheryn.

There was no doubt that Mother Emmet *had* been remiss. For all her apparent kindness and threatened vigilance, she was never there when she was most needed. Katheryn had come to wonder if she absented herself deliberately, wishing to avoid making trouble.

But who was Mr Hastings?

'I have never heard of a Mr Hastings,' she was able to say with truth, although it was also true that she did not know the names of all the young gentlemen who frequented the dorter at night. The others professed ignorance too and gave a good impression of being scandalised that my lady should suspect one of their number of such naughtiness.

'Well, this is strange,' the Duchess said, seating herself on a bench and taking from her pocket a folded piece of paper. 'This afternoon, I found this letter by my pew in the chapel. I will tell you what it says. "Your Grace, it would be advisable if you take good heed to your gentlewomen. If it shall please you, an hour after you go to bed, to rise suddenly and visit their chamber, you shall see that which shall displease you." It is unsigned.' She looked up, her gaze taking in all of them. 'Can any of you think who could have sent this? And why?'

Katheryn could have told her. There was no doubt in her mind that this was Harry Manox seeking to be revenged on her. But she said nothing, while the others shook their heads and said they had no idea who had written it.

'Very well,' the Duchess said. 'It is probably some mischievous prank. I am sorry to have troubled you. Good night!'

As soon as her footsteps had stopped echoing, the young women burst out in anxious speculation.

'Someone knows what goes on here,' Meg said.

'Yes, but it's an outsider,' Kat opined. 'I don't know a Mr Hastings.'

Nor did anyone else.

'The letter didn't actually mention a Mr Hastings,' Alice pointed out.

'Then why did the Duchess ask about him?' Kat wondered.

'I have no idea,' Alice said. 'Maybe she had suspicions of her own.'

'She's barking up the wrong tree there,' Joan told her.

Katheryn turned to Mary, with whom she had made her peace at supper. 'It's Harry, I'm sure,' she whispered.

'I'm sure it is,' Mary murmured.

'Say nothing,' Katheryn told her.

She lay in bed, fretting that Harry would not stop at this. What if the Duchess investigated further and found that the handwriting in the letter was his? There were still old music books bearing his notes and annotations in the house – maybe even letters. No! My lady must not even have the chance to look.

It was the Duchess's custom to hear Mass in her chapel each morning at eight o'clock. While she was thus occupied, Katheryn slipped into her chamber, receiving a jolt when she saw the maids in there, cleaning.

'I thought I left my prayer book in here,' she said, thinking quickly. It gave her a pretext to search the room and, as luck would have it, she saw the letter lying on the top of a pile of papers on the table. Slipping it into her pocket when no one was looking, she hurried back to the dorter and studied it. Yes, she was sure it was Harry's writing.

She showed it to Francis, who reacted angrily.

'By God, he shall answer for this!' He leapt up.

'No, Francis!' Katheryn cried. 'Don't do anything silly, please!'

But he had stormed out. He was too hot-headed for his own good. Didn't he realise that it was a bad idea to draw attention to himself – and her?

She ran after him, all the way up Church Street to Lord Bayment's house, but she was too late. She saw Francis standing at the door, shouting at Harry, calling him a knave – and worse. 'You never loved her!' she heard him say. 'If you did, you wouldn't hurt her. She loves me – just get used to it!'

Katheryn hung back. The mood between the two men was ugly. She saw Harry looking at her.

'One day, Mr Dereham, she'll drop you just as she did me,' he snarled. 'She's a little trollop who'll lift her skirts to any fine fellow who takes her fancy.'

Katheryn gasped, as Francis seized Harry by the throat. Harry punched him in the face. His nose bloodied, Francis went for him like a wild bull and slammed him back against the door. Horrified, Katheryn saw Harry reach for his dagger and screamed. Francis caught his wrist and bent it behind his back, causing him to cry out and drop the knife, then shoved him to his knees.

'You don't want to swing for me!' he growled, as Harry struggled to get up. 'And I'll thank you not to write any more nasty letters to the Duchess!'

'You haven't heard the last of this,' Harry spat.

'Provoke me again and you will regret it,' Francis warned. 'Come, Katheryn, this scum is no fit company for a lady.'

Leaving Harry nursing his twisted wrist and calling out threats behind them, they walked at a brisk pace back towards the Duchess's inn, only to encounter her son Lord William Howard coming out of his house, very fine in his damask gown and feathered bonnet, with two grooms in attendance. He had the thin-faced Howard features and an aristocratic nose like his mother's. He bowed to Katheryn, who dipped a curtsey.

'In the wars, Mr Dereham?' he asked, looking at the bloodied handkerchief Francis was holding to his nose.

'You should see my assailant, my lord,' Francis said, with grim humour. 'Seriously, Mr Manox, who used to be your niece's music master and was dismissed by my lady of Norfolk for imagining he might marry her, is giving her trouble. My lady has asked Lord Edmund Howard if we two might marry, but Mr Manox is jealous. He sent my lady an anonymous letter implying we were closer than we should be, and though she saw there was nothing in it, he won't desist.' He explained what had just happened. 'And I won't repeat what he said about Mistress Katheryn.'

Lord William was frowning. 'I can't allow my niece to be slandered by this Manox, and it is wrong that you are placed in this position, Mr Dereham. You know I think well of you, and we are kin. Does Manox reside with Lord Bayment?'

'No, my lord, he has a house in Streatham, where he lives with his wife,' Katheryn told him. 'They recently married.'

'Indeed?' Lord William raised his eyebrows. 'I would imagine he had better things to do than chase after a former fancy. Look, I have to be at court this afternoon, but I will go this evening to Streatham and warn off Manox. I won't have my kinsfolk harassed in this way.'

They thanked him for intervening and let him proceed to his chariot.

'I'd like to see Manox defying the likes of Lord William,' Francis said.

That night, Francis came to the dorter earlier than usual, to find Katheryn all alone save for Joan Bulmer, who was waiting for Edward Waldegrave to arrive.

'We should go to my chamber,' Katheryn told him. 'The Duchess might come in at any time and check on us. And you, Joan, shouldn't think of entertaining Mr Waldegrave. It's too risky.'

'I'll take my own risks, thank you,' Joan retorted.

'I'm not staying,' Francis said. 'I came to tell you that Lord William just dropped in to say that he went to Streatham and threatened Manox with all manner of punishments if he continued to impugn the honour of a daughter of the Howards and his kinsman. He said he spent a quarter of an hour ranting at him and his wife on their own doorstep.'

'I doubt Harry will dare do anything in the future,' Katheryn said, going into his arms, utterly relieved. 'We're safe now.'

'Yes, and soon, I hope, we will hear from your father.' His mouth bent to hers, while one hand sought her breast.

'What do you think you are doing?' cried a strident voice. It was the Duchess, standing in the doorway, her face like thunder. 'Is this what you call not doing anything wrong? It's a good thing I decided to come here tonight!' She lashed out at Francis, clouting him on the side of the head. As he stood there, dazed and shocked speechless, she lifted her stick and beat Katheryn several times on the back and buttocks.

'Hussy! Foolish wench!' she raged. 'And you too, for allowing it!' She dealt the hapless Joan a blow too, then turned back to Francis.

'My lady—' he began, but she silenced him with a withering look.

'You are no longer welcome in this house,' she told him. 'I won't have you treating it like the King's court, where licence is encouraged. You will leave tomorrow.'

'No!' Katheryn cried, her nether parts smarting. 'My lady, we are to be married!'

'No Howard marries a man who has such little respect for her honour,' the Duchess said coldly.

'Madam, we are troth-plight,' Francis protested. 'There is nothing wrong in a man loving his wife.'

'His wife? Don't talk nonsense!' the old lady retorted. 'How can you be troth-plight?'

'We made a promise to each other to marry,' he told her.

'A likely excuse!' she retorted.

'It's the truth. Katheryn will tell you.' He looked at Katheryn with eyes dark with anger and pain. He really loved her – surely her grandam could see it?

'It is true,' she confirmed, 'and I'm sure my father will give his consent.'

'Fortunately, I have not yet written to him,' the Duchess said.

Katheryn began to cry. She had been expecting a response any day from her father and the thought of more delay was unbearable.

'It is as well,' the Duchess went on. 'He has been dismissed from his post; he is clearly incompetent, and unwell, and Lord Lisle will not suffer him to serve him any longer. He informed me that he hopes to return to England soon. He has enough to deal with without you giving him grief.'

This was bad news, but it carried with it a glimmer of hope, for, if Father was coming home soon, Katheryn had no doubt that she could make him agree to her marrying Francis.

'Tell me,' the Duchess rapped, 'has this gone any further?'

It was best to lie. 'No, Madam,' Katheryn replied.

'We are troth-plight,' Francis insisted.

'No, you are not!' the Duchess railed. 'Don't let me hear you say that again. Now, Mr Dereham, you will pack your possessions and leave. Before you go, I want an assurance from both of you that you will not attempt to see each other.'

Katheryn looked at Francis. He nodded and winked at her. They both gave their word. The Duchess stood there, watching Francis walk out, then followed him, closing the door firmly behind her.

'I will see him again, I will!' Katheryn vowed, drying her tears.

'Don't be a fool,' Joan snapped, rubbing her arm.

'But he means to see me, I know it! We are promised to each other.' She sat down on the bed, wincing at the pain from her beating.

'Methinks the Duchess will be watching you,' Joan said. 'Be careful, Mistress Katheryn.' She wiped her eyes. 'Edward hasn't come. He promised he would. I thought he loved me, but I was wrong. He's been cool to me lately. Anyway, there was no future in it. I . . .' She paused, and Katheryn sensed that she was weighing up whether to confide in her. 'I am married,' she said at length, 'although my husband Will and I have been estranged for some time. He was unfaithful with my maidservant and I would not put up with it. Now he is moving to Yorkshire, to be near his kin. He has asked me to go with him and assured me he no longer loves that woman. He wants an heir, of course; it's the one thing I can give him and she can't. When the Duchess hit me tonight, I made up my mind. I hate this place and I hate her. I'm going back to Will.'

Just then, Edward arrived. He stared at them. 'What's wrong?'

Joan dried her eyes and recounted what had happened.

'Oh, poor darling,' he said, embracing her. 'And you, Mistress Katheryn. I am sorry for your trouble.'

Katheryn started weeping again. 'I can't bear the thought of not seeing Francis.' *Or of not sleeping with him.* By her reckoning, they had spent a hundred nights together. How could she bear to lie alone?

'Knowing him, he'll find a way,' Edward comforted her. 'I would, if I were in his shoes,' he added gallantly.

After a sleepless night, Katheryn got up early, desperate to catch Francis before he left. She did not care that she was breaking her promise to the Duchess.

Crossing the crowded hall, she met her aunt, Lady Bridgewater, the Duchess's favourite – and most pleasant – daughter, who often came to stay. Her three sisters also visited fairly frequently and all brought large trains of attendants who crowded the house and made great demands on the servants, although the Duchess remained oblivious to any complaints.

'I am sorry to hear about what happened,' Lady Bridgewater said kindly. 'My lady told me. I knew about the banqueting that goes on, but I wasn't aware that you were involved. You know, my dear, if you carry on with such pleasures, staying up all night, you will lose your beauty.' Katheryn could not have cared less; all she wanted was to see Francis. She made a hasty excuse and hurried on.

She found him in the buttery, checking the contents of a barrel of ale.

'What are you doing?' she asked. 'Aren't you meant to be leaving?'

He rose and hugged her. 'No, darling. I talked my lady out of it. I said it would not look good if one of her family was cast out on the street and complaining loudly about it. I said people would want to know why, and she wouldn't want any scandal. She saw the wisdom in that and agreed I could stay, but I am not to go near you. As you see, I am her most obedient servant!' He bent and kissed her.

Katheryn laughed. He was incorrigible! Suddenly, she felt happy again. 'There are many ways we could contrive to meet,' she told him.

'There are. We must just be more careful. How would you fancy a walk in the gardens of St Mary's this evening?'

'You will come to the dorter, won't you?'

'Not for a while,' he told her. 'Old Agnes may come prowling again. If she catches us, it really will be over for us. Let's be content, for now, with just being together when we can.' He pinched her bottom playfully.

Covertly, they continued to meet, but not where they might encounter anyone who knew them. St Mary's garden proved too near the Duchess's house for comfort, so they took to walking along the marshes by the Thames, north of Lambeth, or farther afield to Batrichsy, where there was a farm belonging to Westminster Abbey and haystacks in which they could spend stolen hours. Their meetings were few – Katheryn did not dare disappear for too long in case her absence was noticed – so they were all the more precious.

It could not be long before Father returned. Then, she prayed, all this subterfuge would end and, God willing, she and Francis could be married properly. She was counting down the days.

Chapter 12

1539

In March, her brothers came, solemn-faced, to see her. Charles was twenty-three now, Henry twenty-one and George twenty, and all were flourishing in the Duke's service. Katheryn saw them every month or so, but was no longer as close to them as she had been when she was a child. Their lives had taken different directions and they had different interests and different friends – yet there was still a core of affection among them.

'We bear sorrowful news, Kitty,' Charles said, when they were alone in the little parlour. 'Father has died in Calais.'

'Oh, no!' She burst into floods of weeping.

Her brothers comforted her, awkward in the face of her noisy grief.

'What is to become of me?' she cried.

'I am head of the family now,' Charles said, 'although I fear that counts for very little, since I have no money and no lands, because Father died deeply in debt. He's to be buried in Calais, as I can't afford to bring him home.'

'What of Margaret?' Katheryn spared a thought for her poor widowed stepmother.

'She seems to be coping admirably, but she is in penury and reliant on her own kin for financial support. Lord Lisle is being very good to her.'

'What about Place House?'

'It's reverted to Dorothy's family,' George informed her.

'So there is nothing left,' Katheryn said bleakly. But, as she uttered the words, it dawned on her that, penniless though he was, Charles could make her dreams of marriage come true.

The brothers were shaking their heads sadly.

'It's as well we have places with the Duke,' Henry said, 'otherwise we'd be destitute.'

'The Duke has arranged that you will stay here with the Duchess,' Charles told Katheryn.

'Brother,' she said, 'there is a man, a cousin to the Duchess, who will marry me without a portion.'

'And who might that be?' Charles asked.

'Mr Dereham. Francis Dereham.'

Her brothers exchanged looks. 'He's a knave,' Henry said, 'and not popular, I gather.'

'You can do better than that, Kitty,' Charles said, 'even without a dowry. I will look out for you. There are many young gentlemen at Norfolk House and at court. You may leave the matter of your marriage to me.'

'But I love Mr Dereham!' Katheryn blurted out. 'And he loves me!'

'It is not a suitable match for you,' he insisted. 'I would not see you wed a man of dubious character, however well connected.'

There was no point in arguing. She knew Charles of old. Once his mind was made up, he was immovable.

'Very well,' she said, rising, thinking she could not feel any more wretched. 'I must go and put on my black dress and say a prayer for Father's soul.'

Francis took the news that there was no hope well, but Katheryn was desolate. It seemed that the future held nothing for her. It was not enough that she could still meet him in secret, for their trysts left her wanting and unbearably unsatisfied, and made her feel as naught in the world, as if this was all she could expect. When she saw other lovers together, her heart felt as if it was breaking. Why could *she* not marry the man she loved? Why could they not even be seen together?

She slept in her own chamber these days. She could not endure to see the others enjoying bedsports that were denied to her and Francis, or hear them talking about betrothals.

All through the summer, her depression persisted. She could take no pleasure in life and was prone to weeping at the slightest thing. She supposed that her grief for her father had a part in it, although he had been away for so long that she barely missed his physical presence. It was more that she felt cast adrift, an orphan with no prospects – and the one man who was willing to help her was powerless to do so.

Francis was patient with her for a long time, but, as the months passed, relations between them became strained. He often said that things would be better one day, but she couldn't see how.

On the day when they learned that the King was to marry a German princess, they went walking along their usual route northwards. It was early October, and there was a chill in the air – and in Katheryn's heart.

'You're quiet,' Francis observed.

'I'm all right.' She gave him a weak smile.

'Still feeling low?' he asked.

She could not speak.

'I love you, nothing will change that,' he said, gazing at the seabirds swooping over the marshes, 'but you must try and cheer up. I hate to see you so sad, and it's dragging me down too.'

'I just feel there is no future for me, or for us,' she mourned.

'I'm here!' he growled. 'I'm here now, and I love you. That's something, isn't it? Love like ours isn't given to everyone.'

'It isn't enough!' she burst out, and immediately regretted it, for Francis's face closed up and he turned away.

'I want us to be married as much as you do, but, in grieving for what we can't have, you have lost sight of what we do have. And, if it isn't enough, then maybe you would like to end it.' His voice was taut. 'Maybe you would be happier.'

'I don't think I'll ever be happy again.' She was crying now, lost in misery, and upset that he hadn't turned to comfort her, as he usually did. 'Do *you* want to end it?'

'If I'm making you unhappy, it might be best.' Still he looked away from her. 'But I would not leave you of my own volition. It's what you want that matters.'

'I don't know what I want!' she wailed.

'Then it's hardly worth our going on,' he replied. 'If you loved me truly, you would know without a doubt.' And he walked away, leaving her standing there, crying, too stunned to go after him. How long she remained there in the wind she did not know, but dusk was falling as she returned to Norfolk House, aware that she had missed supper. She could not have eaten it anyway.

Three days later, she was sinking in despair, unable to open up to anyone about her woes or to find Francis and make things right between them. She had not seen him since their meeting, and something told her that he would make no move to see her. She knew she had hurt him, but did not know how to mend the harm she had done, for, in truth, she had nothing to offer him but despondency.

Then Mary told her that the Duchess wished to speak to her, and immediately Katheryn thought she had been seen with Francis and was to be rebuked – or worse. But her grandam, seated by the fireside, was beaming when she entered her chamber.

'Katheryn!' she greeted her. 'Sit down, my dear.' She indicated a stool at the other side of the hearth. 'As you know, his Majesty is to marry the Lady Anne of Cleves. One cannot but deplore the fact that Cleves is allied to the Protestant princes of Germany, and I would much have preferred to see a Catholic queen on the throne, but I have always wanted to place you at court. The Lady Anne is expected to arrive in England soon, and, as you may imagine, there has been much jostling for places in her household. You will be pleased to hear that my lord Duke has secured posts as maids-of-honour for you and your cousins, Mary Norris and Katherine Carey.'

Katheryn had been listening with mounting excitement, such as she had not felt in months. She was going to court, that glittering place that drew the greatest in the land like a lodestone! And she would have good company there too. She had lots of cousins, several of whom she had never met, although she had heard of these two, for Mary Norris's father had been one of the men executed for adultery with Queen Anne, and Katherine Carey was Queen Anne's niece, the daughter of her sister Mary. She hoped she would find them to be true friends.

'You are very lucky, Katheryn,' the Duchess was saying. 'Another young lady had already been appointed but was unable to take up her position, so the Duke persuaded the King that you should have it.'

Katheryn drew in a deep breath. The realisation was sinking in. She would live in palaces, have beautiful gowns, dance and make merry – and spend her days in close proximity to the King himself! It was no dream – it was really going to happen, and she suddenly felt dizzy with elation. It was the most sovereign cure for her woes!

She clapped her hands. 'My lady, that is the best news you could have given me!'

'I'm glad,' the Duchess said. 'Going to court will stop you moping around with Mr Dereham. Don't think I haven't been aware of it.'

Katheryn stared at her. After all that subterfuge . . .

'It was reprehensible of you to disobey me,' the Duchess continued, 'but I understand you have been circumspect. It's as well you are going to court. Hopefully, you will attract some fitting suitor there, one who can keep you in the manner to which, as a Howard, you should be accustomed.'

'But, my lady, you were not averse to us marrying, so long as my father agreed?'

'I have a fondness for Mr Dereham, and as things stood it would have been an acceptable match for you. But now that this wonderful chance has come your way, I rejoice that there will be better options open to you. Now, we will forget Mr Dereham, for there is much to be done. The first thing is to get you fitted out for court, and as soon as possible. The Lady Anne is expected to arrive in England soon, and you must be ready. Sir Thomas Manners, who is to be her chamberlain, will inform me when and where you are to be sent. Malyn, Meg and Kat are to go to court too, as chamberers to the Queen. They had hoped to be maids-of-honour, but they are lucky to be going at all! Sir Philip Tilney is to be an usher of the King's Privy Chamber, so he and Malyn will be together at court. Married courtiers are allocated lodgings.'

The Duchess rambled on, but Katheryn was barely listening. It was breathtaking, the speed with which her life had turned around. Suddenly, there was a purpose to it, a future – and a glittering one at that. But before she could enjoy it, there was Francis to be told. She would have to face him.

She found him in the dining hall, supervising the laying of the table.

'Wait for me in the garden,' he told her, his face impassive. She wandered out and waited for ten minutes, her trepidation increasing. Had he thought she had come to apologise for her unhappiness? Did he want her back? And how would he react when she told him she was going to court?

As she gazed out over the river, she faced the fact that she wanted to go to court far more than she wanted to be with him. Their love had become tainted, for her, by hopelessness and the knowledge that it could not flourish. She still had feelings for him, but not the lust and passion she had felt so many weeks ago. She would miss him, she was certain; she was just not sure how much.

It was about a quarter of an hour before he joined her, coming to stand beside her by the low garden wall.

'Hello, Katheryn,' he said. 'How are you?'

'I am well,' she said. 'I have to talk to you.'

'I don't think there's any more to say.' He gave her a hard look.

'It's not about that. I am summoned to court to serve the new Queen.'

He caught his breath. 'You are leaving Lambeth for good?'

'I will visit if I am able.'

'Then it really is over between us.' He turned away. 'If you go, I will not tarry long in this house.'

'I *am* going. My lord of Norfolk has arranged it; I have no choice. You must do as you wish. Believe me, it grieves me to be leaving you.'

'Why should I believe that?' His voice was bitter. 'The court is swarming with eligible men, and you will soon forget me.'

'That's unfair,' Katheryn said, wanting to make him feel better and be kinder to her. 'You will never live to say that I have swerved from you.'

'I wish I could believe that too,' he muttered.

'You can,' she said, feeling sorry for him and taking his hand. He turned to her, his dark eyes full of pain.

'Remember how we plighted our troth?' he said, twisting his hand

and taking hers in his grasp. 'Even if you forsake me for another, you will always be mine, and I will always be true to you.'

'And I will be true to you,' she promised, wanting only to get away. Somehow, her mind had already consigned Francis to the past, and she was eager to embrace her new life. Yes, they had plighted their troth, but that was then, and she did not believe it was as binding as he seemed to think. Certainly, the Duchess had not thought so.

'When are you going?' he asked.

'When I am summoned. It depends on when the Queen is expected. But it won't be long.'

'Then we can see each other in the meantime?'

'Of course,' she said, knowing it was wrong of her to let him hope that all might yet be as it had been between them.

'Then let's go to Batrichsy tomorrow,' he said. 'I have to get back to my duties now.'

'Very well,' she agreed.

He kissed her then, and it felt strange. She was not sure that she wanted to go to Batrichsy with him. As she walked back to the house, she decided to invent an excuse not to.

In the event, she did not have to make up an excuse for, that afternoon, she was plunged into a whirl of preparations for court. The Duchess's tailor came and measured her for six gowns. He laid out length after length of gorgeous fabrics on the long table and my lady pored over them as Katheryn stood there desperately hoping that the ones she liked would be chosen. There was a gorgeous crimson damask . . . but no. The gowns were all to be black or white.

'The late Queen insisted upon it, as did Queen Katherine,' the Duchess told her. 'They didn't want their attendants outshining them. This is a good black, the most expensive. The Duke wants you provided with the best; you will be representing our house at court and must dress fittingly.'

The milliner came with his wires and his buckram to make French hoods for Katheryn. There would be no more running about with her hair loose. A new dancing master was engaged, and Mr Barnes returned to give her music lessons, for she had grown rusty. Lady Bridgewater lectured her on deportment and made her walk up and down with a book on her head to give her poise. Then a jeweller came, and Katheryn was allowed to select three pieces from his wares to adorn her gowns. She chose a pendant depicting the Nativity, a brooch bearing the Howard motto, *Sola virtus invictus*, which meant 'Bravery alone is invincible', and a silver ring. She wished she had not given her mother's ring to Francis, but could not bring herself to ask for it back, fearing his reaction.

She was so busy that she had to send a note saying she could not meet him – and it was the truth. Mother Emmet had ordered fine linen for shifts, and Katheryn was ordered to start making them. There was no time to be wasted, she was told. In fact, she managed just three meetings with Francis in that busy month, none of them very enjoyable for either of them. She suspected that he knew she did not feel the same about him, although she tried to hide it. But there was none of the spontaneous love that they had once shared so passionately.

She had no time to brood, however. In truth, her departure could not come soon enough. Malyn, Meg and Kat shared her excitement, busy with their own preparations, and the other gentlewomen looked on enviously. The bounty that was being lavished on Katheryn made it clear that she was above them all, a noble daughter of the Howards, and that no expense was to be spared in preparing her for her debut at court.

In the middle of November, she was summoned again to the Duchess's chamber, and was overjoyed to find there her cousin Tom Culpeper, whom she had not seen since she was about seven.

'Mr Culpeper has been sent by the Earl of Rutland to inform us that you are to go to the court at Whitehall three days hence,' the Duchess beamed.

Tom bowed. As he straightened, Katheryn stared at him. The handsome boy had broadened and matured into a very attractive man with a strong jaw and high cheekbones. He still had the same shock of curly brown hair and twinkling blue eyes, but there was about him a new air of authority. His clothes were of purple velvet and silk, cut in the latest fashion, and bespoke wealth and status. She would have liked to hug him, but she was no longer a child, while he was now a grand gentleman – and she was aware of the Duchess's eyes on her and of the need to behave with propriety. Besides, she was conscious of a flutter in her breast at his proximity. If he had been one of the gallants who frequented the gentlewomen's chamber, she would have tried him, there was no question of it, Francis or no Francis. It shocked her a little to realise how quickly she had got over her erstwhile lover.

She had perforce to content herself with curtseying to him.

'I was never gladder to see you, cousin,' she said. 'You bring the most welcome news.'

He was looking at her with undisguised appreciation. 'Why, my pretty little cousin has grown into a lovely, graceful lady!' he exclaimed. 'The court will be a fairer place for your presence. You are bound to make a stir there.'

'Not too much of a stir, I hope,' the Duchess said, and Katheryn knew she was thinking of Francis and Harry and all the stir she had caused over them.

My lady bade them both be seated and called for wine.

'I can see from your attire that you are high in the King's favour, Mr Culpeper,' she said. 'The last I heard, only royalty was allowed to wear purple.'

Tom flushed a little. 'His Grace has been pleased to grant me many privileges and honour me with many preferments,' he replied. 'As Katheryn knows, I was brought up in his Privy Chamber. I started as a page, and about six years ago, he made me a gentleman of the Privy Chamber.'

The Duchess was clearly impressed. 'Katheryn, any man who attains such a position is in high favour indeed. The gentlemen of the Privy Chamber have the ear of his Majesty and great influence.'

Tom smiled complacently. It was obvious that he was proud of his achievements.

'These past three years, I have been especially honoured,' he said. 'The King was understandably shocked when Sir Henry Norris was found to have committed treason with Queen Anne. He had been chief gentleman of the Privy Chamber and his Grace's close friend. It was me whom his Grace then turned to for friendship.' He sighed. 'I had thought to succeed Sir Henry, for it appeared I was in like favour, but Sir Thomas Heneage was made chief gentleman in his place; yet I am content, for I have the honour of sharing his Majesty's bed at night. He does not sleep alone, you understand, for reasons of security. I believe he has a genuine liking for me.'

'He wanted a son like you, you know,' the Duchess observed. 'A strong heir, and courtly, with good looks. In that clothing, you could be a prince!'

Tom smiled. Katheryn was aware of his eyes on her. She could hardly drag hers away from him.

'With the King's love, and being so close to him, you are in a position of great influence,' the Duchess went on. 'I imagine there are many seeking your patronage.'

'A few,' he admitted, grinning.

'You are clearly doing well out of it,' she said.

'It can be lucrative,' he told her. 'The King has been pleased to grant me several offices: I am Clerk of the Armoury, Keeper of Penshurst and North Leigh, Master of the Game, Lieutenant of Tonbridge Castle and Steward of Ashdown Forest. I have a fine house in Greenwich and also one at Penshurst.'

'You must be a man of great revenue,' the Duchess said, and Katheryn suddenly realised what all this was about. In nearly every respect, Tom was an eminently desirable suitor. Her grandam was matchmaking.

For all that she fancied Tom, she did not need another suitor now. Things were complicated enough with Francis. Besides, she wanted to go to court and enjoy herself for the foreseeable future; she did not want to be tied down to a husband yet, or be relegated to the country, bearing children year in and year out.

She glanced at Tom. Surely he must have rumbled the Duchess's tactics. Yet he was sitting there, smiling urbanely, clearly enjoying talking about himself. It struck her that he had asked her nothing about her own life in the years they had been apart.

At last, he turned to her. 'You will enjoy the court, Katheryn. But if ever you have need of me, I'll be happy to be of service.'

'That's very kind,' the Duchess said.

Katheryn rose, thanking Tom. 'I crave your leave, my lady, but I have sewing to finish and time is pressing.'

'Run along, then. I'm sure you will see Mr Culpeper at court,' the Duchess said.

The barge stood waiting, bobbing up and down on the choppy water. Katheryn could see it from her chamber window, from which she had watched Lord William Howard walk from the jetty towards the house. He had come to escort her to Whitehall Palace, just a short way downstream.

She was ready to leave, tricked out in one of her new gowns and her new jewels. On the bed lay her fur-lined cloak. She would need it today, for the November wind was cold and shrill. Her travelling chest had already been carried downstairs to the boat. Malyn had boarded, and Meg and Kat were standing in the doorway, pulling on their gloves. All that remained was for them to say their farewells.

The young gentlewomen who had been Katheryn's friends these past nine years hugged and kissed her, enviously begging her to visit and tell them about life at court. Even Joan and Mary seemed sorry to see her go.

'I will come to see you,' she promised, 'and I will remember you all in my prayers.'

They followed as she pattered downstairs; they wanted to wave farewell.

'I must find my lady,' she told them, and sped off in the direction of the Duchess's apartments. As soon as she was well out of sight, she doubled back and made for the steward's room, where she hoped she might find Francis. She could not leave without saying goodbye to him.

He was there and, fortunately, alone. As soon as he saw her, he laid down the silver cup he was examining, presumably for finger-marks. 'You are leaving for the court?' he said.

'Yes,' she replied. 'I came to say farewell.'

He gave her a sharp look. 'Is that farewell for good?'

'Oh, no,' she hastened to assure him. 'I will come to see you whenever I can.'

'Well, I may not be here. I have asked my lady of Norfolk for leave to resign my post. It was only you that kept me here. Now you are departing, I am desirous to be gone too.'

'But where will you go?' Katheryn asked.

'I have not decided yet. Fear not, it won't be for ever. I will come back and claim you, when I have made my fortune!' He gave her a brief smile. A silence yawned between them, one that should have been filled with her telling him she was loath to leave and would miss him dreadfully.

'Katheryn,' he said at length, 'I have a favour to ask, and I ask it as your husband, for it is the part of a husband to leave his wife provided for. I have made a will, and I want you to keep it for me with most of my savings, which amount to a hundred pounds. If I do not return, you are to consider the money your own.'

It was a huge sum, such as her father must have dreamed of, but there was something in Francis's voice that disturbed Katheryn. 'What do you mean, if you do not return? You're not planning to do something dangerous, I hope!'

He grinned. 'Not at all. I want to see the world, that's all, and make some good money while I'm doing it. I was just covering all eventualities. Now, will you look after these things for me?'

'Of course, but where will I keep them? There may not be any safe place at court. I could leave them here, I suppose. There's a loose floorboard in my chamber, in the corner by the window. I hid my own treasures in it. Put the money and the will in there and nail it down when no one is watching. Only you and I will know that they're there.'

'I'll do that,' he said. 'And now, I suppose, it's farewell.'

'Yes,' she said, lamely.

They stood there for a moment, then he took her hand, lifted it to his lips and kissed it. On his little finger, her mother's ring glinted. She could have wept for him and for the loss of what they had once had.

Part Two

'So highly beloved,
far, far beyond the rest'

Chapter 13

1539

Katheryn had often seen the black-and-white-chequered walls of Whitehall Palace from the river and had sometimes walked along the highway that ran through it and led to Charing Cross and the Strand. It was the King's chief residence and said to be the largest palace in Christendom. When they arrived and had been admitted at the gatehouse, Lord William escorted them through the palace to meet the Earl of Rutland, the Queen's chamberlain, and she found herself passing through a rambling labyrinth of magnificent state apartments, lodgings and service quarters, all ranged around several courtyards.

The Earl of Rutland was extremely courteous and looked very much like the portrait of the King that hung at Lambeth. He received them in a picture gallery and waited until Lord William had wished them luck and bade them farewell before conducting them to the Queen's apartments. He was happy to answer their many questions about the palace.

'My lord, where does the King live?'

'His apartments face the river, Mistress Katheryn, and a wonder they are too. You will see them for yourself when you are attending the Queen. A gallery connects them to her lodgings.'

'Will we see his Grace?' Meg wanted to know.

'Not today, I imagine. State affairs keep him busy.'

'I expect he is looking forward to the Queen coming,' Kat said.

'The King is an eager bridegroom,' the chamberlain smiled.

In the Queen's apartments, Katheryn and her friends gaped at the carved and gilded ceilings and mantelpieces, the fine tapestries and furniture. Here were wonders indeed! She saw through the windows the privy garden below, a little paradise into which the Queen and her ladies could retreat. And she was to live here! Life just got better and better.

Waiting to meet them was Mrs Stonor, the Mother of the Maids, who was a far more formidable figure than the lackadaisical Mother Emmet, but welcoming nonetheless. 'Thank you, my lord,' she said to the Earl, as he left them together in the Queen's deserted presence chamber. 'Let me look at you all. Yes, you come well presented. My lady of Norfolk has done you proud.'

Katheryn basked in her praise. She so wanted to make a good impression.

'It goes without saying,' Mrs Stonor said sternly, 'that while you are serving the Queen, you will be models of virtue and exercise impeccable discretion. You will not be bold or loud or do anything to bring discredit upon yourself and your companions. Do I make myself clear?'

'Yes, Mrs Stonor,' they all said, in unison.

'Good.' She smiled. 'Some of the others are here already. I will take you up to the maidens' dorter. Your chests will be delivered shortly. Lady Tilney, please wait here. I have asked your husband to come and show you to your lodging.'

Bidding a temporary farewell to Malyn, Katheryn went ahead of Meg and Kat up a spiral stair in a corner of the presence chamber and came to a large, airy room in which she counted fifteen beds. There were four girls there already, unpacking their clothes. It was not so very different from the dorter at Lambeth, save that it was bigger and a lot tidier. Evidently Mrs Stonor was efficient at supervising her charges. Katheryn could not imagine the goings-on at Lambeth happening here.

'Now, I will leave you ladies to get acquainted,' Mrs Stonor said. 'Choose any bed you like.' As she bustled off down the stairs, Katheryn smiled at the other maids, who came over to introduce themselves.

'I'm Anne Bassett,' the pretty blonde one said, 'and this is Mary Norris.' A tiny girl of about fourteen, with chestnut hair and a proud bearing, smiled graciously at the newcomers. Another very pleasant young lady introduced herself as Kate Carey, then the fourth newcomer, who was a little older than the rest and had a thin face and wiry, dark hair, said she was Dorothy Bray, but that people usually called her Dora.

'We're cousins, I believe,' Katheryn said to Kate Carey. 'I'm Katheryn Howard, and these ladies are Meg Morton and Kat Tilney, another cousin.'

'I'm sure I'm related in some way too,' Meg pitched in.

They fell to chattering, and soon Katheryn learned that Anne Bassett had served Jane Seymour and that her stepfather, Lord Lisle, was the deputy governor of Calais who had shown kindness and forbearance to her own father. Anne had a sister who was desperate to be at court, but had not secured a place. 'So my lady mother expects me to make suit to the King for one,' Anne giggled. 'Fortunately, his Majesty has always been kind to me. He even permitted me to stay on at court after Queen Jane died.' That sounded odd, as even Katheryn knew that there was no place for ladies at court when there was no queen; she wondered if there had been more to it than that. She sensed that Anne would have told them if she could.

Dora revealed that it was her first time at court. 'I'm so glad you are familiar with it,' she told Anne. 'I'd be all adrift on my own.'

'Mrs Stonor would soon put you right,' Anne said. 'This evening, as certain as death, we'll all get a lecture on the rules we must observe and the necessity for being virtuous young ladies and not gossiping or getting too familiar with the gentlemen.'

Mary looked at Kate Carey. 'I'm sure your mother told you all about that.'

Kate coloured. 'I think it unkind of you to say that, Mary.' She turned to Katheryn and the two chamberers. 'You may as well hear it from me, since the whole world knows that my mother was sister to Queen Anne, and that she was the King's mistress for a time.'

'There was no need to taunt Kate with that,' Dora rounded on Mary.

Mary shrugged. 'I too come in for my share of taunts. You ladies may have heard of Sir Henry Norris, who was beheaded for adultery with Queen Anne. He was my father.'

'You know what they say about two wrongs,' Anne put in, unpacking what seemed to be an endless pile of clothes. 'You two should be supportive of each other.'

'I never taunted you, Mary,' Kate said. 'I have great sympathy for you.'

'I don't need anyone's pity,' Mary said. 'Oh, I'm sorry, Kate, I meant no offence. I shouldn't have said what I did. Forgive me.'

'Of course,' Kate said, somewhat offhandedly, and drew out a gown from her chest. 'I have a hem to sew.'

Katheryn was beginning to feel uncomfortable about the tensions in the maidens' dorter. She hoped there wouldn't be unpleasantness like this all the time.

'Our chests are arriving,' Meg said brightly. 'Shall we all choose our beds and get unpacked?'

By the time dusk fell, the other young ladies had arrived. The grandest entrance was made by Lady Lucy Somerset, a haughty fifteen-year-old who boasted of her kinship to the King, which in fact sounded rather distant.

'My father is the grandson of the last of the Beaufort dukes of Somerset,' she told them all.

'Aye, on the wrong side of the blanket,' Anne murmured in Katheryn's ear. It all meant nothing to Katheryn, for she had never heard of the Beaufort dukes of Somerset. 'How is she related to the King?' she whispered.

'His Grace's grandmother was a Beaufort,' Anne told her.

Katheryn soon noticed that Mary Norris would not speak to Lady Lucy.

'And small wonder,' said Anne, who seemed to know everything. 'Lucy's mother was the first to lay evidence about Queen Anne. There is bad blood between those families.'

'Well, I'm staying out of it,' Katheryn decided, and made a point of going over to chat to the other new faces, who introduced themselves as Ursula Stourton, Margaret Garnish, Margaret Coupledike and Damascin Stradling. She also spoke to two chamberers, Mrs Frideswide and Mrs Luffkyn, but found them stand-offish and awkward in the presence of noble girls.

Later that afternoon, they were all sworn to the Queen's service in the presence of the Earl of Rutland and the chief officers of the household. Katheryn pledged herself to be loyal, true, obedient and virtuous, and meant it with every fibre of her being.

Supper was served in a large hall at three rows of trestle tables, with the royal officers sitting at the high table on the dais. Katheryn had thought Lambeth a great household, but it was nothing compared to this. She had never seen so many people gathered together at one meal. It brought home to her the magnificence and wealth of the King, of which she had heard much. Now she could see for herself that gossip had not lied.

The grandeur of the setting did not extend to the table. The plates and utensils before her were made of wood, the bread was wheaten and dark, and ale, not wine, was being served in a leather jug. The food, in large dishes, came in messes, each sufficient for four persons.

'You mustn't finish all your food,' Anne told Katheryn. 'It's uncharitable. The leftovers are collected in a voider and given to the beggars at the gates.'

There seemed to be a lot to learn about life at court.

The great ladies of the household were seated at the higher end of the room. Anne, basking in her superior knowledge of the court, pointed them out. 'The one with red hair is the King's niece Lady Margaret Douglas.' Katheryn could not help staring at her. The last she had heard, the Lady Margaret had been rusticating in grief at Syon Abbey. Now she was chattering and laughing as if she had not a care in the world.

'Next to her is the Duchess of Richmond,' Anne pointed out. Katheryn recognised Uncle Norfolk's daughter Mary, whom she had last seen at Lady Wiltshire's funeral. 'Opposite is the Duchess of Suffolk, and the lady in the tawny gown is your step-aunt, the Countess of Sussex.' Lady William Howard needed no introduction, for Katheryn had met her often at Lambeth. Lady William had seen her too, for she nodded and smiled.

There were many other ladies of the Queen's privy chamber seated further down the table. Anne continued to identify them, as more messes of meats and sauces were carried in and placed on the table. 'My Lady Rutland is the wife of her Grace's chamberlain, and beside her is

Lady Clinton.' She lowered her voice. 'She too was the King's mistress and bore him a son, the late Duke of Richmond. You'll know, of course, that he was married to your cousin.' Katheryn did know, although she had never met the Duke, who had died at the age of seventeen about four years ago.

'The lady in the crimson gable hood is the Lady Rochford.' Anne indicated a slender woman past her youth, yet still comely, with a heart-shaped face and pouting lips. She bent close to Katheryn's ear. 'Her husband was brother to Queen Anne.' Of course. Lord Rochford had been executed for committing incest with his sister, and Katheryn had heard it said that Lady Rochford had laid evidence against them. She wondered if it was true.

'There's Lady Edgcumbe, and opposite, on our side, Lady Baynton.'

Isabel! Katheryn had not realised she would be here, having been too preoccupied with other matters. She leaned forward and saw Isabel's face break into a smile as she caught sight of her. She stared at her half-sister's faintly lined features, realising with a shock that Isabel must be in her mid-forties now.

Isabel rose at once, came over and hugged her.

'How lovely to see you, sister!' she cried. 'I heard you were appointed maid-of-honour, but did not know when you would be arriving. Edward is again made vice chamberlain to the Queen – did you know? We are all serving her together!' They embraced warmly as Katheryn congratulated her.

'Let me look at you,' Isabel said. 'In faith, you are grown very pretty, and that gown becomes you well. We must talk. I'll find you later in the maidens' chamber.'

Katheryn sat down, glad to have her half-sister with her at the court, which suddenly felt like a friendlier place. She was aware of Lady Rochford's appraising eyes on her. She gave her a tentative smile, and the woman smiled back.

'Watch her,' Anne muttered. 'She's a strange one.'

'What do you mean?'

'She's just odd. Ever since that bad business with her husband. You've heard the rumours, of course?'

'Yes.' Katheryn did not like to say too much.

'She's been looked after since, if you take my meaning. It seems to me that she did Lord Cromwell a favour.'

Even Katheryn had heard – who had not? – of Lord Cromwell, the King's chief minister.

'Do you mean she—'

'Not here!' Anne shook her head.

At the next table, she told Katheryn, were seated the gentlewomen of the privy chamber, far too many for her to mention, but she did name those nearest to them, Mistress Anne Parr and Mistress Cromwell, who was sister to the late Queen Jane. Beyond them, Katheryn thought she recognised another of her own half-sisters, Margaret, Lady Arundell, whom she had not seen since she was a child. At the far end, she saw Malyn, Meg and Kat, chatting animatedly to the other chamberers.

It was at once exhilarating and daunting to be part of such a large household – Anne had not even attempted to name the male officers and servants who sat at the far table – but Katheryn reminded herself that she was a Howard, and Howards had long graced the court of England. This was her rightful place, and she would make a success of it.

She had expected an endless round of dancing and revelry, but soon found that life at court was rather boring. With no queen present, they were expected to keep to the apartments set aside for her and amuse themselves. Mrs Stonor explained that the court was the domain of men and it would be a breach of propriety for any young lady to venture there. Katheryn was beginning to appreciate how much freedom she had enjoyed at Lambeth.

They had no duties. Everything was ready for the Queen's coming, down to the last stitch and coat of polish. They occupied themselves as best they could, which meant sewing or making music or playing endless games of dice. Isabel had a backgammon set, and she and Katheryn played together in the evenings. Sometimes Margaret Arundell joined them with her cards. Katheryn, who was always lamenting her own diminutive height, was not a little envious to see how tall her other half-sister had grown.

She was praying that things would liven up when the Queen arrived.

'I wonder what she is like?' she mused, as Margaret dealt the cards one dark, chilly evening.

'The Queen?' Isabel asked. 'Beautiful, I think, and virtuous. The King would not have chosen her otherwise. Edward says his Grace fell for her portrait. Master Holbein went to Cleves to paint her.'

'Well, we'll know soon enough what she is like,' Margaret said. 'She's expected to arrive before Christmas.'

'I hope she'll be a kind mistress,' said Anne Parr, who was watching the game.

'I hope she can speak English!' Katheryn added, and they all laughed.

It was at Yuletide that Katheryn first saw the King. Anne of Cleves was still in Calais, delayed by adverse winds, and Christmas was kept at Whitehall in an atmosphere of eager expectancy. Many lords had brought their wives with them to greet the new Queen, and the presence of so many noblewomen ensured that the rules were relaxed and that the Queen's maids were free to mingle with the crowds that thronged the palace and enjoy the feasting and revelry.

On Christmas Eve, the Yule log was carried into the great hall and ceremonially lit, and wassail bowls were passed around. Then a voice rang out, 'Make way for the King's Majesty!' and a small procession entered through the doorway. There was no mistaking the King: he was taller and broader than everyone else, magnificently dressed in cloth of gold and black velvet, and laden with jewels. Oh, but he was so old – and fat! Katheryn was shocked. He was nothing like his portrait at Lambeth; it must have been painted years ago, when he was a slim and handsome young man, the envy of all. Now, the red hair beneath his velvet bonnet was streaked with grey, and his doublet and padded short gown encased a massive bulk. If he had not been smiling jovially as he greeted everyone, you might have thought he had a permanent scowl on his face, for it looked cruel and sour in repose. And he was limping. Beneath the white hose, Katheryn could see bandages.

144

She felt sorry for the poor Queen. Had Anne of Cleves any idea what awaited her at the end of her journey? King or no, this ageing, obese man had little to offer a young woman. She even found herself feeling pity for him because of what he had once been and what he was now.

He was approaching. Katheryn and the other maids sank into curtseys as he greeted them, then rose at his command.

'Here's a pretty bevy of beauties!' he observed, his eyes full of merriment. 'You must all be as bored with waiting for the Lady Anne as I am.' His eye rested on Katheryn for a moment. 'God grant she will be here soon. A merry Christmas to you all, ladies!' Then he was gone, leaving in his wake the hint of a sweet stink. It came from his leg, Katheryn was sure.

He reminded her of someone, but she could not think who.

After he had passed on, the young women simpered and blushed, thrilled to have been noticed. But Katheryn's thoughts were elsewhere. She had just noticed Tom Culpeper among the gentlemen attending the King, and he had smiled at her.

Later that night, as the maids prepared for bed, Katheryn got a glimpse of Kate Carey in profile and realised who the King had reminded her of. The resemblance was striking. Kate was his daughter; there was no doubting it.

Chapter 14

1540

It was freezing in the chariot, and the young ladies were all huddled together for warmth. The weather was foul, wet and windy beneath a grey sky, and Katheryn's fur-lined cloak was no proof against the chill. They seemed to have been on the road for hours, but, God be thanked, Dartford was now in sight.

Katheryn was so stiff when they arrived that she could barely clamber out of the chariot. She stood there, stamping her feet, as the Queen's household officers and ladies assembled outside the town gate, buffeted by icy winds. A haughty lady swathed in sables approached the maids-of-honour.

'I am Lady Browne,' she informed them. 'I have been appointed to help Mrs Stonor supervise you until we return to Greenwich. The Queen's party has been sighted. You will not be detained here long.'

'She looks like a dragon,' Anne murmured.

'I heard that!' reproved Mrs Stonor behind her. Katheryn giggled. Her teeth were chattering.

The Queen's retinue was at last coming towards them. Katheryn saw Uncle Norfolk and the Duke of Suffolk riding on either side of a wondrously carved gilded chariot. When it drew to a halt, Uncle Norfolk dismounted and offered his hand to the lady who was emerging. She too was wrapped in furs, but the hood of her cloak was down and Katheryn could see that she had on a most peculiar golden headdress that covered her hair and seemed to have wings of gauze. Then the Lady Anne turned to greet the Earl of Rutland and her other officers, and her face came into view. She was not beautiful – her long nose and jutting chin put paid to that – but her eyes were kind and she had a smiling mouth.

'Hmm,' murmured Anne Bassett in Katheryn's ear.

'Shh!' Katheryn hissed, for Archbishop Cranmer and the Duke of Suffolk had begun presenting the ladies and maids to the Lady Anne. When her turn came, she made a graceful reverence and bent to kiss her new mistress's extended hand, which was freezing to the touch. As she did so, she smelt a most unpleasant odour. Heavens, did they wash in Cleves? One thing she had learned about the King was that he was overly fastidious; Mrs Stonor had warned them all not to put food or sticky hands on counterpanes or tapestries, and Katheryn had giggled when it was explained to her that the red crosses painted on the walls of the palace courtyards were meant to deter men from pissing there. Certainly, the King would not appreciate a wife who smelt badly.

Katheryn noticed that the Lady Anne was attended by a lot of German ladies, all wearing the most outlandish, unflattering clothes. She had been told that they were to serve alongside the English ladies.

At last, thankfully, the company processed into the former priory of Dartford, which, like all the other religious houses in England, had been closed down by the King. Katheryn was of the same opinion as the rest of her family, that it was wrong, nay, sacrilegious of his Grace to dissolve the monasteries and appropriate their wealth, but it did not trouble her unduly. She had more pressing concerns. Her duties and her new life were about to begin.

That evening, the Lady Anne summoned her maids and ladies to join her in her privy chamber. She invited them to be seated, the ladies on stools, the maids kneeling on the floor.

'My name is Anna,' she told them, in her halting, guttural English. 'I would like to know you.' With the help of one of her gentlewomen, the Flemish Mrs Gilman, who was to serve her as an interpreter, she spoke to each of them in turn. When Katheryn was presented, she curtseyed and smiled at the Princess, aware that she must be feeling nervous being in a new land and about to marry a strange, awesome and, frankly, repugnant man.

'Mistress Katheryn Howard, your Grace,' Mrs Gilman said. 'She is niece to the Duke of Norfolk.'

'You are welcome,' the Princess said, smiling back. 'You are happy to be here?'

'Oh, yes, your Grace!' Katheryn replied. 'How could I not be? It is an honour to serve you.'

'You haf been at court long?'

'No, I am new here too!' Katheryn laughed. She liked this kind young woman, who was making such an effort to be friendly. Anna was also encouraging her English ladies to make friends with her German women, who were sitting together on one side of the chamber. Katheryn did try, but they knew hardly any English, so she ventured to approach Mother Lowe, the German Mother of the Maids, a stout matron who was very much on her dignity, yet spoke some English.

'Who are you?' Mother Lowe asked, in her abrupt manner.

'Katheryn Howard. My uncle is the Duke of Norfolk.'

Mother Lowe looked unimpressed. 'And your *Vater?*'

'Lord Edmund Howard. He died last year,' Katheryn told her. 'My mother died when I was a child, and I was sent to live in the household of my grandam, the Dowager Duchess of Norfolk.'

'You vere happy there?'

'I was, but I'm pleased to be at court.'

'Your family vill be proud of you.'

'I hope to make them so.'

Later, the conversation, halting as it was, was all of the new Queen's official reception on the morrow. Anna seemed daunted by it, yet she was clearly determined to make a good showing of herself. Katheryn herself could not wait to don the splendid dress of crimson velvet she was to wear.

As the evening wore on, she hoped there would be music and dancing, or even cards, but the Lady Anna went to bed soon after nine o'clock, and so the rest of them had to retire too. Of course, they needed to be up early in the morning to ride to Blackheath, but Katheryn was praying that this would not be the pattern of their future evenings.

Wearing the velvet gown made Katheryn feel like a queen herself. Waiting with the rest of Anna's household before the silken pavilion that had been erected at the foot of Shooter's Hill, she did not care about the cold, although some of the other maids were shivering. They had left Dartford at dawn and ridden ahead, to be ready to receive their new mistress when she arrived.

Waiting with them were what seemed like thousands of people: knights, soldiers, liveried servants and crowds of common people, not to mention the numerous lords and ladies, who were decked out in their best for the occasion. Even the Dowager Duchess was there, standing with the Countess of Bridgewater and the rest of the Howard contingent.

All eyes were on Anna's chariot as it descended Shooter's Hill at noon at the head of an impressive train. When she alighted outside the pavilion, the Earl of Rutland bowed before her and Lady Margaret Douglas, the Duchess of Richmond and the King's other niece, the Marchioness of Dorset, stepped forward with words of welcome. Then Katheryn and the rest of the household made their obeisances.

'I give you all hearty thanks,' Anna said, turning to her chief ladies and kissing them in turn. There was an interminable wait while her almoner made a long speech in Latin, then formally presented to her everyone who was sworn to serve her, which took some considerable time, with each kneeling in order of seniority to kiss her hand. Katheryn was freezing afterwards and grateful to retreat into the pavilion, where scented braziers had been lit and they could all thaw out and partake of the banquet laid out on a long table. Afterwards, they helped Anna to change into a gown of cloth of gold. Katheryn was amazed to see that it had just a circular skirt with no court train, and saw other ladies staring too.

They waited outside the pavilion. Katheryn thought that Anna looked nervous. Last night, the ladies had been talking about their mistress's first meeting with the King and saying that it had not gone well, for his Grace had appeared in disguise and surprised his bride. After that, though, there had been nothing but courtesy between them. Katheryn thought that if the King had surprised *her*, she might have screamed in horror!

Trumpets sounded in the distance. Seeing Anna mounting her

palfrey, Katheryn got on her own horse and followed in procession with the other ladies towards Greenwich Palace. From her elevated position on horseback, she could see the Lord Mayor and leading citizens of London, all bowing low, and behind them the royal trumpeters approaching, heralding the King's procession. As Anna's party halted by a stone cross, Katheryn saw Uncle Norfolk in attendance on his Grace, with the Duke of Suffolk and Archbishop Cranmer, whom she had glimpsed occasionally at Lambeth. Oh, it was wonderful to be at the centre of such a great pageant!

The King looked like some unearthly, majestic being in his coat of purple velvet and cloth of gold. He was glittering with jewels and people were gaping in awe. He beamed to left and right, raising his hand in greeting, then spurred his horse to greet his future Queen.

'My Lady Anna, welcome to England!' he cried for all to hear and bowed in the saddle. Anna responded most humbly. Katheryn could not make out what they said, but she could see the King smiling and saw him embrace Anna, to resounding roars from the crowds.

A great procession was forming, and the Earl of Rutland was signalling sternly to Anna's household to get into place behind him. They followed the King and his bride back to the pavilion, she riding in the place of honour at his right hand. Everyone was cheering and rejoicing.

In the pavilion, Katheryn stood with the other maids as the King called for spiced wine, helped himself to some sweetmeats and presented his chief ministers to Anna. She waited while pleasantries were exchanged, and then it was time to leave for Greenwich.

When the trumpets blared out again, the procession re-formed with the King and Anna at its head. Katheryn was in the second chariot, the one carrying the English ladies, chamberers and laundresses. Ahead, in the first chariot, sat the German ladies. Katheryn thought that the English ladies should have been accorded precedence; after all, Anna was to be queen of England, but she supposed courtesy demanded that the foreigners were made much of.

On they passed through the deer park and up the hill, beyond which the red-brick palace of Greenwich lay on the banks of the Thames.

Katheryn gazed down at the painted roofs and soaring turrets, overawed at the sight. Truly, it felt as if she had died and gone to Heaven! Her old life at Lambeth seemed long ago now. This was what she had been born for.

The river was crowded with boats full of people come to see the new Queen, and music wafted up from the various craft. As the royal procession arrived at the palace, there was a massive crack of guns from the roof of the great tower at the centre of the range of buildings fronting the water, which boasted a fine series of bay windows. The chariots followed the royal couple through the gatehouse at the bottom of the tower and arrived in an inner courtyard, where the King dismounted, assisted Anna out of her litter, and lovingly embraced and kissed her. Everyone clapped and cheered.

The ladies and maids followed as he led Anna to her apartments. As Katheryn passed through the soaring hall, she could smell fresh paint and hear banging. Heavens, they must still be making the palace ready for its new mistress!

By the time the ladies and maids arrived at the Queen's lodgings, the King had gone. They found Anna in earnest conversation with Mother Lowe, but both fell silent at the appearance of the English attendants. Mother Lowe came over and barked out orders in broken English. 'Unpack!' 'Air the bed!' 'Lay her Grace's table!' It was obvious who was going to be in charge. Mrs Stonor would have her work cut out establishing her authority against such a formidable adversary.

Three days later, Katheryn and the other maids helped the ladies to dress Anna for her wedding, with Mother Lowe hovering protectively, pointing out a pearl out of place or a twisted sleeve. Katheryn had got Mother Lowe's measure by now. She wasn't the dragon she had at first appeared to be, just a proud old woman who cared deeply for her mistress and wanted nothing but the best for her.

Anna looked lovely in her wedding gown. Katheryn had marvelled at the sumptuous cloth of gold with its pattern of large flowers stitched with great Orient pearls. It had long, hanging sleeves and a round skirt in the Dutch fashion. She helped to comb her mistress's fair hair. As

151

became a bride, Anna was wearing it loose beneath a coronal of gold set with brilliant gems.

'Pass me that basket,' Mother Lowe commanded, and Mary Norris handed it to her. Katheryn smelt the fresh tang of dried rosemary as Mother Lowe pinned sprigs of it to Anna's bridal gown, saying something to her in German. Then the great ladies of the household came forward with gold chains and a jewelled crucifix, which Mother Lowe insisted on hanging around Anna's neck herself, and a belt adorned with gold and stones, to be fastened at her waist. When she was ready, she shimmered, so glittering was the effect. It was the only time that Katheryn thought she looked beautiful.

Only Anna's ladies-in-waiting were to attend her to the ceremony in the Chapel Royal. Katheryn would have given much to be there but had to stay behind with the other maids and make all tidy. Yet they were allowed to be present in the King's presence chamber, where, following the nuptials, his Grace and his new Queen dined together before the court, with the chief lords and officers of state in attendance. Standing to the right of the Queen with the other maids, all of them wearing their crimson dresses again, Katheryn watched the royal couple. Dinner was served with great formality and eaten mostly in silence. Although the King showed every courtesy to Anna, and spoke to her from time to time, he did not seem as jovial today as he had shown himself at Blackheath. Probably it was because of the solemnity of the occasion. Anna looked terrified – as well she might, given what lay ahead.

After dinner, she retired to her chamber, and the maids whiled away the afternoon making music and telling jokes until Mother Lowe told them to quieten down because the Queen needed her rest.

In the evening, they dressed Anna for her wedding feast. Katheryn could barely suppress her excitement, for this was the kind of court festivity of which she had dreamed, but her mistress did not appear to feel the same way, try as she might to keep smiling.

The food was delicious, the wine potent, the conversation buzzing, and Katheryn was soon in a state of high elation. When, afterwards, the King led a privileged company of courtiers into his presence chamber for a banquet of sweet treats, she was overjoyed when Anna beckoned her maids to follow and attend her. After everyone had partaken of the delicacies and comfits, a masque was performed, called *The Masque of Hymen*. Katheryn had heard of the masques at court and had longed to see one; never had she witnessed anything so wonderful, with the performers in their fantastical costumes, the clever, colourful scenery and the enchanting music. She laughed along with the rest at the bawdy innuendos until she thought the seams of her bodice would split. She was thrilled when, at the end, the players pulled members of the audience on to the floor, asking them to dance.

'Little cousin!' It was Tom Culpeper, dressed as a satyr and looking very much the part. He beamed down at Katheryn. 'May I have the pleasure?' He held out his hand and she willingly took it, not daring to look in the direction of Mother Lowe or Mrs Stonor. They took their places in line for an *allemande* and the music struck up again. How good it felt to be dancing in front of the King and the whole court! Katheryn could not resist the temptation to show off a little and get herself noticed.

'His Grace doesn't seem to be enjoying himself,' she murmured as they moved out of earshot of the dais.

'He has a bad leg,' Tom muttered. 'It gives him hell. He can't dance these days, although he was a great dancer when he was younger and excelled at every sport.'

'It must be terrible to know that such pleasures are behind you,' she said.

'How are you enjoying life at court?' he asked.

'I love it!'

Suddenly, the music stopped and they all stood back to watch the King lead his bride from the dais.

'We will dance a pavane – the King's Pavane!' he cried, and the musicians resumed their playing, slower this time, with a compelling drumbeat. The other dancers fell into step behind the royal couple in a slow and stately measure. When it ended, Katheryn curtseyed as Tom bowed.

'Shall we dance the next one?' he asked.

'Of course,' she said.

She was on the floor for the rest of the evening. Not wishing to confine herself to one partner, she spun around with several gentlemen, all of whom told her how beautiful she was and how divinely she danced. It was a heady experience.

Suddenly, the music stopped for good. The King had risen. It was time to put the bride to bed. Mother Lowe was summoning the Queen's ladies to attend her, but when Katheryn and Anne Bassett hastened over, she told them they were not needed.

'It is not fitting that unmarried maidens witness the bedding,' she told them. 'You may retire.'

'Come along now!' bade Mrs Stonor, still trying to assert her authority.

Katheryn watched wistfully as the King and Queen departed, then trailed along with the other maids, not wanting the night to end.

The Queen looked quite becoming in her new English gown and French hood. She had been nervous about wearing both, thinking them too immodest, but she had looked pleased when the King nodded in approval and complimented her. Katheryn and the other maids took their seats behind them in the royal stand at the side of the tiltyard. The jousts that were to take place today were part of the marriage celebrations.

Katheryn roared with the rest when the knights began charging. It was exhilarating to witness the heart-stopping clashes of challengers and defenders. This was what she had hoped the court would be like. Life was good! She had a kind mistress who was amiable, even lovable. She was making friends at court and attracting admirers; already, she had seen several young gallants with their eyes on her, eyes that hinted of assignations and secret dalliance, and she had taken pleasure in disdaining them all. She was not yet ready to involve herself with another man: she was enjoying herself too much. To Francis, she gave barely a thought. She had not been in touch with him or visited Lambeth; she did not even know where he was. It was strange to think that, this time last year, she had been so deeply in love with him. How strange that passion like that could burn itself out. Well, they had been doomed from the start, she reflected.

In the interval, refreshments were served, and the maids and the young gentlemen of the King's household fell to talking about the tournament and speculating as to who would win. Katheryn soon became aware of a cluster of girls giggling away to her left.

'What's funny?' she asked, swivelling around.

'You haven't heard the gossip?' Lucy Somerset asked.

'What gossip?'

Lucy bent close to her ear. 'People are saying that the King can't . . . you know . . . with the Queen!' she sniggered. 'The word is that he is able to do the act with others, but not with her.'

The other girls rocked with suppressed laughter.

'Is it true?' Katheryn asked, staring at the Queen. Everyone knew that the King had been visiting Anna's bed regularly, and Anna had given no clue that anything was amiss. Not that she would say anything to her maids, of course, but she had seemed happy enough.

'A lot of people believe it,' Dora Bray said, ever fascinated by the subject of sex.

'I wouldn't go about repeating it,' Anne Bassett warned. 'It's treason to impugn the succession.' Several mouths clamped shut. Katheryn decided to give the gossip no credence. It was unkind to make fun of others' misfortunes. Some people just liked to create a drama.

Had she thought that life in the Queen's service would be one round of endless pleasures? How mistaken she had been. For, once the wedding celebrations were over, life quickly settled down into a boring routine. The Queen could not dance, make music or sing. She would not ride a horse unless she had to. Rather than call for entertainments, she preferred to remain quietly in her apartments.

Her ladies found themselves sitting for hours on end, sewing or playing at cards or dice. Katheryn often sat on the floor, playing with the ladies' lapdogs. Occasionally, Anna asked Will Somers, the King's fool, to perform for them, which was a welcome diversion, as was the acrobat who turned triple somersaults. Sometimes, the King would visit, which sent them all a-flutter, sinking into curtseys. He would greet his wife courteously – he had perfect manners – and stay awhile talking to her and her ladies. Anna's English was improving daily, as she was working hard at it, but still she was gauche in his company, while the maids were awestruck, some barely able to respond to his Grace's pleasantries. Katheryn was not one of them. On the one occasion he addressed her, asking if she would pour him some wine, she presented it with a curtsey, saying, 'I hope you enjoy it, Sir.' His eyes lingered on her, and he nodded.

'Thank you, Mistress Katheryn.'

Otherwise, the days were tedious. The gossip in the maidens' dorter was all about the royal marriage. Katheryn was aware of the ladies staring at the Queen or whispering in each other's ears. She wished they would stop, for it was clearly making Anna uncomfortable.

She longed for diversions. The court was out there, but she was cut off from it. She thought she would go mad with frustration. She could not wait for February, for then the Queen would be crowned and there would be more celebrations. And soon afterwards, there would be Easter, when – she had heard – the court made a great festival. Things could only get better.

Katheryn, like all the other maids and ladies, had expected to be involved in preparations for the coronation, but nothing happened. Speculation mounted until Mrs Stonor, deftly stealing a march on Mother Lowe, who was left literally open-mouthed, announced that the ceremony had been deferred until Whitsun. Oh, well, Katheryn told herself; it will still be something to look forward to.

But before then, the Queen was to be formally welcomed in London, as was traditional. In February, her women dressed in their crimson gowns once more and made their way to the barges that were moored on the waterfront at Greenwich. All Anna's possessions had been packed and sent on to Whitehall Palace, where the court would remove today. Katheryn watched the King step unsteadily into his state barge, then came the Queen, who was assisted into hers and made her way along the gangway to the cabin at the back, followed by her chief ladies. It was now the turn of Katheryn and the other maids, who clambered into the barge behind. It rocked alarmingly and the oarsman laughed as the girls squealed and pushed forward into the relative safety of the cabin. It was a tight fit, but Katheryn had a seat by the window.

They were rowed out to the middle of the river, then followed the royal barges upstream towards London. Katheryn's eyes widened at the sight of the crowds on the banks of the Thames; everyone was waving and cheering. She and the other maids waved back. She realised that barges containing the Lord Mayor and the London guilds were following them, all adorned with shields and cloth of gold. Behind those, she could just see a fleet of numerous smaller barges. Every ship they passed let off a deafening salute and, as they neared the Tower of London, there was an ear-splitting salvo from the cannon on the wharf, which seemed to go on for ever.

Past London Bridge, the bells of the City of London were pealing out a welcome and the citizens were massed on the shore, cheering their heads off and clapping. Soon, the barges were nearing Westminster, and Katheryn craned her neck to catch a glimpse of Lambeth, which lay further ahead on the Surrey shore. To her right, she saw the King greeting his Queen at Westminster stairs, to rousing applause from the crowds, and leading her through the great gatehouse to Whitehall Palace.

Chapter 15

1540

That March was unseasonably warm and, in her free time, Katheryn liked to walk in the beautiful gardens at Whitehall. She was praying that, with the coming of spring, life would liven up, for it had been as dull at Whitehall as it had been at Greenwich. At least there was the coronation to look forward to. Or was there? The maids were still covertly speculating among themselves that the Queen remained a virgin; some wondered if the King might divorce her. There was more gossip that he was impotent, which Anne Bassett roundly dismissed. Katheryn had now learned that his Grace had courted Anne herself before he had decided to marry Anna, which was much to Anne's disappointment, and she wondered if Anne was hoping to revive his interest – and exactly what had taken place between them.

Taking advantage of the good weather, she would join the spectators at the bowling alley or go to the tennis play and watch a match. Always, she obeyed Mother Lowe's instructions to be in the company of one of her fellow maids. Usually, Isabel would accompany her, but on one particularly sunny afternoon, when Isabel was busy, Margaret came with her and they paused to watch a bowling contest. Tom was taking part, matched to a baby-faced gentleman in his early twenties. Both were casting not only the ball, but interested glances at Katheryn.

After the game, which Tom won, they wandered over to where she and Margaret were standing.

'Katheryn, may I introduce Thomas Paston?' Tom said. 'He serves with me in the Privy Chamber.'

Thomas flushed and smiled at her. 'It is an honour, Mistress Katheryn. I have been hoping to meet you.'

'This is my sister Margaret,' Katheryn said. Thomas had no personal appeal for her and she did not want to encourage him.

'Will you walk with us?' Tom invited, offering her his arm. As the four of them strolled down towards the river, he held on to her tightly, his elbow on her breast. Was that deliberate? It would surprise her if he was interested in her in that way; he probably still thought of her as his little cousin. Of course, she had already come to think of him as a man, and a very attractive one.

They stood watching the boats going past. Thomas Paston looked a little awkward, having no doubt realised that Katheryn was not going to encourage his advances and that Margaret was married. Presently, he began chatting to another young man standing nearby and Margaret joined in.

'You are still happy in the Queen's household?' Tom asked Katheryn.

'Yes.' There was something in his tone that unnerved her. 'Should I not be?'

Tom hesitated. 'She is a kindly mistress, I'm sure.'

'There is something you are not telling me.'

He lowered his voice. 'I hear things. I am in a privileged position and sworn to discretion. Just keep your ears open.'

'Oh, Tom!' Katheryn was losing patience. 'You can't say things like that and leave me to wonder what you mean.'

He took her hand. 'I am not playing with you; I'm just concerned for your future.'

She met his gaze. He looked sincere enough. And he really was quite beautiful with that dark curly hair, those chiselled cheekbones and merry blue eyes.

'Katheryn,' he said, and there was a catch in his voice, 'I think a lot of you, you know. And I would like to see you more often, if you are willing.'

It threw her. It was all so unexpected. She liked him – indeed, she had always loved him – but did she want a young man in her life just now?

She withdrew her hand. If she had learned anything from her new friends, it was that the woman was supposed to lay down the rules in courtships. 'I'd like to see you,' she said, 'but let us just be friends for now.'

Tom looked crestfallen. 'If that's what you want,' he said.

She nodded. 'And now I must go, or I'll be in trouble with the Mother of the Maids.' It was unlikely, but it would serve as an excuse to get away and think.

She left him there and hastened to catch up with Margaret, who had parted company with Thomas Paston and tactfully left her and Tom on their own. She could see her yards ahead on the path that led to the Queen's lodgings.

'Those two young sirs would like to get to know you better,' said an arch voice behind her. She turned and saw Lady Rochford smiling at her. There was something cat-like and mysterious about her, yet she had always showed herself friendly to Katheryn.

'What do you mean?' Katheryn asked, astounded.

'I've long been a friend of Mr Culpeper,' Lady Rochford informed her, 'and, from what he has told me, I think Mr Paston bears you favour, even though he has never had the courage to speak to you.'

'He spoke to me today,' Katheryn told her, as they strolled back towards the palace, 'but I put him off.'

'That's as well, as I think you are worthy of better than he,' Lady Rochford opined. 'But Mr Culpeper – well, there's a different kettle of fish.'

'He's my cousin; well, my very distant cousin,' Katheryn said. 'I've known him for most of my life. But today, he gave me every reason to believe that I am more than a cousin to him.' She was surprised that she was saying these things to Lady Rochford, but that lady was looking at her so sympathetically – and seemed genuinely to care about her.

'You are!' Lady Rochford replied. 'He told me that he would be much more to you than a cousin. My dear, it is plain to me that he loves you.'

'He has always loved me, but not like that.'

'He is a fine, upstanding young man with a wonderful future ahead of him, and so handsome – and you, Katheryn, are a very lovely young woman. I speak as your cousin and kinswoman, for my late husband was Queen Anne's brother. I know you have no father and mother, and I feel sorry for your lack. If I can help to fill it, I should be honoured. At the very least, you should account me your friend.'

Katheryn was touched, but a dissonant voice in her head was asking why Lady Rochford was showing herself so concerned for her welfare now, when they had been serving together in the Queen's household for four months. Had this interest been prompted by Tom's confidences? If she had long been his friend, maybe she was doing it for him.

'I am grateful for your kindness,' she replied. 'It is good of you to take an interest in me. I was sorry to hear about the loss of your husband.'

Lady Rochford's mouth tightened. 'He was a wicked man in more ways than one. He got what he deserved. As did she.' There was venom in her tone. 'But let us talk of happier things. Like Mr Culpeper! He's a proud man, and justly so, for he has done well for himself. The King regards him almost as a son. The lady who catches him as a husband will be lucky indeed.'

There was a note of envy in her voice that made Katheryn wonder if Lady Rochford fancied Tom herself. But she was too old for him; she must be about forty, and he was a good decade younger.

'Think about it, Katheryn,' Lady Rochford said. 'Do not put him off or dismiss him out of hand. I believe he loves you truly.'

'Has he asked you to plead his suit?' Katheryn asked.

'Not at all. But it would make me so happy to see the two of you come together.'

It didn't quite ring true, but Katheryn could not, for the life of her, think what ulterior motive Lady Rochford could have.

They had reached the palace now.

'I will think about it,' she said as they went upstairs.

After that, Tom seemed to be everywhere Katheryn went – in the gardens, at the tennis play, at the butts. Always, he was hovering. It was flattering to be the object of the attention of such a dashing gallant, and Katheryn was strongly attracted to him. Given that she had always adored him in a cousinly way, it was an easy transition to feelings of quite another kind. She found herself looking forward to their 'chance' meetings and snatched conversations, although it was never possible to speak out loud what their eyes were saying, because they were never alone. Even when she asked Lady Rochford to accompany her on her walks, knowing that lady would afford her every opportunity to spend time with Tom, she could not linger long with him lest someone report her to Mother Lowe or Mrs Stonor.

Tom took to giving Lady Rochford messages for her.

'He says he wants you to be his chosen lady.'

'He is longing to see you again.'

'He wants to see you alone.'

'I would that we could,' Katheryn replied to that last one, 'but what if we were caught? I don't want to lose my place.'

'You can meet in my chamber,' Lady Rochford said. 'I myself will keep watch.'

Katheryn wanted to hear from Tom himself before she committed to seeing him in a bedchamber. Were his intentions honourable? She needed to know. The idea of marrying him was increasingly appealing and she did not want him to think her a wanton. Men of status did not marry wantons. He must never find out about what she had got up to at Lambeth and Chesworth. She had put all that firmly behind her now. She was meant for better things.

One evening, after the Queen had gone to bed, Katheryn sat up late in Isabel's chamber, sipping from a goblet of hot aleberry and talking with her half-sister.

'Tom Culpeper is showing an interest in me,' she confided. She thought Isabel would be pleased for her and glad that she had such a fine suitor in their debonair cousin, but Isabel was frowning.

'Which Tom Culpeper? The one who serves the King or the one who serves Lord Cromwell?'

'The one who serves the King,' Katheryn said. 'I did not know his elder brother was at court.'

'Oh, dear. There are things that Edward has told me . . .' Isabel looked distressed. 'He won't let me have anything to do with Tom.

Our cousin has grown proud out of measure; he has no fear of God, and his sole purpose in life is the pursuit of his own pleasure.'

'That's not the Tom I know,' Katheryn said, 'and you know him too, and what he's really like.'

'Katheryn, there is another side to him that we've never seen – a vicious side.' Isabel was twisting her wedding ring, looking distressed.

'Vicious?' Katheryn echoed.

'I fear so. Within the privy chamber, it's a well-kept secret that, last year, he violated the wife of a park-keeper in a wood.'

'No!' Katheryn was horrified. 'That's a wicked slander.'

'I fear it is true,' Isabel said. 'Horrid to relate, three or four of his friends held her down. Some villagers came upon them and tried to apprehend him, meaning to take him before the justices, but he resisted them and killed one of them. And, for this act of wickedness, he was pardoned by the King.'

Katheryn was speechless. The Tom she knew would never have done such a dreadful thing. She would not believe it!

'There is more. People in the family know about this, and I was told that Tom's father has cut him out of his will. So, although I imagine he is comfortably off, he has no inheritance to offer a wife, save what his Majesty gives him.'

'But why would the King pardon him? Rape is such a terrible crime.'

'I know. Edward says his Majesty regards it as most heinous, along with murder, but he greatly favours Culpeper. Even so . . .'

Katheryn nodded miserably. She still could not bring herself to believe this of Tom, dear Tom, who had long been her hero.

She could not sleep. She had to find out the truth, even if it cost her Tom's love. If he was a rapist and a murderer, she wouldn't want anything more to do with him anyway.

The very next day, she slipped away as soon as her duties were done and went looking for him. She had no idea when he would be free, but she was prepared to wait.

She thought he might come to her in the gardens, as he usually did, so she sat down on a stone bench that gave a clear view of the back entrance of the palace. She had been waiting there forlornly for about half an hour when she saw him emerge. He spied her at once and came hurrying over.

'Katheryn!' he said. 'Are you all right?'

'I can't stay long,' she told him. 'Mother Lowe and Mrs Stonor will kill me if they hear that I was out on my own. But I have to ask you something which is painful to me.'

'What is it?' Suddenly, there was a wary look in his eyes.

'I have heard talk that the King pardoned you for . . . for . . .' She could not bring herself to say the words.

'For what?' His voice was sharp, making her think the worst.

'For r-rape and murder.' It came out as a whisper.

'Who said that?'

'Never mind. Is it true?'

For a fraction of a second, he hesitated. 'It's true that I was pardoned, but all I was guilty of was a bit of dalliance with a girl and some tomfoolery with my friends. There was a little rough-and-tumble, but I wasn't raping her. She was willing, but when she saw her father and the other villagers approaching, she started screaming. They went for us and, yes, I killed one of them, but it was in self-defence, I swear.' He took Katheryn's hand in both of his and squeezed it, but she pulled it away.

'Katheryn, you have to believe me,' he begged, looking anguished. 'I did not intend to harm her. If I had been guilty, the King would never have pardoned me, for he takes a stern view of such crimes. He accepted my explanation. I hope you can too.'

She wanted to, she so wanted to. He was looking at her pleadingly. But his own father clearly hadn't believed him. And the King wouldn't have pardoned Tom if he had committed no offence. She sat there, wringing her hands.

'Katheryn, I swear I am no rapist or murderer!' Tom was beside himself. She had never seen him like this. 'Will that satisfy you?'

Her love for him got the better of her. She nodded, tears in her eyes.

'Oh, darling,' he said, and drew her into his arms. 'I could not bear to have you believe that of me. You are everything to me. I think you know that.'

She looked up at him, searching his face for some sign that he was lying. There was none. His eyes were sincere, full of truth. It had been silly of her to think that her Tom, her beloved, kindly Tom, could do such things.

'I knew you could not have been guilty,' she said. 'I was just so shocked to hear it.'

'Show me the man who told you and I *will* be guilty of murder!' he growled. 'I'll run him through!'

'It was a woman, actually, who heard it from someone with friends in the privy chamber,' she said. She had no intention of naming names.

'Tell her not to gossip!' Tom snapped. 'She had no right to be telling you such things.'

'I'll take the greatest of pleasure in telling her that they are untrue,' Katheryn said.

'Hmm!' he fumed. He still had his arms around her. She knew she should not linger, but it was so lovely nestling against him and feeling his body next to hers.

'I must go,' she said reluctantly and stood up.

'Will I see you later?' He rose too.

'No, I am on duty. Tomorrow afternoon?'

'I'll be there.' He raised her hand and kissed it. 'Until then, my darling.'

Their conversation had released something between them. It had made them closer, more able to talk to each other. Katheryn realised that she was living for their next meeting, and the next, and the next . . .

Isabel had not been as receptive of Tom's denial as Katheryn would have liked. She had been sceptical, unbending, and there was now a coolness between them. Katheryn wasn't confiding in her any more. Instead, she turned to the ever-ready Lady Rochford. They were 'Katheryn' and 'Jane' to each other now, friends as well as cousins, despite a twenty-year age gap. Jane was always so interested in Katheryn's doings, so concerned for her welfare, and so willing to encourage her feelings for Tom.

'You must meet in my chamber, my dear!' she said again, one

morning in late March, when they were in the Queen's bedchamber, tidying away her clothes and jewels.

'But I don't want Tom thinking I am easy game,' Katheryn replied. 'I want him to respect me.'

'He does, my dear, he does! It's as clear as day. And I will be just outside the door, keeping watch. Truly, I don't see how else you will ever be alone together and, if my instinct serves me well, there are things that need to be said in private.'

'What things?' Katheryn asked. Could she dare to hope?

Jane smiled. 'Tom has hinted to me that he would like to be made sure to you.'

'You mean he wants to marry me?'

'Oh, yes. What else could it mean? I know his intentions are honourable.'

'In that case . . .' Katheryn needed no more persuading. 'I will meet him in your chamber, so long as you tell him that I do it for no light purpose. When can it be arranged?'

How could she resist? She was longing for excitement. There were far too few of the entertainments and revels she had longed for, since Queen Anna kept mainly to her apartments. It was tedious spending her days under her mistress's stolid gaze, doing interminable embroidery and wishing that the hours would pass more quickly, or waiting on her at table, or when she stirred from her chamber to go into the court or to the chapel. For the Queen must never be left unattended for a single minute, not even in her stool chamber – and that was one duty Katheryn did not relish. Nor was she best pleased when it was her turn to sleep on a pallet bed in Anna's chamber or wait outside her door on the now rare occasions when the King honoured his wife's bed. She was thankful for the good company of her fellow maids, for at least they could speak English and liven the staid atmosphere. But now she had a chance to enjoy herself – and the prospect was exhilarating.

The meeting with Tom was arranged for two nights hence, after the Queen had gone to bed. Thankfully, Mary Norris and Anne Parr were on duty.

When Katheryn returned to the privy chamber, Jane was waiting for her, a lit candle in her hand.

'He is here.' She led Katheryn to her room, opened the door and closed it lightly, leaving them alone.

'Darling!' Tom held out his hands.

They spent most of their precious hours together seated on the bed, holding each other and kissing as if their lives depended on it. Katheryn could not but marvel at how quickly her priorities had changed. Marriage to Tom, even just seeing him like this, now held far more appeal than the dull life she led at court.

'I love you,' Tom said. 'Not like I loved you when you were a little girl, although you were lovely then, but as the beautiful woman you are.' His lips nuzzled her neck. Her French hood had long since fallen to the floor.

'I love *you*,' Katheryn murmured, clutching him tightly. She raised her face and offered him her lips, and his mouth closed on them, his tongue teasing hers.

'Oh, Katheryn,' he said, as their eyes met. 'You have bound me to you, and I love you above all creatures.'

Her heart was pounding; desire was strong in her.

'I would be bound to you for all time,' he murmured. 'Dare I hope that that is your wish too?'

The moment had come. He would be down on his knees before she knew it.

'I only know that I never want this to end,' she breathed.

They were interrupted by a tap on the door. Of all the moments! Tom gave a deep sigh and rose to his feet, running his fingers through his rumpled curls.

When he opened the door, Katheryn heard Jane say, 'There's someone about. You had best leave now.'

Tom kissed Katheryn quickly and turned to go.

'May I come tomorrow?' he asked.

Jane smiled. 'That's up to Katheryn.'

'Oh, yes!' Katheryn said.

The next night, he asked her to marry him. There was no going down on one knee. He just took her hand and looked into her eyes. In his, she could see everything she could have desired.

'Will you be my wife?' he asked.

She surprised herself by hesitating. His proposal had conjured up memories of Francis calling her his wife – and the realisation that Francis meant nothing to her now. Before him, there had been Harry, and her feelings for him had died too. She loved Tom, she loved him deeply, but they had been courting for less than a month. She could not risk hurting him by saying 'yes' now and regretting it later.

'I want nothing more,' she said, 'but I think we should give ourselves time to make sure that our love is strong and enduring.'

'I know it is!' he said fervently.

'Alas, Tom, I have seen people fall in love so deeply that they think it is for ever – and then fall out of it. My heart is telling me to say "yes" now; my head is telling me to be cautious. A little proving time is all I ask. It will be as nothing in the span of our lives together.'

He looked crestfallen.

'Now I have spoiled the moment,' she said, 'and I didn't mean to. You should be glad that the woman you want to marry is prudent and wise!'

'As long as I can marry you, I don't care what you're like,' he said, and then they were cuddling and kissing again. 'I will wait,' Tom murmured. 'I would wait for you for ever.'

'I'll wager Mistress Katheryn is to be married,' Meg Morton said, one sunny afternoon at the beginning of April.

Katheryn looked up from her mending. She, Meg and Kat Tilney were the only people in the dorter. The others were attending the Queen in her privy garden.

'That's news to me!' she said.

'But we've seen you, arm in arm with Mr Culpeper in the gardens. You're always with him, and he wears his love openly. People are talking about you.'

'*Are* you to be married?' Kat asked eagerly.

Katheryn hesitated a fraction too long. 'No,' she said, feeling herself blush.

'That's not what they're saying!' Meg retorted.

'I think I know more about my affairs than the gossips!' Katheryn flared. 'I wish people wouldn't say such things. What if Mother Lowe heard them? Or the Queen?'

'People have been gossiping about the Queen ever since she was married, and she never hears any of it, so you're safe there,' Kat said, folding her sewing.

'Or she pretends she never hears it,' Meg said. 'I would, if I were her. To save face.'

'Well, I'll thank you not to spread gossip about me,' Katheryn snapped. 'I'm not betrothed to Mr Culpeper and that's that!' She got up, shoved her mending in her travelling chest and left them, giggling, behind her.

When she arrived in the garden, Anna looked up and smiled at her.

'Mistress Katheryn, the Duke of Norfolk has sent a messenger requesting that you attend him at Norfolk House this evening. I have given my permission; you have my leave to go.'

Chapter 16

1540

What could it be about? Katheryn wondered, as Isabel, speaking hardly at all, laced her into her best black damask gown and plaited her hair, pinning it into place before she put on the black-and-white French hood. What matter could be important enough for the Duke himself to send for her? She wished she could confide in Isabel, but there was still that coolness between them.

Could it be that he had arranged a marriage for her? she wondered, as the ferry conveyed her and the messenger across the Thames to Lambeth. She shrank from the prospect of her formidable uncle proposing a match, no doubt one advantageous to himself, but not the one she longed for. She was in awe of him, like most of the family, and feared she lacked the courage to stand up for herself.

She was trembling by the time they arrived at the great gate of Norfolk House. The porter told them that his Grace the Duke was awaiting them in my lady of Norfolk's chamber. In great trepidation, Katheryn mounted the stairs.

She was surprised to find her uncle alone with the Dowager Duchess. The room was glowing with candlelight and a hearty fire crackled on the hearth. She rose from her curtsey and waited, head demurely lowered.

'Welcome, Mistress Katheryn,' the Duke said. His wall-like face with its long nose and pale eyebrows was creased in what passed for a smile. 'You will be wondering why I have sent for you.' He leaned forward in his great chair. 'What we are about to discuss must not go beyond these four walls, do you understand?'

'Yes, my lord,' Katheryn said, swallowing.

'Katheryn, God has vouchsafed you an opportunity to return this benighted realm to the true faith. As champions of the old Catholic religion, we Howards cannot but detest the so-called reformers and their new order in England. I am not ashamed to say that I have never read the Scriptures, nor ever will, but I know the faith of my forefathers must be upheld, and I know too that it was merry in England before this new learning came up!' His lips set in a grimace. 'There is one man in particular who has been the architect of this wickedness.'

Katheryn had no idea who he was talking about, and his mention of her having some part in returning England to the true faith had alarmed her. She was no would-be martyr, but a simple girl who loved God and observed the rites of her faith. She was beginning to wonder if her uncle had gone slightly mad.

'I mean Cromwell!' the Duke spat, his voice choking with venom. 'Him and those arrogant reformers on the Council.'

Lord Cromwell. She had seen him about the court several times, had heard others talking about him, and knew he was very powerful. But she had not been interested.

'*He* arranged the Cleves marriage,' the Duke was saying. 'He pushed the King into it, and now his Majesty wants to get out. And I, the Bishop of Winchester and our friends of the old faith mean to ensure that he does.'

'The King does not love the Queen?' Katheryn asked.

'No, and never has! He did not even want to go through with the wedding, but our friend Cromwell told him there was no way to break the contract. The marriage remains unconsummated.'

So the rumours had been true. Katheryn felt sorry for poor Queen Anna, who was so pleasant and kind. Had she any idea of the danger she was in?

'We no longer need the alliance with Cleves,' the Duke continued. 'The Emperor and the French King are both suing for England's friendship. Our job is to persuade his Majesty that some pretext must be found to divorce him from the Queen – and what better persuasion than to place in his path a young lady of great beauty whom he will find irresistible, especially since he is getting old and must needs speedily marry again and sire more sons to secure the succession. That is where you come in, Katheryn.'

Her first reaction was revulsion. Marry the King! No, it could not be! He was old and fat and he smelt – and he had had four unhappy wives. If she wanted to marry anyone, it was Tom. And how could she betray her sweet, unsuspecting mistress by plotting to supplant her?

'We believe it essential to replace Anna of Cleves with a Catholic queen and bring down Cromwell,' Norfolk stated determinedly. 'I have already seen one of my nieces become queen, and I see no reason why another should not rise so high. Katheryn, you are much prettier than the Boleyn whore and you have charm. The King will be enchanted.'

'We are confident that you have a brilliant future ahead, child,' the Dowager Duchess chimed in, smiling. 'I will be happy to recommend you to his Majesty. Think what it will mean to be queen of this land!'

Katheryn stood there, wringing her hands in turmoil. Her grandam's words had brought home to her the advantages of her uncle's plan. The prospect of becoming queen *was* a dazzling one, even if it did mean marrying an old and ailing man. But . . .

They were waiting for her to be obedient to their wishes, to show herself grateful. She realised that, against such a powerful coalition, any protest of hers would quickly be silenced. She had no choice but to comply. But what of Tom? What of the Queen? They would be the first casualties of her compliance. She was racked with dismay and, already, a strong sense of guilt and loss. How could she give Tom up?

'Have you nothing to say for yourself?' the Duke barked, his eyes steely. 'Most girls would be ecstatic at the prospect of being queen.'

'You should be sensible of the great honour of being chosen by his Grace here for so high a destiny,' the Duchess reproved.

'Oh, I am, I am, I am very grateful,' Katheryn said hurriedly. 'I was too overcome by the honour to say anything.'

They both looked slightly mollified.

'But,' she went on, 'the King has never paid me much attention, so I am not sure that he will be interested in me.'

'By the time we have finished with you, he *will* be interested!' the

Duchess assured her. 'We will take care to see that he cannot but notice you.'

'Thank you,' Katheryn said lamely. 'But I would not see the Queen hurt on my account.'

'The King will take steps to divorce her sooner or later, whatever we do,' the Duke said. 'She'll probably do very well out of it and be happier than she is now.'

'I do hope so.'

'Stop fretting, Katheryn.' The Duchess's tone was firm.

'Now,' her uncle said, 'you will be advised by us on how to behave and how to entertain the King, and how often. After attracting his attention, you will not appear too eager. That should increase his ardour all the more.'

'Encourage him, then draw back,' the Duchess exhorted. 'Don't give too much too soon.'

The Duke regarded Katheryn sternly. 'I am aware that you have some experience in these matters.'

Her face flamed. *What* had the Duchess told him?

'I was most disappointed in you, but whatever has gone before, you will maintain the appearance of being pure and honest, although you will make it clear to the King that you will welcome his embraces *after* he has put a wedding ring on your finger. He prizes virtue in women most highly.'

Who was her uncle to talk? she thought indignantly. What an old hypocrite he was, with his Duchess shut away in the country so that he could disport himself with Bess Holland! What did he know about virtue?

'You must never, ever confess to his Majesty anything about your previous affairs, especially that nonsense about a precontract with Mr Dereham,' the Duchess enjoined. 'There is no need for him to know about these things.'

That was a relief. Anyway, it was all behind her and of no importance now.

There was no point at all in mentioning her love for Tom Culpeper; it would count as nothing against this plan to marry her to the King.

But she felt sick at the thought of ending their affair, for end it she must.

'We must best make a start now,' the Duchess said. 'I will summon the tailor.'

Katheryn was astonished to find that he was already there, waiting in the gallery. He had obviously been well primed, because he came laden with bolts of glorious fabrics. Her grandam chose one of green, which reminded Katheryn of the dress she had loved as a child, and three more of scarlet, yellow and tawny.

'These will suit your colouring,' she said, then turned to the tailor. 'Come with us. You can take Mistress Katheryn's measurements.' She led them into a small closet and closed the door. 'Pray make the gowns in the French style, with hoods to match,' she said, as the tailor took out his tape measure. 'Katheryn, I will lend you some jewels so that you sparkle at court. I will look them out for you later.'

Katheryn stared at the sumptuous materials. They must cost a fortune; even for court, she had never owned such clothing. Her uncle was determined she should succeed, that was clear. And these riches were just a foretaste of what would be hers if she played her part to advantage.

'Have you heard anything of Mr Dereham?' the Duchess asked as Katheryn stood with her arms stretched out.

'No,' she replied, feeling guilty that she had not written to him.

'Well, he has disappeared. Have you any idea where he might be?'

'I know not where he is. I have not heard from him.'

'I suppose that is for the best,' the Duchess replied, then changed the subject.

They returned to the hall to find Norfolk waiting impatiently.

'I will send for you soon,' he told Katheryn. 'You are a Howard. You will not fail us.'

In bed that night, back in the maidens' dorter, Katheryn lay fretting and weeping. She could not fool herself: she did desire worldly glory, very much, but at what cost? There was no guarantee that the King would even notice her, let alone marry her, and she had been sworn to secrecy. What could she say to Tom? If he knew the truth, he would surely understand, but how could she just tell him she did not love him after all? That would hurt him deeply. She did not know how she could do it to him.

And what if the King did want her? The thought of going to bed with him appalled her. He was so old. Beneath the aura of majesty and the gorgeous clothes, he was an ailing man with diseased legs. She had seen for herself that there were days when he could hardly walk, let alone ride. Could she bring herself to endure what her uncle had referred to as his embraces without betraying that she was repelled by him? Maybe the gossip was true and there would be no embraces. That was a comforting thought. And yet, she had heard that he had been a great lover of women in his time. She had never seen him behave in anything other than a kindly and courteous way to Queen Anna and other ladies, and he did have a certain charm.

But he had had her cousin Anne beheaded! And his marriages had all ended in disaster, including, it seemed, this present one. Yet maybe it was not all his fault. Queen Katherine had been stubborn and Queen Jane, whom he had clearly loved, had died. And Anne had probably deserved her fate.

The one thing Katheryn was certain of was that she wanted to be queen. The prospect thrilled her, colouring everything else. To be the first lady in the land, to have everyone showing you deference, to wear the most gorgeous clothes and live in palaces of the greatest splendour, and have servants dancing attention on you and your every whim being law – who could resist it? But every time she saw it becoming reality, she thought of Tom and her heart sank.

Round and round her thoughts went until she fell asleep, exhausted.

She did not say anything to Tom. She could not bring herself to. When they met in the gardens, she showed herself as happy to see him as before – which she was – but she took care to ensure that they were never alone, for then he would try to kiss her, and she would hate herself even more. She loved him, truly she did, but, being strictly honest with herself, the vista that had just been opened up before her had made her realise, as she had realised with Francis, that life held even more exciting prospects.

Another summons from the Duke arrived in the second week of April. Katheryn was to beg leave of the Queen and come to Norfolk House at five o'clock in the afternoon, two days hence, just before the court left for Hampton Court.

The moment had come, and now she must show her mettle. In her heart, she knew that the decision had been made.

She asked Anna if she might have permission to visit her grandam and Anna readily gave it. Katheryn washed her hair and combed it until it glimmered like burnished gold. At the appointed time, she boarded the ferry with her heart pounding, not daring to think of Tom. She was doing this for her family, for its honour, for the true faith – and for herself, admittedly. She must not fail.

It was to be tonight! Destiny beckoned . . .

The Duke had been waiting for her when she arrived. 'Katheryn, his Grace the Bishop of Winchester is entertaining his Majesty tonight at Winchester House,' he told her. 'We are to be honoured guests. The Bishop is your friend and would see you well married.' She knew what that meant. 'All is in readiness for you. Make haste to prepare yourself!'

When she walked down the stairs, dressed in the green gown with its shimmering silk skirts and low-cut bodice, her uncle beamed at the Duchess. 'You have done well, Stepmother. She looks like a queen already. By God, girl, you carry yourself well. His Majesty cannot fail to notice you.'

Holding herself like an empress, Katheryn sat beside the Duke in his barge as it was rowed downstream to Bankside. He was full of advice.

'Niece, the King admires virtue in women. Do not fear that you will put him off by denying him what he wants. Hold out for the greatest prize – and remember what is at stake.'

'Yes, my lord,' she answered, aware that after tonight, her whole life could change.

She wished she had already ended it with Tom. It wasn't fair to lead him on when there might be no future for them.

'We're here,' the Duke grunted as the barge pulled towards a jetty. Beyond, stood a great palace of stone, the London house of the bishops of Winchester, set in beautiful gardens. They were shown to a lofty hall with a rose window of stained glass, where Uncle Norfolk's arrival was announced. A hawk-faced man in clerical robes came forward, bowing.

'My lord Duke! Welcome, welcome!'

Norfolk smiled. 'My lord Bishop, may I present my niece, Mistress Katheryn Howard?'

Katheryn sank into a curtsey, head bowed. The Bishop lifted her chin and gave her an appraising look. 'Welcome, Mistress Katheryn. She is perfect, my lord, perfect for our purpose.'

He personally showed them to their seats. The Duke was to sit in the place of highest honour at the King's right hand, and the Bishop himself would sit on his Majesty's left hand. Katheryn was seated below the salt at the end of the top table, three places away from her uncle, but still in a prominent position. The guests were standing in groups, chattering away, but Katheryn was listening for sounds that heralded the King's arrival. She stood with the Duke, nervous now that the moment was nearly upon her. Pray God the King noticed her!

There was a commotion outside, a fanfare of trumpets and then shouts. 'Make way for the King's Highness. Make way!'

And there he was, glittering in cloth of silver sparkling with rubies, stumping into the hall, where everyone was making their obeisances. Bishop Gardiner knelt before his sovereign, bidding him most heartily welcome, then attended him to the great chair that had been set ready under the canopy of estate bearing the royal arms of England. It was now time for Katheryn and everyone else to take their places. They stood for the Latin grace, then sat down, and the murmur of conversation swelled as the first course was carried in with great ceremony.

Katheryn watched the King, keeping a half-smile of admiration on her face in case he should look her way. He ate most fastidiously, dabbing his lips with his napkin and dipping his fingers in his bowl of rose water every so often, all the time talking to his neighbours at table.

But his narrow blue eyes were roving around the room, and it was not long before they came to rest on Katheryn. And when they did so, they lit up.

'Tell me, my lord of Norfolk, who is that young lady seated at the end of the table?' she heard him ask. 'She serves the Queen, I believe.'

'That is my niece, Katheryn Howard, your Grace,' the Duke replied.

'Another of your nieces,' the King said drily.

'This one, I assure your Grace, is nothing like the other,' Norfolk hastened to assure him.

'Hmm. Her countenance is very delightful. I've noticed her before.' He beamed across at Katheryn. 'It is a pleasure to see you again, Mistress Katheryn.'

'Your Majesty does me great honour,' she said.

'You are enjoying the feast?'

'How could I not, Sir, when your Grace is here?' She gave him the benefit of what she hoped was a radiant smile. Norfolk and Gardiner were watching her approvingly.

'I see you are gracious of speech, as well as having excellent beauty,' the King complimented her.

'She is virtuous too, Sire,' Norfolk added. Katheryn shivered a little, wishing he had kept his mouth shut.

'It is a rare combination,' the King observed. 'You are most fortunate, Mistress Katheryn, that Dame Nature has endowed you with such gifts. Tell me, how old are you?'

'I am nineteen, Sir,' she said.

'Oh, to be nineteen!' the King sighed. 'Youth is so fleeting. Would that I were young enough to play the eager swain with such a beauty.'

'Oh, but your Majesty is not old! You are in the prime of life, Sir.'

He beamed at her again. 'I see that kindness too is among your virtues.' Uncle Norfolk was purring, she would swear.

The King summoned a servitor and lifted his plate. 'Take these choice morsels to Mistress Katheryn. A token of our esteem, Mistress.'

'Oh, how kind of your Grace. Thank you!' Katheryn cried, as if he had given her the moon. He sat back in his chair, basking in her delight.

'And are you contracted to be married?' he asked.

'Oh, no, Sir.'

'She is pure and chaste and free from any matrimonial yoke, your Grace,' Norfolk said. Katheryn's smile froze on her face.

'Hmm,' the King murmured. 'You would be a prize for any man, Mistress Katheryn.'

For the rest of the meal, they exchanged pleasantries and he amused her with his jests, his gaze lingering lustfully on her. It was wonderful being the centre of attention, with every eye in the room on her and people speculating on why the King was showing so much interest in her. Tongues would be wagging tomorrow, for certain! And it had all been so easy. She seemed instinctively to have known what to say and how to flatter his Grace. He was really just a lonely old man in need of a bit of kindness and affection. Would it be so hard to give it to him?

After dinner, he bade her sit by him.

'I have seen you in the Queen's chamber,' he said. 'Are you happy there?'

'Yes, Sir,' she said. 'Her Grace is a good mistress.'

'Yes, she is an admirable lady.' It sounded begrudging.

He asked her if she played music, and she told him she was proficient on the lute and the virginals, which pleased him very much. He was impressed too when she said she could sing and loved to dance, and that she wished she had a horse so that she could go riding or even hunting. 'Alas, I am poor, your Grace. My lord father died in debt.'

'I know,' he said. 'I am sorry for you. Let's see what we can do about finding you a horse.'

He left soon after that, but not before lifting her hand to his lips and kissing it in the most courtly manner. 'I will see you again, Katheryn,' he promised.

'I should love that, Sir,' she told him and curtseyed low.

When he had gone, she hung back with Uncle Norfolk, waiting for the other guests to leave. As the last one filed out and the hall doors closed behind him, Bishop Gardiner was jubilant. 'My lord Duke, things are looking promising! My child, the King is clearly much taken with you. You have done well.'

'You have done exceedingly well,' Norfolk echoed. 'You have made a good beginning.'

'We must capitalise on it,' the Bishop said. 'I will invite his Majesty to a private supper next week and let him know that Mistress Katheryn will be here. If things develop as we hope, I will tell him that he may use my house at any time if he needs some privacy.'

'A capital idea!' the Duke pronounced. Offering Katheryn his arm, he escorted her to the waiting barge along a jetty illuminated by torches. As it glided across the water, Katheryn's head was teeming with memories of the evening, finding it hard to believe that the King himself had paid court to her. When they reached Lambeth stairs, she saw her uncle looking at her, a satisfied smile playing about his lips.

'You have done us proud, niece,' he said. 'Now all that remains is for you to hold the King's interest.'

She trembled at the realisation that they were all counting on her. It felt as if England's future lay in her hands.

'I will do my very best,' she promised.

She hastened through the sleeping house to her own chamber, rousing Dolly Dawby from slumber to unlace her gown. She was so exhausted that she fell into bed, yet sleep eluded her. The King of England had shown her favour and there had been an amorous glint in his eye! She felt giddy at the prospects opening out in front of her. She lay there, hugging her secret.

Over the next two weeks, Bishop Gardiner hosted several suppers, feasts and entertainments for the King, and Katheryn was always present. It was clear that Gardiner, no less than Uncle Norfolk, would never cease striving to achieve their purpose – and they were not alone. Many conservatives wanted to see Cromwell toppled and the King married to an orthodox Catholic. Of course, the Queen was one, but her marriage – as Gardiner explained – represented an alliance with the German Lutherans. He shuddered as he said it. He was a formidable man, persuasive and authoritarian, and Uncle Norfolk had said he was the best champion of the faith in England, beside himself, of course. Katheryn did not doubt that the pair of them would get what they wanted.

She could not believe how quickly the King had fallen for her.

'I cast a fantasy on you, Katheryn, the first time ever I saw you,' he told her on their third meeting, as they sat alone together after the Bishop had ushered the other guests from the supper table. 'What attracted me was your extraordinary beauty and a notable appearance of honour and maidenly behaviour.' He laid his hand, laden with rings, on hers.

'Oh, Sir,' she said, 'I am not worthy of such praise!'

'But you are, Katheryn, you are! You have captivated me by your loveliness and sweetness, your superlative grace and your gentle face. You are so little and so precious to me. Your youth has rejuvenated me. I feel like a new man.'

It was easy to play the role of adoring mistress with such an ardent suitor, and to respond warmly to his addresses. Even after those first two weeks, Katheryn still felt bedazzled at being courted by the King, but she was surprised at how easy it was to be with him – and, she was finding, to love him. How could she help it when he was so loving towards her, so kind and indulgent of her every whim and mood?

Yet she did not love him like she had loved Harry and Francis and still loved Tom; it was a platonic love, of the kind that responds to adoration. And still she could not fancy the King as a man; she did not mind his holding her hand or kissing it, but when he ventured to kiss her on the mouth, she could not respond, which – God be thanked – he took as evidence of inexperience.

'You have never been kissed, sweetheart? I will teach you.' And he proceeded to do so. She endured it, pretending to enjoy having his tongue in her mouth. It would be worth it, she assured herself, not liking to imagine what it would be like to be in his bed, suffering more intimate invasions. But she could always close her eyes and pretend he was someone else! She could do it if she had to. For the first time, she knew herself to be as ambitious as the rest of her family. If submitting to the King's desires was the price of her elevation, she would pay it. In fact, she wanted all the world to know that he was courting her.

He had already given her a horse, a plump palfrey that was eating its head off in the royal stables. They would go riding together one day, he'd promised. The April lilacs and bluebells were in flower when he made her a grant of the confiscated goods and chattels of a convicted criminal. It did not amount to a lot by Howard standards, but she was touched to the point of indiscretion by this proof of the King's esteem.

'His Majesty has made me a grant of land!' she told the Duchess of Richmond triumphantly, for she had no sooner read over the deed than the Duchess had come upon her in the Queen's privy chamber. The Duchess, her cousin Mary Howard, had used to be dismissive of her, but was treating her with a new deference these days, giving Katheryn to believe that Uncle Norfolk had confided in his daughter.

'You have done well,' Mary smiled, her eyes on the King's seal. 'I know his Majesty well, having been married to his son. He was always good to me. Flatter him and defer to him always – that is the way to his heart.'

Katheryn thanked her for the advice.

The King's repeated visits to Winchester House and Katheryn's coinciding absences from court had led to speculation. It was Jane Rochford who told Katheryn that there was gossip about her at Whitehall.

'People are saying that his Grace has crept too near another lady,' she said, making it sound like an accusation. 'Some have it that he is much taken with *you* and that his affections have been alienated from Queen Anna on your account. Is it true?'

'He has been kind enough to show an interest in me,' Katheryn said warily, thinking quickly, 'but the rumours are greatly exaggerated. The Duke, my uncle, mentioned to him that I am an orphan without means or dowry.'

'Then he is not pursuing you for favours?'

'No.' That, at least, was true – so far.

'And you still love Tom Culpeper? Believe me, he loves you truly!' Jane was quite vehement.

'I do.' Even as she said it, she was wondering if it was still true. Her priorities had shifted dramatically. Marrying Tom and consigning herself to a life of domesticity at Penshurst no longer held any attraction for her.

'He is asking to see you,' Jane told her.

'Tell him I will meet him in the gardens tomorrow morning,' Katheryn said. She knew she could not put off much longer breaking it to Tom that it was over between them. But, when she saw him, her courage failed her, and she behaved as if all was still as it had been between them, promising to meet him three days hence in the same spot. Afterwards, knowing she was replicating the miserable endings of her previous affairs, she hated herself for it.

Chapter 17

1540

Late in April, the weather turned warm and the King returned with the court to Whitehall. Almost immediately, he arranged for Katheryn to be conducted to his privy garden by the river, which contained a shady arbour where they could be private. It became the setting for most of their trysts; only when it was raining did they retreat indoors to the King's privy gallery. His ardour was increasing daily. He was plainly entranced. He would clasp her to his broad, gem-encrusted breast, his mouth seeking hers with passion.

'You have rejuvenated me, Katheryn!' he murmured in her ear one balmy evening. 'Your youth, your grace, your beauty — so fresh and pure. Nature made you to shine equal with the stars. I love you!'

It was the first time he had said this to her.

'Could you love me too?' he asked beseechingly. When she looked at that Roman profile and felt the sheer power that emanated from the man, she marvelled that he could be so humble before her.

'I have always loved you, Sir,' she told him. It was not the truth in the way he wanted it, but he took it to be, and crushed her in his arms so that she could barely breathe.

He showered her with gifts: jewels and beautiful silks. She hid them from everyone else, laying them away at the bottom of her chest, but showed them to her uncle and grandam when next she gave them a report on her progress.

'Things are turning out as I anticipated,' the Duke smiled, as satisfied as a cat lapping cream. 'When his Grace takes a fancy for a person or a thing, he goes the whole way.'

The Duchess had had more new gowns made for Katheryn, who

gasped when she saw them, for they were the kind only a queen or princess might wear. Cloth of gold, cloth of silver, crimson tissue and scarlet damask, all edged with pearls and gems or banded with goldsmith's work. They must have cost a fortune.

'To see a good return, you must invest well,' the Duke said. 'It is time to raise our game. It will soon be May Day, and there are to be jousts and entertainments. This will be your chance to shine, Katheryn, and to increase the King's love for you.'

'Has he asked you to bed with him?' the Duchess asked bluntly.

'Not yet,' Katheryn said. 'He is passionate, but respectful.'

'Hmm,' the Duke murmured, his face darkening, and Katheryn thought of those rumours that the King was impotent. Was that why he had not yet importuned her? Had her uncle had the same thought?

'Permit him a few more favours,' Norfolk said at length. 'See if that arouses his ardour. But don't give yourself to him. Make it clear you are saving yourself for marriage.'

It was a bit late for that, she reflected drily. She had nothing to save. The thought of the King pawing at her breasts or attempting closer intimacies still repelled her, but she would allow it if he tried – if he asked her nicely enough. Oh, she was becoming a coquette these days!

When next she was with the King in the arbour, she responded as ardently as she could to his kisses, willing him to go further. And he did. His hand moved to her bodice and began caressing the exposed part of her breast. If she kept her eyes closed, she could almost believe it was Tom doing it, which made it bearable. Emboldened, the King's hand strayed down to her hip. That was enough for now. Gently, she drew it back to her waist.

'Ah, Katheryn, you little tease!' he chuckled hoarsely. 'You know, I would make you my mistress. I would acknowledge you openly before the world.'

'I do not know what your Grace means,' she said.

'I would be your servant!'

'And my lover?' With such words she hoped to inflame him.

'Oh, God, yes!' he breathed. 'If you would permit it.'

She drew back. Her hopes that he would be too infirm for lovemaking were dwindling fast. 'Alas, Sir, I could not. I would save myself for marriage. If I became your acknowledged mistress, people would think I had given myself to you.'

He swallowed, looking flushed. 'It was wrong of me to ask, Katheryn. Forgive me. I was carried away by my desire for you.'

'It is forgotten,' she told him lightly, giving him what she hoped was an adoring look.

'I have something for you,' he announced. 'Compensation for my bad behaviour, but you would have had it anyway.' He drew from his doublet a velvet pouch and handed it to her. She opened it to find two delicate gold chains and a beautiful cameo pendant depicting Venus and Cupid.

'Do you like it?' the King asked eagerly.

'I love it, Sir!' she cried. 'Oh, thank you!' And she gave him a warm kiss.

'How I love you,' he said. 'You are my English rose, my Tudor rose.'

The next time they met, he told her that she must call him Henry in private, and gave her a length of gold silk for a gown. She exclaimed in delight, and he was inordinately pleased.

She showed the jewels and the silk to the Duchess of Richmond the next day, laying them out on a bed when the dorter was empty and everyone else was about their duties. She did not like to show Isabel, for she suspected that she would not approve, even though they were now friends again; nor did she wish to alienate other ladies and maids who might, justly, feel that she was being disloyal to the Queen. But Mary Richmond was a Howard, who could be counted on to applaud the King's interest in her.

To Katheryn's dismay, Jane Rochford walked in and goggled at the bounty on the coverlet.

'Holy Mother, where did you get those?' she asked.

'The King gave them to me,' Katheryn admitted.

Jane stared at her. 'He must be marvellously set on you.'

'I am not his mistress,' Katheryn said, 'not in any way.'

'I've heard that before,' Jane retorted. 'It was what Anne said. She had set her sights far higher. Is that what you are aiming at, Mistress Katheryn?'

There was a pause, broken only when Katheryn laughed. 'And you think I would?'

'I don't know,' Jane said tartly. 'Would you?'

'Oh, be realistic!' Katheryn retorted. 'I'm sure his Grace would never think of me in that way. It is just a passing flirtation.'

She smiled at the Duchess and walked through to her bedchamber, discreetly signalling to Jane to follow. As soon as they were alone, she closed the door. 'Whatever you do, don't tell Tom about this,' she said. 'When the King beckons, it is unwise to say no – you surely understand that – but I have heard that his interest quickly wanes and, when it does, I want Tom to be there waiting for me.'

Jane seemed mollified by this. 'I won't tell him,' she said, 'as long as you carry on meeting him. Otherwise he will smell a rat.'

Katheryn wondered how long she would be able to keep seeing Tom before the King became aware of it. She was beginning to dislike herself for all the lies she had to tell.

It occurred to her later that day that the Queen might have heard the gossip. Yet there had been no change in Anna's demeanour towards her, no sign that she was aware that anything was amiss. Uncle Norfolk had said that the King would divorce her, come what may. It was a question of when, rather than if. Katheryn felt sorry for her, living in ignorance of the fate hanging over her, but she was also a little uneasy because, so far, there had been no hint of any divorce proceedings. Of course, she told herself, there wouldn't be. Such things were conducted in secret. The Queen would probably be the last to know, therefore secrecy was the order of the day.

Katheryn was excited about May Day. She had been told that it was always celebrated with sparkling festivities at court, and she was starved of such things. This year, there were to be four days of tournaments at Whitehall. When she appeared in her new scarlet damask gown on the first day, she attracted many envious looks and compliments. But she was not too conspicuous because everyone else was wearing their best clothes.

She crowded in with the other maids behind the King and Queen and their lords and ladies-in-waiting in the wide oriel window of the new gatehouse at Whitehall and, tense with anticipation, craned her neck to see the triumphal jousts that were taking place in the street below. Being so tiny, she could barely see anything, which was frustrating, as she had heard that the tournament had been proclaimed in France, Flanders, Scotland and Spain, and that the flower of European chivalry was here.

'There are forty-six defenders,' Dora Bray told her, ogling several of them at once. Katheryn caught a glimpse of mounted men in white doublets and hose.

'The Earl of Surrey is leading them,' Anne Bassett added. 'There's your uncle, Lord William Howard!'

'Sir John Dudley is leading the challengers,' her sister Margaret told her, giving Katheryn a sly glance. 'I can see Thomas Culpeper among them.'

Katheryn smiled. It was better if people thought she was being courted by Tom than by the King.

'Mr Culpeper's wearing my mother's colours!' Anne exclaimed. 'I'd have thought she was past all that at her age.'

'She's not the only one to be susceptible to his charms,' Lucy Somerset observed.

Katheryn could not help feeling jealous. Of course, Tom could not wear her colours, for their relationship was supposed to be a secret, but why did he have to wear Lady Lisle's?

Beside her, Elizabeth Seymour was jumping up and down to see her young husband, Lord Cromwell's son, show his prowess in the lists.

Suddenly, the King roared, 'No!' There were gasps from those surrounding him and cries of dismay from the stands.

'What's happened?' Katheryn asked.

Jane Rochford turned around. 'Mr Culpeper has been unhorsed, but he has got up and is walking away from the barriers.'

Katheryn's heart pounded in relief. She could not have borne it if Tom had been seriously injured or killed. She must still love him, to feel like that. Oh, if only life were not so complicated!

When the day's jousts were over, the King presented handsome prizes to the victors. Then word went around that the challengers were keeping open house at Durham House on the Strand and that the King and Queen were attending and there would be a lavish feast. All were welcome.

Katheryn picked up her skirts, fought her way downstairs and joined the crowd of courtiers surging up Whitehall to Charing Cross and the Strand beyond. It carried her to Durham House, which was lavishly adorned with rich hangings and furnished with great cupboards of plate. The King and Queen were already at table in the great hall as everyone filed in and took their seats and servitors came in procession with meat and drink in plenty. Minstrels played and the walls echoed with talk of the day's exploits.

Seated between her tall sister Margaret and tiny Mary Norris, Katheryn saw Tom at the opposite table, looking none the worse for his fall. He smiled at her, but she did not acknowledge it lest the King be looking in her direction. She had seen his eyes on her too, more than once, and was glad she had attracted his attention. Nothing must be allowed to jeopardise Uncle Norfolk's plans.

More tournaments were held over the next few days, and on every evening open house was kept at Durham House, with the King and Queen attending. There were suppers and banquets and Katheryn enjoyed herself hugely. On the last night, Norfolk and the Dowager Duchess were there, keeping a careful eye on how she comported herself. She was glad she was wearing the cloth-of-silver dress, for surely the King could not fail to approve of how it fitted her tiny waist and billowed out in soft folds to the floor. She watched as the Duchess gave the Queen an enamelled box containing a pearl bracelet and the Queen thanked her warmly. She could not but marvel at the duplicity of her grandam.

Tonight, they had gathered in the spacious gardens that bordered the Thames, in the soft glow of lanterns strung in the trees. It was a warm night and servants moved among the guests offering sweetmeats and comfits from gold salvers or pouring wine into jewelled goblets. Katheryn was standing with Isabel and Elizabeth Seymour only a few feet from the King, who was loudly congratulating a group of young men who had fought in the jousts. Queen Anna and some of her ladies were listening avidly, while her maids were casting lascivious glances at the heroes of the hour. Suddenly, Katheryn became aware that the King was looking in her direction

Seizing her moment, she smiled back and was gratified to see his eyes narrow in appreciation as they travelled up and down her figure.

'Come and join us, Mistress Katheryn!' he commanded, and she moved forward, noticing that the Queen was now nowhere to be seen. She did her best to respond prettily to the banter of the King and the young gallants, aware all the time of Henry's unwavering gaze. Then, curtseying, she withdrew, meaning to leave him hungry for more of her company. She took care to circulate among the guests, especially the young knights who had fought in the tourney, and midnight found her standing at one of the long tables, wondering if she really wanted anything else to eat. Reaching for some gilded marchpane, she became aware of a tall presence beside her. It was the King.

'You have been evading me,' he said, only half in jest.

'No, Sir, not really,' she protested. 'I thought it best not to attract attention by being where I wished to be – I mean, by your side. And the Queen's Grace was here.'

'She has gone back to Whitehall,' he said, looking very pleased about it.

Katheryn's hand flew to her mouth. 'I should have attended her! I will be missed.'

The King smiled indulgently. 'She slipped away quietly. She did not want to interrupt anyone's pleasure. She took just two of her maids. And I applaud your discretion.' He leaned in closer and she could smell the wine on his breath. He was a little drunk, she realised.

'Be mine tonight, Katheryn!' he murmured. Fortunately, no one was standing nearby.

'No, Sir, I cannot,' she whispered. 'I mean to preserve that virtue you claim to prize.'

He gave her a rueful smile and sighed. 'I stand well rebuked. Will you come to the privy garden then, tomorrow afternoon?'

'If I can get away,' she said.

'I shall live in hope,' he replied, his eyes glittering with desire.

He moved away and joined a circle of nobles, who all greeted him heartily. Katheryn put the marchpane and some candied fruits on her plate and went in search of her friends. Suddenly, Tom was standing before her, barring the way.

'Tell me it isn't true what people are saying,' he muttered, looking wild and fraught.

She swallowed. 'What are they saying?'

'That the King is in love with you. Is it true?'

'Keep your voice down!' she hissed. 'Come over here, it's quieter.' Luckily, the King was at the other side of the garden, separated from them by a great crowd of noisy, chattering people. She led the way to a stone bench beneath an overhanging branch and sat down.

Tom joined her, sitting a good foot away. 'Well?'

She owed him some honesty at least. 'It is true that he thinks himself in love with me, but I am not in love with him. He has asked me to be his mistress, but I would not.'

'And yet you have let things progress that far!'

'Tom, I have no choice! When the King beckons, we all have to jump. You must know that; you serve him daily.'

'I understand, but you must have given him some encourage-ment.'

She hesitated. 'It's complicated, Tom. I have been sworn to secrecy.'

'It's always complicated,' he snorted, 'and I didn't notice his Majesty taking much trouble to keep his interest in you secret to-night. It's what half the people here are gossiping about.' His eyes bored into hers. 'Tell me truthfully, Katheryn. Have you encouraged him?'

She was silent for just a little too long. 'I did what I felt I had to do,' she said at length.

'Don't play with me,' he growled, and grabbed her wrist so tightly that she wondered if there had been any truth to the story about him committing rape and murder.

'Let go,' she muttered. 'People are looking.' She stood up. 'We cannot be seen here together.'

'Why, are you afraid that the King will notice us? Or that someone will tell him we are together?'

'You don't own me!' she retorted. 'Stop hectoring me.' And she walked off towards the house.

He caught up with her in one of the deserted state rooms. He was beside himself, actually crying. 'Katheryn, is it over between us? Be honest, please!'

She felt like crying herself. The last thing she wanted to do was hurt him, but, with the King's pursuit of her progressing so speedily, and the outcome looking hopeful, he would be hurt much more if she gave him false hope now.

'It has to be over, Tom. The King, of all men, will not brook a rival, and I do not know what the future holds.'

'You are putting his love before mine?'

'I have no choice!' Tears were streaming down her cheeks now.

'Then he has deprived me of the thing I love best in the world!' Tom flung at her. 'I thought to make you my wife. Now you are lost to me. I could die.' He sank down on a stool, sobbing. She did not know what to say or do to comfort him.

She knelt at his knee, grateful that no one had overheard them and come to investigate what was going on. 'I'm so sorry, Tom. If it were up to me, this would not be happening. But I really have no choice in the matter, believe me.'

He raised a wet, ravaged face to her. 'Yes, you do. You could tell the King that we are in love and promised to each other.'

'But we are not. It would be a lie, because I never promised to marry you.'

'I'm asking you again now.' He took her hand, gently this time, his eyes earnest, pleading.

'The answer must be no,' she told him, and saw him wince. 'I am not free to make my own choices, believe me. But I will always love you, as I always have.' She broke down again.

Tom stood up and walked to the door without a word, leaving her kneeling there.

A few days later, Katheryn was among the maids and ladies attending on the Queen at a performance by Anna's new consort of musicians, the Bassanos of Venice, in her privy chamber. She was conscious of the King's eye straying upon her from time to time as she sat on the floor between Kate Carey and Anne Bassett, and of Tom Culpeper too, standing with the other gentlemen, darkly brooding and never looking her way.

Anne Bassett had been in a morose mood too, all morning, and the music did not seem to be doing anything to cheer her. During one particularly poignant piece, she suddenly fell to weeping on Elizabeth Seymour's shoulder. At a signal from the Queen, Mother Lowe hauled the girl to her feet and led her out, clucking sympathy. The King was frowning, but the company soon settled down.

Later, as Katheryn was helping to clear the table after Henry and Anna had shared a private supper, she heard him say that he had had Anne's stepfather, Lord Lisle, the deputy of Calais, arrested for treason, which would certainly have accounted for Anne's tears. It upset Katheryn too, for Lord Lisle had been good to Father, even in the face of his incompetence. She could not imagine what his lordship could have done to deserve being arrested, and it brought home to her how great and far-reaching the King's authority was. This was not her humble suitor who whispered sweet words imploring her to love him. This was a man who wielded terrible power over all his subjects, high and low, and could crush any of them if they displeased him. She shivered, wondering if it was wise to entangle herself further with him. Lord Lisle had been riding high in a position of the greatest trust; then suddenly he had fallen with his whole world crumbling about him.

She heard the Queen ask, 'Should I dismiss her?'

'No, Anna,' the King answered. 'She has committed no treason, and I like the little minx. You may tell her that my displeasure does not extend to her.'

Katheryn had to return to the servery then, so she did not hear the rest of the conversation, but she felt comforted. There was kindness in the King after all. She was worrying about nothing.

She had avoided going into the palace gardens after that horrible scene with Tom at Durham House. She felt guilty and could not forget the look on his face as she dashed his hopes. But the weather was warm on the last day of May and she was fed up with being indoors or confined to the Queen's privy garden; when Isabel and Margaret asked her to walk with them, she thought, why not? They would be there for her protection, should Tom approach her with harsh words, although she doubted he would do that anyway.

'There's still been no announcement about the Queen's coronation,' Margaret said, as they strolled along a gravelled path between flower beds enclosed by low rails with tall coloured poles at each corner bearing statues of heraldic beasts. 'Not long ago, people were talking about little else.'

'She was supposed to be crowned at Whitsun,' Katheryn recalled. In truth, she had been so preoccupied with her own affairs that she had forgotten about the coronation. She wondered if Uncle Norfolk and Bishop Gardiner had convinced the King that he should set the Queen aside.

'Yes,' Isabel said, 'but, if you ask me, there won't be a coronation – or not yet. Queen Jane never had one. First there was plague, then the Pilgrimage of Grace – and then she died in childbed. But Edward reckoned that the King would not have gone to that expense until she had borne him an heir. Had she lived, I'll wager she'd have been crowned. But this Queen . . . Methinks there is no likelihood of an heir. The King does not come to her bed these days.'

'But he needs another son,' Margaret said.

'Has he said anything to you, Katheryn?' Isabel asked. It was a tacit admission that she – and many other people, no doubt – knew about Henry's pursuit of Katheryn, and it showed that she had no intention of pretending it wasn't happening. Whether she approved or not was another matter. Katheryn knew that her half-sister had her interests at heart, but she so wanted her approval.

'He never mentions the Queen,' she said, 'and I want you to know that nothing improper has taken place between us.'

'You are holding out for marriage?' Isabel asked. 'It's what people are saying.'

Katheryn was taken aback by her bluntness.

'You wouldn't be the first to use such tactics,' Isabel said. Her tone was disapproving.

'Has it occurred to you that I might have no choice but to receive his courtship?' Katheryn asked, unable to bear Isabel judging her without knowing the truth. She bent close to her half-sister's ear. 'My lord of Norfolk and Bishop Gardiner constrained me to it. My heart was elsewhere, but I dared not tell them. I cannot say more.'

Isabel stared at her, then turned to Margaret. 'You go on, dear. I can see Dora and Ursula ahead. I need to talk to Katheryn.' Margaret obeyed, with an understanding smile.

'You don't have to do this,' Isabel said.

'I do. Much hangs on it. And I have ended it with my other suitor, much to his grief.' Katheryn looked around nervously, as she had been doing all the way from the palace, for any sign of Tom.

'Oh, my poor girl,' Isabel said, and squeezed her hand. 'Has the King mentioned marriage?'

'No, he—' She broke off because there, striding along the path towards them, was Francis. He was the second-to-last person she wanted to see – or had expected to see. Only last week, her grandam had told her that he was in Ireland, adding mysteriously that it was on Katheryn's account. When Katheryn had pressed her to say more, the old lady had said he had gone to make his fortune in the foolish hope that he might marry her. 'I sent him off with a flea in his ear,' she'd snorted.

'Is this the suitor?' Isabel asked.

'No,' Katheryn faltered. 'This is Mr Dereham, who was in my lady of Norfolk's service at Lambeth.'

Francis doffed his cap and swept an exaggerated bow. 'At your service, ladies.' When he stood up, his mouth was upturned in a wolfish grin, but his eyes were not smiling.

'Good day, Mr Dereham,' Katheryn managed to say. 'This is my half-sister Lady Baynton, the wife of the Queen's chamberlain. Isabel, may I present Mr Dereham?' Francis bowed again.

'I am no longer in the Duchess's service,' he told them. 'I am here in attendance on Lord William Howard, who has been a good patron to me.'

'I have not heard from you in some time, Mr Dereham,' Katheryn said, admiring at his roguish good looks and feeling still that pull of attraction.

'I have been in Ireland,' he told her.

'Ireland?' she echoed, feigning surprise.

'You have family or business there?' Isabel asked politely.

'I had business there,' he replied, 'and it concerned Mistress Katheryn. If, by your leave, Lady Baynton, I might have a word in private with her . . .'

Isabel looked at Katheryn. Clearly, she was wondering if it was proper to leave the two of them alone together.

'It's all right,' Katheryn said. 'Mr Dereham is my cousin, and the Duchess's. I have known him for a long time.' She saw a fleeting smirk on his face.

Isabel smiled politely. 'Well, it was a pleasure to meet you, Mr Dereham.' She walked off in the direction of the others. Katheryn was horrified to see Tom standing a little way beyond them, staring at her and Francis with a grim look on his face. She could guess what he was thinking.

'Why don't we go down by the river?' she suggested, and led the way along a path that wound behind a hedge.

'So what was your business in Ireland?' she asked lightly, once they were out of Tom's line of sight.

'I turned pirate!' Francis replied. There was an edge to his voice. 'I went to Ireland soon after I heard from Meg Morton that the King's Grace was in love with you. I also heard from Kat Tilney that there was talk at court that you were to marry a gentleman of the King's Privy Chamber. I thought I would combine my thirst for adventure with making lots of money so that I could compete with such grand company.' There was a sneer in his voice. 'I spent my savings on a boat and tried holding merchant vessels to ransom. I didn't have much success and had to come home.' He paused, his eyes narrowing. 'Is it true, this talk? What is going on, Katheryn?'

Katheryn took a deep breath. 'It is true that this gentleman, Mr Culpeper, paid court to me, but there was no talk of marriage between us. If you heard such a report, you heard more than I know. Besides, I put him off when the King showed an interest in me. I could not say no to the King.'

'Are you the King's mistress?' He flung the words at her.

'No, and never will be.'

Francis's eyebrows narrowed. 'I don't know what game you're playing, Katheryn, but you need to remember two things. One is that I still love you; the other is that you are precontracted to me and not free to marry anyone else.'

'Not that again!' she cried. 'Why are you troubling me with this now? It's over between us. I will not have you!'

He gave her a severe look. 'I know you better than that, Katheryn. I could make you mine if I willed it, although I dare not, for the King is after you. But, if he were dead, I would marry you.'

'Hush!' she hissed, looking around nervously to check that no one had heard him. 'Don't you know it's treason to speak of the King's death?'

'You're not going to tell on me, are you?' Francis retorted. 'Fear not, I'm leaving and will not trouble you again. Just remember that bigamy is frowned upon.'

She walked back towards the palace in turmoil. Isabel had waited for her.

'Thank goodness you're here,' Katheryn said. 'That man is hounding me. He took an unwelcome interest in me at Lambeth and is behaving as if he was all the world to me.'

'Do you want me to speak to him?' Isabel asked, taking her hand.

Katheryn looked behind them to check that Francis was not following. 'No. I just want to avoid him without making any fuss. Least said, soonest mended. Hopefully, he's got the message.'

'Well,' Isabel said doubtfully, 'if you need my help, you know where I am.'

They walked on in silence along the gravel path. It was unbelievable that Francis was here at court. Why were there so many entanglements in her life? At that moment, she didn't want to be involved with anyone – Francis, Tom or even the King. She just wanted to be left alone. But there, waiting for her in the antechamber to the Queen's lodgings, was an usher in the royal livery.

'His Majesty requests that you meet him in his privy garden at five o'clock tomorrow, Mistress Katheryn. I myself will come to escort you.'

Her heart sank. She had no choice but to go and look happy about it.

The next morning, when she emerged from the dorter, Mother Lowe was waiting for her in the Queen's presence chamber. 'Mistress Katheryn, the Duke of Norfolk would be grateful if you would wait on him in the great hall,' she said. Her tone was cold and Katheryn guessed she had heard the gossip. Mother Lowe would have lain down and died for Queen Anna. Naturally, she would hate anyone who caused her any hurt.

Katheryn glanced at the clock on the court cupboard. 'I am due to wait upon the Queen in five minutes,' she said.

'Her Grace has given you leave to see your uncle.'

'That is kind of her,' Katheryn said, and sped off.

Norfolk was seated alone at the table on the dais. Further down the hall, servants were stacking the trestle tables used at breakfast against the walls. The Duke stood up and ushered Katheryn into a window embrasure with a cushioned seat.

'Sit down,' he bade her. 'I wanted to ask if all goes well.'

'Very well, my lord,' she replied. 'I think the King fancies himself in love with me.'

'Indeed.' He smiled at her. 'That is good progress. Has he mentioned marriage or divorcing the Queen?'

'Not yet, Sir.'

'Well, give it time. He will come to the point, I have no doubt. When are you seeing him again?'

'Later this afternoon.'

'Good.' The Duke leaned closer. 'Cromwell is tottering. The King might have made him Earl of Essex, but he has a habit of showing favour to those he means to destroy. Mark me, that man's days are numbered. If you get the chance, use your wiles to convince his Majesty that Cromwell is no good to him.'

Katheryn felt uncomfortable. 'But I know nothing about him!'

'You know that the Cleves marriage was his doing. Granted, you can't criticise him for that until the King gives a sign that he is thinking of ending the marriage, but you can say you have heard gossip that Cromwell is a heretic Lutheran. All you need to do is plant the seed in his Grace's mind. He is very suggestible and, if he is as besotted with you as you say, he will be receptive.'

'All right,' Katheryn agreed, fearing nevertheless that she would be out of her depth. 'I will do my best.'

'Continue as you have begun and you'll have a crown on your head before you know it!' Norfolk grinned.

Chapter 18

1540

The King was sitting in the arbour when Katheryn arrived in the privy garden that afternoon.

'It's a beautiful day, Sir,' she said as she rose from her curtsey and went to sit beside him.

He sighed. 'You are a feast for the eyes, Katheryn, and it gives me the greatest pleasure to see you. But I am, in a manner, weary of my life. I am not well handled by those who advise me.'

Katheryn seized her moment. 'Do you mean the Earl of Essex?'

He looked at her in surprise. 'Why do you say that, sweetheart?'

'Well, there are rumours, Sir. I shouldn't repeat them to you; they are probably nothing.'

'No, go on, Katheryn. I need to know what people are saying.'

'They say he is a Lutheran heretic, Sir, who does your Grace no good service. I'm not quite sure what they mean.'

'Hmm.' The King's face had flushed. 'That is interesting.'

'I meant no harm,' she said.

'Of course not,' he assured her. 'But I didn't summon you to hear my woes or talk about my lord of Essex. I wanted to ask you something.'

She held her breath.

'Katheryn, are you truly free from any entanglements?'

'Entanglements, Sir?' She affected innocence, but she had a good idea of where this was going. Her pulse began to race.

'I mean, are you betrothed or promised to anyone?'

Fleetingly, she thought of Francis, but pushed the thought resolutely away. 'No, Sir.'

'It is a marvel to me that some young gallant has not snapped you up,' the King said, laying his hand on hers.

'I have no dowry,' she told him.

'Ah. But what would that matter against such beauty and charm?'

She laughed. 'It seems to matter very much.'

'It is the misfortune of those of high birth to be married for profit and advantage. I speak from experience, as one who has married both for policy and for love. Love is the more important. Never forget that, Katheryn. What good is policy when you are forced to spend your life sleeping with a woman you cannot love?'

She guessed who he was referring to. 'It can only bring unhappiness to both spouses,' she said. He nodded sadly.

He said no more about marriage, but went on to tell her about the summer hunting progress he was planning; she would be going too, in attendance on the Queen.

Presently, it was supper time and she had to leave. The King kissed her hand, his eyes drinking her in.

'I will send for you again, very soon,' he said.

Had she any entanglements? His question went round and round in her head. He would not have asked it, surely, if he did not have marriage in mind – unless, of course, he meant to find a husband for her, which she very much doubted was his intention. No, he must be thinking of proposing!

She sought out Uncle Norfolk as soon as she could to tell him about the conversation. She found him in his lodging with Bishop Gardiner and, over a glass of wine, told them what the King had said – and how she had brought up the subject of Cromwell.

'You have done well, Mistress,' Gardiner pronounced. 'Our faith in you was not misplaced.'

'He *is* thinking of marriage,' Norfolk said. 'All is falling out as we intended.'

It was. Not two weeks later, news went winging about the court that Cromwell had been arrested for treason and heresy, stripped of his honours and carried off to the Tower. Katheryn wondered if what she had said to the King had been instrumental in bringing this about, and felt a pang of guilt, but Uncle Norfolk and Bishop Gardiner were triumphant.

'That's an end to the blacksmith's boy!' the Duke exulted. 'Now the governance of England will be in the hands of those who were bred to it!'

It was a hot, dry summer, the hottest Katheryn could remember, and there was no rain. By the third week of June, the grass was looking parched and there were fears that plague might break out.

The King had not mentioned Cromwell to her and there was no longer any need for her to speak of the fallen minister. She could sense the anger in Henry, suppressed for her sake, and thought it had probably been simmering for all those months since he had married the Queen.

It was hot, even in the shade of the arbour, and Katheryn had worn her light gown of green silk, yet still it clung to her. She would have sat there in her shift if she had been let! The King was in his shirtsleeves, his collar of black-work embroidery unlaced, exposing the red hairs on his vast chest. He was sweating a lot – and, she soon guessed, not just from the heat.

'Katheryn,' he said, interrupting a conversation about masques, 'I have to talk to you. Before I married the Queen, I was assured that there were proofs of the breaking of her previous betrothal to the Duke of Lorraine. But the envoys of Cleves did not bring those proofs when they escorted her to England, which made me reluctant to proceed with the marriage. The Duke of Cleves promised to send them to me, but he has not done so and it is clear that they do not exist. So I am resolved to have the marriage annulled.'

Katheryn tensed. He was going to ask for her hand.

'The Queen does not yet know about this,' Henry continued, 'and I want to make it as painless as possible for her – and for you. There is talk of us, and I would not want it thought that this divorce is on your account. I was set on it before ever I became your servant. So I am sending you back to my lady of Norfolk at Lambeth.'

Katheryn nearly burst into tears. She did not want to go back to Lambeth. She loved being at court and – she realised – she had come to have feelings for Henry. Not the kind of feelings she had had for any of her other suitors, but affection all the same, and there was something very special about being courted by so powerful a king. But he had not said anything about marriage, so she would be going away without any assurances for her future – and might never come back.

'Do not look so downcast,' Henry enjoined her. 'I will come and visit you privately.'

'I would like that,' she said, brightening.

He kissed her gently. 'As will I.' He sat up. 'You will leave in two days. Say to the Queen that your grandam needs you at home. You might hint that a marriage is in the offing.'

Yes, but what marriage? And would the Queen would guess that this was just a bluff?

They strolled down to the river, where Henry beckoned a group of young lords and gentlemen to join them. As they stood there chatting and jesting, Katheryn basked in the open admiration of the handsome gallants – until she looked up and saw a figure at an upstairs window. It was the Queen, staring at her, her face a mask of sadness. She prayed that her mistress would think she was with one of the young men. Even if that got her into trouble, it was better than Anna thinking that she had betrayed her.

She had already noticed a new wariness towards her on Anna's part and suspected that the Queen had heard the gossip. Yet she had not been treating Katheryn any differently and remained pleasant and courteous. Katheryn felt sorry for her, for Anna did not know what was in store. She felt guilty too. Yet she knew that the King would have ended the marriage anyway, and not on her account. She detected fear in the Queen's demeanour. Anna must have guessed that something was afoot. How could she not, when the King rarely came near her? Of course, she would be worrying that he might get rid of her as he had Queen Katherine, or even – Heaven forbid! – Queen Anne. She might easily conclude that he was setting her aside so that he could marry Katheryn.

Katheryn was aware that some of the ladies and maids had become hostile towards her. Anna was a kind mistress who inspired loyalty and protectiveness. Mother Lowe's manner towards Katheryn was now positively icy. Even Jane Rochford was no longer as friendly, but that was probably because of the way Katheryn had treated Tom Culpeper. And, of course, there was a certain jealousy among those who would have given much to be courted by the King. It was probably as well that she was leaving court.

Yet she did so with a heavy heart, and when she asked the Queen for leave to go, it was hard not to cry. Anna noticed her distress and asked if anyone had been unkind to her.

'No, Madam,' Katheryn sobbed.

'But I thought you were happy here?'

'Madam, I was.'

'Is it a young man?'

Katheryn dabbed at her eyes. 'No, Madam. My lady of Norfolk needs me.'

Anna seemed surprised. Of course, she would be wondering why the Howards would permit one of their blood to leave court just to help her grandam. But she made no protest, and Katheryn had not expected her to. The Queen was probably relieved to see her go.

When she got back to her chamber, Malyn was waiting for her, ready to offer a sympathetic shoulder to cry on. Katheryn needed it. She could not bear to think of herself being rusticated at Lambeth when Malyn, Meg and Kat were staying on at court.

Lambeth seemed relatively quiet after the court. There was the usual household bustle, but on a much smaller scale. Familiar faces were missing. Of those who had been there in Katheryn's time, only Dorothy Berwick, Margaret Bennet, Dotty Baskerville and Dolly Dawby remained in the gentlewomen's dorter, and she had never been par-ticularly friendly with any of them. Disinterestedly, they told her that Mary Lascelles had married a Mr Hall and gone to live in Sussex, Joan Bulmer had returned to her husband and was now in York, and Alice Wilkes had married Mr Anthony Restwold and moved to

Buckinghamshire. Katheryn was sorry that Alice had left; she missed the young woman's cheerful presence.

It was a good thing that the Duchess had kept her old chamber free for her. Mournfully, she stowed away her gorgeous court gowns in the chest at the foot of the bed, wondering when she would ever wear them again.

She was grateful that Francis was absent – thank goodness he had gone to serve Lord William Howard – but pleased to see Edward Waldegrave, Robert Damport and William Ashby, who all expressed pleasure at her return. And the Duchess welcomed her warmly when she answered the summons to her chamber.

'It is I who will, God willing, be curtseying to you soon!' she declared.

'I am not so sure, Madam,' Katheryn said. 'His Majesty has said nothing about marriage – and he has sent me away.' Her voice broke.

'He is protecting you from scandal, child,' the Duchess said briskly. 'The Duke has told me about this coming divorce and it is most proper that you are here, away from the court. You must not go reading the worst into it. He sent your cousin Anne home when his divorce from Queen Katherine was thought to be imminent.'

Katheryn felt better hearing that. Yet still she found herself moping around the house, bored and in need of distractions. The hot summer days seemed very long.

There came an evening when, enjoying the cooler air in the gardens, she saw a small boat making its way across the Thames towards Lambeth. There were people standing on the riverbank watching it. She let out a gasp when she saw the King sitting in the boat, and her spirits soared. There he was, climbing out onto the landing stage, with just two gentlemen in attendance, and striding towards her with his arms held out.

'Katheryn!'

'Your Grace!' she cried, and ran to him, almost forgetting to curtsey in her joy at seeing him – at not being forgotten. And he would probably not have noticed, so pleased to see her did he look.

'I have missed you, sweetheart,' he told her, curling a beefy arm around her slender shoulders. 'But all is going well, and I look to have a good end to my matter soon.'

Was he telling her that soon he would be free to marry her? It sounded like it, but she dared not let herself believe that, in a few short weeks, God willing, she might be queen. It was not just the prospect of a crown that thrilled her, though. She was genuinely pleased to see Henry. No other man had ever been as kind to her, or as humble in his courtship. She knew he would give her the moon if she asked for it.

The King's arrival had been noticed and the Duchess's chamberlain had come racing out of the house to welcome him. My lady herself was waiting in the hall and swept a deep curtsey as her sovereign entered. She smiled when she saw Katheryn on his arm.

'My lady of Norfolk! Greetings!'

'Welcome, your Grace, to my poor house,' she said, indicating the fine furniture, the costly tapestries and the buffet groaning with gold plate behind her. 'Will you take a goblet of wine while I arrange for food to be prepared?'

'Wine would be most welcome,' Henry said, 'but do not go to any more trouble, for I have eaten supper already. I came to see Mistress Katheryn and, by your leave, will take the air with her in the gardens.'

'By all means, Sir,' the Duchess said, beaming at them both.

Henry stayed for two hours, most of which they spent sitting on the stone bench fronting the river.

'I have sent the Queen to Richmond,' he told her, 'for her health.' He placed the slightest emphasis on the last phrase, which Katheryn took to mean that Anna too had been got out of the way while divorce proceedings went ahead. He said no more of the matter, but went on to speak of his love of ships and the sea, of the rivalry between himself and the King of France, of his sadness at the death of his champion horse, Governatore, and of a myriad other things. Katheryn told him about her childhood at Moreton and Lambeth and Oxon Hoath, and of her brothers, who were doing so well in Norfolk's service, and of Mary, the little sister she had rarely seen, who was now twelve and being cared for at Oxon Hoath.

'I had four sisters,' the King said. 'All gone now, except one, and she the most troublesome. I must find your Mary a place at court.'

When it grew late, he bade Katheryn a fervent farewell, holding her tightly in his arms and kissing her as if he would drink her in.

He came frequently after that, often in the daytime, and sometimes in the evening. She also saw him at Winchester House, where Bishop Gardiner provided feasts and entertainments for them. On these occasions, she was aware of the stares of the Londoners watching her barge pass along the river, not all of them friendly. It made her realise with a jolt that her fame – or, rather, notoriety – had spread beyond the court. She feared that people were drawing the wrong conclusions about her. Those fears deepened one evening when, returning from Winchester House, she stole past the porter's lodge and heard him say to someone she could not see, 'The King's Grace has been banqueting these two nights with Mistress Katheryn there, and I suspect they were enjoying more than comfits.' Her cheeks burned.

By the end of June, Henry was coming nightly to see her. Because it was still so hot in the early evening, they talked in the little parlour by the hall. One night, he told her that, despite every effort having been made to maintain discretion, word had got out that he was planning to divorce the Queen. 'Worse still, two of my own lawyers were speculating that Cromwell is in the Tower because he will not consent to it. My lord of Canterbury came to hear of this and had them severely reprimanded by my Council. Sweetheart, it would be a kindness if you would write to thank the Archbishop.'

Nervously, Katheryn fetched writing materials. She did not want the King to see how difficult writing was for her; it might give him cause to think twice about making her queen. But she made a creditable effort, she felt, assuring Cranmer that his prompt action had left him in greater favour than he had ever been. Hard-line reformist though he was, she was desirous of obtaining his friendship. He would not relish a Catholic queen on the throne, but he might come to like her for herself.

At Lambeth, little was spoken of but the likely fate of Cromwell.

'He'll be executed as he deserves,' Robert Damport predicted.

By the end of the first week of July, such talk had been superseded by excited speculation about another royal divorce. It was no secret that the King was coming a-courting every day, and people tended to look at Katheryn when the subject was mentioned. It both embarrassed and excited her, but she said nothing. After all, there was nothing to say, was there?

'I hope to goodness this divorce doesn't take as long as the last one,' Mother Emmet said one day at dinner in the hall. 'Seven years it was, by my reckoning.'

Katheryn hoped so too. It was hard enough to bear the waiting as it was. How had her cousin Anne coped?

Towards the middle of July, there came an evening when the King arrived and told Katheryn he desired to speak with the Duchess in private. When he had disappeared into her grandam's chamber, she walked restlessly up and down the gallery, desperate to know what was being discussed. It seemed like ages before Henry emerged and asked her if she would walk with him in the gardens.

'We can speak freely there,' he said.

The sky above the silhouetted rooftops of Westminster was streaked with pink and gold as they strolled along the gravelled paths, the King leaning heavily on his stick. His leg was giving him trouble this week, but he was in a buoyant mood, squeezing her hand and complimenting her on her gown. It was the green one, his favourite.

When they had come some way from the house, he bade her sit beside him on a wooden seat. 'I have good news, darling,' he said. 'Today, Parliament confirmed the annulment of my marriage.'

Katheryn's heart began to race. 'I am pleased for your Grace,' she said.

'Henry!' he reminded her.

'It is a comfort to have your doubts resolved – Henry,' she ventured, and laughed.

'Already, my Council have petitioned me to marry again,' he told her. Surely, she thought, the idea had been in his mind already. 'They wish me to frame my heart to the love and favour of some noble lady with whom I can be joined in lawful matrimony, so that I can secure the succession to the comfort of my realm.' He took her hand. 'Tonight, I asked my lady of Norfolk if you, my sweet Katheryn, are worthy to become my queen.' His blue eyes were warm in his tanned face.

Katheryn's head was spinning. She could not speak for excitement.

'She told me she knew no wrong of you,' the King continued, 'and commended your purity and your honesty. My darling, now that I am assured you are chaste and free from any entanglement, I wish to honour you with marriage.' He bent forward and kissed her reverently on the lips. 'I would go down on one knee, as is proper, but I doubt I would get up again. Katheryn, say you will have me!'

Still she was speechless. It was what she had been longing to hear, what Norfolk and Gardiner had schemed for; it would mean a crown for herself and the pinnacle of success for the Howards, and she *was* elated. But, in those heady seconds of Henry's proposal, all she had thought of was that the Duchess had lied. She was not pure or honest. She would be marrying the King under false pretences.

For a mad moment, she thought of confessing all. But that would be the end of everyone's hopes and the ruin of her future. Besides, the King was eagerly awaiting a reply.

'It is such an honour,' she said, her voice little more than a whisper. 'Truly, Henry, I am overwhelmed.'

'Then you will consent, my darling?'

'With all my heart,' she replied.

Tears streamed down his cheeks as he enfolded her in his arms and kissed her with new ardour.

'Thanks be to God!' he breathed. 'It is a marvel to me that, in my old days, after so many troubles of mind caused by my marriages, I have obtained such a perfect jewel of womanhood, a sweet lady who shows such perfect love towards me, to my peace of mind, and that I can again look forward to the desired fruits of matrimony.' He drew away and gazed into her face. 'I have never seen such honour, purity and maidenly behaviour in a young lady.'

A great lump of guilt rose in Katheryn's throat. They had, all of them, colluded to deceive him – and there was nothing to be done about it. Too many hopes rested upon her. Well, from now on, she would be all those things he admired. What had happened in the past must be consigned to the past.

Henry kissed her tenderly. 'I know I can be content with you, Katheryn. And you will easily win the hearts of my subjects, for your beauty surpasses that of all the ladies in England. You have such a gentle face, and you are so gracious of speech. They will love your modest bearing and courteous conversation.'

'I do hope I will live up to your expectations of me,' Katheryn said, caressing his cheek.

'Oh, Katheryn, Katheryn, how could you doubt it?' he cried, and kissed her passionately.

That night, she lay wakeful, fretting about deceiving the King. What was it Francis had said about bigamy? That it was frowned upon. But they had not been wed; they had merely promised themselves to each other, and the Duchess had dismissed it as being of no significance, so Katheryn was sure that Francis had got it wrong. She wished she knew more about such things, but she dared not ask anyone now.

She smothered the proddings of her conscience by indulging in a reverie about being queen. The prospect of riches, influence and fame was a heady one, and she had found that it did not come at such a high price after all. The King was a sweetheart, loving, kind and protective, and she had grown very fond of him. The prospect of sharing a bed with him was not one she relished, but he had shown himself an ardent lover so far and might yet surprise her. As long as he did not suspect that she was no virgin, all would be well. She remembered the blood spots on the sheet after she had surrendered her maidenhead to Francis and resolved to prick her finger before she went to sleep on her wedding night, so that there would be similar evidence on her uprising the next morning.

All would be well. Finally, she slept, worn out by her restless tossings and turnings.

The Duchess was the first person at Lambeth to hear the news. She had retired before the King left, so Katheryn broke it to her the next morning after Mass.

'My lady,' she said, following her grandam into her chamber and

210

closing the door behind them. 'The King has proposed! I am to be queen!'

For the first time ever, the Duchess threw her arms around her and kissed her.

'I feel as if I have been visited by the Angel Gabriel!' she exclaimed. 'You have triumphed, Katheryn! I knew you would not let us down.'

Immediately, she sent her usher to summon the Duke, Lord and Lady William Howard and the Countess of Bridgewater, to tell them the news. Norfolk arrived from court within what seemed like ten minutes, with Bishop Gardiner in tow. When he heard the glad tidings, he embraced Katheryn with unusual warmth.

'Well done, niece! It is marvellous to think we will have a Howard queen on the throne again. It will be to the great benefit of this realm.'

The Bishop congratulated her. 'My dear, there is no doubt that you will be the handsomest of his Grace's wives. He is a lucky man indeed.' Behind him, she saw her brothers, looking so tall and debonair and jubilant. They kissed her and told her how clever she was.

'I cannot take it all in!' she told them.

Lord William, arriving in haste, bowed low, his eyes shining, a foretaste of the deference that would soon be shown to her.

When Henry called that evening, the Duchess was quick to voice her appreciation of the honour he had done her house. He beamed at her evident joy and said that it was Katheryn who had honoured *him* in consenting to be his Queen.

'When is the marriage to be announced, Sir?' the Duchess asked.

'Not yet,' the King said. 'There is a lot of idle talk about my divorce from the Lady Anna, so I think it best to let that die down.'

When he was alone with Katheryn in the gardens, he bade her sit with him and kissed her. 'My little Queen is looking beautiful tonight.'

'Beautiful and very hot!' she replied, giggling.

'It's still stifling,' he complained, and shrugged off his gown, sitting there in his shirtsleeves. 'You know there are rumours about us all over the court, and beyond. I'm told that the French ambassador thinks we are already married! He has informed his master that the divorce of the Queen was hastened because I had to wed you.'

'No!' Katheryn cried, flushing. 'I would not have anyone think that.'

'Time will prove him wrong,' Henry said. 'You must accustom yourself to this kind of speculation. As queen, you will live on a public stage and the world will watch everything you do.'

'I know,' Katheryn replied.

'Anyone with any sense, and who knows me, could not credit that I would make you my mistress. They'd know that I would never compromise the legitimacy of any child of mine born in wedlock. Besides, my queen must be a model of purity, the very mirror of the Virgin Mary.'

Katheryn's heart sank again. She was so unfitted to be the kind of queen Henry wanted.

'I thought we could be married towards the end of this month, after I've dissolved Parliament,' Henry said.

So soon!

'If that is your pleasure,' she answered.

'Is it yours, darling?'

'Of course!' she told him, setting aside her fears and giving him a radiant smile.

'It will be a quiet ceremony, just for us,' he said. 'My treasury is empty. I hope you won't mind. I won't have our marriage proclaimed until a week or so later, to give us time to enjoy a honeymoon in private.'

'Whatever you wish,' she assured him. 'I am content.'

In the third week of July, a letter addressed in a strange hand arrived for Katheryn. Breaking the seal, she saw that it was from Sir George Seaford, a friend of her grandam. He informed her that he was away on business in York and had visited Joan Bulmer, who had sent her the enclosed note.

Katheryn unfolded it and read Joan's message. Sir George must have told her about the King's divorce and that it was thought Katheryn was to be queen. Uncharacteristically gushing, Joan wished her all the wealth and good fortune she could desire. 'You will be worthy to have that honour,' she had written, before mostly heartily desiring Katheryn to remember the love she had always borne her. She went on to relate how a change of fortune had brought her into the utmost misery and she was now leading the most wretched life. She could not express her sorrows in writing, and there was no remedy for them, unless Katheryn, of her goodness, found the means to get her to London, which she would find very difficult to do herself.

But, if you write to my husband and command him to bring me there, I think he will not dare disobey you. If it could be arranged, I would like to be with you before you attain your high honour. In the meantime, I beseech you to save some place for me in your household, whatever you think fit, for the nearer I am to you, the happier I will be. I would write more to you, but I dare not be so bold, considering the great honour you are to have. But, remembering the honesty I have always known to be in you, I have felt encouraged to write this. I beseech you not to be forgetful of my request for, if you do not help me, I am not likely to have any joy in this world. I desire you, if you can, to let me have some answer to satisfy my mind; for I know the Queen of Britain will not forget her secretary, and favour you will show.

Your humble servant, with heart unfeigned, Joan Bulmer

Katheryn's heart was racing. This was intimidation, nothing less. The pointed reminders of her past, couched in the most flattering terms, that taunting mention of her honesty – a sly reference to her chastity – and the reminder that Joan had occasionally acted as her secretary, not only writing the occasional letter for her, but knowing her secrets. Her words were loaded with meaning. 'I would write more to you, but I dare not be so bold' – what could this be, but a threat, a reminder that Joan knew about Katheryn's misconduct with Francis and Harry? The peremptory, dictatorial tone of her demands and the last, menacing line were so unlike the manner in which a petitioner was supposed to approach one of higher rank. And it was all couched in the most friendly, flattering terms, so cleverly composed that no one else reading the letter could guess at its hidden subtext.

Katheryn stared at it for a long time. Would granting Joan's request be the price of her silence? Or would Joan want more, holding her implied threats over her mistress's head like a sword of Damocles? Katheryn dared not contemplate having the woman in her household, certainly not after this. Joan would be a constant reminder of a past she was trying to forget. But did she have a choice?

Yes, she did! She would not be bullied like this.

She fetched pen and ink and retired to her chamber, where she wrote a short note to Joan, thanking her for her kind letter and saying that the King had already appointed her household (which was not true), but that, if a vacancy should arise in the future, she would send for her. That should content her, or at least buy her silence! Resolving that she never would send for Joan Bulmer, she sealed the letter.

She had much to do. The new gowns Uncle Norfolk had provided would serve for a queen, but the Duchess insisted she should be fitted for more. My lady's jeweller was a frequent visitor to Lambeth, bringing tray after tray of his wares. When Katheryn baulked at the cost, her grandam smiled at her.

'Remember to think of it as an investment, my dear,' she said, 'in earnest of the bounty that is to come.' Katheryn hoped that the King would be as generous to her family as they expected.

She spent hours sitting in the shade in the garden, embroidering smocks and coifs. The young gentlewomen clustered around, offering to help, all eager to be her best friends now. Naturally, they were hoping for places at court. Isabel and Margaret came to visit her and helped with the endless sewing. And, all the while, July was drawing inexorably towards its close.

On the 27th, Sir John Russell arrived from the King to say that his Majesty was moving to the palace of Oatlands for the hunting, with just a small riding household in attendance, and requested that Mistress Katheryn join him there with all haste. She would find that everything was in readiness for her. He himself would escort her.

214

She knew what the summons betokened.

'I am going to Oatlands to be married,' she told the Duchess, who clasped her to her flat bosom and kissed her warmly.

'God be thanked!' she said. 'You are an honour to our house!'

Katheryn's belongings were all packed. As they were being loaded onto the sumpter mules that had been sent by the King, she changed into a riding habit of tawny damask with a matching bonnet sporting a jaunty feather. Sir John looked at her admiringly as she descended the stairs.

The Duchess was waiting for her. 'Farewell, my child. May God go with you. Remember us all in your prayers, and never forget that you are a Howard!'

The weather was oppressively warm, but the cabin of the barge that took them upriver to Walton-on-Thames offered shade and there was a good breeze from the river. Late in the afternoon, they alighted to find horses awaiting them, and rode the three miles to Oatlands. The palace, with its turreted gatehouse and gabled roofs, was secluded in an extensive deer park, and Katheryn could see why Henry had chosen it for their nuptials. She was surprised to see how big it was, and how new.

They crossed the arched bridge over the moat and found Sir Anthony Wingfield, Vice Chamberlain of the King's household, waiting to greet them at the gatehouse. As he led them into a large courtyard, he told Katheryn that the King had acquired the old house three years previously and had been extending it ever since.

'This is only the first of three courts, Madam.'

In the second one, irregularly shaped with an octagonal tower, which Sir Anthony told her was called the Prospect Tower, they came to the royal lodgings. Inside, Katheryn was surprised to find that there was no great hall.

'His Majesty had it demolished,' Sir John said. 'He prefers smaller, private lodgings these days.'

As they ascended the stairs, Katheryn caught a glimpse of orchards beyond the windows. Truly, this was a delightful house.

Henry was waiting for her in his presence chamber. When she

curtseyed low, he raised her joyfully and embraced her. 'I have been longing for this day!' he declared, waving away Sir Anthony and Sir John.

He called for wine to be served as Katheryn gazed at her surroundings, the fine French tapestries, the Turkey carpets and the furniture upholstered in velvet and cloth of gold.

'You approve?' he asked, seeing her wonderment.

'It's beautiful,' Katheryn said.

'A fitting place for a honeymoon,' he observed. 'Wait till you see the Queen's lodgings! I have summoned your half-sisters, Lady Baynton and Lady Arundell, to attend on you until your household is formed. We must see to that while we are here.' Katheryn was delighted that she was to have two people she loved to serve her.

There was a sudden sound of hammering in the distance. 'Pay no heed,' Henry said. 'Works are still going on here, but I made them finish the royal apartments first. The hunting hereabouts is excellent. And I've had a road built linking Oatlands to Hampton Court so that I can travel here with ease.'

The wine was poured and, as soon as the page had retired, Henry raised his goblet to Katheryn's. 'To us, darling, and our future! May our marriage be blessed with much happiness and many children.'

'To us!' Katheryn echoed, realising with a start that she might very soon be a mother – the mother of a prince! Suddenly, her fears seemed unimportant. All would be well, she knew it.

'I have sent for my chaplain, the Bishop of London, to come and marry us,' Henry told her. 'We will be wed tomorrow.'

It really was happening. Until now, Katheryn had only half believed it.

Her apartments were as sumptuous as Henry had promised. Isabel and Margaret were waiting in her presence chamber and would have curtseyed, had she not flung her arms around them and whirled them about.

'It's so wonderful to have you here!' she cried.

'I hope you won't treat all your ladies so familiarly!' Isabel laughed.

They walked with her through the suite of rooms that comprised her privy chamber, admiring the tapestries with scenes from antiquity, the Turkey rugs and the gilded panelling. They drank some wine, then dressed Katherine in cloth of gold and brushed her hair until it shone like burnished copper. She walked through to the dining chamber, where a table had been laid with a snowy-white cloth, silver-gilt cutlery and Venetian goblets. Only when the King arrived did Isabel and Margaret discreetly withdraw.

After a delicious supper of salmon and chicken, Henry and Katheryn walked in the terraced gardens, cupped their hands and drank water from the fountains, then found a seat in a delightful walled pleasance. The King gathered her in his arms and kissed her reverently.

'I am counting the hours until tomorrow,' he murmured. 'I love you so much, my Katheryn.' And he kissed her again as if he could not get enough of her.

Chapter 19

1540

The following afternoon, Katheryn was escorted by Sir Anthony and Sir John to the chapel closet, with Isabel and Margaret walking behind, carrying her train. She was wearing her cloth-of-gold gown and the King's pendant depicting Venus and Cupid. Henry was waiting for her, resplendent in silver and white, and raised her hand to his lips before turning to face his chaplain. Katheryn took one look at the portly, fleshy-faced Edmund Bonner, Bishop of London, and disliked him on sight. There was a coarseness about him, and his manner was somewhat fierce and overbearing. Yet he observed all the courtesies, even if he did conduct the marriage rite as if he were casting out demons. But the King seemed impervious and showed only the greatest joy when he and Katheryn were pronounced man and wife.

Afterwards, when Henry had released her from his embrace, everyone made reverences to Katheryn and congratulated her.

'I am so happy for you!' Isabel said, her eyes damp. 'That I should live to see this day!'

Katheryn felt dizzy with elation. She was queen now. She really was queen!

The casements in the large bay window had been left open and the bedchamber was pleasantly temperate. Outside, the rooftops of the palace were silhouetted against a moonlit sky.

Katheryn turned away and walked towards the ornate pearl bed that Henry had specially commissioned from a French craftsman and brought here for their wedding night. The sheets were embroidered with the initial K, a nice touch.

Deftly, saying little, Isabel and Margaret undressed her, then lifted over her head the almost diaphanous lawn night-rail embellished on the low neckline and cuffs with tiny flowers she had embroidered herself in gold thread. Then they combed her long auburn hair until it shone.

There was to be no bedding ceremony. The King had insisted on complete privacy, which was a relief as Katheryn would have hated the fiery Bishop Bonner blessing the bed as she lay in it.

When they were done, Isabel and Margaret kissed Katheryn good night, curtseyed and left her alone. Quickly, she drew a needle from her sewing basket and stuck it in the mattress beneath her pillow. Then she stood by the window, wondering if she should get into bed. She had not been there long when the door opened softly and she turned to see the King, dressed in a long night robe of crimson damask. He was gazing at her in wonder, his eyes raking her figure in the thin night-rail.

'Katheryn! Oh, my darling . . .'

He lurched towards her and crushed her to his broad breast, pressing his mouth on hers and running his hands down her body. She closed her eyes, pretending it was Tom, and was surprised to find herself responding.

'Let me look at you.' Henry's voice was hoarse with desire. He undid the ribbons of her night-rail and it gaped open, partly exposing her breasts. 'Oh, you are beautiful . . .'

He slipped the garment off her shoulders and it fell to the floor, leaving her naked before him. His eyes narrowed with lust.

She had not expected a man of Henry's age and weight to be virile; she had wondered if, when it came to it, he would be capable of the marriage act. So she was surprised when he almost fell upon her, cupping her breasts and kissing her as if he would devour her. Then he drew her towards the bed. She lay down and he heaved himself on top of her, his need for her urgent against her thigh. She could barely breathe with his weight crushing her into the mattress, but then he moved slightly to one side as he reached his hand down to enter her. She remembered to gasp, as if it was painful, held her breath as if she was bearing the discomfort, and then allowed herself to smile. And, really, it was not as repellent as she had feared. There was only the faintest odour of corruption from Henry's diseased legs, and when he had spent himself and rolled away, his thoughts were of her pleasure and his fingers moved between her legs. He knew exactly how to arouse her, and she climaxed very quickly.

They lay together panting gently, his hand flat on her thigh.

'I had not thought to enjoy such bliss,' she whispered.

'My physicians say that a woman has to experience pleasure to conceive,' Henry murmured. 'But I want you to enjoy lovemaking for its own sake too. I trust I did not hurt you, sweetheart?'

'Only a little,' she said, 'and then I started to like it.'

He kissed her, tilting her chin so that he could look into her eyes. 'I think myself in Paradise,' he whispered.

'Paradise, for me, is where you are,' she replied, wondering where she got the inspiration to say such things to him.

'Oh, my darling . . .' He buried his head in the crook of her shoulder. 'I thank God that you are mine, my sweet Tudor rose. And I love you far, far beyond the rest. At last, I have a wife who embodies everything I admire in women: beauty, charm, a pleasant disposition, obedience and virtue. I am blessed indeed.'

Katheryn swallowed. 'I am glad to bring you happiness after the mishaps of your other marriages.'

'This is a new beginning for us both. And I am glad that we are going to be spending time alone together here. I want to enjoy you and get to know you better before we have to return to court and you are proclaimed queen. There's precious little privacy there.'

'When do we have to be back at court?'

'Not for five days. Five days that are just for us.' He kissed her again. 'And now, sweetheart, it is time for sleep.'

He was snoring within moments. Katheryn reached for the needle.

She was awoken by Henry kissing her, his beard rough against her chin, his breath sour. His hands were exploring her body. Obediently, she let him do as he wished, and soon he rolled over on his back and pulled her on top of him.

'Mount me, like a horse!' he commanded, and she climbed astride him, guiding him inside her. The sight of her body in motion held him spellbound, and then his eyes closed in ecstasy.

Afterwards, he pleasured her as before, and then, when they had rested a little, he kissed her and heaved himself out of the bed.

'I have something for you,' he said, like a child eager to reveal a wonderful surprise. She sat up, the sheet falling down to her waist, and watched him unlock a small carved chest on the table under the window. Then he carried it over to the bed, opened it and tipped the contents into her lap.

'The jewels of the queens of England!' he said triumphantly, watching avidly for her reaction.

She gasped at the cascade of riches that lay before her. There must be well over a hundred pieces, she thought, all gleaming gold and precious stones. Her fingers rifled through gems of uncalculated price, ropes of pearls, watches, pendants, brooches, rings . . . and all hers to wear.

'They are fabulous!' she cried. 'Oh, thank you, thank you, Henry!'

He was almost beside himself with happiness. 'Some of these were given by my ancestors to their beloved consorts. They come with my love. I am so glad you like them.'

'How could I not?' she asked, her eyes wide with wonder.

'And these I have had made especially for you,' he said, laying a bulging velvet pouch on top of the jewels and opening it to reveal yet more. She picked up, in turn, a gold brooch with scenes from the life of Noah crafted in diamonds and rubies, a gold ship garnished with diamonds, and a rich collar with her initial set in diamonds. There were gem-studded crosses, a necklace of table diamonds, pomanders, girdles and jewelled books and purses. There was even a gold tablet depicting the Pope lamenting the King's break with Rome.

'Oh, Henry!' she breathed and kissed him lovingly.

She spent a very happy hour with him, admiring the jewels and trying them on, all naked as she was, until the sight of her became too much for him and he claimed her again, although with less vigour this time.

Afterwards, he grinned at her. 'We should be celebrating your uprising as a wife! It is traditional for a husband to give his wife a gift.'

'But you have given me so many already. The jewels . . .'

'Those are but your due, as my Queen. These are your morning gift.' He bent down and retrieved a silk-wrapped bundle he must have had placed on the step of the bed the day before, concealed beneath the curtains. Katheryn sat up and undid the ribbon that bound it, and the silk fell away to reveal four books, exquisitely bound and tooled in purple and crimson velvet, leather, silver and gilt. She read the titles: there were two Mass books, a New Testament and a little book in French, a language she could not read.

'They are beautiful, Henry,' she said, kissing him, although her heart was sinking because he clearly thought her better educated than she was. She had never read a book for pleasure in her life. Reading, like writing, did not come easily to her. 'I will treasure them.'

'They are aids to devotion that I know will bring you spiritual comfort,' he said. 'I have commissioned more for you, but they await the engraving of your initials. They are Latin works by the Church Fathers, Erasmus, St John Chrysostom and Pope Gregory the Great – and there's an excellent book on the difference between royal and ecclesiastical power by the Provost of King's College, Cambridge.'

Latin! She could barely read English.

'You are too good to me,' she said, 'but I may need some help with the Latin.'

'Of course,' Henry smiled. 'I did not expect you to know it. These are the kind of books that ought to be owned by the wife of the Supreme Head of the Church. I myself have enjoyed them and will have much pleasure in discussing them with you.'

That would be amusing, she thought dismally.

But she could not stay dismal for long. It was time for her uprising. When Henry had kissed her and gone off to the ministrations of his gentlemen, she pulled on her night-rail and robe and sent for Isabel and Margaret. She felt happy. Her wedding night had not been as bad as she had feared, and she had experienced the pleasure a wife should feel. She was queen now, and the possessor of great riches and a husband who adored her and was good to her. And this was just the beginning!

Isabel and Margaret were discreet.

'Your Grace is looking radiant!' Isabel said, regarding her wistfully. 'Oh, what it is to be young with your life ahead of you. I wish you every happiness, my dear.'

Katheryn stood impatiently as they dressed her in her scarlet gown, eager to select some pieces from her treasure chest to go with it. She chose rings, pearls, chains and an ouche set with three rubies, which Margaret pinned to her breast. Then Isabel began plaiting her hair.

'No, leave it loose,' Katheryn said.

'But a wife must bind up her hair and cover it, Madam, from the day of her uprising. Only her husband may see it in its glory. I think the King would expect you to put it up.'

'Very well,' she said, resolving to ask Henry to indulge her wish to keep her hair unbound beneath her hood, as she had always worn it. She suffered Isabel to pin up her plaits and cover them with a French hood of black velvet and scarlet with a white band and a pearl biliment.

'Your Grace looks every inch the Queen,' Isabel declared when she had finished, then hesitated. 'May I ask a favour?'

'Of course,' Katheryn said.

'My brother John is still in the Tower. It's been months now and no word. If you feel able, could you ask the King if he will release him?'

'I will,' Katheryn promised. 'I will wait for the right moment.'

She joined Henry for breakfast, which was served to them in the little pleasance, by his order. The morning was fair, with the sweet scent of roses perfuming the air.

'You look beautiful,' he said, his eyes gleaming.

'But I had to put my hair up. Henry, do you think I might still wear it loose?'

'You may do whatever you wish, sweetheart. You are my Queen now, and as such, you are invested with a spiritual virginity, as the mirror of our Blessed Lady, and may wear your hair as you please.'

His words brought home to Katheryn the gravity of her high rank. She now occupied the most powerful and desirable position to which a woman could aspire, and she was going to love every minute of it. But she was also the wife of the Supreme Head of the Church, and that would be reflected in the ceremonial that surrounded her and people's expectations of her. She must not only be virtuous; she must strive to emulate the Virgin Mary's example in all things: in loving the King, bearing him children – heavens, she might be pregnant already! – and in the charities and acts of mercy expected of a queen.

'I want to be worthy of you,' she told Henry, buttering a piece of manchet bread and filling it with a slice of cold beef. 'I mean to carry out my duties as befits the wife of a mighty sovereign, but I am aware that I lack experience in running a great household.'

'Do not worry,' Henry said, finishing his ale. 'You will have officers to do that for you. When we get to Hampton Court, I will appoint them. In the meantime, start thinking about who you want to serve you. I assume you would like your sisters to remain with you, and Sir Edward Baynton as vice chamberlain?'

'Yes, please,' Katheryn nodded.

'Most of those officers appointed to serve the Lady Anna of Cleves can remain with you,' he told her, 'but we can make changes if you would like.'

It seemed that her every wish was to be his command.

'You must choose a badge,' he said.

She had not thought of this. 'What do you recommend, Henry?'

'I thought a crowned rose – for my fair Tudor rose.'

'I love it!' she cried.

'And you need a motto.'

She thought for a few moments. He had been so good to her. 'I want something that shows I place my whole reliance on you. I know! "No other will than his." Does that please you?'

His smile was broad. 'Indeed it does. But it must be in French. *Non autre volonté que le sienne.* I will have it engraved on a bracelet that you can wear for all to see. And we will have your badge and arms set up in all my palaces, replacing the Lady Anna's. I will give the order today.'

There was a discreet tap on the wooden gate.

'Enter!' the King called. And there was Tom Culpeper, looking very pale. Katheryn was shocked to see him. But, she realised, as one of Henry's most favoured gentlemen, of course he would be here. And they had done nothing wrong, nothing to be ashamed of.

Tom did not look at her, but fell on one knee, his face expressionless. 'Your Grace, I have come to inform you that the deed you ordered was carried out yesterday.'

Henry's smile vanished. 'Thank you for letting me know. You may go.'

Tom got up, bowed and left without a glance at Katheryn.

Henry's face was set like stone. He sat there, pensive, not speaking.

'What's happened?' she asked.

He started. It was as if he had forgotten that she was there. 'Alas, darling, I would not have anything bad darken our honeymoon, but you will have to know sometime. Cromwell was executed yesterday. I told them not to trouble me with talk about it because it was our wedding day.'

He had had Cromwell executed on their wedding day? She could not believe it. And yet, it was oddly appropriate. Cromwell had entangled Henry in a marriage that was no marriage and caused him great trouble and grief. No wonder Henry had thought it fitting that he should pay for it on the day he took another wife.

She should be pleased that Cromwell was no more. Uncle Norfolk and all her Howard relatives had loathed him and vowed to topple him. They would be rejoicing that he was dead and that their way to power was unobstructed. Her elevation to queenship had helped to make that possible and Cromwell's death had left a vacancy that the Catholic party would surely fill – and Norfolk and Gardiner were the men to do it. She thought of all the people who had come to grief because of Cromwell – Queen Anne sprang immediately to mind, and Sir Thomas More and Bishop Fisher, saintly men who had died by the axe for supporting the old order. Now he had been struck by his own staff.

'Never again will I rely on any one minister,' Henry was saying. 'After Wolsey and Cromwell, I've learned my lesson. From now on, I will rule alone.' He dabbed at his mouth, laid the napkin on the table and rose slowly to his feet. 'Let us think of more pleasant things, darling,' he said. 'Will you walk with me on the terraces?'

* * *

That afternoon, while the King was having a nap in his apartments, Katheryn ventured into the park. She could not get Cromwell out of her mind and kept wondering how it had been for him at the end and if he had suffered. He was lucky it had not been the stake for him, for Henry had told her that the late minister had been found guilty of heresy as well as treason. She supposed she ought not to feel sorry for him, yet common humanity demanded it.

The weather was still sweltering, and she was hot and uncomfortable in her damask gown. She pulled off her hood, unplaited her hair and let it drift in the breeze. It was tiring walking about in the heat and she surveyed the wide vista of the park, looking for a shady tree under which to sit for a while. A grove of them stood to her left and, as she approached, she saw the remnants of coloured lanterns clinging to the branches. This place had been used for some open-air feast or revel.

She sat down on the grass in a sheltered spot, leaned back against a tree and closed her eyes. She had not been there five minutes when she heard a deep sob coming from somewhere behind her. Startled, she leaned round to see who was there and caught sight of a black puffed sleeve sticking out from behind a tree trunk. It was a man's sleeve, she was sure.

What should she do? Creep away and leave whoever it was to his misery? Maybe that was best, for he might not appreciate her intruding. But, as she got to her feet, a twig cracked beneath her sole and she heard a rustling behind her. When she turned around, she saw Tom Culpeper staring at her, his face ravaged with pain.

'Katheryn!' He was clearly amazed to see her. 'I'm sorry, I mean your Grace.'

'Tom!' She was shocked to see him thus. 'What on earth is the matter?' She knew the answer even as she spoke, and could have kicked herself for being so insensitive.

He shook his head. 'You should know! When I learned that you were to wed the King, I was much grieved. I have not felt well since. And when I saw you lost to me, I was like to die. I cannot eat and I have barely slept. And I have to attend the King daily and hear him sing your praises.'

Katheryn held up a hand to stop him. 'Tom, I am truly sorry for the pain you suffer, but I should not be hearing this. Forget me. I am his wife now and nothing can alter that. Now farewell. I must go.'

Picking up her hood, she turned and walked back towards the palace, leaving him standing there. She felt bad doing so, but she could not be caught talking to him alone.

Henry could not keep his hands off her. Whether they were sitting talking or walking in the gardens or lingering at table after meals, he would caress and kiss her, telling her how much he loved her and how it pleased him to be her servant. And this from the man who was not only a king to be obeyed on earth, but the Supreme Head of the Church, almost a god to be worshipped. It left her in awe.

They spent the time getting to know each other better. Henry liked to talk about religion and knew far more about theology than Katheryn did. She tried to show an interest, but found it hard to stop herself from yawning.

Sometimes, when he was talking about himself and what it meant to rule a kingdom, he came across as somewhat sanctimonious. For him, there was no middle ground, only moral absolutes.

'When I compare my own honesty, openness, simplicity and chivalry with the perfidy and deceit of others, I am amazed,' he told her one day while they were sitting in the pleasance drinking ale cooled in a water bucket. 'I would keep in favour with everybody, but I do not trust a single man. I keep my own counsel. I learned when I was young that fear engenders obedience, and I rule on that precept.' Suddenly, he smiled at her. 'But I would not want *you* to be afraid of me, Katheryn.' His hand touched her cheek.

'Oh, I am not, Henry,' she told him.

During the course of their long conversations, she discovered many facets to this remarkable man she had married. He was highly opinionated, which was not surprising because for years his opinions had been the ones that mattered. He had no conception of ever being wrong. She realised that, in the four months she had known him, she had never heard anyone contradict him.

He was also highly suggestible. For all his insistence that he did not listen to court gossip, it was plain that the impressions he got from it were never effaced. He was intensely jealous of everyone, which predisposed him to think the worst of people. In executing Cromwell, who had been his right arm for years, he had demonstrated that those he had raised high could be destroyed at a stroke. It was a chilling thought.

And yet, there was in him an almost childlike simplicity. He was devout in his religious observances. Once, when his leg was paining him, Katheryn heard one of his chaplains say that he need not kneel to adore the body of his Saviour, but could receive the sacrament sitting in a chair. He'd refused, saying, 'Even if I lie flat on the ground, or under the ground, I should not think I have sufficient reverence to His blessed sacrament.'

That day, he showed Katheryn his psalter, which contained seven exquisite miniature scenes, one portraying him as King David slaying Goliath, others showing him playing his harp or reading a devotional book in his bedroom. On the page where the thirty-seventh Psalm appeared, against the verse 'I have been young and now am old, yet have I not seen the righteous forsaken', she saw a Latin note in Henry's own hand.

'What does that mean?' she asked.

'"A painful saying",' he said, and his eyes were sad. She knew then that, more than anything else, he regretted the loss of his golden youth.

It was inevitable that she would see Tom in these honeymoon days, for Henry had brought very few gentlemen with him and liked to have Tom in attendance anyway. He waited at table, followed at a discreet distance when the King and Queen took their walks, or carried one of the torches that lit Henry up the stair to Katheryn's bedchamber. More than once, she caught him staring at her mournfully, leaving her in no doubt as to his suffering. Even Henry noticed.

'Are you ill, Culpeper?' he asked one supper time as Tom, looking wan, placed a platter of meats before him. 'You have not been yourself lately.'

'Your Grace is kind to ask,' Tom said. 'In truth, I am grieving. I did not like to intrude on your Grace's happiness by telling you, but my father died last month.'

'By God, man, you should have spoken up.'

'I am so sorry,' Katheryn said, wondering if Sir Alexander Culpeper had been reconciled to his son before he died, or if Tom was still disinherited.

'Culpeper, you are excused from your duties at court,' the King said. 'You will go to your house at Penshurst to recover, and you shall have two thousand crowns for your expenses.'

Katheryn loved to see this side of Henry, loved the kindness and generosity in his heart.

'Your Grace, I cannot fully express my thanks,' Tom said, almost swaying on his feet. 'With your leave, I will depart in the morning.'

Katheryn felt sorry for him. She knew his grief was not all for his father. It was for her.

After five blissful days of peace, Henry and Katherine left Oatlands and moved to Hampton Court. The palace was breathtaking. Katheryn gasped at the sight of the vast great hall with its magnificent carved ceiling and at the sumptuous apartments prepared for her. She stared at walls decorated with gold and silver carvings, cherubs frolicking along friezes, and the gorgeous tapestries that hung in the spacious chambers. Everything that could be gilded had been, and her arms, impaled with the King's, were everywhere: on hangings, embroideries and furniture, and even in the glass of the windows. The floors were laid with priceless carpets, and the ceilings set with mirrors.

After she had hugged and kissed him and told him how wonderful he was to her, Henry disappeared into his new secret lodgings, which extended beyond his privy chamber, and to which access was permitted only to the highly privileged. Katheryn dined there with him on that first evening and was surprised to find the presence chamber almost deserted and the privy chamber beyond it crowded with those who no longer had a place in the King's intimate circle.

'I value my privacy,' Henry told her over the roast beef. 'I have long wanted to live in a secluded lodging with only my gentlemen and grooms of the chamber to serve me.'

Katheryn suspected that this need had arisen on account of his episodes of ill health and immobility; that he did not want to be seen as weak in any way or have people think he was losing his grip on affairs.

He helped himself to more sauce. 'I have decreed that, in future, petitioners must not molest me with their suits, but must send all claims in writing to my Privy Council.'

It sounded like a retreat from public life. She hoped it would not mean an end to all court festivities, for she was longing to play her part as queen to the full.

Her own lodgings were sumptuous, extending along the north side of Cloister Green Court, opposite the King's; a range of shared reception rooms connected them. She marvelled at the grand beds, the walnut furniture, the Flanders tapestries and Turkey carpets. With just herself, Isabel and Margaret to occupy them, the rooms seemed vast. Soon, though, they would be filled with people – her new household and the courtiers who would come flocking.

Her belongings had just been unpacked and put away when Henry came to escort her to the old Queen's apartments and bade her look out of a window overlooking the Inner Court of the palace.

'See yonder,' he said. 'My new astronomical clock! It has just been installed. It shows the hours, the month, the date, the number of days since the beginning of the year, the phases of the moon, the movement of the constellations in the zodiac, and the time of high water at London Bridge, which is most useful for planning journeys by river. And look, Katheryn, there is the sun revolving around the earth.'

She was astounded. The clock was a marvel, and it was beautiful too. How anyone had devised it was beyond her. But Henry loved astronomy and astrology, and had many clocks; they fascinated him.

'I have something else to show you,' he said. She followed him through the chambers and galleries that led to his lodgings and then down the stair to his privy garden. There, in the centre, stood a new sundial.

'I designed it myself,' he told her, eager as a schoolboy. 'It shows the hour of the day, the day of the month, the sign of the moon, the ebbing and flowing of the sea, and many other things.'

She was amazed that he knew how such things worked. He was extraordinary. Every day, she was finding out new and marvellous things about him.

She had not yet been proclaimed queen; Henry wanted a few more days to enjoy their privacy before letting the world in. They kept to her chambers or his, and tried to avoid being seen by too many people, but one day, Uncle Norfolk was announced by the usher who guarded her outer door.

'Welcome back, niece, or should I say "your Grace"?' His greeting was jubilant. She had never seen him so elated.

'You should, my lord!' she replied, extending her hand for him to kiss, which he did fervently. 'You are clearly aware of what has come to pass in my absence.'

'His Majesty himself wrote to inform me. I was delighted to hear the news, as you may imagine. We have a Howard queen – and the false churl is dead. It is a victory for the Catholic faith! Watch now as the reformers scuttle underground like rats. Only yesterday, that Lutheran Robert Barnes was burned as a heretic. Now you shall see the King clamp down on reform and heresy.'

Katheryn shrank from the prospect of anyone suffering such a dreadful death, and from the thought of Henry giving the order for it, although she knew that a taste of hellfire on earth might prompt a heretic to recant at the last minute and spare them eternal damnation.

'Our hour has come!' the Duke was saying. 'When it comes to appointing your household, think of your family and your house.'

'I had already intended to do that,' she told him. 'Do not think me unmindful of what you have done for me.' As she spoke, she realised she would never have spoken so confidently to her uncle a few short months ago. The King's love, and becoming queen, had done wonders for her.

* * *

'I am going to Richmond today, darling,' Henry told her as he rose from her bed on a warm morning in early August. 'I must see the Lady Anna and obtain her signature on the deed ending our pretended marriage.'

Katheryn had no qualms about his going. She knew he had never loved Anna, and that she was no rival. She spent the day practising dance steps and ordering more gowns.

Part Three

'To be a queen, Fortune did me prefer'

Chapter 20

1540

On the eighth day of August, the highest peeresses of the realm dressed Katheryn in royal robes of purple and ermine. She could barely stand still for she was both excited and nervous. Today, her marriage was to be announced to the world. From henceforth, she would enjoy all the privileges of a queen. She was praying that the courtiers – and the country at large – would welcome her.

As the procession formed in her apartments, the Dowager Duchess of Norfolk placed a gold coronet on her step-granddaughter's head. Then, with the heralds going before, Katheryn walked through the great doors of her lodgings, her long train trailing behind her, and processed through Hampton Court Palace to the Chapel Royal. The galleries and the chapel were packed with courtiers, craning their necks to see her. Many were smiling or clapping; only a few were staring at her doubtfully.

She took her place in the Queen's chair beside the King's empty throne in the royal pew, gazing up at the ornate blue-and-gold ceiling. Mass was celebrated and she was prayed for as queen. Afterwards, still very much on her mettle, she dined in her great chamber, sitting alone beneath the cloth of estate bearing the royal arms quartered with her own, and a herald proclaimed her queen of England. There was applause from the crowds of people watching, and she smiled at them with as much graciousness as she could muster, feeling quite dizzy with elation at being the first lady in the land.

The rest of August was given over to celebrations. To her delight, there were feasts, sports and banquets, all in her honour. She hunted most days with Henry, exhilarated by the thrill of the chase and the triumph of the kill.

'All I want, sweetheart,' Henry told her, as they rode back to the palace early one evening, 'is to reign in peace with you by my side. I swear you will want for nothing if my love might procure it. You are so highly beloved, far, far beyond the rest.' He leaned across from his saddle and kissed her hand.

When her household was appointed that month, many of those who had served Queen Anna, and Queen Jane before her, were recalled. Henry's cousin, the Earl of Rutland, was chamberlain, and, as he had promised, Isabel's husband, Sir Edward Baynton, was vice chamberlain. The King's niece, Lady Margaret Douglas, was made chief lady-of-honour.

At Katheryn's wish, the Howards received a goodly share of places. Norfolk's daughter, the Duchess of Richmond, whom she liked well, was restored as one of the great ladies of the household. She also asked for Lady William Howard, the former Margred Gamage, who was lively company, and the Countess of Bridgewater, who had been kind to her at Lambeth. She feared that the Duke's sister-in-law, Mary Arundell, Countess of Sussex, a very intense girl with almond eyes, might be hard work, and Katherine Willoughby, Duchess of Suffolk, might think her mistress an ignoramus, the Duchess being famed for her learning. But both young ladies proved to be good company.

The middle-aged Lady Rutland, the wife of the Queen's chamberlain, was a grand dame of the old school, kindly, level-headed and generous. She was to head the nine ladies of the privy chamber, chief of whom were Isabel and Margaret. Katheryn did not forget her stepmother, Lady Edmund Howard, who came to Hampton Court almost weeping with gratitude. Among the other ladies and maids were Elizabeth Seymour, Anne Bassett, Lucy Somerset and two newcomers: the fair Bess Harvey and the very beautiful Elizabeth Fitzgerald, who had been recommended by Katheryn's cousin, the Earl of Surrey. Because Bishop Gardiner had been so zealous in making her queen, Katheryn appointed his niece, the demure Lady Wriothesley, to her privy chamber.

Altogether, she felt comfortable with her ladies, which was why she did not reappoint Jane Rochford. She feared that Jane might be angry at her abandoning Tom Culpeper, although surely she'd understood why she had had to do it. Katheryn had let their friendship go and felt awkward about it.

Serving as chamberers were some of the young women who had been her companions at Lambeth: Meg Morton, Alice Restwold, Mrs Luffkyn and Mrs Frideswide. Katheryn offered Kat Tilney a place too, for she and Meg were normally inseparable, but Kat's mother was ill and she felt she should go to her.

Katheryn blushed as her old friends thanked her for her graciousness to them. She had felt honour-bound to offer them places, hoping to buy their silence, for they had all been privy to the secrets of her past. Her heart plummeted when she thought of all the people who knew about her affairs with Harry and Francis. What if they gossiped? For the first time, it occurred to her to wonder what Francis might do now that she had married the King. Surely he would not dare claim her for himself?

Too many people, too many secrets. The smile never left her face, but she was realising, with dread, that she would never likely know peace of mind again while there was a chance that someone might talk and the King get to hear of it. This was brought home to her when Alice Restwold rose from her curtsey and declared, with a sly smile, 'I'm sure your Grace has never forgotten the good times we shared at Lambeth.'

That night, Katheryn summoned Alice ahead of the others who were to make her ready for bed. 'I want you to have these,' she said, handing her biliments of goldsmith's work for a French hood, and a tablet of gold, rich gifts that, ordinarily, chamberers did not look to receive. 'For the good times we shared.'

Alice's eyes widened at the treasures that lay in her hands. 'I understand, Madam. Thank you. You can rely on my discretion.'

Lying in bed, waiting for the King, Katheryn reflected that it was better to have these old acquaintances under her eye. She would make sure that they had no cause to betray her.

* * *

Her days were one long round of amusements: she did nothing but dance and rejoice and bask in the adulation that came her way and the approval of Uncle Norfolk and her family. She was not interested in trying to involve herself in state affairs; she had not the head for politics, or for court intrigue. When her ladies began gossiping about the Lady Anna of Cleves, as her former mistress was now called, wondering what that lady was doing now, or what it was about her that the King had disliked, she silenced them, for she would not hear a bad word said about Anna.

Each evening at six, Sir Thomas Heneage, the King's Groom of the Stool, brought her news of her husband, for which she always thanked him prettily. But, more often than not, she had already seen Henry in the day, for he spent as much time as he could with her.

He doted on her. He was constantly touching or embracing her, and he came to her bed every night. She was used now to his body and his need for her, and tried not to wish that he was younger, slimmer and more virile. Sometimes he had difficulty in penetrating her, and would withdraw, frustrated and humiliated. Then she would use her wiles, and her fingers, to arouse him again, usually with success.

'Alas, Katheryn, I wish I could be a better husband to you,' he would murmur. 'You should have known me when I was young. No man could touch me, in the field, at the jousts, or in bed.'

She always smiled at him. 'I love you just as you are.'

'Was ever man so blessed?' he would sigh, kissing her.

Her every whim he gratified. Each day, she wore new gowns. She had completely captured his heart.

It moved her to hear the new bidding prayer that was being read not only in the Chapel Royal, but also in all the churches in England, with her name superseding Queen Anna's. It brought home to her the gravity of her queenly rank and made her realise she was ill-prepared for it. But she would learn. She had the King's love, unlimited riches at her disposal, power at her fingertips, and an army of servants at her beck and call. She tried not to let it all go to her head. Pride, she knew, went before a fall. Yet she was aware that she was changing, growing in confidence and becoming more demanding and particular, and she could hear the imperious tone in her voice when she was giving orders.

One day, when her dressmaker, Mrs Josselyn, brought her a finished gown for inspection, she saw that the woman looked troubled.

'Is everything all right?' she asked.

'Oh, yes, Madam. I was just worrying that my work would not please your Grace.'

Katheryn wondered if the dressmaker had heard of the sharp reprimand she had given her tailor the previous day for making a kirtle that was too short. She really must learn to watch her tongue; it was all too easy to lose her temper when things were not exactly as she wanted them.

'It's a gorgeous dress,' she said, smiling. 'Thank you for your hard work.'

Henry could see no fault in her. 'You are the perfect wife in every respect,' he told her. 'Soon, God willing, you will be with child.' They were in his barge, enjoying an evening cruise along the Thames, with musicians playing for them in the stern. The hot weather still showed no sign of abating, and they were enjoying the breeze from the river.

It was not the first time Henry had expressed the hope that she would give him sons. Tonight, she knew she must disappoint him. Her flowers had arrived that morning.

She had always loved children and liked the idea of becoming a mother. It would give her immense status. She felt so blessed and lucky, she was sure that God and His Holy Mother would protect her through the perils of pregnancy and birth. Her children would be next in line to the throne after Prince Edward. It was a thrilling thought. Not that she wished any ill to that precious little boy, of course. She looked forward to meeting him, and the King's daughters.

'You're quiet, darling,' Henry observed, as they passed the torchlit streets of Kingston.

'I think we have not been blessed this month,' she said.

He patted her hand. 'No matter. We have not been married four weeks. God moves in His own time. Maybe He will bless us soon.'

'I pray for it,' she said.

A servant brought them wine and gilded marchpane, and Katheryn settled into the crook of Henry's arm to enjoy them and the journey. People were lazing on the riverbank, their day's work done, enjoying the balmy evening, and she waved to them. The King smiled indulgently.

'This is meant to be a private trip!'

'They don't know who we are.' There was no coat of arms on the barge.

'They will probably guess. Look, they are standing up!' He raised his own hand in salute, and some of the people on the banks knelt to him. 'See, they do know who we are.'

When they had rounded a bend in the river, Katheryn saw a large complex of buildings ahead on their left. The grounds were overgrown and the place looked abandoned and creepy in the twilight.

'That was the monastery of Syon,' the King said. 'It was dissolved last year.'

'Is no one living there?' she asked.

'No. I have not yet decided what to do with it. It stands on prime land.'

Katheryn felt sad that such a great religious house had been brought low. She shivered a little. She would not like to go inside that empty, echoing monastery. But there was something else on her mind.

'Henry,' she said, gazing up at him, 'I have a favour to ask.'

'Ask anything you like,' he told her.

'It is for my brothers. They have been brought up in my lord of Norfolk's household. They are now very proficient at knightly skills, and it would mean a lot to me to have them at court.'

Henry beamed. 'I can accommodate three more gentlemen in my Privy Chamber. They will have good wages and new robes, and your uncle Lord William can show them their duties.'

'Thank you!' Katheryn cried, and gave him a kiss.

'Anything for you,' he said, squeezing her hand. 'I have a mind to give your uncle, the Earl of Sussex, the office of Lord Great Chamberlain, which has been vacant since Cromwell was arrested. It is an influential post in the Privy Chamber, and I know I can rely on him to fill it well. And young Surrey is to be a Knight of the Garter.'

Uncle Norfolk would be pleased! Katheryn flung her arms around

Henry. 'You are so good to me and mine!' She could not wait to tell her cousin Surrey the good news. They were much of an age, and she was fond of him and his wife, Frances.

'There is one other thing I would ask,' she ventured. 'My half-brother John Leigh has been in the Tower for some time. I have always thought him a good man. Would your Grace consider freeing him?'

Henry frowned. 'Hmm. I will look into the matter, sweetheart, and consider it.'

He sat there thoughtfully for a while, then changed the subject. 'I have a mind to ask Master Holbein to paint you. I would like a miniature of you to carry around with me.'

'I should be very happy to sit for him,' she replied.

They were nearing Hampton Court now and the oarsmen were pulling in towards the landing stage. The night sky was dark blue and velvety, patterned by stars, and the palace lit up by torches. Henry helped Katheryn out of the boat and gave her his hand. Together, arm in arm, they strolled into the palace.

For her portrait, she dressed in a French hood and a tawny gown with a deep jewelled biliment that Henry had given her. She wore fur sleeves, which she would take off later because it was too hot to wear them for long. She chose a golden ouche with a table diamond from which hung a ruby and a pearl, and a heavy pearl necklace, all pieces from the Queen's jewels. When she was ready, she seated herself in her presence chamber. Her brothers were arriving at court today and she wanted to greet them before she summoned Master Holbein.

They bowed low, then embraced her. They towered above her and she marvelled at how manly they had become. Charles was twenty-four now, Henry twenty-two and George twenty-one.

'How well you have done for yourself, and for us, sister,' Charles said.

'We are very grateful,' Henry told her. 'My income from my new post will enable me to marry.'

'Marry?' Katheryn echoed.

'The fool thinks himself in love!' George teased.

'I am in love. Grow up!' Henry retorted. 'Her name is Ann and she is very comely.'

'I hope to meet her,' Katheryn smiled.

'You are looking every inch the queen, Kitty,' Charles said. 'I assume I may still call you that?'

'Of course,' she smiled. 'Is there any news of our sister Mary?'

'Yes, she too is to be married, to Mr Trafford, a young gentleman of Lancashire. My lord Duke arranged it.'

Katheryn was startled. 'It's hard to believe she is twelve years old and about to become a wife. I have not seen her since she was tiny. I would not recognise her, I'm sure. And now she is going to live in the north, so I doubt I will see her for a long time – and I had hoped to have her at court. It's sad. I have a sister, but I don't know her.'

'I hear she is quite happy to be wed,' Henry said. 'Trafford is only fourteen. They will live with his parents. Maybe Mary can come to court one day.'

'Who is that young lady over there?' Charles asked, indicating Margaret Douglas, who was sitting in a window seat with Mary Howard.

'That's the King's niece, the Lady Margaret Douglas,' Katheryn told him.

'What a beauty she is!'

'No, Charles, she's not for you,' Katheryn declared. 'She will be married off to the King's advantage one day.'

'But I can dream . . .' He winked at her. It was good to have her brothers at court.

After her sitting with Master Holbein had ended, she joined the ladies in her privy chamber and several young gentlemen came to keep them company. As some played cards and others played music, her cousin Surrey came over and seated himself on a stool beside her great chair. He was of a mercurial, artistic temperament and could be quite wild sometimes. Everyone knew what his opinions were, for he was loud to voice them, but he had a great wit and had always been kind to Katheryn.

'How is my cousin enjoying being queen?' he asked.

'Wonderfully,' she enthused.

'My father sings your praises all day long, and that's not like the old curmudgeon.' He grinned. 'In truth, we are all grateful to you. It is no mean thing to ensnare a king.'

Katheryn laughed. 'I think his Grace did the snaring.'

'And now the reformists are muzzled!' he smiled. 'The days of Archbishop Cranmer and the upstart Seymours are numbered. I hear they're squabbling among themselves now, which leaves us conservatives a free hand.'

Katheryn bristled a little. 'And you think the King is not master of them all?'

'He is highly suggestible and easily led, and it is our job to see that he is not led in the wrong direction. That is why your role is so important. While he loves you so deeply, we have nothing to fear, so it is essential that you keep his affection.'

'He is not as simple as that,' Katheryn said coldly, angry at Surrey for thinking that Henry could be manipulated so easily. 'He is very suspicious and finds it hard to trust people. He worries about those around him embracing Lutheran ideas, especially the younger generation, like us. He is wary of ambitious courtiers. He likes it when people are unsure of him. It is unwise to judge him as you do, for he is no puppet.'

'You *have* been observant,' Surrey observed. 'Yet he is still suggestible – and dangerous. He burns Catholics for supporting the Pope, and Protestants for heresy. We all have to watch our step lest we get fried! And if the King will not curb the reformers at court, then we must.'

She shook her head. 'You had best watch your tongue, my lord, lest it get you in trouble.'

He gave her a sharp look. 'You would not tell him what I said?'

'No, but I can see you fear that I might. And that is the measure of the King's power!' She smiled at him defiantly.

'All right, I concede you the victory,' he laughed. 'His Grace should know what a loyal champion he has!'

* * *

The summer remained hot and dry; there was plague in London, and the court moved to Windsor Castle, which seemed old-fashioned and gloomy after the glories of Hampton Court. Henry ordered the bishops to exhort the people to pray for rain and an end to the pestilence, and there were processions of clergy and supplicants in the streets.

'We are going away,' he told Katheryn. 'It is time to continue our honeymoon with a hunting progress.'

Excitedly, Katheryn ordered her women to pack, herself choosing what she would take. When Henry walked into her bedchamber and saw the gowns piled on the bed, the shoes all over the floor and hoods on every surface, he clapped his hand to his forehead.

'It's no wonder my treasury is empty!' he groaned in mock anguish. Then he put his arm around a giggling Katheryn. 'But you look lovely in them all, my darling, so it is money well spent.'

They left Windsor on 22 August and rode through Berkshire to Reading. There they stayed in the deserted abbey, where the lodgings once used by numerous kings and queens were still in good repair. Katheryn found it eerie, peering into the great empty church, imagining invisible monks and the echo of plainchant. How sad it was that there were no religious houses left now. She was glad when it was time to leave.

They rode on into Oxfordshire and Ewelme, a beautiful village nestling in lush countryside, where they stayed in the old royal manor house.

'I was conceived here, so my father told me,' Henry said, as they walked in the gardens. 'It used to belong to my sister Mary, the French Queen. She died seven years ago.' He looked wistful; he had clearly been fond of her. 'It's a good base for hunting.'

With some courtiers in attendance, they walked through the village to see the church. There, Henry showed Katheryn the magnificent tomb of Thomas, the son of Geoffrey Chaucer the poet. 'He was once lord of the manor of Ewelme, and fought at Agincourt,' he said. Katheryn wished she knew more about England's history, because it would please Henry, but she had vaguely heard of Agincourt.

Henry had moved on. 'And this is the tomb of Thomas's daughter, Alice Chaucer. She married the Duke of Suffolk. My grandmother, the

Lady Margaret Beaufort, was married for a short time to their son. The last Duke of Suffolk proved to be a traitor, which is how the manor came to the Crown.' Katheryn thought the white marble effigy of Alice Chaucer very beautiful.

Outside, crowds had gathered to see them. By the village pond, an old woman told Katheryn that the fairies played there and the water had healing powers. Just then, Henry stumbled on a stone and nearly fell into the pond, getting his velvet shoe wet.

'They'll have to call it the King's Pool now!' he said, and everyone laughed.

That evening, after he and Katheryn had dined in private, a messenger arrived from the Council and handed him a sealed document. His eyes narrowed as he read it and he waved the man away.

'What is wrong?' Katheryn asked.

'Nothing to bother yourself with, sweetheart,' he said. 'Just malicious gossip.'

His words chilled her. Too many people knew too many things about her.

'If it is about me, I should like to know what has been said,' she told him.

Henry hesitated for a moment. 'A priest has been brought before the magistrates at Windsor for having spoken unbefitting words about you.'

'What words?' What could a priest at Windsor possibly know about her?

'The Council does not say. But I will not have it. No one will be allowed to impugn your honour. He shall be confined to his diocese and admonished to be more temperate in the use of his tongue.'

She wondered what Henry would say if he knew that her honour had already been impugned, as he would see it. Again, guilt struck her.

They journeyed on, stopping at Rycote, Notley and Buckingham, and, at the end of August, came to the royal manor of Grafton in Northamptonshire.

On the first evening, as they supped together in a panelled chamber overlooking open fields, Henry told Katheryn that his grandfather, King Edward IV, had married in secret at Grafton. 'His nobles wanted him to wed a French princess, but he loved a widow, Elizabeth Wydeville, and defied them. It caused a lot of trouble.' He chuckled. 'It seems that marrying for love runs in my family!' He raised her hand and kissed it.

They had been married for a month now and he was more loving and amorous than ever, and so openly demonstrative. His hands must always be touching and caressing her. He would gaze into her face and tell her how beautiful she was, not caring who was nearby.

'I have had this gold medal struck to commemorate our marriage,' he told her, and placed it in her hand. It was embossed with Tudor roses and true lovers' knots entwined, and carried the inscription: *HENRICUS VIII: RUTILANS ROSA SINE SPINA.*

'What does it say?' she asked.

'It says you are my red rose without a thorn,' he told her.

Thorns were spikes; they hurt. She would never hurt him, for she thought too highly of him and loved him in her way, so the inscription was apt. Yet, again, she felt guilty, for he thought her perfect and she wasn't.

In the second week of September, they travelled south to Ampthill, where they stayed for a fortnight. Henry went hunting, while Katheryn sunned herself in the pretty garden with her ladies and maids.

'I was here before with the late Princess Dowager after she was banished from court,' Anne Parr told her one morning. It took a moment for Katheryn to realise that she was talking about Queen Katherine. 'I was very young and had not long lost my mother, who was very close to the Princess Dowager. We were all prisoners, really. Fortunately, the King allowed me to leave and found me a post at court. I felt bad about abandoning my kind mistress, but glad to be gone, for Ampthill was a dismal place to be back then.'

'It is best not to dwell on such things,' Lady Suffolk advised, fanning herself with the veil she had removed. It was hot and the garden looked parched.

'If the Princess Dowager had not defied the King and had agreed to an annulment, he would have given her the world,' Lady Rutland observed. 'Such misplaced courage!'

Katheryn did not want to hear any more of this talk. She did not like to think of Henry sending a queen from court to a lonely exile in the shires. There was to be dancing after dinner and she needed to decide what she would wear.

'I hear that Will Somers is to entertain us this evening,' she said. When she became queen, she had been disconcerted to find that the King's eccentric little fool, with his wicked wit, was an almost permanent fixture in Henry's chambers and never far from his master's side. He was privy to many of his master's private thoughts. No one dared to speak to Henry as familiarly as Somers did, yet his discretion was absolute. Katheryn wasn't sure she liked him, being wary of his barbed tongue, which she had seen used to effect on others, but he was always pleasant to her. Of course, he knew how much Henry loved her.

Dinner was excellent and Somers very funny. He had the court holding its sides and crying with laughter.

'What beast is it that has her tail between her eyes?' he cried. 'It is a cat when she licks her arse.' Henry roared at that.

At one point, Thomas, the King's juggler, entered the hall.

'Time for my performance!' he said to Somers. But Somers was having none of it. Out he stormed and came back carrying a jug of milk and a bread roll.

'Will you give me a spoon, Harry?' he asked the King, as Thomas glared at him.

'Alas, I have none,' Henry told him.

'Ooh . . .' went the courtiers, and the King laughed.

Somers grinned at them and, handing his master a piece of the bread, burst into an impromptu song:

> 'This bit Harry I give to thee
> And this next bit must serve for me,
> Both which I'll eat apace.'

He grabbed back Henry's share and handed it to Katheryn.

'This bit Madam unto you,
And this bit I myself eat now,
And the rest upon thy face.'

So saying, he turned to Thomas, raised the jug and threw the milk at him, then ran cackling out of the hall, with Thomas, bawling insults and dripping with milk, running after him. Katheryn laughed so much she could barely catch her breath. Henry, too, was in fits, as was everyone else present.

When the tables were cleared, the musicians played and the dancing began. Katheryn was partnered in turn by most of the gentlemen of the Privy Chamber, while the King, whose leg was paining him a little, looked on indulgently, flushed with wine.

When it grew late, he stood up, took her hand and bowed to the company, then led her off to bed.

'I hope you will not mind if I do not play the husband tonight,' he said as he lay down beside her. 'This wretched leg is getting worse and I think I shall have to see my physician tomorrow. Just let me hold you, darling.'

She sank into his arms and began to drift off to sleep. But the quietness of the night was abruptly shattered by shouts and laughter from outside their window. Henry disengaged himself, sat up and reached for the sword he always kept by the bed in case some would-be assassin attacked him in the night.

'What's going on?' Katheryn asked.

The carousing – for that was what it sounded like – continued in a rowdy fashion.

'What the devil . . .' Henry heaved himself to his feet, stalked over to the window and opened it. Katheryn joined him and was shocked to see, sprawled below in the garden, Sir Edward Baynton, as drunk as might be, with a group of other men, whom she recognised as members of the King's and her own privy chambers. They were passing around flagons of ale and ewers of wine, and some were singing a bawdy song.

Henry's face had turned puce. He pulled on his night robe, ordered Katheryn back to bed and flung open the door. 'Send for Sir Anthony Wingfield!' he commanded the young knight who had been sleeping on a pallet bed outside.

When the King's Vice Chamberlain presented himself, Henry barked at him, 'Look out of that window and see yonder fools below. I will not have *anyone* drunk and disorderly in my presence or that of the Queen. You will advise them of my pleasure concerning the sober and temperate behaviour I would have them use at all times in my household.'

'You will not dismiss Sir Edward? He is a loyal officer,' Katheryn said when Sir Anthony had gone.

'Not this time,' Henry said, returning to bed. 'But I shall be watching him.'

Isabel was full of apologies when she came to attend Katheryn in the morning.

'Be assured I have given Edward a piece of my mind!' she said. 'What was he thinking of, acting as if he were some young knave trying to impress his fellows? The great fool!'

'Think no more of it,' Katheryn urged. 'I thought it was funny, but I didn't dare tell the King that.' In truth, she had not thought Edward had it in him to put off his dignity and act like an idiot.

'Well, *I* didn't think it funny!' Isabel declared. 'Edward and every other man involved will be on their knees this morning, apologising to the King.' She jabbed a pin in a cushion as if she was stabbing her errant husband.

Elizabeth Seymour came in. 'Your Grace, one of his Majesty's ushers is here. He says the King is unwell and has taken to his bed.'

Katheryn pulled on the hood she had chosen to wear. 'I must go to him.'

She hastened to the King's lodgings, but was stopped in the antechamber by Dr Butts, one of his doctors.

'Your Grace, you may not enter. His Majesty is indisposed. His leg is inflamed and he has a fever. My colleagues are with him now. I will bring you word later.'

'But I must see him! He will want me to be there.'

Dr Butts looked at her kindly. 'I fear, Madam, that he would not have you see him looking poorly. He has ordered that you stay away, and bids you take your pastime with your ladies until he is better.'

She hesitated. She wanted to do Henry's bidding, for she hated sickrooms, but felt that she owed it to him to try to see him. He would approve of that, surely.

'Let an ailing man keep his pride,' the doctor murmured.

'Very well,' she said, 'but tell me, is he in danger?' She shied away from the thought of Henry dying. She had grown fond of him and could not imagine a world without him.

'Not at present, Madam, but we are concerned. I will send word, or come to you, if there is any change.'

She sat listlessly on her favourite shady bench, listening to her women chattering. Abruptly, she got up and went to the chapel, where she knelt to pray for Henry's recovery. There was something else on her mind too; something for which to beseech God. Her flowers were late, only by a few days, but she was beginning to be hopeful. She imagined herself telling Henry the glad news that she was with child. How pleased he would be with her!

As she left the chapel, Dr Butts was waiting for her.

'Your Grace, we think there is an infection in both the King's legs. We have applied plasters and bandages and are hoping to see an improvement soon.'

'May I see his Majesty?'

'Not yet. Allow the treatment time to work. We have given him a draught and he is sleeping now.'

She wondered if she dared mention her secret hope to this kind doctor and ask his opinion. She was desperate to confide in someone. But maybe it was best to keep silent until she was sure.

The next day, they told her that Henry had suddenly rallied and was asking for her. Again she sped to his apartments, wondering if it was too soon to cheer him by telling him her exciting secret.

To her surprise, he was up and dressed and sitting in a chair by an open window, his legs stretched out on a large footstool.

'Katheryn! Oh, what a joy it is to see you!' He held out his arms and she ran into them. He kissed her lovingly.

She could not resist the temptation. 'There is something I have been longing to tell you,' she said as she knelt on the floor at his side. 'I think I am with child.'

She had never seen anyone's face light up so quickly.

'You are sure?' Henry asked, grasping her hand tightly.

'Almost,' she said.

'Then I will pray that you are right and that God has indeed blessed us,' he said, kissing her soundly. 'But not a word of this to anyone else, mind. Let it be our secret for now.'

They moved on to Dunstable and then The More, which Anne Parr said had been another residence of Queen Katherine in her exile. Katheryn was pleased that they would be there for only two nights.

It was now early October, and every day Henry asked Katheryn if she still thought herself with child. He examined her body for signs, but there were none – yet there was no sign of her flowers either. It was, after all, early days and, as those days went on, he became increasingly hopeful, and protective of her. Her every whim was to be gratified. He gave her two rosaries adorned with crosses and tassels, and a gold brooch with rubies and diamonds encircling a gold relief depicting the story of Noah. To please her, he granted her brother George a pension of a hundred marks and some manors that had lately been the property of Wilton Abbey, and appointed him and Charles gentleman pensioners – members of his own elite guard. Isabel received a gift of money for her good service to Katheryn, and Sir Edward was given a manor, a sure sign that his recent transgression had been forgotten.

On the eighth day of October, the first rain since June fell. Hearing it spatter on her window, Katheryn and her maids ran down into the garden and twirled about, revelling in it. The chapel at The More was crowded that day with people giving thanks for the rain. The drought had been dreadful, the relentless heat exhausting, but now it was cooler

251

and very pleasant. And soon they would be home. At the King's insistence, Katheryn travelled in a litter, nursing her secret. She was sure now that she was with child.

Chapter 21

1540

Later that October, they arrived at Windsor. Henry assured her that she was quite safe, for the plague had died down and he had given orders that anyone who had been in contact with it was to leave the town.

Katheryn was glad to alight in the upper ward and go into her apartments. It had been a long journey and she decided to rest on her bed before having a wash and changing her clothes. Later, attired in a crimson gown with a black velvet partlet and one of the new stand-up collars, she joined the King for supper in his dining parlour and was surprised to find him looking ill at ease.

'What is wrong?' she asked, when the servants had left them alone.

'There is something you should know, Katheryn, and I'd rather you heard it from me than from idle gossip.' A shiver went through her; pray God no one had betrayed the secrets of her past.

Henry sighed. There was a slight flush to his cheeks. 'I am told that rumour credits me with getting the Lady Anna of Cleves with child when I visited her in August. There is, of course, no truth in it.'

Relief flooded Katheryn. 'Of course not,' she said. 'I would not believe it for a moment.' How anyone would credit such a calumny was beyond belief, for no one could doubt where Henry's heart lay. And he had never loved or fancied Anna.

'Why would anyone spread such a rumour?' she wondered, as he served her some chicken.

'The Lady Anna was laid up in bed with a bad humour of the stomach. I am told she is better now. But some fool put two and two together and made five, and let it be known that she was suffering the sickness of pregnancy. If they are discovered, they will know my displeasure!' He downed his wine and refilled the goblet. 'You will not let this upset you, sweetheart?'

'Not at all,' Katheryn told him.

He raised her hand to his lips. 'No sign yet of your courses?'

'No,' she smiled. 'And I don't think there will be.'

Two days later, they returned to Hampton Court. That night, as Henry snored beside her, Katheryn was awakened by a cramping pain in the bottom of her stomach. With mounting dismay, she thought she knew what it portended.

Rising to go to the close stool, she saw blood on the sheets. The sight was so awful that she burst into tears. Henry sat up suddenly, his hand already reaching for his sword.

'What is it?' he asked. 'What is wrong?' Then he noticed the blood. 'Oh, darling . . .'

Katheryn was sobbing uncontrollably. 'I am so sorry, Henry. So sorry! I so wanted to gladden you with a prince. I really did think I was with child. I'm so sorry . . .'

He rose stiffly and came to her, folding her in his arms. 'And maybe you were with child. There are many babes lost early on, as I well know. Do not distress yourself, Katheryn.'

He gentled her until she had calmed down a little, then sent for Isabel.

'Her Grace needs you,' he said when she arrived in her night robe, her greying hair loose about her shoulders. Then he was gone.

'Oh, Isabel . . .' Katheryn began weeping again and, between sobs, explained what had happened.

'It is not unusual to lose a first baby,' Isabel said. 'I did, and I know several others who have. It usually happens very early on. Or you may have just had a delayed course. That can happen when you commence married life. It is all the upheaval and adjusting to the, um, physical side.' Katheryn could not tell her that she had been well used to that long before she wed the King.

'But I went on to have a healthy child,' Isabel comforted her, 'and so do many other women. Don't let this upset you too much. Now let's find you some cloths and a clean night-rail.' She got up then saw that Katheryn was weeping again.

'Come on now,' she said gently. 'It's not the end of the world.'

'But he called me Katheryn!' She could not stem the tears.

'What's wrong with that?'

'He always calls me darling or sweetheart. He's angry with me, I know it.'

'He didn't seem angry when he spoke to me,' Isabel said, rummaging through the chest. 'He was very concerned. He must be upset too, and when people are upset, they don't always behave as you expect them to. You are reading too much into this, Katheryn. Now, take these through to the stool chamber. I'll be with you in a moment.'

Isabel stayed with her for the rest of the night. The cramping pains got worse and the blood flow was heavy, but, by morning, things had settled down. Katheryn, though, was exhausted and decided to lie in bed for the day. And then Henry was there, come to see how she was, tears in his eyes and a red rose in his hand.

'For you, sweetheart,' he said. 'Lady Baynton tells me that all is well.'

She held the rose to her lips; its fragrance was exquisite. 'You have forgiven me?'

'There is nothing to forgive.' He bent forward and kissed her. Isabel stood there, beaming.

'I told you,' she said, when Henry had gone to Mass. 'There is nothing amiss.'

'You are so kind,' Katheryn said. 'I want you to have this. She took from the table by the bed a gold brooch. 'It's a thank-you.'

Isabel stared at it in wonder. 'I couldn't possibly—'

'Yes, you can! I want you to have it. You're the best sister anyone could have.'

Isabel hugged her and took the brooch. 'Thank you,' she smiled. 'I will treasure it.'

Katheryn lay in bed trying to sleep, but she could not. She had got the idea into her head that God had punished her for fornicating with Harry and Francis – and for concealing it from the King. There was nothing to be done. It was far too late now to confess, and the consequences would be disastrous, so she must continue to live with her guilt and her fear of exposure. She was sure she had seen the last of Harry; he had married and would not want to risk raking up old scandals. But Francis? She had not heard a word of him in months, which was a comforting thought. Yet he might still be nursing the conviction that they were man and wife. Would he, at some point, feel so grieved about losing her that he had to say something?

Panic gripped her. She could see the whole glittering edifice of her life crumbling around her – and not just that. She stood to lose Henry's love and all that flowed from it, and that she could not have borne.

She felt helpless. She was desperate to take steps to protect herself, but what could she do without giving herself away? There was no one she could talk to, not even Isabel. Tom was still away from court, or she might have thought of confiding in him. He could not think any less of her than he already did. Then again, he might well believe that his duty to the King required him to reveal her secrets. No, it was as well that Tom was still convalescing.

She lay there, trying to still her fears. They would pass, she assured herself, as they had on earlier occasions. She was overreacting again. If Francis wanted to expose her, he would surely have done so by now.

Towards dinner time, Lady William Howard came to help her dress. As they chatted, it occurred to Katheryn that Lady William might have news of Francis.

'Do you know where Mr Dereham is these days?' she asked, hoping it sounded like a casual enquiry about an old acquaintance.

'Madam, he is here with my lord,' Lady William replied.

'Oh,' Katheryn said, panicking at the knowledge that Francis was near at hand, at court, and frantically searching for something to say to justify her interest. 'It's just that my lady of Norfolk has asked me to be good to him, and I will be.'

'He'll be pleased,' Lady William said.

'I'm sure, but don't say anything to him as I haven't decided what I shall do for him.'

Lady William stood back to admire her handiwork. 'I shan't say a thing. My lord will be pleased to hear of your kindness. He thinks well of Dereham.'

Damn! Katheryn thought. What a fool she had been to let her tongue run away with her. She would now have to show some favour to Francis – and how would he interpret that? Maybe it was best just to forget about her voiced intention and hope that Lady William did too.

Early in November, Richard Jones, the High Master of St Paul's School in London, begged an audience with Katheryn and, on his knees, presented her with a book, looking up eagerly at her. She thanked him and opened it to see the title, *The Birth of Mankind, otherwise named the Woman's Book*. It was a treatise on childbirth and midwifery, dedicated to 'our most gracious and virtuous Queen Katheryn', with an exhortation to all men to use it in a godly fashion.

How she stopped herself from weeping she did not know. Grief for her lost hopes was still raw. But she managed to smile and thanked Master Jones for the compliment he had paid her. When he had gone, and she was back in her privy chamber, she handed the book to Isabel.

'Take it away, please. You keep it.'

Isabel hugged her. 'Try not to dwell on your loss,' she whispered. And then the other ladies were coming into the room, so they broke apart and Katheryn announced that they would spend the afternoon practising their dance steps.

She was glad when, towards the end of the month, Henry took her away to Woking in Surrey for the good hawking to be had in those parts. They were accompanied only by a small riding household and four privy councillors: the grim-faced Earl of Southampton, the Lord Privy Seal; Sir John Russell, the Lord High Admiral; the gallant Sir Anthony Browne, Master of Horse, and Sir Anthony Wingfield, the Vice Chamberlain. With them were Monsieur Chapuys and Monsieur de Marillac, the Imperial and French ambassadors.

'His Majesty seems like a new man,' Browne told Katheryn as they watched the Master of the King's Hawks tie the jesses of the royal falcon to Henry's wrist. 'He has been rejuvenated by his marriage to your Grace.'

It was true. Henry had adopted a new daily regime. He was up between five and six, heard Mass at seven, then rode out hawking with Katheryn until dinner was served at ten o'clock. In the afternoons, he was closeted with his councillors, attending to state affairs, while she and her ladies made merry with the gentlemen of the Privy Chamber. Mercifully, Tom Culpeper was not among them; he was better, Henry had told her, but was attending to duties that took him away from the court. She wondered if Henry had sent him away on purpose, having an inkling of Tom's feelings for her. She had made sure to suppress hers, knowing that to think of him in that way was futile now.

'I feel much better in the country than near London,' Henry said, as they trotted out of the stables one morning. 'My leg is better and I think I've lost weight.' It was hard to tell if this was true, since his clothing was so padded and puffed, but he did look better. It was all this good fresh air, Katheryn thought. After the hot summer, they were enjoying a pleasant autumn with lots of pale sunshine.

One afternoon, as Katheryn was strumming her lute, Isabel came to her, looking worried.

'Kat Tilney is here, asking to see you,' she said. 'She is seeking a place in your household.'

'I'm sure I can find one for her,' Katheryn smiled.

'Mr Dereham is with her,' Isabel told her.

Katheryn's heart plummeted like a stone. 'What does he want?' she hissed, more sharply than she had intended.

'Nothing, Madam,' Isabel answered. 'He escorted her here. He did not speak to me.'

'Send her in alone,' Katheryn ordered. 'Tell him he may obtain refreshment at the servery and be on his way.' She was praying that he would not demand to see her and that he had no sinister intent in coming here.

To her relief, Kat came in by herself and curtseyed before her. Katheryn welcomed her warmly and asked after her mother. Kat said that she was better and that she herself was keen to return to court.

'You shall be one of my chamberers,' Katheryn told her, thinking that Joan Bulmer could not possibly hear of this in faraway York. 'Meg will show you to the maidens' dorter and explain your duties. Remember, I require strict discretion and loyalty from those who serve me.' Her eyes held Kat's. She hoped her meaning was clear. Kat had been a witness to things Katheryn would rather forget.

'Of course, Madam,' Kat smiled. 'I am so grateful to be serving you.'

'You may send Mr Dereham back to Lambeth,' Katheryn said, needing to know that he had left court.

'I will tell him, Madam,' Kat said, with a knowing smile.

As yet, Katheryn had not met the King's children. Three-year-old Prince Edward had his own establishment; like his sister, the Lady Elizabeth, who was seven, he lodged in turn at the various nursery palaces surrounding London, where the air was cleaner and more healthful than in the city. Katheryn hoped to meet them both soon; Henry had promised that she would, for he loved them very much and was eager for them to know their new stepmother, but both plague and progress had prevented him from sending for them.

'Soon I will,' he promised.

Katheryn was nervous about meeting the King's elder daughter, the Lady Mary. At twenty-four, Mary was five years her senior and, while people sang her praises, saying she was devout, virtuous and kind, it was also murmured that she was embittered because of her parents' divorce and her lack of a husband. She had found solace in the faith she shared with Katheryn, but it sounded as if she lived like a nun. She did not seem like the kind of companion who would fit into the Queen's merry, pleasure-loving circle and so Katheryn had done nothing to cultivate her friendship; she had not even written Mary a letter.

She was apprehensive, therefore, when her stepdaughter visited court early in December. Sumptuously attired in velvet and furs, and glistening with jewels, as unlike a nun as could be, Mary entered Henry's presence chamber and curtseyed low before him. She was a plain young woman with red hair, a snub nose, tight lips and peering eyes, as if she was short-sighted, and her manner was poised yet timid.

She regarded Katheryn warily as she rose from her curtsey. Katheryn felt herself under scrutiny. Nervously, she smiled, and Mary reciprocated, although her smile did not reach her eyes.

'I will leave you ladies to get better acquainted,' Henry said, beaming, and left the Queen's chamber. At once, the other women gathered around Mary, paying as much court to her as they normally did to Katheryn, and, for the rest of that day, she was the centre of attention. Katheryn sat aloof, by choice, feeling left out and wishing that Mary wasn't staying for three days. As for the two maids who had come in attendance on her, they ignored Katheryn entirely!

At one point, Mary came over to her as she sat at the virginals, hitting the keys as loudly as she could.

'May I sit with your Grace?' she asked.

'Of course,' Katheryn replied stiffly.

'I hear you are a friend to the true faith,' Mary said. 'It needs such a champion in these difficult times.'

'Indeed,' Katheryn answered, unwilling to unbend.

'I was glad to hear that my father's Grace is so happily married,' Mary continued. 'I trust your Grace is happy too. If you ever need any advice or help, I would be pleased to give it. You are very young and inexperienced in the ways of the court. My mother was queen and a wonderful example to all.'

'Thank you,' Katheryn said, angry because Mary had clearly found her wanting beside that paragon of a mother of hers, and was implying that she herself was too young and inept to make a good queen. 'I am nearly twenty and have the King himself to guide me. You know how attentive he is.'

'Indeed. I have known him a lot longer than your Grace,' Mary said, leaving Katheryn seething.

Before she could think of a retort, Lady Suffolk came and sat with them, and took Mary's hand. 'My dear mother loved your Grace's mother so much,' she said. 'You will be sad to hear that she died last year.'

'That is indeed doleful news,' Mary said, tears welling in her eyes. 'I loved her; she was always kind to me. And my sainted mother adored her.'

As they continued reminiscing and others joined in, Katheryn again felt excluded. She had nothing in common with Mary except their faith, no shared history. Her ladies were supposed to be there to attend on her and keep her entertained, not to fawn endlessly over Mary! She said as much to Henry at supper that evening. 'They ignored me for most of the afternoon,' she complained.

'Forgive them, darling; some of them knew my daughter in her younger days.' He looked wistful for a moment as if he was thinking back to that far-off time when he was young and married to Queen Katherine, with an adored daughter – and still hopeful of a son. If Katherine had borne that son, how different the course of history would have been. Katheryn might not be sitting here today.

'It was not just my ladies! The Lady Mary herself did not treat me with the respect that is my due. And the two maids she brought with her just ignored me too!'

Henry sighed. 'I see. Well, if you wish it, Katheryn, I will send Mary away to join her brother Edward at Ashridge. I will tell her that we are leaving for Oatlands. And I will order that those maids be dismissed.'

'Thank you, Henry,' Katheryn said, resting her hand on his. He looked unhappy. Of course, he enjoyed seeing his daughter. Now she felt bad for having made him send Mary away. But Mary was to blame. She should have made her maids show the Queen her proper due, and not spoken so patronisingly.

In the morning, Henry arrived late at the stables with Monsieur Chapuys in tow.

'My apologies, darling,' he said, seeing Katheryn waiting for him, wearing a green velvet riding habit. 'I will not be a moment.'

He turned to the ambassador. 'So the Lady Mary has asked you to intercede for her maids?' He put an arm around Chapuys' shoulders and drew him a little apart from the hunting party. But not far enough, for Katheryn could still hear what was being said.

'Your Majesty, she fears that the order to send them away proceeded entirely from the Queen.'

'We will not have anyone show disrespect to her Grace,' Henry countered.

'She insists it was not intended, Sire,' Chapuys replied.

'Well, maybe I was over-harsh. I will rescind the order. Tell the maids to make ready to leave with the Lady Mary tomorrow.'

Katheryn's anger too had dissipated. She made no complaint when Henry rejoined her and they rode out into the park. He was sending Mary away. It was enough. But, during the hunt, she was disconcerted to hear Monsieur de Marillac observing to Chapuys that the pure atmosphere surrounding the Lady Mary was in marvellous contrast to the tainted air of the court. Was he referring to her? She almost taxed him with it, but caught herself in time. It was better to keep silent about such matters.

To please Henry, when Mary left the following morning, Katheryn gave her a jewelled pomander. 'It is a token of my esteem,' she told her stepdaughter. Mary, who had barely smiled when bidding her farewell, looked nonplussed.

'This is most kind of your Grace,' she said. 'It is a beautiful gift and I shall treasure it.'

Henry was beaming broadly, delighted that Katheryn had made the gesture. Basking in his approval, she decided to send something to Elizabeth too. From her great store of jewels, she chose some pretty beads, and a gold cameo brooch studded with rubies and emeralds, colourful pieces a child would love. The King was thrilled.

'You have a generous heart, darling,' he told her.

Oatlands in December was a place of magic, coated with layers of snow beneath a hazy bright sky pierced by the sun's rays. It was hard to believe that it was more than four months since she and Henry had been married here. To mark their return, he gave her two rosaries.

It was lovely to be back and capture once more those brief days of privacy they had shared on their honeymoon. The only thing that marred their stay was Tom Culpeper's presence. He had finished with whatever business had taken him away from court and was constantly in attendance on Henry, who treated him almost like a son. Katheryn was courteous whenever she was obliged to speak to him, but she took care to ensure that their eyes never met, lest Henry suspect that there had been something between them. She was constantly aware of Tom's gaze on her, and wished he would look away. She still felt attracted to him, to his manliness and his vigour, but loyally she tried to avoid comparing him to Henry. Tom could not give her what Henry could, and Henry did love her so. But then, whispered a disloyal little voice in her head, Henry could not give her what Tom could! It upset her to realise that she might never again have a younger lover.

They were at Oatlands for three weeks before they left to spend Christmas at Hampton Court. On arrival there, Henry surprised Katheryn with a gift of a rope of large pearls, for which she thanked him with many grateful kisses. He was in high good spirits and dined and supped with her every day in her apartments.

The Christmas revels were even more magnificent than they had been a year ago when everyone was awaiting the arrival of Anna of Cleves. Trumpets sounded every time the King and Queen appeared for a feast or a revel; the royal musicians played for the court on sackbuts, drums and viols; the Gentlemen and Children of the Chapel Royal sang like angels; there was dancing, hunting and disports, and heralds distributed the King's largesse to all. Katheryn had never been so happy or entered into festivities so joyfully.

Chapter 22

1541

On New Year's Day, Henry woke Katheryn with a kiss and pulled her to him. She submitted to his lovemaking with open arms and a willing smile; she was used to it now. His ageing body held no terrors for her, and he knew how to please a lady. If he had been twenty years younger, he would have been the perfect lover.

Afterwards, sitting up in bed, he gave her eight exquisite jewels as New Year's gifts: pendant laces with fair table diamonds, ropes of pearls, a square pendant with clusters of diamonds and pearls, and a gorgeous black velvet muff lined with sables and ornamented with rubies, hundreds of pearls and tiny gold chains. She cried out in delight when she saw this treasure trove, and glimpsed tears in Henry's eyes.

She sat beside him that morning through the long presentation of gifts in the presence chamber, marvelling at the riches his courtiers bestowed on him. Then she went to her own presence chamber to distribute presents to her ladies and servants. Margaret Douglas was thrilled with the Venetian glass beads she received, while Isabel gasped out loud at the girdle of goldsmith's work Katheryn gave her.

At dinner, Henry was in an expansive mood. 'I've sent money to the Lady Mary and the Lady Elizabeth. They will know better than I what to buy with it. Oh, and I've rewarded your minstrels and players, darling.'

'That was kind,' Katheryn smiled, pouring sauce on her roast fowl. 'You are good to me, Henry.'

He leaned back in his chair, regarding her devotedly. 'Darling, the Lady Anna is nearby at Richmond, so I thought we could invite her to court to share the festivities. She has been so amenable in regard to the

264

annulment, and when I told her of our marriage, she did not begrudge me my happiness.'

Katheryn did not, in principle, mind Anna coming to court, for she had always liked her, but she could foresee some awkwardness between them. How could it be otherwise when she had supplanted Anna as queen? And Anna had been raised in courts; she might find Katheryn lacking in the dignity of a queen.

She smiled. 'Of course she must come,' she said.

Henry was looking at her curiously. 'Is it my imagination, or have you put on weight?' he asked.

Katheryn flushed. She had indeed put on weight, with all the rich fare that had been served to her these past months, and her ladies had been unable to lace her gowns as tightly as they had back in the summer. She had hoped that Henry would not notice.

'Could it be that you are with child?' he asked eagerly.

'I know I am not,' she said, hating to disappoint him.

'Never mind,' he said briskly. 'I will continue to live in hope.' It sounded like a reproach. At nearly fifty, he, unlike her, had no time to waste.

'Oh, so will I!' she cried. 'I pray for it every day.'

'Then we will have to make sure that there is every chance of it happening,' Henry said, winking at her, and all was well again.

The Lady Anna's gifts to the King preceded her – two great horses with purple velvet trappings. Henry was ecstatic.

'At least she's spending the fortune I pay her wisely!' he observed, stroking the animals' manes as he, Katheryn and a host of courtiers stood in the stables courtyard, admiring the horses. 'These are fine mounts indeed!'

Anna followed that afternoon. Apprised of her approach, Katheryn sent the Duchess of Suffolk, the Countess of Hertford and other ladies to greet her and conduct her to her lodgings. Henry had commanded that she be given a spacious apartment with rich furnishings. Nothing was too good for her. Katheryn thought it remarkable that his dislike had so soon turned to esteem.

In her own chambers, Katheryn paced up and down in her gown of cloth of silver, still anxious about receiving her predecessor. She could not forget that she had been Anna's maid-of-honour and that she had betrayed her trust. She had summoned Lord Chancellor Audley and her uncle, the Earl of Sussex, who was Lord Great Chamberlain, and asked for their advice as to how she should treat her visitor.

'Your Grace is the Queen now,' they told her. 'The Lady Anna will understand that. Have no fear.'

Katheryn entered her presence chamber and stood on the dais, her ladies grouped around her. She did not sit, feeling it was inappropriate, given Anna's high rank as a princess of Cleves. Then Anna was announced and, to Katheryn's mortification, fell to her knees in front of her with as much reverence and ceremony as if she herself were the most insignificant damsel at court.

'Oh, please, my Lady Anna, do not kneel to me, I pray!' Katheryn cried, bending forward to help her to her feet. 'I am so pleased to see you! I have dearly hoped that we can be friends. You were always a kind mistress to me, and now I long to do you favour in return.' She embraced Anna and kissed her. Anna reciprocated warmly, and for the first time Katheryn wondered if the annulment had come as a welcome blessing to her. There was no rancour in her eyes, only goodwill.

'Make way for his Majesty the King!' cried an usher, and Henry entered the room, smiling broadly.

'Welcome, Anna, my dear sister!' he said, opening his arms to his former wife and pressing his lips to hers. 'I see you two ladies are pleasantly according together. The horses are splendid – I cannot thank you sufficiently. My love . . .' He let Anna go and embraced Katheryn, kissing her heartily and making her blush. Maybe he wanted to give the lie to those rumours and show the world which of the two of them he really loved.

As the trumpets sounded, he escorted them both into the presence chamber for supper, Katheryn on his right hand and Anna on his left. The fresh aroma of evergreens filled the room and candles glimmered amidst festive table and window decorations of pine cones, spiced dried oranges and juniper berries.

Katheryn seated herself next to the King at the high table. She saw that Anna was placed at a seat near the end, below the salt yet close enough to converse with her and Henry and the Lady Mary, who had come up from the country. She watched as Anna sat down, smiling at those around her, looking as unconcerned as if there had never been anything between her and Henry.

Supper was a very merry and convivial occasion, with much laughter and wine, and Katheryn found herself enjoying Anna's company in a way she had never been able to before. She even managed to share a jest with Mary, whose manner towards her was much more friendly and respectful than on the previous occasion. Excitedly, Katheryn told them both about the lavish Twelfth Night celebrations that were being planned and discussed the ever-fascinating subject of clothes – she was pleased to mark that Anna was wearing an English gown – and the gifts the King had given her.

She was itching to be up and dancing. 'Are we going to dance?' she asked. 'Oh, Henry, please say we can dance. I love it when you lead me out before the court.'

Henry smiled at her, but shook his head. 'I think I am rather tired and would prefer to go to bed,' he said. 'But you ladies can dance together.' He signalled to the musicians in the gallery, and they began playing.

'Oh, thank you, Henry!' she cried.

'Don't be too late,' he said, caressing her cheek as he rose to leave. Everyone stood, but he waved them down. 'Be seated, my friends! Enjoy the rest of the evening.'

When he had gone, Katheryn and Anna sat together, talking as they emptied their goblets. As soon as the wine was drunk, Katheryn extended her hand. 'My Lady Anna, please dance with me!' She was a little tipsy and desperate to be out on the floor.

Anna looked uncertain and Katheryn wondered if she had placed her new friend in an embarrassing position. She could recall seeing Anna dance hardly at all. But Anna rose. 'It will be my pleasure,' she said, taking Katheryn's hand.

'The pavane!' Katheryn cried, and the musicians changed to a slow and stately tune. She enjoyed showing off her skill as a dancer, and noticed that Anna was moving about with increasing confidence. When Katheryn called for a lively *branle*, she joined in enthusiastically, clearly enjoying herself. Everyone was clapping and Katheryn bade the gentlemen lead out their ladies. Soon the floor was crowded. It was a wonderful evening and, at the end of it, she sank happily into bed.

The next day, Henry invited Anna to dine with him and Katheryn in his privy chamber, and again the conversation flowed, with much merriment. Afterwards, Katheryn and Anna played backgammon in the Queen's privy chamber. They were interrupted by the arrival of an usher with two tiny lapdogs. He bowed to Katheryn.

'Your Grace, the King has asked me to bring you these gifts.' He handed her the leads and a pouch, from which she pulled a ruby ring. She did not know which to admire first.

'It's beautiful!' she exclaimed, holding out the ring in her palm, as Anna bent forward to gaze at it. The puppies were sniffing at the rush matting.

'Oh, they're adorable!' Katheryn cried, sweeping them up onto her lap, where they crouched, quivering, as if they were frightened of her. 'You silly things, you mustn't be afraid of little Kafwyn,' she murmured, nuzzling their smooth heads, their fur silky against her lips. She looked up. 'Anna, don't you just love them?'

Anna reached over to fondle the puppies. 'I do. They are so pretty.'

'They are yours!' Katheryn announced impulsively, lifting them onto Anna's lap.

'Oh, but I couldn't—' Anna protested.

'I want you to have them,' Katheryn insisted. 'And the ring!'

Anna could not hide her pleasure. Perhaps she too had been dreading their meeting. 'Thank you!' She bent forward and kissed Katheryn. 'I'm so grateful.'

Katheryn turned to the usher. 'Pray thank his Majesty for his goodness to me, and say I will thank him properly when I see him later.'

All in all, it was a very satisfactory and pleasant afternoon and, at the end of it, she was sorry to see Anna depart.

* * *

A week later, Katheryn was disconcerted to hear her maids gossiping about rumours that the King might take Anna back as his Queen. She was about to join them in the privy chamber, the door of which was ajar, but held back when she heard what they were saying.

'I suppose they think that, because he has sent her presents, he is regretting having divorced her.' That was Elizabeth Fitzgerald.

'But, seeing how he caresses the Queen, that could never be!' Damascin Stradling said.

'I think people have drawn conclusions because the Lady Anna seemed so happy in the King's company – and her Grace is not yet *enceinte*,' Margaret Garnish chimed in.

'It's absurd!' retorted Lucy Somerset. 'The King will never leave Queen Katheryn; he loves her too much.'

Katheryn was pleased to hear that, but it offended her that people were willing to believe that Henry might discard her. Was it not obvious to them what he thought of her? They must be blind!

A week later, she was practising dance steps in her privy chamber when Norfolk was announced. He was still basking in the glory of being uncle to the Queen and still brimful with approval.

'I hope you can help me, Katheryn,' he said, when she bade him be seated. 'A year ago, the Captain of Guisnes died, and I sought to obtain the post for Lord William, but that knave Cromwell blocked it. The post is still unfilled, and I should be grateful if you would put in a good word for Lord William with the King.'

'Of course,' Katheryn said, always happy to do good to her kins-folk.

That night, in bed, she relayed Uncle Norfolk's request. 'I am fond of Lord William and he is eager to serve you,' she added.

'Anything for you, darling,' Henry said, replete with lovemaking. 'I will give the order.'

It had been that easy. It was a heady thought. Not that she was hungry for power, but she did want to use her influence for good. Never, she vowed, would she abuse it. And when Lord William came to thank her for her intercession, she was thrilled that, by a simple action, she had been able to make him happy and obtain for him a lucrative post. That was the best part of exercising patronage.

She had another opportunity of doing so three days later. Her sister Margaret came to her, full of apologies. 'Your Grace, I am with child again and crave leave to resign my post and go home. I feel constantly exhausted and sick and little Charles needs me – he is ailing again.' Margaret's second son had never thrived, although her eldest, Matthew, was a lively little boy.

'Of course you must go,' Katheryn said, embracing her. 'It would be selfish of me to ask you to stay. Does this mean you are leaving my household for good?'

'It does,' Margaret said sadly. 'I am very sorry. I will miss you, my dear sister.'

When she had gone, Katheryn gave thought to who might replace her. She broached the matter with the King at supper that evening.

'Why not appoint Lady Rochford?' he asked. 'She is very experienced, having served the last three queens.'

'Of course,' Katheryn said quickly, pre-empting his asking why she had not appointed Jane Rochford in the first place. 'I will ask her myself, with your leave.'

'By all means,' Henry smiled, and tucked into his venison pasty.

Jane stood before Katheryn, a little stiff in her manner. She had arrived that morning from her father's mansion in Essex and Katheryn wondered what she had been doing these past six months. She realised it must have been hard being cast into the shadows after serving for so long at court. No wonder Jane seemed so unbending.

'A vacancy has occurred in my household. I should like to offer you the post of lady of the privy chamber,' Katheryn told her. 'His Majesty recommended you.'

Jane smiled her cat-like smile. 'I shall be grateful to accept, Madam,' she said.

'I am sorry that our former friendship lapsed,' Katheryn said, wanting things to be right between them before Jane took up her duties. 'I am sure you understand that events overtook me; my life had changed before I knew it. But I hope that we can be friends again.'

'That is my hope too,' Jane said, still smiling. 'I have ever had a deep affection for your Grace. Might I ask after our mutual friend? Is he well?'

It chilled Katheryn to hear her speak of Tom Culpeper so. 'I assume so,' she said. 'I have little to do with him these days, of course, although the King thinks more highly of him than ever and, I hope, will always do so.' She hoped Jane would take her meaning – and the warning. She was trying her hardest to forget Tom. It wasn't easy when she saw him in attendance on the King every other day or so, and she didn't want Jane getting the wrong impression.

'I am pleased to hear that,' Jane said. 'I did like him, as you know. And I would never hurt him.'

She had got the message. Katheryn smiled and felt reassured.

Early in February, Henry went to London to attend to state business, leaving Katheryn and his household at Hampton Court. It was the first time they had been apart since their marriage and Katheryn found herself missing him, which made her realise how fond of him she had grown. She was genuinely pleased to see him return after three nights away.

About ten days later, he complained of feeling shivery and unwell. Katheryn waited anxiously in her apartments until his doctors came to report to her.

'It is a slight tertian fever, Madam,' Dr Butts pronounced. 'Wine is the sovereign remedy and we have recommended that his Grace drinks as much of it as he can.'

'Will he get better soon?' she asked.

'Of course, Madam. He has had it before and recovered. There is no need to worry.'

Slight the fever might have been, yet Henry was not well enough to attend the masques that were staged on two successive nights at Hampton Court, and Katheryn had to preside over them alone, seated on her smaller chair next to the great empty chair of estate.

After that, fortunately, Henry rallied, and the fever subsided.

'I think I might visit my castles on the coast towards France, to have the ramparts repaired, for I'm told that some have fallen,' he announced one evening, looking up from his book. Katheryn, seated opposite, sewing, was pleased to hear it.

'I particularly want to look at those at Dover,' he went on. 'You must come with me, darling. We'll make a holiday of it.'

They never went. The very next morning, Henry complained of pain in his leg. Pulling away the bandage, he revealed a swollen, black, angry-looking wound. Katheryn drew in her breath, horrified.

'It's closed up again,' he explained, wincing. 'My physicians have tried to keep it open, to maintain my health, but it has suddenly closed.' He drew in his breath. 'By God, Katheryn, it is agony, and dangerous. Five or six years ago, the same thing happened, and I thought I would die. I will go back to my apartments now and summon my physicians.'

He tried to rise, but sank down, defeated, sweat pouring from his brow.

'Stay here, Henry!' she cried, alarmed. 'I will call the doctors.'

'No, I will go back,' he insisted, struggling to his feet. How he managed it, she did not know. Calling for the guards outside the door, he had them help him into his night robe and bonnet and assist him to his bedchamber, while Katheryn, wrapped in her own robe, looked on helplessly.

'If there is anything I can do for your Grace—' she began, but he silenced her.

'You must not worry about me, Katheryn. I will be all right.'

Then he was gone. Hearing his footsteps receding painfully, she found herself crying.

The doctors came to her later that morning. She felt faint when she saw the grave expressions on their faces.

'Your Grace, it is not good news,' Dr Butts told her. 'We fear for his Majesty's life. The ulcer is clogged and he is feverish and black in the face. The danger lies not so much in the fever, but in the leg. It is diseased because he is very stout and drinks and eats excessively. We have opened the wound and drained off the fluid to relieve the swelling, but it was a very painful process. Let us pray that it proves effective.'

She was near to tears and frightened. The prospect of losing Henry, the husband who adored her, was unbearable. What would happen to her? What did they do with redundant, widowed queens? The same as Henry had done with Anna of Cleves? She pictured herself pensioned off, laden with wealth and great houses. But beside that was another image, of her leaving court, mournful in her widow's weeds, no longer a queen and bereft of Henry's love and protection. And then she saw herself as a bride again, kissing Tom in a church porch. No! It was wrong to think such things. She loved Henry, she did! She wanted him to recover.

'Oh, I will pray for him!' she cried. 'And you, kind sirs, please do everything in your power to make his Grace well.'

'We will, Madam,' they assured her. 'And you should rest. This is trying for you as well.'

God answered her prayers. When Henry summoned her two days later, on Shrove Tuesday, his leg was on the mend and he was sitting up in his chair by the fire, with the offending limb resting on a footstool; but he was not himself. He did not hold out his arms to her, as he usually did, but merely gave her a mournful smile.

'Alas, Katheryn, whom shall men trust?' he sighed. 'I have an unhappy people to govern, who I will shortly make so poor that they will not have the boldness nor the power to oppose me.'

She had no idea what he was talking about. 'What has happened?' she asked in alarm and jumped as Will Somers, the fool, crawled out from behind Henry's chair.

'Harry's councillors have been enjoying ruling England without him,' he said, pulling a face.

'Get out!' Henry snapped. 'Go on, you varlet!' With a woeful look on his face, Will capered away. He knew how far he could go with his master.

'Is it true?' Katheryn asked when he had gone.

'More or less,' Henry growled. 'Most of my Privy Council, under pretence of serving me, only temporise for their own profit. I know their tricks. They are all striving for supremacy, each one over the other, thinking to rule me thereby. But I know the good servants from the flatterers and, if God lends me health, I will take care that their projects do not succeed.' He was working himself into a temper. It was not good for him.

'You will be up and well again soon,' she said soothingly, 'and then I am sure you will deal with those who have offended you.'

'Hmm.' He sat there brooding.

'Shall I call the musicians?' she asked.

'No.'

That startled her. Music was one of his passions. 'Shall I play for you then?' she offered.

'Katheryn, you mean well, but I am not in the mood. This leg is so painful. When I think how I used to be, riding and jousting and playing sports at will. And now I can hardly walk around my chamber. God's teeth, I am sick of it, sick of being ill, sick of my councillors – sick of it all! When I think of everything I have done for my people and how I am repaid, it makes my blood boil. I'll have their heads if they so much as squeak about taking things off my shoulders!'

He rambled on, making so little sense to Katheryn that she wondered if his fever had returned. Just then, the door opened and Tom Culpeper entered, carrying a tray.

'Forgive the intrusion, your Graces,' he said, placing it on the table and bowing, his face impassive. 'I have come to lay the board for dinner.'

'You wouldn't betray me, would you, Tom?' Henry said plaintively.

Tom, smoothing the cloth, looked startled. 'Of course not, Sir.'

'Others do!' Henry growled, looking around angrily as if seeking someone to fight with. 'By God,' he exploded, 'they shall know my wrath!'

Both Katheryn and Tom jumped. Their eyes met briefly. He shook his head, almost imperceptibly, as if warning her that there was no point in trying to calm the King.

'Was ever prince so unhappy in his councillors?' Henry's voice was more measured now, but bitter. 'Upon a light pretext, by false accusations, they made me put to death the most faithful servant I ever had.' He was referring to Cromwell, Katheryn realised, and the men he was blaming could only include her uncle. She felt a sharp stab of fear. She too had colluded in the plot.

'Cromwell was above factions!' Henry said, fierce. 'He would have kept them in check.' He slumped in his chair, his face in his hand. 'Oh, God. Don't listen to me, darling. I am being an old bear. It is the pain, not my ministers, that arouses my anger.'

'Can I help in any way, Sir?' Tom asked.

'No. I would be alone. Go away, the both of you. Tom, find some way to divert my poor Queen. This will be a quiet Shrovetide for her. I cannot face any entertainments or merrymaking. Just send my confessor to me, so that I may be shriven.'

As Tom bowed, Katheryn curtseyed, then bent forward impulsively and kissed Henry's cheek. 'Get well soon, Sir,' she said. 'You will be in my prayers.'

In the antechamber, after the door had closed behind them, Katheryn let out a sigh. 'I have never seen him like this.'

'He gets peevish when his leg troubles him,' Tom said, his eyes never leaving her face. He lowered his voice. 'Tell me, Katheryn, how do you bear it?'

'Bear what? I've only seen him behave in this manner today.'

'No, I mean being his wife.' It was the concerned way he said it that did it. Something of what she had once felt for him flickered and flared up.

'I love him, Tom. He has been more than good to me.'

'You *love* him?' There was anguish in his gaze.

'Yes, I do.' It was true. But being with Tom made her realise that she was not *in* love with Henry, which was a rather different thing.

His tone became brisk. 'Well, what can I do to divert your Grace?' There was a pause.

'A walk in the gardens, maybe?' she suggested, with some reluctance.

'If your Grace wishes. I'm playing tennis at two o'clock, if the King will give me leave.'

'Then I will come and watch.' She would bring some of her ladies with her. There would be safety in numbers. 'I think I will leave the gardens for now.'

Chapter 23

1541

She hastened back to her lodgings in turmoil. She had no business to be thinking of Tom in that way, yet she could not help it. He was so debonair, so handsome. He drew her in, as he always had. But for a turn of Fortune's wheel, he would have been her husband and she would have been in bliss. Yet she had given him up for a crown and it had cost her dearly. But she had really had no choice.

She had thought herself happy, married to Henry, and in many ways she was. But he was old and she was young, with the clamorous blood of youth coursing through her veins – and she had known passion. Seeing Tom, talking to Tom, had awakened something in her, something she thought had died.

Stop it! she admonished herself. You can't have him. Forget him, as you did before.

She did not want to go to watch him play tennis, but she had said she would, and it was small enough compensation for what she could not give him. So she went, then spent the whole time drinking in the sight of his lithe, athletic body dancing this way and that.

'He's a handsome gentleman,' Lucy Somerset murmured in her ear. 'I'd like to catch his fancy!'

'No you wouldn't,' Lady Wriothesley said. 'I'm told he has eyes for none but Bess Harvey.'

'Bess Harvey?' Katheryn echoed, shocked. And she had imagined him pining away in grief for her . . . So there was no reason to feel sorry for him after all! The pretty, vacuous face of her maid came to mind, and she would have liked to slap it. But she must be careful. No one must guess that she was jealous.

The court was quiet that week. It was so empty that it resembled more a private household than a king's train. Katheryn was bored, and there was too much time to think – yet she was afraid where her thoughts might lead her.

When next she went to visit Henry, the guards outside his door crossed their halberds at her approach.

'What are you doing?' She put on her most imperious voice. 'I wish to see the King!'

'I'm sorry, your Grace,' one officer said. 'We have orders to admit no one, even yourself.'

Her face flushed and she walked away, smarting at such a public rejection. Why would he not see her? Had someone told him how she had feasted her eyes on Tom at the tennis? Or, worse, had their conversation in the antechamber been overheard? She had said nothing wrong, but she had not castigated Tom for his boldness.

'The King refuses to see me,' she confided to Isabel when her sister found her sitting alone in her bedchamber, fretting. 'And I don't know why!'

'Isn't it obvious?' Isabel asked gently. 'It's pride. He won't want you seeing him in a poorly state. And maybe he knows he is not good company.'

'Maybe,' Katheryn said, but she was not convinced. She had seen how easily Henry could become suspicious, how impulsively he shouted threats at those he believed had offended against him. She prayed that his displeasure had not fallen on her. But there was no way of finding out.

Or was there? Tom was in tune to all Henry's moods. He would know.

She went to the Chapel Royal. It was Lent and no one would think it remarkable if she was at her prayers more often than usual. She knelt in the royal pew, where she could not be seen from the nave below. From time to time, she looked over the parapet to see who was down there.

A week passed, ten days, and still she went daily to the chapel. By now, she was mad with anxiety. The doctors had told her that Henry was still in low spirits and still refusing to see anyone. She read all kinds of horrors into that.

She could not be in the chapel all the time, but she spent as long as she could there. Oh, when would Tom come? He must come soon!

Some of her ladies were at prayer when next she entered the pew. She heard them get up and leave, heard them talking about her. The sibilant whispers carried.

'He's been nearly two weeks without seeing her, when he couldn't be a moment without her,' one said.

'Maybe he has tired of her,' someone else replied.

'There can't be *another* divorce!'

'Surely not? Lady Rutland thinks her Grace is with child.'

The footsteps receded, leaving Katheryn aghast. Was that what people were thinking? And could it be true, that the King was contemplating divorcing her? If so, why? Had someone talked about her past or about Tom? Or was it because Henry believed her to be barren?

She was shaking when, as luck would have it, Tom walked into the chapel. She flew down the stairs and was relieved to find that he was alone.

'Your Grace!' he said, startled. 'I was just snatching a few moments' quiet. His Majesty has been very poorly and we've all been kept busy.'

Katheryn looked around to see if anyone was concealed in the shadows and lowered her voice. 'Tom, I must know! Has he mentioned me?'

'He calls for you sometimes in his sleep,' Tom said, 'and he did say that he hoped he would be well soon because he wanted to arrange your state entry into London. Why are you so upset?'

'Because I have heard talk that he is tired of me.' She must not let Tom see her cry. Who knew where that might lead?

'Well, that's the first I've heard of it,' he said, regarding her with those beautiful eyes. 'Right now, he's preoccupied with finishing the fortifications at Calais and Guisnes. Remember, when he wanted to be rid of the Lady Anna, he talked of little else. It's just gossip, Katheryn. Take no notice of it.'

'I won't,' she said, aware that he had used her Christian name and not her title. 'Thank you. You have set my mind at rest. It's just that, what with his Grace refusing to see me . . .'

'He does not want you to see him laid so low. In your eyes, he wants to be all-powerful, the very image of vigorous manhood. I'm sure that's the only reason. Anyone can see how he dotes on you. Indeed, it is painful to see.'

Their eyes locked. He had admitted that he still had feelings for her. There was a long pause.

Katheryn was the first to look away. 'I'm sure Bess Harvey has helped you to forget that I ever meant anything to you,' she said.

'What was I to do?' he asked. 'Live like a monk?'

'No.' She sighed. 'I am not reproaching you in any way. But there can be nothing between us now.'

'I am well aware of that,' he said bitterly.

'I must go,' she said. 'No one must see us talking alone together. I thank you for the reassurance you have given me, I feel so much happier now. We must pray that the King gets better quickly.'

She turned and left the chapel.

She knew she would not be fully reassured until she had seen and spoken with Henry. She was glad, therefore, when, two days later, he finally sent a message inviting her to dine with him.

Isabel came to help her dress, looking worried. 'Madam, you will remember that our brother John was accused of conspiring with Cardinal Pole?'

'Yes, I do.' John Leigh was still in the Tower, and Katheryn felt guilty for not having secured his release.

'The Cardinal's mother, Lady Salisbury, has been imprisoned in the Tower for over two years,' Isabel went on. 'It is said that she is held in a cold cell with no warm clothing – and it's freezing outdoors at the moment. She's an old lady and I can't bear to think of her suffering. Would you intercede for her with his Majesty – and for John?'

'Of course I will,' Katheryn agreed, shuddering to think of Lady Salisbury's plight. 'I'll do all I can for them – when the right moment comes.'

When she arrived in Henry's privy chamber, with just Anne Bassett in attendance on her, she found him at a table by the fire, his bad leg hidden beneath the damask cloth.

'Be seated, Katheryn,' he bade her. She searched his face for any sign of displeasure, but could see none.

'I am so glad to see you looking better,' she told him. 'I have missed you.'

'The sickroom is no place for a young lady,' he told her. 'There was nothing you could do, and I fear I was very fierce with my physicians. It is ever thus when my leg pains me. Thank God, I have my appetite back. Try this trout – it's excellent.'

He served her to a portion. She was so suffused with relief that she was near to tears.

'What ails you, darling?' Henry asked, all concern.

'Oh, Henry, I have been so worried,' she confessed. 'I heard a rumour that you were tired of me.'

Henry frowned. 'Who's been saying such things?'

'I don't know. I overheard people talking below the pew when I was in the chapel.'

'God's blood, they take a crumb and call it a loaf! Darling, you must not believe such things or attach faith to rumours.'

Katheryn sagged with relief. She was hoping that Anne Bassett would report the King's words to those ladies who had gossiped.

'I shall give them no more credence,' she said, brightening. 'But I was also sad for another reason. I have heard that old Lady Salisbury lies in the Tower in harsh conditions, with inadequate clothes and heat in this bitter weather.'

Henry's smile vanished, making her wish she hadn't spoken. 'She is a traitor,' he barked. 'She is lucky that I let her live.'

'Forgive me,' Katheryn begged, alarmed at his change of mood. 'I don't know what she has done wrong, and I do know you will have dealt her just punishment. But our Lord teaches us to succour prisoners and I was moved by her plight, as she is an old lady.'

Henry sighed. 'You have a kind heart, darling, but your sympathy is misplaced in this case. Lady Salisbury is my cousin and has a dubious claim to the throne. Some years ago, her son Cardinal Pole wrote a treasonable treatise against me, for which reason he is now in exile in Italy. Not long afterwards, his brothers and their friends plotted to kill me. I had them executed and the rest of the family imprisoned in the Tower.'

'Was Lady Salisbury involved in the plot?'

Henry refilled his goblet. 'I am convinced of it. When her castle at Warblington was searched by my officers, they found a silk tunic embroidered with the royal arms – undifferenced, as if they belonged to a reigning monarch. I have no doubt that the aim of the plot was to put Lady Salisbury or her sons on the throne in my stead. That is why she was condemned by Act of Attainder to lose her life and possessions. But, on account of her great age, I spared her the axe.'

'Your Grace is always most merciful,' Katheryn said, deeming flattery the best course, 'but, traitor though she is, it upsets me to think of her suffering such privations, for she is but human. Might I send her some warm clothing?'

Henry frowned. She waited, hoping she had not angered him. 'Very well,' he said at length. 'But you will pay for them out of your privy purse.' It was the money he gave her for her pleasures.

'Oh, thank you, Henry! You are so kind!' she cried, rising and kissing him.

'Hmm,' he grunted, mellowing. 'You'll have me lodging traitors in the Tower palace next! I can deny you nothing.' He took her face in his hands and kissed her back. 'How I love you, my little Queen!'

Katheryn was thinking that now was not the time to speak for John Leigh.

The next morning, she summoned Master Scutt, her tailor, and ordered him to make up garments to be sent to Lady Salisbury. A furred night-gown was a priority, and it should be lined with satin; she also asked for a kirtle of worsted, a furred petticoat, a bonnet and frontlet in the old gable style, four pairs of hose, four pairs of shoes and a pair of slippers. What she spent could have paid a craftsman's wages for a year, but it was all in a good cause, she told herself.

The tailor got to work at once and the garments were delivered to the Tower. Of course, Lady Salisbury was not allowed writing materials, so could not thank Katheryn, but it was enough to know that she would be warmer and more comfortable from now on.

The messenger had just been dispatched when Bess Harvey came to Katheryn, looking tearful. 'Madam, I crave your leave to resign my post.'

Jealousy flared in Katheryn. She could not look at Bess these days without imagining her with Tom. 'Why?' Her voiced sounded sharper than she had intended. 'Are you unhappy here?'

Bess's face flushed. 'No, Madam, it is a personal matter that makes it necessary for me to go home.'

Katheryn did not probe any further. She was happy to see the girl go. 'You have my leave,' she said. 'I wish you well.' She forbore to thank Bess for her good service.

'Thank you, Madam.'

When she had gone, Katheryn smiled to herself. She'd wager a lot on this having something to do with Tom. Had he lost interest in Bess? Or was Bess upset because there really was a problem at home and she had to leave him behind at court?

It was now March and Henry was well on the mend, although he had not yet left his rooms.

'Let Tom Culpeper take you to the tennis play or the bowling alley,' he urged Katheryn, one sunny morning. 'Spring is at hand and you should be out enjoying the fresh air.' He smiled at Tom.

'I shall be honoured to escort her Grace,' Tom said.

Why did Henry insist on pushing them together? Katheryn asked herself as she returned to her apartments to fetch her cloak and two maids to follow at a respectable distance. It was as if he was encouraging them! But then he knew nothing of the love they had shared – the love she feared was blossoming anew. Because of this, she did not want to spend time with Tom. It might break her resolve to put the past firmly behind her. But how could she explain that to her unsuspecting husband?

Tom was waiting for her in the King's privy garden. 'What would your Grace like to do?' he asked.

In her dreams, she could have told him. He looked so attractive, standing tall and broad-shouldered in his elegant black gown and silver-striped doublet and bases, his cap in his hand and his dark hair curling about his shirt collar. With an effort, she dragged her eyes away. 'Let us walk to the alley and watch the bowling,' she said.

They strolled through the gardens, past trees budding with blossom, speaking of how the weather had improved and how much better the King was. No one, watching them, would have suspected that there was anything between them.

The bowling alley was unfortunately deserted, so they sat down on one of the seats near the river, watching the boats, with Katheryn's maids occupying another seat, chattering gaily. But Katheryn could think of no safe way to begin a conversation. So much that was unsaid lay between her and Tom. For months, she had resolutely thrust away all thoughts of him; now those dammed-up feelings were inundating her to the extent that she was frightened of what she might say or do. She really should not be here with him.

She was about to rise when he spoke.

'Katheryn, I am dying for love of you.' He said it in a whisper, so none could have heard, but the longing in his voice shocked her.

'You must not say such things to me!' she reproved him. 'We are both bound by ties of loyalty to the King.'

'The King is ailing. Surely he cannot be a proper husband to you? But I – I could make you happy.'

'Hush!' She looked around nervously. There was no one in sight, only her maids, a few yards away, giggling among themselves. 'I *am* happy. The King *is* a proper husband. I pray you say no more. I will not hear it.' She rose to her feet. 'It grows chilly. I'm going back to my lodgings. Do not follow me, Tom. Farewell.'

'Katheryn . . .' His eyes were pleading.

'*Farewell!* And let that be an end to it!' She walked away, beckoning her maids to follow her. Her heart was thumping and her body trembling. She had been so near the brink, so tempted . . . She must never be alone with Tom again. It had been madness to think they could just be friends.

Jane Rochford was brushing Katheryn's hair. The other women had finished preparing their mistress for bed and left. Soon, Katheryn hoped, the King would come to her; he had not yet done so since his illness. She wanted him to make love to her, to make her forget her yearning for Tom and assuage the desire raging in her.

'Your Grace is quiet tonight,' Jane remarked. 'Could it be that you are thinking about a certain mutual friend of ours?'

In her mirror, Katheryn could see the flush creeping up from the neckline of her night-rail. She had done nothing but think of Tom's words to her. *I am dying for love of you.*

'Our mutual friend?' she echoed.

'Mr Culpeper,' Jane said, her slanted eyes gleaming. She loves him herself, Katheryn thought.

'Why should I think of him?' she replied.

'You know why. He has come to me and told me all. Will you not just speak with him?'

'I *have* spoken to him, and I have made it clear that there can be nothing between us. I am married to the King. I will not be unfaithful to him. Besides, it would be dangerous. I have never forgotten what happened to my cousin Anne – and you, Jane, should not be constraining Tom to love me, or me to encourage him!'

'Anne fell because Cromwell feared her,' Jane said. 'And she deserved what she got. But knowing that you and Mr Culpeper love each other, I would be more than willing to watch out for you and protect you both.'

And what would be in it for you? Katheryn wondered, unable to think of an answer.

'No,' she said. 'Tom must forget me, as I have forgotten him. Now you may go, as the King might be here soon.'

Jane left with a curtsey, making no protest, but she did not desist. When they were next alone in the bedchamber, she seized her chance. 'Mr Culpeper desires nothing else but your love,' she said. 'Will you not even consent to meet him?'

Katheryn turned on her. 'Trouble me no more!' she hissed. 'I do not want him lusting after me, or even looking at me, if it makes him want me!'

'You must give men leave to look, for they *will* look upon you,' Jane retorted. 'You are very beautiful.'

'Are you encouraging him in this folly?' Katheryn snapped.

'I know what lies between you,' Jane smiled. 'I would be your friend as well as Mr Culpeper's.'

One day, Meg Morton came into the bedchamber with some clean linen, just as Jane was singing Tom's praises. Meg shook her head contemptuously and walked out. Later that day, when she came back to help make up the Queen's bed, Katheryn was sitting at her mirror, searching in her casket for jewels to wear at supper. She looked up and their eyes met.

'I know what Lady Rochford is doing, Madam,' Meg said, 'and she should stop, for it is foolish – and wrong.'

'So I keep telling her!' Katheryn replied. 'Yet she will not desist.'

'Your Grace could send her away.'

'On what grounds? It could get her into trouble – and Mr Culpeper, if she makes a fuss.'

Meg nodded. 'It could. But why is she doing it?'

Katheryn sighed. 'I have asked myself that many times. Maybe she expects a reward.'

'What, for getting the Queen of England to commit adultery?'

That, stated baldly, took Katheryn aback. 'Well, in gratitude, I suppose.'

'I think she's a born meddler who can't refrain from nosing into other people's business.'

Katherine held up a pendant to her breast. 'That doesn't begin to describe it. She is so zealous in the matter. She clearly adores Mr Culpeper herself, yet she is urging me to love him.'

'Doesn't she realise how dangerous that could be?' Meg asked.

'If she does, it doesn't deter her. She says she will protect us.'

'Do you know what I think, Madam?' Meg hesitated. 'I think she gets her pleasure from imagining you and Mr Culpeper together.

I believe she has a wicked imagination. What else could account for her conduct?'

Katheryn pondered this notion. She had come near to thinking the same herself. Had it not been for Jane's many small kindnesses and her warm interest in Katheryn, she would have dismissed her, and wondered about doing so now, but Henry might ask questions. No, it was too risky. She must just speak firmly with Jane and put a stop to this foolishness.

Her opportunity came the next day when Jane approached her as she was sitting on a window seat strumming her lute. Her ladies were playing a very noisy card game and she was feeling irritated because they were drowning out the music.

'Your Grace, I would speak with you again about Mr Culpeper,' Jane said in a low voice, so that Katheryn had to strain to hear her.

'I want to talk to *you* about him!' she replied.

'Madam, I think you have misunderstood. He desires nothing more than to speak with you, and I would swear upon a holy book that he means nothing but honesty.'

It occurred to Katheryn that it might be worth meeting with Tom, if only to get him to stop Jane pestering her on his behalf. 'Look, I will see him,' she said. 'And I will put an end to this.'

Jane's face lit up. 'I will tell him,' she said. 'I will bring him to my chamber at midnight.'

Katheryn had grave misgivings. What if Henry came to her bed that night? Well, then, Tom would just have to wait until another time!

But Henry did not come. When all was dark and Hampton Court lay sleeping, Katheryn rose from her bed, put on her damask night robe with the high stand-up collar and crept along the gallery to Jane's room. When she opened the door, Tom was waiting for her, alone. She recoiled. She had expected Jane to be there.

She dared not stay out in the gallery, so she stepped into the room and closed the door quietly behind her.

'Katheryn, you came!' Tom breathed, looking at her with longing.

She had vowed to be impervious to his charisma, but it was not easy. 'I cannot stay. I came to tell you that you must stop making Lady Rochford press your suit on me.'

'*I* must stop? I assure you, Katheryn, she provokes me often to love you; she keeps telling me how much you love me.' He was plainly nonplussed.

'I have never told her that I love you. She does nothing but urge me to see you. Be honest, Tom – have you put her up to that?'

'Well, I suppose I have,' he confessed. 'Can you blame me if I am gripped with a kind of madness?'

'This must stop right now!' Katheryn said firmly. 'That is what I came to say. I would not hurt you for the world, but there is no future for us, and we are putting ourselves in danger by meeting like this.'

'I know,' he said, looking anguished. 'But I love you, Katheryn, and I would risk all for you.'

'And I am the King's wife!' she reminded him.

'Do you think I can forget it, attending on him daily as I do? He never stops talking about you. It galls me to hear it. Just let me kiss you, please—'

'No,' she answered, stepping back. 'I *must* go. There cannot be anything between us, Tom. Now fare you well.'

'Katheryn . . .'

But she had gone, her heart beating wildly.

Jane was waiting for her in the gallery. Katheryn could just make out her shape in the darkness. 'Did it go well?' she whispered.

'I finished it,' Katheryn told her.

'But you can't!' Jane was vehement.

'Alas, will this never end?' Katheryn hissed. 'I pray you, bid him trouble me no more and be done with it!'

She was angry about Jane's reluctance, but the next day, she found out that Jane had done as she was bidden.

'He will not take no for an answer,' she murmured, joining Katheryn in her privy garden, where the blossom was now in full bloom. 'He bids you remember what you meant to each other and that you might have been his wife.'

'Shh!' Katheryn hissed. 'No one must ever know that.'

But *she* remembered. She could think of little else, and of how she had hurt him. She was utterly torn. She kept reminding herself that they had got away with meeting in secret last night, and that it had easily been achieved. Dare she . . . ? Could she do it? Possibilities opened out to her. The temptation was great. Henry would never know. No one apart from Jane need ever know.

No, it would be risking too much. It was madness to contemplate it.

But she wanted Tom so much. She had been sleeping alone for weeks now. She yearned to touch him and have him pleasure her. Imagining him inside her made her feel faint with desire.

She *must* resist. She could not betray Henry, dear Henry, who loved her so and was good to her way beyond what she deserved. And – she must never lose sight of this – he was not only her husband, but her King. In betraying him with Tom, she would be committing not just adultery, but treason.

But Henry might never find out . . .

Tom had ignored her warning. Still he was asking Jane to urge her to at least see him and talk with him, and Henry, whose leg was still keeping him largely confined to a chair, went on playing an unsuspecting Cupid, often suggesting that Tom look after Katheryn for him. This evening, as he watched them fondly from the dais, Tom was partnering the Queen in the dancing the King had ordered. Katheryn was making a tremendous effort to act in a regal manner and suppress her feelings for him, but, when he clasped her hand, she felt him press something into it. It was a folded paper, which she quickly slipped into her pocket, hoping that no one had seen.

She could not wait to get back to her chamber. The evening seemed to drag on interminably. But at last – at last – she was alone and could read it. He had written of his love for her, how it had been born when she was but a little girl, and how it had deepened when he first saw her at court. Could they not meet? he begged. He would ask nothing of her but her friendship.

Again, she was tempted. She wrote a reply. 'Have patience, and I will find a way to comply with what you wish.'

There was to be dancing again the following evening and it was inevitable that Tom partner her. She managed to pass her note to him and saw that he was overjoyed beyond measure and barely concealing the fact. She prayed no one would notice. 'I am so glad to hear the good news about your brother, Mr Culpeper!' she said in a loud voice.

She noticed Thomas Paston watching them. She had almost forgotten meeting him on the day she had first realised that Tom saw her as more than his little cousin. Jane had said recently that past on still bore her, Katheryn, favour, and it was probably true, for he was looking daggers at Tom. Well, you can look! she thought. She had never fancied him.

Two days later, at supper, Henry was grumbling that some servants of Tom and Thomas Paston had been brawling. 'They made a riotous and unlawful affray in Southwark, over God knows what!' I think I do, Katheryn thought. 'I've sent Paston to the Fleet prison for inciting it.'

At least it wasn't Tom's fault. Henry could see no wrong in Tom.

Jane was eager to arrange another meeting, but still Katheryn held back. She was not sure that she wanted to take any more risks.

The court moved to Whitehall for Easter, and Henry was much his old self again, happily making plans for Katheryn's official reception in London. He had said nothing about her being crowned, and she did not like to ask. Maybe he could not afford it, or maybe he was waiting for her to earn the privilege by bearing him a son.

He had decided that she was to be presented to the citizens of London in a river pageant. As she made her preparations, choosing what gown she was to wear, she was thinking of Queen Anne's river pageant seven years earlier and how splendid that had been. She hoped that hers would be the same.

The evening before, as she returned to her apartments after Vespers, she found her cousin Surrey waiting for her in the gallery.

'Good evening, my lord,' she said.

'I have a favour to ask of your Grace,' he told her, his eyes dark and brooding. 'I need your help.'

'What can I do for you?' she asked.

Surrey fell, rather dramatically, to his knees before her and clutched her hand, pressing it to his lips. 'You may have heard that my friends

Sir Thomas Wyatt and Sir John Wallop are in the Tower. Malicious persons have persuaded his Majesty that Sir Thomas is a Lutheran and that Sir John has praised the Pope, and that both are guilty of treason. But I know them well, Madam, and I can say, hand on heart, that none of it is true. Poor Wyatt is being held in a foul prison. Of your charity, will you intercede with the King for them?'

'Of course,' she said, thinking that on the day of her triumph, Henry would be inclined to grant her request.

'May God bless your Grace for your goodness!' Surrey cried, kissing her hand again.

She smiled at him. 'Get up, cousin. I'm happy to help. Now, walk with me to my lodgings and tell me something more of the circumstances.'

Wearing white damask and cloth of gold, she carried herself as a queen should when she entered the King's barge at Whitehall stairs and seated herself beside him in the cabin.

'You look beautiful!' he told her, taking her hand and holding it on his knee. The oarsmen pulled away and they were carried along the Thames towards Greenwich, past riverbanks crammed with cheering, waving crowds. Henry was in his element, smiling broadly from left to right, acknowledging the acclaim. At three o'clock, they passed under London Bridge and found waiting for them, in barges hung with tapestry and banners, the Lord Mayor and all the aldermen and craft-guilds of the City. They escorted the royal barge past the Tower, where there were great salvoes of artillery, and, when they arrived at Greenwich, all the ships docked there let off their guns in salute. The noise was deafening.

'A great triumph, darling,' Henry commented. 'My people love you.'

'Sir, I have a favour to ask.'

'What is your wish, sweetheart?'

'Might I entreat your Grace for the release of Sir Thomas Wyatt and Sir John Wallop? My cousin Surrey has explained all to me, and has convinced me that they have been slandered by false persons.'

'Hmm.' Henry looked doubtful.

'Please, for me? I beg of you, Henry!' She tried to get down on her knees, but he pulled her back.

'You'll have the boat over, Katheryn!' Suddenly, they were laughing. 'All right, I will pardon them both. I have come to have doubts myself about their guilt. And, on this day of all days, I cannot refuse you.'

'Oh, Henry, I am so grateful!' she cried. 'You have such a godly nature and are always inclined to pity and mercy. Thank you!'

He beamed at her, basking in her praise. 'But there is one condition,' he said, 'which is that Wyatt should return to his wife, from whom he has been separated for many years. It is not fitting that spouses live apart.' His lips pursed in that prim way he had. 'And he will be warned that he must be true to her henceforth on pain of death.'

She was aghast. 'But, Henry, from what I've heard from my cousin of Surrey, *she* was unfaithful to him.'

'He has been living in adultery with Bess Darrell, who used to serve the Princess Dowager, and it has to stop. Two wrongs can never make a right. He must return to his wife and follow the path of virtue.'

'Sir, I beg you to reconsider! I doubt he has seen his wife for many years.'

But Henry was immovable. There was no more that she could do.

Many people came to congratulate her on securing the pardoning of Wyatt. Henry himself was clearly impressed by her compassion for the prisoners and seemed to revel in the role of indulgent husband and merciful sovereign. In the wake of her successful intercession, Katheryn seized her moment and gathered her courage to beg him again to release her half-brother John Leigh, who was still in the Tower. Henry had not responded to her last pleas, but now he readily granted her request, and Katheryn had the pleasure of seeing John reunited with their sister Isabel, who cried tears of joy. Prison had subdued him; he was no longer the ebullient man Katheryn had known in her younger years, but it was heart-warming to be embraced by him and thanked for her wonderful kindness.

'Could you spare your good lady to be my gentlewoman?' she asked him.

His drawn face lit up. 'Elizabeth will be honoured, Madam!' Katheryn liked his wife, who was a warm, kindly soul.

'Then it is settled,' she said. 'She shall come to me when you have had some time together.'

On 21 March, Henry rode off to Dover to inspect the fortifications, leaving Katheryn and her ladies at Greenwich.

'I'll be back by Palm Sunday,' he told her, as she handed him the stirrup cup and bade him farewell. 'It won't be long before we are together again.'

Her flowers did not appear that month. She said nothing to Henry when he returned; she did not want to raise his hopes, only to dash them again. As the days wore on, she spent an increasing amount of time in her closet or the chapel, praying that God would send her a son. I will never see Tom Culpeper again! she vowed. Jane was still badgering her to meet him, reminding her that she had promised to do so, but she was now taking care to avoid being alone with Jane.

Her flowers did not come in April either. When Henry came to her bed, for the first time in weeks, and started caressing her, she had to tell him.

'We ought not,' she said. 'I think I am with child.'

He gathered her in his arms and held her tightly. She could sense the emotion in him. 'Oh, darling,' he breathed, 'if that is so, it will be a very great joy to me. And I will have you crowned at Whitsuntide.'

The very next day, he announced it. Her coronation was to take place on 5 June. Suddenly, everyone was astir, making preparations for it. An army of embroiderers were set to making furniture and tapestry for Westminster Abbey and Westminster Hall, where the coronation banquet was to be held. Copes and ornaments were borrowed from churches. The young lords and gentlemen of the court began practising for the jousts and tournaments Henry was planning.

Suddenly, Katheryn was gripped with fear. Someone mentioned Queen Jane, and she was forcefully reminded that Jane had died in childbed, like her own mother. She had never forgotten that terrible loss or the still figure on the bed. At a stroke, all her joy in her pregnancy was gone. If she could have wished the child away, she would.

And then . . .

She lay on her bed, weeping bitterly, reproaching herself. She had lost the baby. It lay, a tiny, curved blob of matter, no bigger than her fingertip, in a dish in her stool chamber. And it was all her fault. God had sent her a child in response to her prayers and He must be angry with her for wishing it away. She was not fit to be a mother.

Her ladies gathered around, trying to soothe her, but she would not be comforted, for Henry had yet to be told. Someone must have sent for him, for he came in a hurry.

She felt a hand on her shoulder.

'Hush now, Katheryn,' he said in a shaky voice. 'It is God's will. Maybe He does not intend for us to have children.'

That just made her cry more. It sounded like a death knell, as if he had given up hope. But she was still young. Surely God would let her conceive again.

'Rest now,' he said. 'I will come to you later.' But he did not. And soon she realised that all preparations for her coronation had ceased.

Part Four

'Breaking the fetters of
fame and chastity'

Chapter 24

1541

Henry's love for her had cooled, she knew it. She had disappointed him. Isabel tried to comfort her, saying that he had doubtless ceased coming to her bed because she was not yet over her miscarriage.

'But he could hold me, couldn't he, and reassure me that he still loves me!' she burst out. She could not bear to think that she had lost his love and his favour.

'Some men don't think like that,' Isabel said, patting her hand.

'If only he would come to dine with me!' Katheryn sobbed. 'I haven't seen him for three days.'

'He will come soon, I'm sure,' Isabel soothed. 'Now try to rest, so that you look your best for him when he does. Let me put some drops of distilled lavender on your pillow. That will help to calm you.' She sprinkled the bolster and drew the curtains against the daylight, then left, closing the door quietly behind her.

Inhaling the sharp scent of lavender, Katheryn lay there fretting. Please come, Henry! she prayed. God, please make him come. At the root of her distress was the fear that he would cast her away.

There was a soft tap, and someone entered the room. She sat up and saw Jane Rochford smiling at her in the dim light.

'I do hope your Grace is feeling better,' she said. 'I'm sure the King is grieving too for your sad loss, and that when he is himself again he will visit you.'

'I do hope so,' Katheryn whispered.

'But here is some good news,' Jane said, sitting down uninvited on the bed. 'His Grace has granted Mr Culpeper four manors in Gloucestershire and one in Wiltshire, as a reward for good service.

Our friend is becoming quite the man of property!'

'Jane, I am pleased for him, but I would like to be left alone to sleep now,' Katheryn said.

'Of course,' Jane replied. 'I will leave you in peace.' She tiptoed out.

A week later, when Katheryn had stopped bleeding and was feeling calmer, Henry came to supper. One look at his face told her that he too had been suffering.

'I trust you are recovered now, Katheryn,' he said, sitting down at the table. 'I am sorry I did not come to see you or send to you, but I have been ill myself.'

'I hope you are feeling better,' she said, wondering why they had suddenly become so formal with each other.

'I do well enough,' he sighed.

Their conversation seemed forced, with intermittent silences. Neither of them mentioned their lost child. At nine, earlier than usual, Henry rose, kissed her hand and left. He did not return the following evening.

She was distraught, convinced he would put her away. But how? Could he divorce her for being barren? She had no idea. Surely he had loved her too much to do anything worse? But, if he was angry with her . . . Icy shivers shot down her spine.

Jane came to her again as she sat, staring into space, in her window seat, apart from the others, and bent to her ear. 'I know something that will cheer you,' she murmured. 'I know of an old kitchen here where you can safely speak with Mr Culpeper.'

Katheryn wondered why she allowed herself to listen to Jane, but she knew the answer. It was because she liked to fantasise about what it would be like to have Tom love her. It excited her to have Jane dangle the possibility before her. She felt so dejected that she longed for the comfort of his arms. And why should she not avail herself of it? Henry didn't want her any more!

She lay all night thinking about it. By morning, she had made her decision.

* * *

298

The next day was Maundy Thursday. Early in the morning, she sent for her tailor. Fortunately, he had exactly what she wanted. Then she had to make ready to accompany Henry to the Maundy service in the Chapel Royal. There, clad, like him, in a voluminous white apron, she stood by holding a golden basin as he sat on a padded stool and washed the feet of fifty poor men and women, one for each year of his life. Of course, they had all had their feet thoroughly scoured beforehand, and been given clean clothes. They looked on in awe as the King of England bent to their footstools with a damp cloth and kissed their feet in emulation of Christ. Afterwards, he distributed among them leather purses filled with coins.

Katheryn found it hard to hold her patience during the long cere-mony. She was building up to what she had planned for the afternoon, which could not come soon enough. But then, when the last poor fellow had left the chapel, bowing his thanks, Henry said he would dine with her and the waiting was prolonged until she thought she would scream with frustration. By noon, though, she was free, Henry having gone to meet with his Council.

After a safe interval had elapsed, she sent her usher, Henry Webb, to escort Tom to her presence chamber, where her ladies waited with her. When Tom arrived, he was flushed, regarding her quizzically. As he fell on one knee, Katheryn stood up. 'Please rise, Mr Culpeper. I wish personally to thank you for the good service you have rendered to his Majesty during his illness.' She turned to her women. 'I would speak privily with Mr Culpeper. You may go.'

The door closed, leaving them alone.

'You sent for me!' he said.

'I was awaiting the right opportunity,' she told him. 'And I really do wish to express my appreciation for all you have done for the King's Grace. I want you to have this.' She placed in his hands a fair cap of velvet garnished with a brooch, three dozen pairs of aglets and a chain. 'Put these under your cloak, so that nobody sees them,' she charged him.

She waited for him to shower her with thanks. He must have known that a gift like this from a lady to her suitor was an exceptional favour.

Instead, he looked at her with something like exasperation. 'Alas, Madam, why did you not do this before you married the King?'

Anger flared up in her. She had risked much to give him what he had repeatedly asked for. Even now, her ladies might be wondering why she had insisted on their leaving her unattended. 'Is this all the thanks you give me?' she cried. 'If I had known you would speak thus, you would never have had those gifts!'

'Oh, forgive me, Katheryn,' he capitulated. 'It torments me that you could so easily have been mine. Yet you put your desire for a crown before our love, which is infinitely more precious.'

'I know,' she said. 'I *was* dazzled by the thought of being queen. I do love being queen. But, as I've told you, I had no choice in the matter. My lord of Norfolk and Bishop Gardiner were determined that the King should love me and gave me many good reasons why I should encourage it. I was to help save the true faith! How could I go against them? But what's done is done. Can we begin anew?'

He had raised his eyebrows at her revelations. 'It is my heart's desire,' he told her, taking her hand. 'Forgive me, I should not have sounded so ungrateful. These are fine gifts and I will treasure them.'

'Let none know who gave them to you!'

'Never!' He smiled at her. How she ached to go into his arms. But it was too public a place. 'I had no idea,' he said. 'Forgive me for judging you harshly. Of course you had no choice. But there is always another day. How can we meet?'

'Lady Rochford will help us. I'm sure she will let us use her chamber. But I'd rather not go to that kitchen.'

'Kitchen?'

'You didn't know? She said she knows of a disused kitchen where we could meet in secret.'

'You are worthy of better than that,' Tom said, raising her hand and kissing it. 'Tell me . . .' His eyes, dark with longing, sought hers. 'What may I hope for?'

She felt a flutter of panic. 'Don't hope for too much, please. Remember what I am. There are risks I dare not take. I hope you understand.'

'I do, Katheryn. I can be patient. For you, I would wait for ever.'

Jane was more than accommodating. Of course, they must use her chamber! She would keep watch in the gallery. She was so pleased that they had become friends again.

The first time they were alone together in the moonlit room, Katheryn felt awkward. The big tester bed beckoned, but she had made her position clear. Tom kissed her, reverently at first, then more demandingly, but she broke away. 'Let's just talk,' she said.

'Whatever you wish,' he said. So they sat on the bench at the bedfoot and reminisced about the old days at Oxon Hoath and Lambeth.

'I had lovers before,' Katheryn confessed.

'That does not matter,' he told her. 'They cannot be rivals to me now.'

Neither of them mentioned the greatest rival of them all, who was sleeping, unsuspecting, in his great bedchamber beyond the door at the further end of the gallery.

'Do you still see Bess Harvey?' she asked.

'No,' he said. 'It was a passing fancy. I hope we can be more than that.'

Why was it, she asked herself, that she wanted Tom so desperately, was drinking in every aspect of him and feeling quite faint at being together in such intimacy, yet could not communicate her feelings to him? 'That is my hope too,' she said, knowing it conveyed nothing of the desire she felt.

'I have brought you a token,' he said, and gave her a garnet ring. 'A token of my love. You know, sweet Katheryn, I love you more than the King or any other person ever could. My only hope is that you could love me half as much.'

His mention of Henry had made her feel so disloyal that she heard little else of what he said. When she remained silent, he put his arm around her. 'Tell me I may hope,' he whispered.

'Yes, you may hope,' she said. 'But now I must leave. It grows late and my ladies will wonder where I am.'

'Must you go so soon?' He looked appalled.

'Yes! Good night, Tom.' She left the chamber with tears in her eyes. It was galling that she, who had never lacked for things to say or do to entice her admirers, should be so gauche with the man she loved. And it was love; she was certain of it. An entirely different love from that which she felt for Henry. Pray God Tom would not be put off! It was her last waking thought that night.

Some days later, Jane brought her word that Tom was sick. 'Our friend has a high fever and is confined to his chamber.' Katheryn longed to go to him, to bully the doctors and do everything in her power to make him well. What if he died? She might die herself, for sorrow.

All she could do was send him, through the good offices of Morris, her page, the kind of gifts that might be sent with propriety to any servant who was ill: red meat to strengthen the blood, and fresh fish, so heartening for an invalid. Morris reported that Mr Culpeper was very pleased with the gifts and had promised him a reward.

She knew she was running a risk, but she could not resist sending Tom a letter, which she planned to conceal in a basket of manchet rolls. Hating to write anything, she began by dictating to the ever-willing Jane what she wanted to say. Then, needing to seize this golden chance of making her feelings clear, and wanting to keep them private, she decided to continue it herself.

When it was finished, she read it over.

Master Culpepper, I heartily recommend myself to you, praying you to send me word how you are doing. I was informed that you were sick, which troubles me very much, and will do until I hear from you, for I never longed so much for anything as I do to see you and speak with you, which, I trust, shall happen shortly. The thought of that comforts me very much every time I think of it; and when I think that you will have to depart from me again afterwards, it makes my heart die to think what ill fortune I have that I cannot be always in your company. Yet my trust is always in you, that you will be as you have promised me, and in that hope I trust still, praying that you will come when my Lady Rochford is here, for then I shall be at leisure to be at your command.

Thank you for having promised to be good to that poor fellow, my page. I pray you, keep him with you, that I may sometimes hear from you. Thus, I take my leave of you, trusting to see you shortly. I wish you were with me now, that you might see what pain I take in writing to you.

Yours as long as life endures,

Katheryn

Tom made a speedy recovery, much to Katheryn's heartfelt relief, and she contrived a second meeting in Jane's chamber, to which Jane led him up the privy stair at dead of night once it was certain that the King was not coming to visit Katheryn's bed and her women were asleep. As soon as the door had closed behind him, he kissed and embraced her.

'You could not know what a health your sweet letter was to me,' he breathed. 'I have read it so many times that it's in danger of crumbling away. Did you mean it all, Katheryn?'

'Every word,' she said. After that, she felt more relaxed in his company and better able to express herself – and what she lacked in demonstrativeness, he more than made up for, though not in a disrespectful way. She marvelled at how restrained they both were, especially when she remembered how free she had been in her passions before she came to court. Once, when she was in Tom's arms, his hand cupped her breast, but she pulled it away. 'Not yet!' she whispered. She could feel the sexual tension in him, but he made no protest. And, when he bade her farewell in the first light of dawn, after they had talked for hours, he kissed her hand and said, 'I promise I will presume no further.' She loved him for that.

There were as many meetings as they could contrive after that, mostly in Jane's chamber, but sometimes in Katheryn's. Always, Jane stood guard for them. She did everything she could to encourage them, arranging their trysts and acting as a go-between and confidante. Katheryn confessed to her how deep her love for Tom ran, and Jane explained to him how difficult Katheryn found it to express the strength of her feelings. Before long, however, her rapturous welcome at their reunions could have left him in no doubt of the love she bore him.

She was well aware of the risks she was taking. 'If this is spied one day, we will all be undone,' she told Jane. 'But if none of it ever comes out, then I need fear nothing.'

'No one will hear of it from me,' Jane vowed.

'I know that.' Katheryn kissed her. 'If anyone asks if something is going on, just deny it utterly.'

They had no choice but to trust each other. Sometimes Katheryn would lie in bed at night and ask herself what she thought she was doing, carrying on a love affair behind the King's back. It was folly for the Queen of England to behave so rashly. Her cousin Queen Anne seemed to be much in her thoughts these days. Yet she loved Tom so much, and they weren't doing any harm, were they? Anne had committed adultery with many lovers. Katheryn and Tom hadn't ever been lovers, even though both of them desired it. Love for the King had held them back – and fear of the consequences.

In the mornings, she would feel bold again, convinced that it was possible to enjoy the love of both the men in her life. In such a mood, she would send Tom word through Lady Rochford that she was languishing and dying of love for him, or would send him a loving present. More often than not, Morris, whom she had sworn to secrecy with the threat of dismissal if he talked, would bring her pretty gifts in return.

Early in May, Katheryn went by barge to the royal palace at Chelsea to ensure that all was in readiness for the coming visit of her stepdaughter the Lady Elizabeth. In response to her pleas, Henry had decided it was high time that she met his younger children, and Katheryn was looking forward to it. Elizabeth was seven, just a child, and would surely not be as difficult as her sister, the Lady Mary; and she was Katheryn's own cousin on her mother's side.

She wished Tom could come with her, but it was impossible. He had no business escorting the Queen, unless Henry commanded him, and Henry had not. But how lovely it would have been to walk together in these beautiful gardens and dine in the shade of those trees by the river!

Satisfied that the best plate was on display, the furniture polished to a shine and the sheets crisp and bleached, she lodged at Baynard's Castle, one of her dower properties, a massive white stone edifice with tall towers, rising majestically from the River Thames, a few streets down from St Paul's Cathedral. Two days later, she returned to Chelsea to be informed that Elizabeth had already arrived and was walking in the gardens. Proceeding along a gravelled walk, her ladies following, Katheryn saw ahead of her a little girl with long flame-red hair and a woman wearing black – the nurse, Mrs Astley, she assumed. Henry was always singing her praises, saying how learned she was and how well she looked to the welfare of his daughter.

The child turned at her approach and Katheryn was startled to see how old a face she had. There was a regal wariness about her, and no wonder, given her bastard status and what had happened to her mother. She curtseyed gracefully, head bowed. Katheryn had intended to take her into her arms and play the good stepmother, but instinct told her that there would be no cuddling of this child, who was much on her dignity. So she bent forward and kissed Elizabeth lightly on both cheeks, smiling a welcome.

Within an afternoon, she had realised that there was an unbreachable gulf between them. Elizabeth was advanced for her years and ageless in her wisdom. Her learning was formidable. Katheryn was at a loss to compete with her. The only thing they shared was vanity, and there was a limit to how long you could spend talking about fashion. The woman whose blood they shared could not, for obvious reasons, be mentioned. Besides, Elizabeth was restive. She was longing to be off to Waltham, where Henry was waiting for them with Prince Edward. It was quite obvious that Henry was Elizabeth's hero and that she had little time for her stepmother. Katheryn made an effort to get closer to her, but it was hard work. She reminded herself that Elizabeth had had two stepmothers already and neither had lasted long. Could you blame her for not wanting to give her heart to another one? And the ironic thing, Katheryn told herself, is that *I'm* probably going to be the one who lasts.

The next day, they travelled to Dallance, the King's house near Waltham Abbey in Essex. There, in the hall, Henry was waiting for them with the Lady Mary, who was holding Prince Edward's hand. Henry opened his arms to Elizabeth and, omitting to curtsey, she ran into them.

'And Katheryn, my sweetheart, welcome!' he cried, embracing her. There was no trace of the awkwardness that had lain between them before. She knew herself forgiven. 'How I have missed you!' Henry told her. He released her and gave his son a gentle push in her direction. 'Allow me to present the Prince of Wales.'

Katheryn watched, enchanted, as the sturdy three-year-old toddled towards her and made a good attempt at a courtly bow. Then, because he was the heir to England, she bobbed him a small curtsey, which made him chuckle with pride.

'What a lovely boy your Grace is!' she said. 'I have brought you a gift.' And she took from her pocket a silver horse and rider, small enough to fit in her palm.

Henry was smiling his approval. 'What do you say, Sir?'

'Thank you, Queen Kaffewyn,' the child said. His sweet, heart-shaped face with its chubby cheeks and pointed chin was pink with pleasure. He held out the toy to his half-sister Elizabeth. 'Isn't it pretty, Bess?' he asked her. For answer, she gave him a tight hug.

'May we go and play, Sir?' she asked her father.

'Off you go,' he replied. 'Mrs Astley, take them into the garden.' The nurse stepped forward and took their hands. They looked so vulnerable, those two motherless children, for all their rich clothes and servants.

'They are inseparable,' Mary said. 'It is touching so see how much they love each other.'

'They are delightful children,' Katheryn enthused, 'and so like you, Sir. They have your colouring.' She wished she could be the mother of one such.

Henry looked as proud as could be. 'They are good children too,' he said. 'Now, you will be hungry after your journey. Let us go in to dinner.'

The three of them dined in his privy chamber, with Tom and another gentleman in attendance. Katheryn was careful not to let her eyes stray in Tom's direction. 'Your Grace is looking very well,' Mary said to Katheryn.

'Thank you. I trust that you yourself are in health?'

'I am not so bad. The autumn is my worst time. I get all sorts of ailments then, for some strange reason.'

'I told you to keep taking that cordial I made up for you,' Henry said. He loved concocting medicines and seemed to be quite expert at it. He had a remedy for everything.

He turned to Katheryn. 'Darling, I have decided to give Mary permission to reside at court whenever she wishes.'

'Of course,' Katheryn replied, with good grace. 'We shall be companions for each other.' Mary looked gratified.

'I am having new apartments built for her at Hampton Court,' the King went on. 'I hope, daughter, that we shall have the pleasure of your company soon, and that you will join us for this summer's progress. It will be the greatest ever, for we are going to Lincoln and York. I mind to bring my subjects in those places to submission following the late rebellion.'

Katheryn had heard of the Pilgrimage of Grace because her Uncle Norfolk had helped to crush it. The so-called pilgrims had marched four years earlier in a desperate bid to halt the King's religious reforms and the dissolution of the monasteries, and been ruthlessly suppressed. She remembered hearing tales of the mass hangings that had followed it. She hoped they would not be riding into hostile territory.

'And I want to meet my nephew the King of Scots,' Henry went on. 'He has agreed to ride south to York.'

'I should love to accompany your Graces,' Mary said.

'That's settled, then. I plan to leave at the end of June. Let's hope the weather will be kind to us. It's going to be a long journey.'

Chapter 25

1541

Henry and Katheryn returned to Greenwich to prepare for the progress. They would be away for several weeks and Katheryn was very busy planning her wardrobe. She would need dozens of new gowns and kirtles and hoods – the list seemed endless.

Isabel helped her, but she seemed preoccupied.

'Is something wrong?' Katheryn asked.

Isabel smiled at her. 'I've noticed that you've been spending a lot of time with Lady Rochford recently. I think you should be wary of her. She has a poor reputation.'

Katheryn froze and had to take a moment to collect her thoughts. 'You mean it's true that she laid evidence against her husband?'

'That, yes – and her unbridled dealings with men. She was notorious when she was younger.'

'I know nothing of that,' Katheryn said firmly, 'so she can't have been that notorious. She certainly isn't free with her favours now.'

'Well, just be prudent. There's something unsavoury about her.'

Isabel was jealous, Katheryn concluded, sorting through her jewels. *She'd have preferred it if I'd confided in her.* If she had, she knew what would have happened: Isabel would have told her to cease all contact with Tom. And that was why she hadn't made her sister privy to her love for him. Isabel would have tried to make her put her duty before her pleasure.

She felt a tremor of excitement, anticipating that the long trip would afford her opportunities to be alone with Tom. Henry had reeled off a list of the places where they would be staying; surely there would be somewhere it would be possible to be together. Jane could help spy out the land. Katheryn sighed with longing. It was all the more desperate because it was unsatisfied and probably never could be. And since Henry had recovered and been visiting her bed every night, intent on getting her with child again, she had barely seen Tom at all.

Now Henry had gone to Whitehall to deal with pressing matters of state and taken Tom with him. She was sleeping alone and – she sighed again – pleasuring herself.

She was on her knees in her closet, rummaging through chests for an embroidery pattern she wanted for a night-rail, when she heard her maids talking in the bedchamber next door.

'Is it true what I heard someone say at the tennis play today, that his Grace is going to set aside the Queen and take back the Lady of Cleves?' Elizabeth Fitzgerald asked.

'If it's true that she is barren, then he has cause,' Damascin Stradling put in. 'But what will become of us?'

'Hush!' warned Lucy Somerset. 'I think the Queen is in there.' This was in a whisper, but it carried.

'Oh, dear,' Elizabeth said and whispered something Katheryn could not hear. Their footsteps receded, leaving her kneeling there, trembling, the tambour forgotten in her hand. Not these rumours again! She had thought them all put to bed weeks ago.

Could it be true? Henry had given no hint that he was tiring of her, but then you never knew with Henry. They said he had shown a smiling face to Cromwell right up to the morning of his arrest. He might well be dissembling with her too. After all, she *had* lost their child.

Yet who had been spreading these rumours? Someone with inside knowledge? No, they must be pure idle gossip, spread by people who had nothing better to do. Henry would be cross with her for heeding them. She tried to put what she had heard out of her mind, but failed.

When Henry returned from Whitehall that evening and arrived to have supper with her, she was aware of not being her usual happy, flirtatious self. Instead, she was watching for any sign that he no longer loved her.

'What's the matter, darling?' he asked at length, covering her hand with his. 'You've been sad and thoughtful ever since I arrived.'

She hesitated to tell him what was on her mind in case it was true, or he thought her a fool for believing it, yet she had to say it, otherwise she would go on torturing herself. 'You'll think me silly, but I heard my maids repeating a rumour that you are about to take back the Lady Anna.'

'Oh, Katheryn! When will you learn not to give credence to gossip? You are wrong to attach faith to reports of that kind. Iif I ever did have to marry again – which Heaven forbid – I would never take my lady of Cleves.'

His words reassured her. He pulled her onto his knee and began kissing and caressing her. 'Let this put your mind at rest,' he murmured. Then he led her to her bedchamber and himself acted as her tirewoman, untying her sleeves, unlacing her gown and pulling off her stockings. When she stood naked before him, he ran his hands over her body. Closing her eyes, she imagined that it was Tom doing it, and became very excited and wanton, surprising Henry with her boldness. Soon they were on the bed, making love quite passionately, and she was enjoying it, welcoming Henry into her and sending him into raptures.

Afterwards, as she lay in the crook of his arm, she felt guilty because the thought of Tom had inflamed her. But Henry was happy and oblivious, and that was really all that mattered.

That May, there were several days when she hardly saw Henry and, when she did, he was distracted and irritable.

'There's been an uprising in Yorkshire,' he told her, when he made time to sup with her. 'It's the Papists, of course. They wanted to depose my Lord President of the North and restore the old forms of religion. Well, they're not so bullish now. We've got them on the run, and as soon as they're caught, they will be executed.' He hesitated. 'It is my belief that they meant to take Lady Salisbury from the Tower and set her on the throne.'

'No!' Katheryn said, laying down her knife. 'I cannot believe it.'

'You know nothing of her,' Henry said, with unusual severity. 'I know her of old. She is a very dangerous woman. Even if she wasn't involved, she is a lure for dissidents and, while she lives, I can never be truly safe on my throne.'

'Henry, she's an old lady! What can she do against you?'

'She can sit on my throne and wear my crown! I'm sorry if it upsets you, Katheryn, but I intend to have the sentence on her carried out without delay.'

'You're having her executed?'

'Yes.' He was adamant. 'This disaffection among my northern subjects could lead to more plots for a restoration of the old royal line. Lady Salisbury is a threat to the security of the realm – and my throne. She must die.'

'Please, Henry, don't do this, I beg you!' Katheryn slid to her knees by the table and grasped his hand with both of hers. He regarded her with a mixture of pain and exasperation.

'This is one request I cannot grant you. I loved Lady Salisbury. She is my cousin and she was governess to Mary, and I thought her the saintliest woman in England. But that was long ago, before she nurtured a nest of vipers and turned against me. Now I must do what is necessary – the matter touches me too near.'

Katheryn knew herself defeated. She dared not press him further. It was awesome, the power he wielded. One word from him, and someone would die. She could not bear to imagine what it would be like for poor Lady Salisbury, being told that her time had come, after two years in the Tower, during which she must have imagined that imprisonment was the worst she would suffer. How would she feel, learning that she was to die imminently, to walk to the scaffold knowing that the seconds were petering out and that she would have to lay her head on the block and wait for the axe to descend? How would she find the courage to face that horror? Katheryn had often tried to imagine what it had been like for her cousin Anne – and she had had a cleaner death by the sword.

She got up, very distressed, then sat down again.

'When will you give the order?' she asked.

'Tonight,' Henry said. 'She will die in the morning.' As Katheryn felt tears welling, she noticed that he had stopped eating and wondered if beneath the tough statesman lay a heart that shrank at such necessary measures. She was beginning to understand why Henry's name struck dread into many. And this was the man she had married, and whose trust she was betraying.

While her ladies were packing for the court's removal to Whitehall, which was planned for the afternoon, Katheryn spent much of the next morning in her closet, on her knees in prayer before the altar hung with cloth of gold.

'Let her not suffer!' she beseeched the statue of the Virgin Mother. 'Vouchsafe her a quick passage into Heaven!'

She emerged at dinner time and seated herself at table in her privy chamber, but waved the food away, for the last thing she felt like was eating. Then Henry arrived and sat down heavily opposite her. His face was grey.

'Ladies, you may leave us,' he said, and her women curtseyed and were gone.

He took Katheryn's hand. 'Darling, Lady Salisbury died this morning. I want you to hear what happened from me before you hear it from anyone else, because you should know that it was not of my doing.'

She tensed. 'What happened, Henry?'

'The Constable of the Tower escorted her to Tower Green. Because of her high rank, I had ordered that the execution take place in private. There was no time to build a scaffold, so the block was on the grass. She took her fate calmly and commended her soul to God, desiring the Lord Mayor and others present to pray for me and you, and for Prince Edward and the Lady Mary.' He paused, seemingly reluctant to go on. 'The public executioner is away in the north, dealing with the rebels, so the Constable had found some wretched, blundering youth to perform his office. Alas, he did not do the job cleanly. I fear death was not instantaneous. By God, they shall know my displeasure in this!'

'Oh, no!' Katheryn's hands flew to her face. 'That is terrible!' She could barely imagine just how terrible. She broke down in floods of tears.

'Don't!' Henry said, getting up and gathering her to him.

'It was bad enough that she had to die,' she sobbed.

'It was a necessity,' he said gruffly, 'but I did not wish this on her.'

He held her for a few moments, then gave her his kerchief to mop away the tears.

'Come, eat something. We'll be leaving for Whitehall soon and I don't want you feeling sick if you sail on an empty stomach.'

She made herself eat some meat and drank some wine to try to steady herself, but she could not get the ghastly image she had conjured of Lady Salisbury's last moments out of her head. It was with her as she boarded the royal barge and seated herself next to Henry in the cushioned cabin, and as they sailed westwards up the Thames. When the Tower came into view, she could not stop shuddering.

Henry put his arm around her. 'I have some good news for you. I'm giving your brothers licences to import wine from Gascony and timber from Toulouse. That will bring them a very good income.'

She knew he was doing his best to distract her from all thought of what had taken place behind those grim walls only that morning. Was Lady Salisbury's poor body buried yet? she wondered.

'That is most generous, Henry,' she said, although she knew she was not reacting as he had hoped. Normally, she would be flinging her arms around him and kissing him. 'They will be so grateful.'

He slid his arm away. 'Come, Katheryn – the woman was a traitor. You should have saved your tears for gratitude that I was not overthrown by these rebels.'

'But the manner of her dying—'

'That was not my fault!' Rarely had he spoken so sharply to her. She turned away and stared out of the window, fighting back tears. They were passing London now. Soon, they would be at Whitehall and she could get away from him and weep.

He said no more apart from commenting on how fine the City looked with all its church spires pointing up to the sky. She nodded, but said nothing, and he lapsed into silence again. She could sense that he was angry with her.

'I am on your side, Henry, really I am,' she blurted out. 'I know that traitors have to be punished. But if you hadn't ordered Lady Salisbury's execution, she would not have suffered as she did.'

'So it *is* my fault!' he flared. '*I* did not wield the axe.' His face had flamed a dangerous red. 'A fine thing it is when my own wife takes the part of a traitor who would have had my throne!' He was tense with anger.

'But you don't know that—'

'By God, Katheryn, she was attainted by Parliament. You've said enough. Be silent!'

Never had he been so harsh with her. She sat there, tears streaming down her cheeks, not caring if anyone noticed.

The oarsmen were pulling in at Whitehall stairs.

'Compose yourself,' Henry muttered. Katheryn dabbed at her eyes and followed him along the gangway. He handed her out of the barge and they walked together through the gallery to the royal lodgings, putting on smiles for the courtiers waiting to greet them. Katheryn caught Tom's eye and saw him look again at her for a second or so. He must have seen that she had been crying. Heavens – he might be thinking that they were discovered!

At the door of her lodgings, Henry kissed her hand and bowed. 'I will see you anon, Madam.' As she curtseyed, he walked away.

He did not come that night – had she really expected him to after their first real quarrel? She realised she had been foolish to argue with him, and over such a sensitive subject. Their conversation kept repeating itself in her head, vying for room with the horrific image of Lady Salisbury being chopped to death. She did not think she could feel more wretched.

When midnight had passed with still no sign of Henry, she sent for Jane Rochford.

'Can you get word to Mr Culpeper, asking him to come here?' she asked.

Jane smiled. 'Of course, if he is not sleeping in the King's bedchamber. We have a prearranged code. If he gets a message from me saying that I would beg a favour, which is nothing unusual, for he gets many such, he will know that you wish to see him.'

'And is it all right if we use your chamber?' Katheryn asked.

'Madam, for you and Mr Culpeper, it is a pleasure.'

Katheryn could not stop herself. 'Why are you doing this for us?' she asked.

Jane returned her gaze. 'Because I love you both. You are a sweet girl, Madam, and deserve to be happy.'

'And Mr Culpeper?'

'I have long liked him, ever since he first came to court as a beautiful youth at the time of the King's Great Matter.'

'Is that all? You are taking dangerous risks for us.'

Jane hesitated and lowered her voice. 'Madam, it is treason to speak of the King's death, or even to imagine it, as Queen Anne found to her cost. But anyone can see that he is not a well man, and the Prince is very young. If there were to be a regency, you, as the Queen, might find yourself a rich widow in a position of influence and needing good friends – and, maybe, a new husband after a suitable interval. That is all we wish to be to you: good friends.'

Katheryn stared at her. Was Tom using her as a stepping stone to power and riches? Had he and Jane planned this together? Had they played her like a puppet? She was so appalled she felt a little faint.

'So he does not love me after all?' she countered in a voice that was shaking. 'He just wants what I can give him – and you want your share too!'

'No!' Jane protested. 'No! He loves you deeply, never doubt it. He would have married you before, remember? God knows, you had nothing to offer him then in the way of riches and power. He was heartbroken when you wed the King, preferring glory and fame to him.'

It was true. And Tom would have had to have been a good actor indeed to have kept up the pretence of loving her during the past weeks.

'It was the King's illness that made him realise what might happen if . . . Well, I dare not say it. Mr Culpeper has a powerful position in the Privy Chamber and knows the ways of the court well. He could protect and advise you. He wants to marry you more than anything in this life, and he is willing to wait. Together, you would enjoy great influence and wealth and be very happy. We could all benefit. Truly,

Katheryn, we are not using you. I have ever been your friend.'

We again. Katheryn did not like that. She wished they had confided to her their aims from the outset. It still seemed to her that Jane, in particular, was using her. As for Tom . . .

'I need to see him,' she said. 'Send for him now.'

When Tom crept into Jane's chamber, his face lit up to see Katheryn waiting alone there.

'Is Lady Rochford on watch?' she asked.

'Yes. She is sitting in the gallery. Oh, Katheryn . . .' He went to embrace her, but she drew back.

'I was used by those who wanted to marry me to the King for their own ends,' she said. 'Now it seems I am being used again, by one who should love me. Do you think to gain power through me?'

Tom looked aghast. 'I seek only to love you – and to marry you. It can only be a matter of time.'

'Keep your voice down! The walls have ears in this place. Jane says you hope for influence in the event of a regency, and she hopes to profit from it too – from me!'

Tom clasped her tightly and would not let go, even though she struggled to free herself. 'Katheryn, I would marry you if you were a kitchen maid. The fact that you are queen makes no difference to me. You cannot doubt that I love you. But you *are* queen, and if we marry, we can all prosper. Even if Jane is helping us for mercenary reasons, we have cause to thank her. And remember, she helped us long before the King decided to marry you.'

Katheryn allowed herself to relax in his arms. 'I've been thinking about that. I've wondered all along what her motive was.'

'Between ourselves, she's a frustrated woman who takes a vicarious pleasure in the love lives of others. I've often had the impression that she is in love with me herself, but if so, why does she encourage me to love you?'

'I've thought the same thing,' Katheryn said. 'It's a bit strange.'

'Never doubt me!' he urged, and she let him kiss her.

'Forgive me for thinking ill of you,' she murmured. 'It's been a terrible day and I was upset anyway. You've heard about Lady Salisbury?'

'Yes,' he said, holding her against him. 'I was horrified. Everyone is.'

'The King is angry with me because I criticised him for it. I had pleaded for her life, but he would not listen.'

'That was brave of you. He has been in an uncertain temper of late.'

'It was the least I could do.' She shrank from the memory of how Henry had spoken to her.

They sat on the bed and talked for a long while, then fell to kissing until the first light of dawn broke.

For much of June, Henry did not visit her table or her bed. In chapel or when she sat enthroned beside him in the presence chamber, he was courteous and smiling, and no one would have known that he was displeased with her. But she was aware that he was avoiding her company. For all she knew, he was seeking his pleasures elsewhere. It was a fine way to get a son, she fumed.

She kept to her lodgings. Tom visited her almost every night, and Jane kept watch. Once, when there were servants coming and going along the gallery – someone must have been ill – she sat in the room with them with her back turned. It was inhibiting, and Katheryn felt awkward when Tom tried to embrace her. 'For God's sake, Jane is too near us!' she cried. She had not been so modest at Lambeth, she remembered with some shame. But Tom was special. She loved him more than she had ever loved anyone, and she did not want anything sullying that love.

'Edward tells me that his Majesty is taking with him to the north his richest clothing and the most sumptuous tapestries and plate from Whitehall,' Isabel revealed one morning, as she served Katheryn's breakfast. 'He believes you will be crowned at York.'

Katheryn was startled to hear that. But she began to believe it when she encountered Henry in the gardens that morning, as she was out walking with her ladies, and he welcomed her with a resounding kiss. She was bewildered by the change in his manner, unable to account for his sudden warmth towards her. Maybe he had not been angry with her, but ill? He was limping quite badly today.

'What a fair sight on such a beautiful day!' he exclaimed. 'Well met, Katheryn!'

She curtseyed as the gentlemen in attendance on him grinned, doffing their caps and bowing. Only Tom was unsmiling.

'Come, darling, we will walk together,' Henry said, leading her ahead of the rest. 'Are you all prepared for the progress?' he asked.

'Yes, Sir. My new gowns arrived yesterday.'

'I know. I received the bill. You will be the ruin of me yet!' He gave her a sideways glance.

'I am very sorry if I have displeased you,' she said.

He took her meaning. 'I could never be angry with you for long, darling,' he assured her, tucking her hand in the crook of his elbow. 'This journey north is to be an important one. I usually go away for the hunting, and there'll be plenty of that, but I intend this progress to be especially magnificent, to overawe and impress my northern subjects and teach them that I am not to be flouted. Regrettably, there are still a lot of Papists in those regions who dislike my reforms. I mean to reinforce my authority in the north and collect the fines levied on those cities that supported the Pilgrimage of Grace.'

'Have you visited the north before, Sir?' she asked.

'No; there, I am just a name to the people. Well, they will know me better soon! And I look forward to meeting my nephew King James and establishing a better friendship between us. It will serve to protect my northern border from a Scottish invasion.' He turned around to his gentlemen. 'Aye, we'll make such a display of England's might that they'll all cower in terror!' The courtiers cheered, clapping each other on the back.

'Oh, Sir, I do hope you will not be placing yourself in danger,' Katheryn fretted. 'You are making me fearful to go on this journey.'

'Nonsense!' Henry roared, as the men laughed. 'I'm taking such a force of men-at-arms that my train will be more like a military camp than a court. And you, my Queen, can expect to be well received, for your family is well known in the north. The people there have not forgotten how your grandfather vanquished the Scots at Flodden.'

That was true, but Katheryn was aware that their most recent memory of the Howards would be Uncle Norfolk's bloody suppression of the Pilgrimage of Grace. She made herself stifle that thought. With an army in attendance, she would surely be safe.

Katheryn was in a good mood as she and her ladies selected the clothes she would take on the progress. It dissipated when an usher brought her a sealed package. She was astonished and dismayed to see that it was from Francis Dereham. What could he possibly have to say to her now?

Going into her closet, she broke the seal and found ten pounds in gold enclosed in a letter. He had addressed her with all the proper courtesies and was craving a favour. Could she see her way clear to offering him a post in her household?

The money was a bribe, no less. It made her feel much as she had felt a year ago when Joan Bulmer sent her that threatening letter; mercifully, she had heard no more from Joan and she prayed that happy state of affairs would continue. There was no implied threat here, no reminder of their shared past, but sending her such a large sum carried its own message.

She did not want Francis anywhere near her. He was the living embodiment of everything she was keen to forget. She did not think she could trust him to keep silent about what they had shared; she had not forgotten how loose-tongued he could be when he was in his cups. The further away from Henry she could keep him, the better. She did not want him watching her, wanting her, going on about her being his wife . . . And what if he got wind that there was something between her and Tom? That did not bear thinking about.

She had to refuse his request. What could she say? Then she remembered that she was the Queen and need say nothing. All she had to do was ignore the letter and hope that he would get the message.

Chapter 26

1541

She had never seen so many people and horses assembled together. They were saying that it was the greatest royal retinue the country had witnessed since Henry had met the French King at the Field of Cloth of Gold twenty-one years earlier before she was born.

'There are five thousand horses here and one thousand soldiers,' Henry told her, as they stood on the palace steps surveying the scene before them. He was dressed for riding and eager to be on his way. The entire court was to accompany him – an astonishing number of people. Those who could not be accommodated in the houses where he, Katheryn and the Lady Mary were to stay would sleep in tents. Prince Edward, of course, was to stay behind – Henry was obsessively anxious about his health and safety – and Archbishop Cranmer, Lord Chancellor Audley, the Earl of Hertford and Sir Ralph Sadler were remaining in London to attend to matters of state.

'A more dangerous bunch of heretics you could not hope to meet,' Norfolk growled in Katheryn's ear, watching them conferring with the King. 'We'll be lucky if England hasn't turned Protestant by the time we get back.'

'Uncle, you worry too much,' Katheryn chided him. 'The King would not have appointed them if he didn't trust them.'

'He trusted Cromwell,' the Duke reminded her.

'Yes, and he lived to regret it,' she replied.

'God send that he does not live to regret putting that lot in charge,' Norfolk humphed.

It looked as if the King was ready to depart. Seeing him walking towards his horse, Katheryn hastened to join him. Around them, everyone was mounting, saying farewells or shouting out last-minute orders. Seated in the saddle, Henry gave the signal, trumpets sounded, and he and Katheryn rode forth side by side at the head of their great train – five thousand persons in all, he told her.

He was looking up anxiously at the grey sky. 'It's unseasonably cold for late June. I hope it won't rain. We've some miles to go before we can seek shelter.'

Katheryn hoped so too. She did not want her green velvet riding habit ruined.

The rain held off for the first few days. They rode northwards, lodging at Hatfield, Dunstable and Ampthill on the route to Grafton, hunting and hawking on the way. At every town and city, people flocked to see them. Henry would ride ahead, mounted on his great horse, with his chief lords in front, two by two, and sixty or eighty archers with drawn bows following. Katheryn, the Lady Mary and the other ladies followed behind. Streets were gaily bedecked and there were speeches, lavish receptions, and banquets. Henry won hearts by exerting his compelling charm and making himself accessible to all who sought his justice.

Katheryn marvelled at the efficient arrangements that had been made for transporting such large numbers of people. The various departments of the royal household provided mountains of food for all, supplemented by game, fish and fowl caught by the hunting parties and prepared in field kitchens.

After a good start, their progress was slow. As Henry had feared, rain and storms hampered it. The roads leading north were all flooded and the baggage carts proceeded only with great difficulty. Everyone was drenched daily, and soon Katheryn gave up worrying about the state of her clothes. There was nothing she could do about it. Every night, she was so cold that they had to light fires in her rooms – and this was July!

'I had reckoned to be in Lincoln by this time,' Henry grumbled, when they had been on the road for three weeks. 'This rain has been incessant. It grieves me to see the crops so damaged.' He waved a hand in the direction of the fields stretching into the distance.

That day, Katheryn went down with a streaming cold and they had to stay an extra night at the royal manor house at Grafton to allow her time to recover. Her maids were wondering if the King would give the order to turn back, but she knew he wouldn't. The progress meant too much to him. Yet, at this rate, they wouldn't reach Lincoln until the middle of August.

After Grafton the weather cleared, and the royal procession was able to press on to Northampton at a faster pace. Katheryn was feeling better and Henry was in a buoyant mood. So far, there had been no opportunity to arrange a tryst with Tom and, by the time they reached Loddington Hall in late July, Katheryn was going out of her mind with frustration. It had been weeks since they had been alone together, and she had caught only glimpses of him in the procession or hurrying in or out of their lodgings. They had barely had time to exchange glances. At Loddington, fearing he would think she had cooled, she took pains to compose a letter to him, telling him that she would arrange a meeting as soon as she could. She sealed it and left the outside blank, then called Meg Morton to carry it to Lady Rochford.

'Tell her I am sorry that I can write no better,' she said.

Back came Meg, saying that Lady Rochford had promised an answer the next morning. Katheryn was in a fever of impatience and dispatched Meg to Jane, even before breakfast. Meg returned with a sealed note.

'My lady prays your Grace to keep this secret,' she said, clearly agog to know what was in it.

'Thank you,' Katheryn smiled, determined to throw her off the scent. 'The King will be pleased with this!'

When Meg had gone, she tore off the seal and read that Tom had said he would wait for ever, if need be, so long as he could see her in the end. That was all. Smiling to herself, she burned the letter.

She travelled to Collyweston on wings, hardly hearing Henry telling her that it had been a favourite residence of his grandmother the Lady Margaret Beaufort, Countess of Richmond. He added, rather wistfully, that his bastard son, the late Duke of Richmond, had owned it too. She was glad to see that all trace of the Duke had been cleared away, for she did not want to see Henry grieved by reminders of him. Nothing must be allowed to upset the holiday mood.

At Grimsthorpe Castle, the Duke and Duchess of Suffolk entertained them lavishly. The Duchess was one of the great ladies of Katheryn's household, and proudly showed her the improvements they had made to the ancient stronghold.

Henry was tired that night and sent a message to say that he would not be joining Katheryn in her bedchamber in one of the old towers. Immediately, she sent Kat Tilney to ask Jane Rochford when she would have the thing Jane had promised her. The answer was that Jane was sitting up waiting for it, and tomorrow she would bring the Queen word herself, rather than trouble Kat again.

When all was dark, Katheryn got up, put on a night robe of black damask and made her way down the spiral stair to Jane's chamber on the lower landing. Tom was there, waiting for her. He drew in his breath at the sight of her, for her hair was loose and her feet bare. There was no time for words. He gathered her into his arms and they kissed as if they would have devoured each other. His hand strayed to her breast, but she moved it away. Denial only fed their passion, and it was two in the morning before she was back in bed.

The next night, their plans were frustrated because Henry came to her with bedsport firmly in his mind. 'Let's see if we can't make another prince for England!' he challenged her, flushed with wine. That was his resolve on most of the nights that followed, but, at every stop, Katheryn tried to meet Tom in secret, even if only for a few snatched moments.

Jane contrived these meetings. She was still encouraging them, acting as a messenger between them and sometimes conveying gifts, only now, it was Katheryn who bade her send for Tom. In every house, instead of getting Jane to do it, Katheryn would seek for the back doors and back stairs herself, and tell Jane how convenient they were for an assignation. Sometimes she got her maids to help her, saying they might need to make an exit in case of fire; if they suspected anything amiss, they said nothing. When Tom visited at night, Katheryn always ordered Jane to stay nearby, because Jane had got into the habit of wandering off. It occurred to Katheryn that she might be trying to distance herself from a situation about which she had become uneasy.

One night, when she and Tom were lying on the bed, fully dressed, whispering to each other, he produced from his pocket a cramp ring, one of several the King had blessed on Good Friday.

'I stole this from Jane,' he announced. 'She said it was yours.'

'It isn't,' she said. 'What is she trying to do?'

'I have no idea!'

'I will send her to you with one of mine. You should have two, as it is a bad omen to wear but one cramp ring.' She sent it by Jane the next day.

Nine days into August, they came to Temple Bruer, seven miles from Lincoln, where a great dinner had been prepared for them. Henry wore Lincoln green, as a compliment to the people of Lincolnshire, and Katheryn appeared in crimson velvet. Their silken tent had been set up at the furthest point of the city liberties and they went in procession to it, preceded by trumpeters, drummers, archers marching with drawn bows, and the Yeomen of the Guard with their pikes and axes.

'The city fathers are already gathering in Lincoln, your Majesties,' Sir Robert Tyrwhitt, the High Sheriff for Lincolnshire, told them, as they seated themselves in their tent for the feast. Katheryn felt some trepidation. Lincoln had risen against the King in the Pilgrimage of Grace and been savagely punished into submission. Would there be demonstrations, riots, even? But Henry did not look perturbed. He was tucking into his food with gusto.

After they had eaten their meal and the local worthies had dispersed, Henry and Katheryn prepared for their reception in Lincoln. He changed into a glittering suit of cloth of gold; her gown was of cloth of silver. When they emerged, they found their ladies and gentlemen waiting for them with six children-of-honour, dressed in cloth of gold and crimson velvet. Tom was in attendance on the King and Katheryn could not help but notice how handsome he looked in his outfit of dark red damask.

A procession of dignitaries was advancing towards them, headed by the Dean of Lincoln and the cathedral clergy. An archdeacon made a speech in Latin and presented a basket of local delicacies: sage sausages, haslet, gingerbread and plum loaf, for which Henry thanked him heartily. Then he and Katheryn mounted their richly trapped horses. Lord Hastings walked ahead, bearing the sword of state, the King following, his mount led by the Master of Horse. Then came the children-of-honour riding great coursers, and, after them, the Earl of Rutland, then Katheryn herself and all the ladies, with the King's guard bringing up the rear.

At the gates of Lincoln, they were received by the Mayor and his brethren, who fell to their knees, crying, 'Jesus save your Grace!' The Recorder read a speech from a scroll, which he presented to the King, who handed it to the Duke of Norfolk. Katheryn was watching the citizens, some of whom were regarding her uncle with ill-concealed hostility; God knew they had no reason to love him. The knot of tension in her stomach tightened. But the Mayor was presenting the sword and mace, while the chief citizens and the knights and gentlemen of the county were taking their places at the front of Henry's train. Then the great cavalcade set off again and, as the King and Queen entered Lincoln, all the church bells began pealing.

They ascended the steepest hill Katheryn had ever seen. Looking round at the slope falling away behind her, she felt a little dizzy. Fixing her eyes resolutely ahead, she nodded and smiled at the crowds on each side of the road. At the top of the hill, the procession wound its way to the right and there, in front of them, stood the mighty cathedral with its magnificent arched facade. It seemed that all Lincolnshire had gathered around it to greet them.

The Mayor and the chief citizens now knelt on the ground as Henry gazed down at them from his horse; all around, the people were falling to their knees. The Mayor cleared his throat and spoke in a ringing voice. 'Your Majesty, we, your humble subjects, the inhabitants of this your Grace's county of Lincoln, confess that we wretches, for lack of grace and of sincere knowledge of the truth of God's word, have most grievously, heinously and wantonly offended your Majesty in the unnatural, most odious and detestable offences of outrageous disobedience and traitorous rebellion. We beg your bountiful forgiveness and promise that we and our posterity will henceforth pray for the preservation of your Majesty, Queen Katheryn and Prince Edward.'

Henry looked down on the sea of bowed heads. 'Good people of Lincolnshire, my loving subjects,' he cried in a ringing tone, 'I formally pardon you for your disobedience and forgive you. I pray you all rise and depart in peace.'

He spurred his horse and rode through the crowd with Katheryn following, beaming down at those who were calling out blessings on her for obtaining the King's mercy. By St Mary, she thought, they think I interceded for them! I do not deserve this. She would not think about the other reasons why she did not deserve their acclaim.

They had reached the west door of the cathedral and it was time to dismount. Within, the Bishop of Lincoln, who was also the King's confessor, was waiting with his cross and his clergy to receive them. A carpet had been laid along the nave and two prayer stools with cushions of cloth of gold had been set facing the high altar. As Katheryn knelt beside Henry, she saw that crucifixes had been laid there for them. She kissed hers fervently, thankful that the day had gone so well and that there had been no trouble. The Bishop censed them; then they received the sacrament and prayed while the choir sang the *Te Deum*.

They were lodged in the adjacent Bishop's Palace, a very old building, but much embellished over the years. That evening, Bishop Longland hosted a feast in their honour in the great hall.

Late that night, when she was certain that Henry was not coming to sleep with her, Katheryn stole out of her chamber, fully dressed, intending to go up to Jane's room and ask her to summon Tom. She was climbing the two short flights of stairs when she heard Kat's voice behind her: 'I'm so sorry, Madam, we did not hear you call us.' She looked around to see Kat and Meg standing in the gallery.

'I'm just going up to see Lady Rochford,' she told them.

'We should be attending your Grace,' Meg said, and they came after her. She did not dare deter them, lest they smelt a rat. When they got upstairs, she smiled at them.

'You can go to bed now. I will call you if I need you.'

They went back downstairs and Katheryn slumped in relief as she opened Jane's door. Jane had her plans laid. 'We have arranged that he shall wait below my window for a signal,' she explained. 'If I don't appear by midnight, he will go to bed.'

When Tom arrived, Katheryn went into his arms and he kissed her as if he would never stop. Their need for each other sated a little, they stood talking for over an hour in a little gallery at the stairhead, because Jane was tired and Katheryn had felt obliged to send her to bed. At one point, they thought they heard someone on the stairs below, but, when Katheryn went down to look, there was no one there. She fell into bed around two o'clock, thoughts of Tom filling her head.

The next day, she accompanied Henry when he was shown around Lincoln Castle and the ancient city. He was in fine spirits and especially interested to see some Roman remains and the tomb of his ancestress, Katherine Swynford, in the cathedral.

'She was the mother of the Beauforts, my grandmother's family,' he told Katheryn, gazing at the brass. 'She was much beloved by John of Gaunt, who made her his mistress and then married her. It was an extraordinary thing for a royal duke to do, but then love makes fools of the best of men!' He winked at Katheryn. 'She was very beautiful, it says here.' He was reading the Latin epitaph. 'As are you, my love.' He reached for her hand and squeezed it.

She thought he would come to her that night, but his leg was playing him up; he had walked for too long, he told her. Eleven o'clock found her standing with Jane just inside the back door of her lodgings, waiting for Tom. They were peering out when one of the watch came with a light, and drew back inside just before he locked and bolted the door from the outside. They stared at each other in dismay.

'How will Tom get in?' Katheryn whispered. But presently they heard someone fiddling with the lock and the sound of footsteps retreating. Soon afterwards, the door opened, and Tom stood there grinning. Jane pulled him inside and hastened to shut the door.

'My man picked the lock,' he told them. 'Don't worry, he's gone.' Katheryn marvelled at how resourceful he had been.

'Go on up and wait for me in Lady Rochford's chamber,' she said, and hastened to her bedchamber, where her women were waiting to prepare her for bed. 'Ladies, you may retire,' she said.

'Does your Grace not need help to undress?' Kat asked.

'You may attend me in due course,' Katheryn said hastily. It would not do for anyone to suspect that something was amiss. 'But I will be late to bed, so you must wait.' Judging that Jane would now have smuggled Tom into her chamber, she led Kat Tilney up the stairs and bade her wait on the landing with Jane's maid. 'I have private business to discuss with my Lady Rochford,' she said. 'Do not disturb us.'

Tom was waiting in the bedchamber with Jane.

'I've just thought that you could be private in your stool chamber,' Jane said. 'No one can hear you or discover you there. I will stand guard outside in the bedchamber.'

Needing to be alone with Tom, Katheryn agreed without hesitation. When all was clear, the three of them slipped downstairs and Jane dismissed the maids who were waiting to assist Katheryn to bed.

The stool chamber, which led off the Queen's bedchamber, was spacious, having space for hanging clothes, and it had been cleaned and aired. The close stool stood in a corner, upholstered in padded red velvet secured by brass studs. Tom dragged a bench in, and they sat down and talked, oblivious to the passing of time. They spoke of their lives before they had met at court, and of their loves. Katheryn played down the feelings she had had for Francis and said nothing about their plans to marry or how close they had been.

'They made me do things I did not want to do,' she said. 'I could not tell the King about them because I was too frightened to, but I am being honest with you because I truly love you and want there to be no secrets between us.'

'Did you bed with them?' Tom asked sharply.

'Only with Francis,' she said, 'but I was careful. He only went as far as I let him.' Let Tom think it had not been that far.

'They took advantage of you, those knaves,' Tom seethed. 'You were young and naive. Manox was your tutor! He betrayed everyone's trust. He should have been horsewhipped!'

Katheryn did not like to say that she had encouraged him. 'Let it be.

It's all in the past now. I hope you don't think any the worse of me for it.' She looked at him pleadingly.

'How could I? You were more sinned against than sinning. Forget it, sweet Katheryn. We shall never speak of it again.' He drew her to him and began kissing her; and all the while she was thinking that she had not been wholly honest with him. But what he did not know could not hurt him.

'You must have fancied many young ladies in your time,' she said, deftly changing the subject.

Tom kissed her again. 'A few,' he said, still looking annoyed. 'Before I loved you.'

'Did you love any of them?'

'I thought I did at the time, but most, like Bess, meant little to me. I only pursued her because I couldn't have you. I haven't seen her since March.'

That was when Bess had left Katheryn's service.

'Did you tell her you had tired of her?' she asked.

'I fear I did, and that I hurt her,' he admitted.

Loving him as much as she did, Katheryn suddenly felt sympathy for one who had loved and lost him. She wished she had been kinder to Bess back in March.

'She left court because of you?'

He nodded. 'I knew then that I still loved you and that no one could replace you. It wasn't fair to lead her on any more.'

'I will send her a gown,' Katheryn said impulsively. 'As compensation for her loss. I feel sorry for her.'

'That's more than generous!' Tom was surprised. '*I* should be giving her the gown.'

'Oh no, you shouldn't! I shall send it to her and say that I hope all is well with her now.'

There was a noise in the bedchamber beyond. Katheryn held her breath. It would be Jane, of course. But what if Henry woke in the night and took it into his head to visit his wife? He had been in an affectionate mood today, caressing and kissing her quite publicly. Yet he had never arrived to see Katheryn so late.

She put her head around the door. There was only Jane there, sewing in the candlelight, thanks be to God!

Another sound, from the stairwell this time! Katheryn jumped. Jane looked up questioningly as she crept across the room, opened the door a crack then peered down the stairs. No one.

'It was probably a mouse,' Tom said, when she returned. 'There's no need to look so frightened.'

'I must indeed love you,' she told him, 'to risk all for you.'

'I am taking risks too,' he reminded her. 'But you have bound me to you, as you did before, so that I must love you again above all creatures!'

They fell to kissing once more, but sprang apart in terror when there came a loud banging from outside.

'Wait here,' Katheryn whispered. She peeped into the bedchamber, to see an ashen-faced Jane standing in the middle of the room. Someone was knocking loudly on the outer door. Katheryn's blood froze.

'Open it!' she hissed, diving back into the stool chamber and closing the door. She and Tom stood there, holding their breath.

She heard the latch being lifted and the voice of Mrs Luffkyn, the chamberer. 'The Queen is not abed yet, my lady. Do you know where she is?'

'She's in the stool chamber,' Jane replied.

'Oh. That's a relief! We were wondering where she had gone. Do you know what time it is?'

'I heard the watch calling three o'clock,' Jane said.

'It's nigh four now.'

'Her Grace would not have expected you to wait up this late for her. Tilney is waiting to put her to bed.'

'Tilney is asleep on the stairs.'

'Just go to bed, Luffkyn!' Jane snapped. They heard the door shut.

'I'd better go,' Tom said. 'I don't want to, but it does grow late.' He kissed Katheryn on the lips. 'May God give you good rest.'

'I need it, in truth.' Staying up late so often had left her tired and drained, and she had even found herself falling asleep in the saddle. Isabel had enquired whether she was well, and Henry himself had told her she looked peaky. She must get some sleep!

* * *

Two days later, they left in procession for Gainsborough, with the Earl of Derby bearing the sword of state before the King. Katheryn loved Gainsborough Old Hall, where they stayed, even if she was a little daunted by their host, the red-faced, plain-spoken and frankly terrifying Lord Burgh. Flanked by his numerous children and his nervous wife, he received the King as if he were the one bestowing the favour. Lecherously, he eyed Katheryn up and down.

'A good breeder her Grace'll prove, eh?' he chuckled, oblivious to the dangerous flush creeping up from Henry's collar. But congenial relations were restored when his lordship led them into his lofty, timbered great hall and offered them goblets of his best wine, then pressed them to accept large refills. Lady Burgh showed Katheryn to the chamber that had been prepared for her at the top of the tower that led off the great hall. It was obvious as they climbed the narrow spiral stairs that Henry would never manage them, and Katheryn sent up a prayer of thanks when her hostess said that his Majesty was being accommodated in the best chamber on the ground floor.

Tom, however, would have no difficulty in negotiating the stairs. As soon as the bedchamber door closed behind her that night, Katheryn was seized with longing for him. It was a longing both emotional and physical and would not be denied.

'Send Lady Rochford to me,' she ordered her maids, then dismissed them.

Jane came, puffing up the stairs. She was not as nimble as Katheryn.

'Can you arrange for Mr Culpeper to come here in secret?' Katheryn asked.

'I'm not sure where he is lodged,' Jane said doubtfully.

'You must get a message to him, then. Tell him I am pining for him. No, say I am dying of love for him – and for his person!'

Jane gave her a searching look. 'You know what you are saying? I mean, what he might take dying to mean?'

'It's how I want him to take it.'

'Madam, I did not realise that the two of you had gone so far.'

'We have not – that's why I'm dying for him!'

'Be careful, I beg of you.' Jane looked frightened. 'What if he gets you with child?'

'We won't go *that* far! But there are other ways of giving pleasure.'

'Don't I know it.' Jane's voice was bitter.

'What do you mean?' Katheryn realised she knew very little about her friend.

'My late husband did things to me I could never bring myself to describe, and never will,' Jane muttered. Rarely did she mention Lord Rochford to Katheryn, and it was now easy to see why. 'Of course, Mr Culpeper is not like that,' she said hastily. 'All I ask is that you be prudent. I would not deny you your pleasures.' Her voice turned brisk. 'I will go and find Mr Culpeper. If the coast is clear, I will bring him to you.'

That night, Katheryn let Tom discover the secrets of her body and pleasure her. The ecstasy he aroused in her was such that it was almost like a spiritual experience, consuming her whole being. She was tempted to give herself to him, but she had retained some vestige of reason and made him desist before they both got completely carried away.

Afterwards, they lay together on her bed. How long would they have to go on like this? she asked herself. How long before she could be his completely?

Then she realised what that would mean, and guilt flooded her. It was something she was growing accustomed to living with daily.

At Hatfield, near Doncaster, a week later, they stayed in an ancient Norman manor house that afforded them little beyond the spartan comforts of another age. But the hunting at Hatfield Chase was excellent: Henry and his companions shot nearly four hundred deer in two days.

Katheryn had not gone with them. She was suffering menstrual pains and had to lie down for a while with a hot brick wrapped in flannel pressed to her belly. Another month gone with no sign of a child. How long would Henry's patience last? He had been so loving to her lately – but he might not continue so if she failed him in the one thing that counted.

In the afternoon, she felt better and got up. She walked in the gardens with her ladies for an hour, then sat doing some embroidery in her chamber. Around six o'clock, she heard horses' hooves and the hunting party returning. Going to the window, she saw Henry riding into the courtyard and waved to him. He raised his hand in salute and dismounted, disappearing into the house. Amidst the crowd of men and horses, Katheryn caught sight of Tom. She could not draw her eyes away from him. He looked so gallant in his leather riding clothes with his dark hair blown about by the wind. He glanced up and saw her, then quickly looked away. She watched him until he was out of sight. As she left the window, she saw Meg Morton watching her in no very friendly manner. It occurred to her that Meg, and perhaps Kat Tilney, was beginning to suspect something. She should not have looked upon Tom for so long. She would not do so again, she vowed. How easy it was to give yourself away.

'We went out on the river,' Henry told Katheryn afterwards, eating his supper with relish. 'We took a great quantity of young swans, two boatfuls of river birds, and as many great pikes and other fish.' He was very pleased with himself.

She sat there fretting about Meg, hoping the girl had not jumped to conclusions. But that could only be speculation, she reminded herself. She had not done anything wrong in looking, and her gazing at Culpeper could be interpreted in other ways. She could always say that she looked tenderly upon him because he was her cousin and was dear to the King.

'Are you all right, darling?' Henry said suddenly. She realised she had been miles away, distracted by her fears.

'Perfectly!' she said, recovering herself. 'I was thinking that I might ride out with you tomorrow, if I may?'

'Of course!' Henry beamed. 'We'll have good sport, sweetheart.'

He did not come to her bed that night or the next; he never slept with her when she was having her courses. On the third night, he himself was indisposed with one of the blinding headaches he suffered intermittently. It was then that Jane brought Tom to her room and stood guard outside. That night, Katheryn and Tom lay together for five or six hours. They were lovers now in all but the most intimate way and knew the secrets of each other's bodies.

'I want you, Katheryn,' Tom sighed, holding her tightly against him. 'I want all of you. It's killing me, having to hold back.'

'I want you just as much!' she breathed. 'I want to feel you inside me.'

'I will have you one day!' he vowed.

She wanted to say that she longed for that day, but knew it would make her feel guilty again, because that day could only come when Henry died. 'I mind to have you too,' she told him. 'I long for you all the time.'

He was touching her now, quickly bringing her to such a pinnacle of pleasure that she cried out. They slept a little afterwards, until Katheryn woke with a start.

'Heavens, what is the time? I didn't mean to sleep!'

'Hush, my love,' Tom soothed. 'Our good friend is watching out for us.'

'I should go back,' she said, still nervous. He helped her to dress and held her tightly before kissing her goodbye.

When Katheryn emerged from the bedchamber, she found a very agitated Jane.

'Morton was here,' she said. 'She heard you cry out. What were you doing?'

Katheryn felt her cheeks redden. 'What do you think? Oh, dear God, did she say anything?' Coming on top of what had happened the other night, this was too much! They would be discovered!

'She asked if you were all right, and I had to think quickly,' Jane said, clearly shaken. 'I said you were suffering terrible monthly pains, but I know that's not true.'

'It's not! She'll know that I put out the last stained clouts for the chamberers to wash two days ago. You don't think she's guessed what's going on?'

'I hope not. And what *is* going on?' Jane asked sharply. 'You've lain with him, haven't you? I've heard you.'

Katheryn resented being spoken to as if she were a naughty child; she was the Queen, after all, and she was no fool, for had she not refused Tom the ultimate favour?

She rounded on Jane. 'I swear in the name of God and His Holy Angels that I have not given myself to him. I would not so abuse my sovereign's bed.' As she said it, she knew that she *had* abused it, and that there were more ways than one of being unfaithful.

'That's a relief,' Jane said. 'And I pray you never will! But in future, Madam, take care. If there's the merest hint that others suspect, it will have to stop!'

Chapter 27

1541

Henry and Katheryn had been hunting and were clattering through the gatehouse at Hatfield when Katheryn spied a familiar figure in the courtyard, just entering the house. It was Francis Dereham!

She felt faint and gripped her saddle to steady herself. What was he doing here? The last thing she wanted was Henry noticing him – or Tom, for who knew what Tom might do if he saw him?

As the groom came forward, she slipped from the saddle.

'I must hurry to my chamber, Sir,' she said to Henry. 'I shouldn't have drunk so much ale at dinner!' They had eaten in the open, enjoying the sunshine.

As she went indoors, she looked around warily, expecting to see Francis waiting for her, but he was nowhere to be seen. She mounted the old stone stairs to her presence chamber – and there he was, bowing. Her ladies were regarding him with interest, for he was a handsome man. But his rumpled looks no longer held any appeal for Katheryn.

'Mr Dereham!' she said crisply. 'What do you here?'

'Your Majesty.' There was a slightly ironic emphasis to the words. He bowed again and handed her a letter. It bore the crest of the Dowager Duchess. They had kept in touch but rarely since Katheryn's marriage to the King, and Katheryn wondered why her grandam would be writing to her now and why she had chosen Francis, of all people, as her messenger. Had she taken leave of her senses?

She broke the seal and read, in mounting disbelief. The Duchess asked a favour. Her daughter, the Countess of Bridgewater, and Lady William Howard had made suit to have Dereham in the Queen's service and begged her to speak to Katheryn for them. 'Therefore, I most humbly ask your Grace to grant my request, on account of the good service Dereham has rendered to myself and Lord William. I pray you be good to him on my account and renew your favour?'

The Duchess had done much for her and had never asked her for anything, so she could hardly refuse; it would be churlish. She wondered if Francis had put pressure on Lady Bridgewater and Lady William to make suit for him and, if so, what his motive had been. Surely he did not hope for any special favour at her hands – or, God forbid, a resumption of their relationship? Had it never occurred to him that she might not want him in her household? Pray God he would not resurrect that nonsense about them being man and wife!

He was standing there nonchalantly, looking at her with that rakish grin. Had he no idea of the danger in which he was placing them both? But there had always been a streak of the devil-may-care in him. He liked taking risks.

'Walk with me in the garden, Mr Dereham,' she said. 'Lady Cromwell and Lady Herbert, please attend me.' There was no way she was going to be alone with him.

He bowed again – he really was overdoing it – and she led the way outside, then walked ahead with him, her ladies following at a discreet distance, just out of earshot.

'Why have you come here?' she asked. 'Is it to ill intent?'

'Why would you think that of me?' he asked.

'Don't imagine for a moment that I think of you as I once did.' She must make that plain right now. 'I would not have you thinking that I wish to return to my old life.'

He made no answer, only smiled knowingly at her. She had forgotten how infuriating he could be.

'I don't know what my lady of Norfolk was thinking of when she recommended you,' she said.

'It's simple,' he replied. 'You remember that letter Manox wrote to her, about some young lady dallying with a Mr Hastings, whoever he was? Well, back in the spring, I told her the truth, that it was about me and you. She should have realised that – she knew how close we were – but she got very angry and commanded me out of her gates.'

'So how come she recommended you to me?'

'I asked Lady Bridgewater and Lady William Howard to intercede for me. I reminded them how close you and I had been.' He turned and smiled at her. 'My lady changed her tune then!'

Katheryn recoiled from the implied threat. By such means, Joan Bulmer had tried to inveigle herself into the Queen's household. And Francis had come all the way to Yorkshire to press his suit; clearly, he meant business. If only, if only she had never let him love her. Because of her great folly, he had power over her. He knew too much about her past for her to risk offending him by a refusal. He could do untold damage to her reputation and position. And she had no way of knowing if she could trust him not to exploit that knowledge and use it to his advantage. Was this but the beginning?

She dared not refuse his request.

'You hesitate, Madam,' he said. 'Do not forget that this marriage of yours is a sham. You were my wife before you were the King's. But, not being content with that, you have looked upon another with favour, I hear. I have my friends in your household. They keep me informed.'

She froze at his words. Who knew? Who had talked? She and Tom had taken such pains to keep their love a secret.

'I have no idea what you are talking about,' she said coldly. 'I have looked upon another? It is nonsense. Who told you that?'

'Surely you don't think I would betray a confidence, Katheryn?' he smirked, and she noted how he had omitted to address her by her title. 'But, if you think to betray the King, you may as well do it with your *lawful* husband!'

'I love the King; I would not betray him!'

He looked at her quizzically, as if he thought she was lying. *Oh, God, who had betrayed her? And to Francis, of all people!*

'This is not the way to go about getting a post in my household,' she reproved him. 'You presume too much upon our past association, which is over.'

'We are still married,' he said. 'You made your vow to me. And I am a jealous husband.'

338

'What vow?' She glanced nervously behind her to check that her ladies were still out of earshot.

'You promised to take me for your husband; that is as binding as a marriage made in church.'

'I don't believe you!'

'Ask any priest. Ask Archbishop Cranmer, if you will!'

'Oh, stop bothering me with your nonsense!' Katheryn snapped. 'I want you to leave – now.'

'That would be a pity,' Francis said, giving her a sly glance. 'One word from me and your marriage would be exposed for the charade it is.'

His words chilled her to the marrow. She knew he had it in him to do it. She dared not refuse him. 'If I give you a post, you must promise me never to speak of the past to anyone. I want your word of honour.'

He chuckled. 'For what that is worth, I give it. You ever were naive, Katheryn.'

The next day, she summoned him before her as she sat on her chair under the great canopy of estate and waited as he bowed low with exaggerated grace.

'Mr Dereham, I have decided to make you an usher of my chamber,' she informed him. 'You will receive visitors and petitioners, perform errands for me and write letters when my secretary is away.'

He smiled and bowed again. 'Your Highness is most gracious,' he said. 'Please accept my humble thanks.' He was laughing at her, she knew.

'My treasurer will give you money to buy a new gown,' she said.

'I will inform my lady of Norfolk of your Grace's goodness to me,' he replied.

Within a day or so, she realised that his duties would occasion his attendance on her in her privy chamber more often than she would have liked. The maids-of-honour, and even some of her younger ladies, were all a-flutter whenever he appeared, for he was so good-looking in his rakish way and always had a wink and a cheery word for them.

They had been told the bare truth, that he was their mistress's cousin who had been recommended for a place by the Duchess of Norfolk.

'Who's that new usher?' Henry asked, after Francis had announced his arrival for supper and departed.

Katheryn felt a tremor of fear. It was disconcerting to have Francis in such close proximity to the King, not to mention Tom. 'He is kin to me and my lady of Norfolk. He served her at Lambeth. She asked me to be good to him – and so I will.'

'He looks like a popinjay in that coat of white satin!'

'Yes, indeed.' She had been annoyed that Francis had spent the money she'd given him on such a showy gown. 'I mentioned it to my chamberlain, but he said that ushers at court are permitted to wear satin.'

'Keep an eye on him,' Henry said. 'Don't let him get above himself.'

If only you knew, she thought.

Annoyingly, Mr Huttoft, Katheryn's secretary, happened to go down with a fever soon afterwards, so she was obliged to rely on Francis to deal with her personal correspondence and write confidential letters. That necessitated him waiting on her in private, in her closet, with no one else present. Wary of him as she was, she took care to keep strictly to business and did not respond when he came out with the occasional familiarity.

That first morning, as he was writing, she noticed that he had on her mother's ruby ring. Anger burned in her that such a villain should be wearing it. And yet she herself had given it to him, at the height of her passion for him. Was he sporting it to remind her of that?

After a while, he laid down his pen, stretched and stuck out his leg. 'See, my hose are in holes; for old times' sake, Katheryn, could you give me a little money to buy more?'

'Will five shillings suffice?' she asked.

He chortled. 'You never did have any idea of how much things cost. I could not get good hose for less than three pounds.'

'Three pounds?' She was sure he was wrong.

'I buy mine from Master Cotes of Lambeth; he's the best. You have to pay for quality.'

Wondering why she had agreed to this, she gave him the money out of her privy purse.

Katheryn could not sleep. She was being used again, she knew it. It had dawned on her that Francis had never exposed her because it would have rebounded on him too, if they really had been precontracted, as he insisted. Henry would take a stern view of them both for not confessing it and thereby compromising the succession. No, Francis was using their so-called precontract to gain power over her and extract favours. Like Tom, he was probably hoping to marry her after the King died, which was another reason why he kept bringing up that wretched precontract. Well, she would not be manipulated thus. If she married anyone after she had been widowed, it would be Tom.

Towards the end of August, the court arrived at Pontefract Castle. Henry decreed that they would lodge there for six days to recuperate after enduring two months on the road. Pontefract was a mighty, forbidding stronghold, yet one, Katheryn discovered, with many secret stairs and disused rooms – perfect for assignations with Tom.

She and Henry were lodged in the King's and Queen's Towers at either end of the great hall. Each tower had four floors, and a spiral staircase leading off Katheryn's bedchamber gave access to the floors above; another door led to a passage to the hall. Jane's chamber was on the third floor – and the rooms above that were empty. Yet, Katheryn enjoined, they, and Tom, must all take great care to be even more discreet than before – especially, she thought fearfully, as someone in her household had got wind that she had a lover.

'I don't like it here,' Damascin confided on their first night at Pontefract, as she helped to prepare Katheryn for bed. 'It's too dark and eerie. They say a king was murdered here.'

'Richard the Second,' Anne Bassett supplied. 'My stepfather told me he was brought here after he was deposed and starved to death.'

'Ooh, don't tell me that!' Damascin shuddered. 'He might haunt the place.'

'Don't talk nonsense!' Lady Rutland chided her.

'It happened a long time ago,' Anne said.

Katheryn was glad when they had gone and left her in peace. She lay in bed, wondering if Henry would come. When a distant clock chimed midnight, she knew he would not. He had been tired at supper after hunting all day.

Rising from her bed, she pulled on her night robe, crept up the stairs past the room where Lady Rutland was sleeping, then ascended to Jane's chamber and tapped lightly on the door. Jane, still dressed, beckoned her inside and closed it.

'I have been expecting you,' she said. 'The upstairs door is unlocked. Do you want me to take a message to Mr Culpeper?'

'Yes,' Katheryn whispered. 'Tell him that it is open and that it is safe for him to come.'

Jane left her there and tiptoed downstairs. She was soon back.

'I found him outside and gave him your message, but there was a watchman lingering at the bottom of the stair.'

Katheryn's hand flew to her mouth. 'Oh, no! Are we discovered? Has the King set him to watch at the back door, the way Tom would come? My God, are we undone?'

'Calm yourself,' Jane urged. 'The man did not see me speaking with Mr Culpeper, for we were in the shadow of that tower to the left, and he did not look as if he was watching for anything. Maybe he was just waiting until he has to cry the hour.'

'I pray you are right!' Katheryn was trembling.

'I will set Morris to watch the door to see if any of the watch or someone else goes in or out,' Jane said.

They sat there on Jane's bed, waiting for what seemed like hours. Katheryn was worried that Tom would come and be caught entering the Queen's Tower, but Jane assured her that he was too sensible for that.

'He knows the risks as well as you do,' she said, holding Katheryn's hand.

Katheryn tried to reassure herself that Henry would not have behaved so lovingly towards her today if he had suspected her of being unfaithful.

At about three o'clock, Morris returned to report that the watchman had long gone and that no one else had ventured near the door. Heartily relieved, Katheryn went back to bed. Tom would not come this late, and that was as well. She had been badly frightened and resolved yet again to be more careful in future.

The next night, when she and Jane had made certain that there was no danger, Katheryn sent for Tom again and they met in the chilly, dusty chamber on the fourth floor. All they had time for was talking, because he had to go to help prepare the King for bed.

But, the following night, Henry went to bed early. Not wanting to use the horrid little attic room, Katheryn wondered if she dared admit Tom to her own bedchamber. Jane said it would be safe. The door to the hall passage could be locked, and she herself would keep watch outside the door to the stairs. So Tom came and held Katheryn tightly as she kissed him hungrily and his hands caressed her back and hips. Soon, they were writhing on the bed, enjoying as much of each other as they dared.

'I love you!' she cried in his ear. 'I love you above all men!'

Later, as she sponged his seed from the counterpane, hoping the stain would not show, she teased him. 'You are so handsome, Mr Culpeper, especially with no clothes on. A wonder it is that no fair lady has borne you off to the altar.'

'That is because my heart has always been yours, my love.' He stretched lazily. 'Although I had to console myself with others, since you so cruelly forsook me.'

'Others?' He had led her to believe that Bess Harvey was the only woman he had taken up with after she had married the King. 'What others?'

He had the grace to look sheepish. 'Well, I did have a flirtation with Lady Herbert.'

Her own gentlewoman! Right under her nose!

'I did not know Anne Parr to be an unfaithful wife,' she said stiffly, stunned, pulling on her robe. 'What do you mean, a flirtation?'

He looked uncomfortable.

'You slept with her! When?'

'Just after you married the King. Katheryn—'

343

'I marvel that you could say you loved me and yet lay so soon with another!' she hissed.

Tom leaned forward and caught her hand. 'But you were married before I loved her, and I had found so little favour at your hands that I was moved to look elsewhere.'

'If I chose, I could put a lot of other strumpets your way! Like that trollop Dora Bray, who has my Lord Parr in thrall, yet I am sure would be ready to accommodate you!' Katheryn shrilled. 'Doubtless you only see me as another such and value me accordingly!'

'I do not!' Tom protested.

'No? Know this then, if I had still been in the maidens' chamber at Lambeth, I would have tried you, as I did Francis!'

'But you said—'

'If we're talking about honesty, we're both equally remiss.'

He swallowed. 'Katheryn, she meant nothing to me.'

'She must have meant something!'

'My love, you are being unreasonable.' He tried to pull her into his arms, but she broke away. 'Katheryn, I respect you – and Anne Herbert meant nothing to me. But man cannot live on bread alone and you had chosen to leave me for the King. Since we have been together, there has been no one else.'

She allowed herself to be mollified. Her brief spell of temper soon abated and she joined him again on the bed, knowing she had over-reacted. And, of course, the making-up of their quarrel was all the more passionate . . .

One night, while they were still at Pontefract, Katheryn insisted that all her other ladies and maids go to bed, leaving Jane Rochford to attend her. The rest looked a little askance at her, but said nothing. It was not usual for the Queen to be prepared for bed by only one lady, but it had happened before. Tom was waiting to be admitted to her bedchamber and, once it was dark and they were certain that the King would not come – he had visited Katheryn's bed the night before and had probably not yet recovered from his exertions – Jane slipped downstairs to let him in.

When she brought him into the bedchamber, she locked the door and bolted it.

'The chamberers are still about,' she said. 'It must look as if I am still in attendance on your Grace.'

She sat down at the table with her back to them. Crestfallen, because she had been longing to lie with Tom, Katheryn let him fold his arms about her and kiss her. It was awkward with Jane present, now that they had become intimate.

Suddenly, there was a light tap on the door. All three of them stared at each other in dismay, frozen into indecision. The tap came again, more insistent this time.

'In there!' Jane mouthed, indicating the privy, and Tom vanished.

Katheryn sat at the table, trying to compose herself, as Jane opened the door. Outside stood Mr Dane, one of the King's ushers.

'Madam,' he said, bowing, his face impassive, 'his Majesty has sent me to inform you that he is on his way to visit you.'

Katheryn prayed that her panic did not register on her face. She glanced at Jane's white face. They were trapped! Henry was bound to use the privy. He always got up several times in the night. How could he fail to see Tom?

'I will look forward to receiving his Grace,' she said, as evenly as she could, thinking quickly. She must plead an indisposition. One that would put Henry off.

Jane curtseyed and made herself scarce when the King arrived.

Katheryn curtseyed too. 'Henry!' she cried, rising, and held up her face for his kiss.

'My Katheryn,' he said, as he stroked her cheek.

'Oh, Henry!' she said and clutched at her middle. 'I think I have eaten something bad. Ooh, the pain is griping.'

He was all solicitude. 'You must rest, darling. I will have an infusion of chamomile sent to you. I find it always works. Now you get to bed, and I will see you in the morning. While I'm here, please excuse me for a moment.' He began making for the privy. Struck with terror, she cried, 'No, please, Henry – it's not very nice in there just now.'

In a heart-stopping instant, he turned. 'Forgive me, darling. I did not mean to embarrass you. I will return to my own lodging.' He kissed her and was gone, leaving her light-headed with relief.

In seconds, Jane was back. 'Oh, my God,' she breathed, hand to her mouth. 'I thought we would be undone.'

'I had visions of myself being arrested and taken to the Tower,' Katheryn gasped. 'I think the King loves me too much to punish me as he did Anne Boleyn, but he would have been very hurt and angry, and there is no telling what he would do to Tom.'

Jane moved to the privy door. 'Mr Culpeper, you can come out,' she murmured. Tom emerged, looking ashen.

'Holy Mother of God, I thought I was done for then,' he muttered.

'So did I!' Jane gasped. 'And we would all have suffered for it, whatever her Grace thinks.'

'But the King loves me!'

'Oh, you are so naive!' Jane had never spoken so sharply to Katheryn. 'That love would soon turn to hatred if he discovers that you have betrayed him.'

Fear gripped Katheryn. She'd always known that this was dangerous – indeed, the danger made it more exciting – but somehow she had never believed they could be caught. Tonight had been too close, and their secret suddenly seemed impossible to keep. She looked at Tom, agonised. 'Maybe we should end it now,' she whispered.

'No!' He was adamant. 'I will not let you go. I would risk all for you, you know that!'

'Little sweet fool!' she retorted, touched, but still scared. 'But we must be even more careful from now on. None of us must breathe a word to anyone, not even in confession, for the King is Supreme Head of the Church and will surely get to hear of it.'

'I will say nothing, my love,' Tom promised her.

'I give you my word,' Jane declared.

Katheryn was still feeling jittery the next night and asked Jane to let Tom know that it was best not to come to her for the moment. It was as well she did so, since her chamberers, Mrs Luffkyn and Mrs

Frideswide, took it upon themselves to enter her bedchamber without knocking, in defiance of her orders.

'What do you think you are doing?' she cried. 'I will have you both dismissed if you come in again without permission. In future, you are forbidden to attend me in my bedchamber.' She was aware that fear had made her overreact. But, after they had left, sullen and muttering apologies, she wished she *had* dismissed them, for then she could have replaced them with ladies of Jane Rochford's choosing, who could be relied upon to be discreet.

She had been wondering lately – was it her imagination, or did her ladies and maids suspect her of conducting an illicit affair? Was she reading too much into the way they looked at her or watched her? Pray God she had not been discovered!

Francis's behaviour was not helping. Ever unpredictable and volatile, he was proving a troublesome addition to her household. Having received that excessive payment for his hose, he now asked her for more money – ten pounds this time, a much larger sum – without a trace of shame.

'You would not begrudge an old friend,' he wheedled. 'Besides, I hope to be more than an old friend to you before very long.'

'No!' she cried. 'That will never happen. Have you forgotten that I am married to the King?'

'No, but *you* seem to.'

She was taken aback by his candour. 'You have no right to hold me to ransom like this.'

He gave her the benefit of his wolfish smile. 'I have every right. I am your true husband.'

She dared not risk offending him. What if he talked? He had never been very guarded with his tongue. Well, if she must bribe him to buy his silence, so be it. She gave him the money, telling him that this must be an end to his demands. He merely grinned at her.

What was almost worse was his being over-familiar with her in the presence of others, even to the extent of calling her Katheryn. Given the amount of time she was obliged to spend with him, she feared people might think she was giving him preferential treatment – or worse.

'Your officers despise me, you know,' he told her the next day, once she had itemised the letters he was to write for her.

'What makes you think that, Mr Dereham?' she asked.

'Because you favour me.'

'That is not the case and well you know it. I need someone to do Mr Huttoft's work.'

'And there I was thinking that you enjoyed my company!'

She recoiled. 'You have given me no choice but to endure it. If you hadn't constrained me to give you a place, I would have sent you packing!'

'We have turned into a little firebrand!' he chuckled.

'You should learn the manners that are expected of you at court, Mr Dereham, and the proper courtesy to be observed towards your Queen. Then you might be a little more popular.'

He seized her wrist. 'Don't forget that I knew you at Lambeth when you were nothing but a waif – and that I knew you very well.' He was not laughing now.

'I could report you to the King!' she cried, outraged, pulling her hand away.

'But you won't, because he thinks you are virtuous and would be horrified to discover that you are not.'

His words struck fear into her. 'What do you mean?'

'I mean what went on at Lambeth. And that you are flighty.'

'What makes you think he doesn't know?' she challenged.

'Your face, Katheryn. You look terrified.'

'I'm not!' She could feel the telltale flush. 'Why are you being so horrible to me?'

His grin faded. 'You forget that you and I are wed and that you walked away from that without a backward glance.'

'Oh, don't start that again!' she snorted. 'I will not listen to it. You may go.'

He rose and made her an exaggerated bow. '*I* do not forget it,' he said, 'and, one day, when you are no longer encumbered . . .' He left the sentence unfinished and walked out, leaving her shaking with rage.

Two days later, it became clear that he would not be easily contained.

Mr Johns, her gentleman usher, asked for a word with her in private.

'Madam,' he began, looking uncomfortable. 'Something must be done about Mr Dereham. He has taken to remaining at table with the officers of your council after everyone else has risen, and it is not his place to do so. He is not of your council and he is deliberately being disrespectful.'

Katheryn sighed, exasperated. Was there no end to Francis's presumption?

'When I sent to ask whether he were of the council,' Mr Johns went on, 'he said he was of your Grace's counsel before I knew you and would be when you have forgotten me.'

He had said that? She began to tremble and struggled to concentrate on what Mr Johns was saying.

'Then he picked a brawl with me, Madam, in which I fear I did not give a good account of myself. I had no choice but to look to my defence. See this . . .' He drew back his sleeve to reveal a nasty cut and pointed to a bruise on his jaw.

'He drew blood!' she said, appalled. Suddenly, she saw a way of being rid of Francis. Violence done in close proximity to the King was taken very seriously indeed – and the penalties were ruthless. A man who struck another and drew blood within the verge of the court could incur a fine, imprisonment and the loss of his right hand. This had been vividly demonstrated earlier in the year, when a serjeant porter had assaulted one of the Earl of Surrey's retainers in the tennis court at Greenwich. The serjeant porter had been sentenced to lose his right hand and forfeit his lands and possessions. All had been in readiness for the punishment to be carried out – Katheryn remembered that large crowds had crammed into the great hall – but the porter had thrown himself on the King's mercy, begging that someone go and ask his Grace if he might lose his left hand rather than his right, for if his right hand were spared, he might do the King much good service. Henry had been so impressed by his loyalty that he had graciously pardoned him, though he had afterwards expressed the opinion that the sentence of amputation should be mandatory.

She would not wish that on Francis, ever. But the threat of it might be sufficient to make him pack his bags and flee her service.

'Tell me, Mr Johns,' she said, 'did this fight take place within the verge of the court?'

Mr Johns was regarding her fearfully. She knew, without being told, that he had drawn blood too.

'It is no matter,' she said, sighing inwardly. 'I will speak to Mr Dereham.' For all the good it would do.

He came at her summons and she received him in the closet where they worked on her correspondence. 'I have just learned about what happened with Mr Johns,' she told him, 'and what you said to him. Take heed what words you speak! And remember that you could lose your right hand if you pick a fight and draw blood within the verge of the court.'

Even that did not seem to ruffle him. He just stood there grinning at her.

'Well?' she snapped. 'What have you got to say for yourself?'

'Please accept my humble apologies,' he said, bowing with a flamboyant flourish.

'Oh, go away!' she cried, exasperated.

Tom seemed subdued when he arrived in her chamber that night. He did not embrace or kiss her, but just sat down at the table glowering.

'What is wrong, darling?' she asked.

'Why is Mr Dereham in the court?' Tom asked.

Katheryn froze. She had been dreading something like this.

'My lady sued for a place for him. I could not very well refuse. It would have seemed churlish.'

Tom glared at her. 'Foolish, more like! He's been hinting that he knows you rather well.'

Oh, God. She had feared that Francis would not be able to hold his tongue. He did not know what discretion was.

'Has he indeed?' Her indignation was genuine. 'He was ever a rogue.'

Tom was scrutinising her face. 'Today, at supper, some of my fellow gentlemen of the Privy Chamber were saying that he is over-familiar towards you and scants his courtesies. Apparently, your servants have been complaining of it. We'd heard him ourselves, from further along the table. God knows, he was loud enough. He was saying that if the King died, he was certain that you would marry him. Is this true, Katheryn?'

'Of course not! If anything befell the King, it would be you I would marry. I assure you, Tom, you have no need to be jealous of Francis. I have eyes only for you. I do not love Mr Dereham and I would never encourage him to think so.'

'You need to make that very clear to him,' Tom told her, 'because he's labouring under a dangerous delusion. He ought to know too that it's treason to speak of the King's death. If he was reported, he would be in serious trouble indeed.'

She half hoped he would be, if only to shut him up. But she would not wish a traitor's fate on him, even though he was proving a serious liability. Only yesterday, he had asked for more money, and she had sent Kat Tilney to him with a purse of silver – and rewarded her for doing it.

'He is a fool,' she said, recovering her composure, 'and I have told him he can be nothing to me.'

'Then tell him again!' Tom flared. He gave a long sigh. 'I'm sorry, my love. It struck me to the heart to hear that knave boasting. I could have strangled him.'

'Forget him,' she urged. 'I don't want him intruding in any way on our precious time together.'

Soon she was in Tom's arms again, and all was as it should be. She prayed fervently that Francis would keep his mouth shut in future. He really was dicing with death and might learn his lesson the hard way – and take her down with him.

Chapter 28

1541

Early in September, the court left Pontefract and moved on to the ancient castle of the archbishops of York at Cawood. As they approached on horseback, Margaret Douglas leaned forward in the saddle, her long red hair flying in the breeze, and told Katheryn that Cardinal Wolsey had been arrested here. It was a sad, ancient pile and they were glad to leave the next day for Wressle Castle, which had been confiscated from the powerful Percy family after they had supported the Pilgrimage of Grace. They stayed here for three nights and Henry came to Katheryn's bed on two of them.

'It's about time we got ourselves a son!' he said, heaving himself on top of her and fumbling between her legs. She dared not think of Tom at these times, or afterwards, when Henry gently cradled her in his arms, his beard rasping her cheek, and told her how much he loved her and how blessed he was to have such a wife. She hated herself then, knowing how she was deceiving him.

As the days wore on, she lost count of the places they stayed. Leconfield, Hull, Leconfield again, and back to Wressle. Then they were on their way to York and Henry's long-anticipated meeting with the King of Scots. It was the middle of September by the time they arrived, and they were a long way behind schedule.

'We should have been halfway back to London now,' Henry said, as they saw before them York Minster rising in splendour above the city walls. 'At least, given how far behind we are, the workmen will be finished.' Before they came away on the progress, he had ordered the refurbishment of the former abbot's house in the dissolved Benedictine abbey of St Mary's in York, which was now to be called the King's

352

Manor. 'I've had fifteen hundred men working night and day.'

Ahead, they could see crowds massed around the great Micklegate Bar, the royal entrance to England's second city. Henry looked pleased.

'A fine welcome lies ahead, I see. I'm told that the good people of York have seen the lavish preparations for our visit and concluded that they betoken some extraordinary triumph. They expect me to have you crowned in the Minster, Katheryn. It will do no harm to let them think that, or hope that you will bear a duke of York.'

'I pray for it daily,' she said, feeling guilty because she had not conceived again since her miscarriage in the spring.

They had dressed in their most magnificent clothes, as had the citizens, who put on a brave show for their coming. There was as much solemnity as there had been at Lincoln. Henry and Katheryn were formally welcomed by the Archbishop of York and three hundred clergy, then two hundred men who had rebelled against the King and been pardoned came to make further submission, kneeling in the street before him and offering purses bulging with gold. Then the procession moved on into the city at a stately pace.

The King's Manor was magnificent. The army of workmen had done a wonderful job. Katheryn gazed up in amazement at the newly rebuilt great hall, which was furnished with the tapestries and plate that had been brought from Whitehall to impress King James. Henry had also transported from London his richest clothes and new liveries for his archers, pages and gentlemen. Colourful tents and pavilions had been erected in the grounds of the old abbey to accommodate the members of both courts, and vast supplies of food had been purveyed from the districts round about York.

Katheryn knew at once that it would be difficult for her and Tom to meet. The manor house, large as it was, was crammed with courtiers and servants. The best Jane could contrive was a brief assignation at the top of the back stairs, with herself on guard on the landing below.

It was wonderful to be alone with Tom, if only for a short time.

'We haven't long,' Katheryn whispered, looking fearfully up and down, 'but I have been yearning to see you, my dear heart, and to tell you how well I love you.'

'I thought to die of longing,' Tom muttered, holding her tightly.

They barely had time for a few kisses, and then Jane was there, saying that Katheryn should leave.

The next night, when they snatched an hour in Jane's chamber, Katheryn told Tom more about her years at Lambeth. 'When I first was there, when I was a young maiden, I hated it. My grief was such that I could not but weep in the presence of my fellows.'

'But you were happier later on?'

'I thought I was. But I know what real happiness is now.'

'How is that?' He smiled at her.

She pretended to think about it. 'Well, there is this gentleman who keeps coming a-courting. And I have a store of other lovers at other doors as well as he!'

He stared at her in disbelief for a moment until she started giggling. Then he snaked one arm around her and smacked her bottom with the other hand. 'Wicked wench!'

She squealed, loudly enough for Jane to tap on the door and hiss, 'Be quiet!'

They were unable to meet after that. Henry claimed her nights for himself, fired up with the idea of siring a duke of York, conceived in the city.

One evening, Jane handed Katheryn a pretty ring. 'It is a gift for your Grace,' she said, 'from Mr Culpeper. And costly too. He gave it to me this afternoon, after returning from Sheriff Hutton, where the King was hunting.'

Katheryn admired the bright scarlet garnet in its gold setting. It fitted her finger perfectly.

The next day, Tom sent a pheasant for her dinner.

'Your Grace should buy something for him in return,' Jane said, and there was something in her tone that made Katheryn wonder yet again if she was half in love herself with Tom. It would explain how protective she was of him and his interests.

'I know!' she said. 'I will go and buy something myself. We can go in disguise into York and look in the shops.'

Jane's eyes gleamed. 'Do you think we'll get away with it?'

'Trust me!'

Wearing hooded cloaks to disguise themselves, Katheryn and Jane slipped out of the King's Manor and went to explore the streets of York. Katheryn had forgotten what it was like to have the freedom to wander where she would. It felt strange now to be jostled in crowds and have men whistling after her. If only they knew who she was!

They enjoyed walking the narrow, bustling streets, where the upper storeys of half-timbered houses nearly met above their heads. They passed beautiful churches and fine civic halls, and marvelled at the range of wares in the shops and the marketplace.

Near Minster Yard, they found a goldsmith's shop. Displayed among his wares was a pair of bracelets.

'These will be a suitable gift for Tom,' Katheryn said, counting the coins out of her purse. 'Will you take them to him? Tell him they are to keep his arms warm!'

That set them both laughing. They strolled back, taking care to pull their hoods over their faces as they neared the King's Manor.

Katheryn had divested herself of her cloak and was washing her hands for dinner when Henry arrived in an angry mood.

'He's not coming!' he growled, stumping around the room. Thankfully, he was so preoccupied that he did not ask where she had been.

James had not arrived when expected. Henry's frustration had been mounting for some days, as time went by and the Scots King failed to appear. Now he was puce with anger.

She took his hand. 'What's happened?'

'The Scots have raided England! They've burned houses and murdered at least seven people. And this after my nephew expressed friendship to me and the desire to see me. If this is friendship, I'm the Pope!' His expression was fierce. 'By God, I'd have something to say to him if he were here. People have no honour these days. When I consider all the fanfares for his visit and all the outlay on preparations . . .' He was quivering with anger. 'Well, he shall know my displeasure. This is not the way to court my friendship!'

He ranted on for a while, as Katheryn made soothing noises. She didn't pretend to understand Scottish politics; in fact, she was getting bored. And she was weary of travelling. They had been away for three months now and she was ready to go home. There was nothing to stay for now, after all.

She was glad when they left York. It was now nearing the end of September and the weather was growing chilly. They spent an uncomfortable night at Holme-on-Spalding-Moor in a manor house that had been confiscated from Sir Robert Constable, one of the leaders of the Pilgrimage of Grace, whose body had hung in chains above the gates of Hull. The house had an eerie atmosphere – Katheryn could easily imagine Sir Robert's unhappy ghost walking here – and she was glad of Henry's solid presence beside her in bed.

They rode east to Hull so that he could plan fortifications; he was always expecting the French to invade. He enjoyed anything to do with military matters; the exercise restored his good humour, and he was again in a holiday mood during the five days they lodged at Hull Manor House. He could not bear to be without Katheryn for long and spent every night with her. There were no opportunities for dalliance with Tom.

From there, the great, but somewhat fatigued, procession travelled south into Lincolnshire, where the court was entertained and feasted at Thornton Manor, Kettleby Hall, Bishop's Norton, Ingleby, Nocton Manor and Sleaford. By the middle of October, they were back at Collyweston, and two days later they arrived at Fotheringhay Castle, which was one of Katheryn's dower properties. Although every effort had been made to make the ancient stronghold habitable, even comfortable, and it was obvious that the royal apartments had once been palatial, it was cold and damp and everything looked faded.

Katheryn was interested to learn that King Richard III had been born in the castle, a long time ago, when Fotheringhay had been one of the chief residences of the royal House of York, Henry's kin on his mother's side. He didn't want to hear about it, however. He had a very low opinion of his great-uncle Richard, who had murdered his young uncles, the Princes in the Tower, and had apparently stopped at nothing to steal the crown.

Henry was also uncomfortable in the nearby church, where some of his Yorkist ancestors were buried. Katheryn thought it fitting that she should visit because she was patroness of the collegiate foundation of Fotheringhay, but Henry told her that the college had been surrendered to the Crown two years ago, so there was nothing for her to do.

The church was one of two places she did not like at Fotheringhay. On the second night, Jane arranged for Tom to be waiting there, deeming it the safest place for a meeting. Katheryn donned her cloak and, concealed in its deep hood, slipped past the guards at the castle gates. They hooted after her, thinking her a serving wench keeping a tryst with a rustic swain. She ran along the moonlit street and pushed open the heavy church door. Tom greeted her, carrying a lantern, but she could tell from his face that something was wrong.

'I have heard from my brother,' he said. 'My mother is ill. She has made her will, but she has made no bequests to me, or even mentioned me in it.' He started walking up and down the chilly nave, his face twisted in anger. 'I had hoped that my parents would come to believe me innocent of rape and murder, but clearly they do not. I looked for at least some sympathy from my own mother.'

Katheryn put her arms around him; she could feel the underlying hurt in his tense body. 'Would you like me to write to her? I can tell her that the King himself believes in your innocence.'

Tom hesitated. 'It is best left alone, but thank you for offering, my darling. You are so good to me.'

She wondered why he was turning down her offer. Did his family know something she didn't? Did he fear they might tell her? No, that was disloyal of her. He was innocent, and much wronged by his parents – she was sure of it.

'It's worth a try,' she pointed out. 'Especially as your mother is ill.'

'No. I will write to her myself,' he said. 'If all else fails, I will take up your offer.'

He was too downcast to be in the mood for lovemaking, so they left, pulling the door shut behind them. It was quiet as the grave in the village, but suddenly, as they began walking towards the black bulk of the castle, they heard male voices singing faintly somewhere behind them, which stopped them in their tracks. They stared at each other.

'What's that?' Katheryn whispered.

'It sounds like monks chanting,' Tom said. 'It's coming from the church, but all is in darkness – and there was no one there a minute ago.'

They stood there listening for a while, Katheryn feeling as if her hair was standing on end. Abruptly, the music stopped, but they could hear a man's voice intoning. It sounded like Latin.

She was trembling. 'Let's go back to the castle!'

'You go ahead,' Tom bade her. 'I'll follow in a little while. We can't be seen together. Good night, my love.'

But Katheryn had gone, running towards the castle as if the hounds of hell were at her heels.

The other bad place at Fotheringhay was in the great hall, near the vast fireplace. The fire was kept stoked, but, every time Katheryn passed, it was cold there, and she found herself full of fear for no reason.

'You feel it too,' said a voice behind her, as she paused there, shivering. She wheeled around. It was Francis and, for once, he was not smiling. 'Something bad happened here.'

Anne Parr, who was in attendance on Katheryn with Dora Bray, regarded him coolly. 'My mother and I served the late Princess Dowager, who owned this house, and she complained of it being damp and inhospitable, but she never spoke of any dark deed taking place here.'

'It could have happened long ago. The castle is very old.'

'There's definitely a cold spot here,' Katheryn said, keeping her distance from Anne. 'If I move over here' – she took a few steps to the left – 'it is warmer, and yet I am further from the fireplace.'

'And here, too, it is warmer,' said Francis, moving to the right. 'It could be a portent of something bad that will happen in the future.'

'Oh, stop talking nonsense, Mr Dereham!' Anne reproved him.

Just then, Tom entered the hall and visibly bristled at the sight of Francis, who glared at him. For a moment, Katheryn feared that they might fall to blows.

'Mr Dereham, I have letters for you to write,' she said quickly. 'Attend me in my closet. Come, ladies.' So saying, she led them away, pretending not to notice the venomous looks on both men's faces.

They were soon on their way south to Higham Ferrers, where they were guests of Lucy Somerset's father, the Earl of Worcester. After a very convivial evening, Katheryn ran into Francis on the stairs. She could smell alcohol on him.

'Well met, wife!' he smirked.

'Hush!' she hissed. 'My ladies are not far behind.'

He sidled past her on the narrow spiral, sliding a hand around her waist. 'I'll have you again yet,' he murmured.

Angrily, she twisted out of his grasp, nearly losing her balance. 'Never!'

'We'll see about that,' he drawled. 'If anyone is going to enjoy your favours, it is me, who has the right to them.' He kissed her soundly on the mouth, then was gone, clattering down the stairs.

She was still fuming when the royal train moved on to Willington, but by the time it reached Ampthill Castle and Chenies Manor, where she and Henry were accommodated in a stately new wing, she had convinced herself that Francis was all bluster. He had as much to lose as she did by betraying her. He just enjoyed playing cat-and-mouse with her, the knave. Well, it wouldn't get him anywhere.

At Chenies, Alice Restwold asked for leave to visit her husband at The Vache, their country house. 'It's only five miles away, Madam. I can be there and back in an afternoon.'

'Of course,' Katheryn agreed.

Alice remained standing there. 'I wonder, Madam, if you could help me,' she said, smiling, 'for the sake of the good times we shared at Lambeth.'

Katheryn went cold. 'What can I do for you?'

Alice smiled. 'I was thinking that it would be lovely if I could turn up at home looking like a great lady. It would impress my husband! A fine biliment . . . perhaps a pretty jewel?'

It was a blatant demand and it was outrageous, not least because chamberers were not supposed to dress like great ladies. But Katheryn dared not show her anger.

'I will see what I can do,' she said stiffly.

'Thank you, Madam,' Alice said, dipping a curtsey.

Katheryn watched her go, fuming. She had had no choice but to comply with her demand. Gritting her teeth, she looked in her travelling chest and found a biliment of goldsmith's work she had meant to use for a French hood, and a little golden tablet pendant. Giving them to Jane, she ordered her to take them to Mrs Restwold. Thank God she could trust Jane not to take advantage of her!

She wandered into her privy chamber, where her ladies and some gentlemen were enjoying a lively game of cards. Margaret Douglas was sitting apart. It took a moment for Katheryn to realise that she was weeping.

'What's wrong, Margaret?' she asked in a low voice, sitting down beside her.

'My lady mother has died,' Margaret said, her fair face taut with pain. 'We were never close, and I had not seen her for years. I came into England as a young girl – my childhood was unhappy, for my parents were always at odds, and then my father fell foul of King James. I had been hoping to see my half-brother, King James, in York and ask for news of our mother, but it was not to be. Now it is too late. Forgive me. The news has come as something of a shock.'

'There is nothing to forgive,' Katheryn said warmly, putting her arm around Margaret's shoulders.

Just then, Katheryn's brother Charles came in, looking to join the card players, as she thought. He was twenty-five now, broad and good-looking, and drew admiring glances from the ladies wherever he went. He was doing well in the Privy Chamber and was held in high favour by the King, who had recently granted him a dissolved priory and two manors in Hampshire.

But he did not join the group at the table. Instead, he paused, looking Margaret's way, and she met his gaze, her eyes filled with yearning. There was obviously something between them, and it looked serious. Clearly, Charles had not heeded Katheryn's warning. And no good could come of this, especially given who Margaret was, and that she had already suffered for that disastrous affair with Lord Thomas Howard. Katheryn couldn't very well censure them, for what she was doing with Tom was far worse, but she understood how they felt. Yet she must speak!

'I hope you know what you are doing,' she murmured.

'I know, I should know better,' Margaret admitted, never taking her eyes off Charles, who was still standing in the doorway, obviously reluctant to approach while the Queen was with Margaret. 'There is all the comfort I need,' she whispered.

'Be careful, I pray you!' Katheryn urged her.

Standing up, she greeted Charles with a kiss. 'I'm trusting you not to put her in danger,' she muttered, and left.

After four months away, it was a relief to see the squat tower of Windsor Castle on its distant eminence. They stayed there for four nights before moving on to Hampton Court. It was good to be back in familiar surroundings after their long, long journey. But there was no time to relax, for a mud-spattered messenger was waiting with an urgent message for the King.

'Your Majesty,' he said, falling to his knees. 'I have just arrived from Hunsdon. The Prince of Wales is sick of a quartan fever.'

Henry's normally rosy countenance turned white. 'My son is sick? How sick?'

'The fever had not broken when I left, Sire.'

'Summon all my physicians!' Henry barked at his lords and gentlemen. 'They must attend him at once.'

Katheryn touched his arm. 'Should we go?'

'No, darling. It's the doctors he needs.'

'But he is only four; he should have someone close to him to liven his spirits.'

'I said no! I will not risk any further infection. Think where we have been travelling of late; who knows what evil humours were in the air. No. Much as I long to go to Edward, I must do what is prudent. His safety comes before all else. He is my only heir!'

His words were not said in reproach, she knew that, but they brought home to her how badly she had failed him. It must be some fault in her, because it was not for the lack of effort on his part.

'I am sorry, Katheryn,' Henry said, squeezing her hand, looking distracted. 'You must forgive my rough manner. It was fear for Edward that made me sharp.' His eyes were brimming with tears. 'I understand enough of medical matters to know that this is a dangerous malady for a child of his age. God grant he will withstand it!'

Dr Chamber and Dr Butts, the King's chief physicians, went riding off at speed to Hunsdon. All their reassuring words on departure had not masked their fears for the Prince. Henry shut himself in his prayer closet and began beseeching and bargaining with the Almighty to spare his son. He was there for hours. When he emerged, his knees were so stiff that he could barely stand. He spent the night lying in Katheryn's arms, sobbing on her shoulder.

Two days later, they were toying with their dinner when another messenger arrived and handed the King a letter. He read it hastily and gave a shout of jubilation.

'God has heard my prayers! The Prince is making a good recovery.'

'Praised be God!' Katheryn breathed. 'Oh, Sir, you must be so relieved!'

He was pressing coins into the messenger's hand. 'Take this for your pains and for bringing us such joy. And go to the servery and tell them I command them to give you a hearty dinner.'

When the man had gone, he turned to Katheryn. 'When Edward is fully restored to health, I shall send him to Ashridge. The air is beneficial there. And I will limit the number of servants in attendance. I daren't risk him catching anything else at this time. But now we must celebrate. I shall bring some of my gentlemen and join you and your ladies in your privy chamber this afternoon, and we will all be merry!'

They were indeed. Henry brought Will Somers with him and soon everyone was doubled over with laughter at the fool's droll jests. Isabel, Meg and Kat had tears streaming down their cheeks.

'What did the gardener say when the flower threatened to drop its petals?' Somers cried, mercilessly firing off one joke after another. '"Thou wilt not!" What of the miser who left everything to himself in his will?' On and on he cackled, dancing about the room and brandishing his stick of jingling bells.

'Enough!' Henry cried, breathless. 'You will kill us all, Fool!'

'Just one more, Harry?' Will cocked his head to one side, looking at his master pleadingly.

'Begone!' The King waved his hand. 'Go and get me some wine. Make yourself useful for once.' There was more laughter.

'Oh, the pity of it,' Will muttered, making for the court cupboard on which stood the wine ewer. But he was grinning. There was much affection between him and Henry.

The gathering broke up shortly before Vespers.

'I must go and give thanks to God for restoring the Prince to health,' Henry said, as he took his farewell of Katheryn. 'Then I think I will have an early night. I will see you in the morning, sweetheart.' He cupped her face in his hands. 'Thank you for your sweet kindness to me at this time. You are a jewel of womanhood – the jewel of my age – and I thank God for sending me such a wife.' He paused, gazing into her eyes. 'You do not know this, Katheryn, but while we were away on progress, I gave orders that, tomorrow, on All Hallows' Day, special thanksgiving services are to be held up and down the land, so that my people may render thanks for my happiness with you. For your virtue and your good behaviour, the whole realm shall do you all honour.'

She was overwhelmed – and filled with shame. She did not deserve this great distinction he had laid upon her; she was not worthy.

'I wish only to love you and do you service,' she said, aware that her cheeks had grown warm. She hoped Henry had not noticed that she had taken his magnificent gesture amiss.

God would not be mocked. There would be a reckoning, she was sure of it.

Part Five

'How dreadful is the jewel of brittle beauty'

Chapter 29

1541

Katheryn sat in her rich chair next to Henry's in the royal pew in the Chapel Royal at Hampton Court. It was All Saints' Day and they had just received Holy Communion. She had been moved to hear her husband, still kneeling before the altar, offer his Maker most humble and hearty thanks for the good life he led, and trusted to lead, with her. He had desired his confessor, the Bishop of Lincoln, to give thanks with him. Now the Bishop was praying aloud: 'Almighty God, we thank you for having provided the King our sovereign lord with so loving, dutiful and virtuous a queen.'

'Amen,' the congregation murmured.

Her eyes shut in prayer, Katheryn heard Henry's voice ring out. 'I render thanks to Thee, O Lord, that, after so many strange accidents that have befallen my marriages, Thou hast been pleased to give me a wife so entirely conformable to my inclinations as her I now have.'

There was spontaneous applause from the courtiers gathered in the nave below.

Katheryn wished the floor would open up and swallow her. She was going to Hell, that was for certain.

Could she give Tom up? But she loved him too much; she needed him constantly; his love was life itself to her. She loved Henry too, but not in the same way, and she had been manoeuvred into her marriage through no choice of her own. God, who knew the secrets of people's hearts, would know that. Yet how could He approve of her breaking the solemn vows she had made at her wedding?

In pricking her conscience, God was showing her the way. She knew what she should do, but she knew too that she could not do it. When the service was over and she went in procession with Henry to the presence chamber, where a feast awaited them, the moment passed; and when she saw Tom, bending forward with a golden ewer in his hands to pour wine for the King, she knew she was irredeemably lost.

On the morrow of All Saints, Katheryn again attended Mass with Henry. As they seated themselves in the royal pew, she noticed a sealed letter lying on the arm of the King's chair. Henry slid it inside his doublet and the service proceeded. Afterwards, he bade her a loving farewell in the holy day closet behind the pew and went off to receive some ambassadors. Katheryn returned to her apartments to have dinner.

It was at three o'clock that the door to her privy chamber was flung open to admit Lord Chancellor Audley and a deputation of privy councillors, attended by four of the King's guards.

'Katheryn, Queen of England, you are under arrest!' the Lord Chancellor informed her. He held out a warrant bearing the King's signature.

The room began spinning; there was a rushing of blood from her head and she felt faint. Terror gripped her. And yet she was not surprised.

She saw Isabel staring at her in horror, Jane Rochford's ashen face, and knowing looks on those of Meg and Kat. They had guessed! Had they betrayed her?

'Ladies, you may leave us,' Audley said. Her attendants filed out in silence, casting furtive glances at her as she stood there, wringing her hands in distress, barely able to breathe.

'Secure the apartment!' Audley ordered the guards, and they took up their places, halberds crossed in front of the door to prevent her from leaving.

'You are under house arrest and will remain here until further notice,' he told her, not meeting her eyes, but speaking to her with as much distaste as if she were a clod of dirt stuck to his shoe.

It came to her that he was acting on the King's orders. Oh, great God, what had she done? Why had she been so stupid? Lust weighed little now in the scales against fear and shame, exposing her love for

Tom as the tawdry, sinful thing it was. She could not imagine how Henry must be feeling, especially if he had discovered what had been going on – and so soon after he had publicly thanked God for blessing him with so virtuous a wife! What a fool she had made of him!

But how much – and what – did he know?

She faced the councillors. Her voice shook as she spoke. 'My lords, what is the reason for my confinement?'

'Madam, you are accused of misconduct before your marriage to the King,' Audley said gravely.

Francis! Francis must have talked. She had nourished a snake in her household. She had known it had been a grievous mistake to employ him, yet what choice had she had, enmeshed as she was in the chains of her past, and at the mercy of others? Oh, what a fool she had been to underestimate his malice!

But, she told herself, all was not lost. The Lord Chancellor had mentioned only misconduct *before* her marriage. This was not about Tom. She might have brought eternal shame and ignominy on herself, but she had committed no crime with Harry or Francis.

A thought struck her. If it had been Francis who had betrayed her, then he might well be under arrest too! But what, if anything, did Francis know about Tom? What had he meant that day he'd told her she seemed to have forgotten she was married to the King? What gossip had he heard?

Of course, he might have been making it up; you never knew with him. But if people had been gossiping, had it been about her and Tom? The thought chilled her to the marrow. And she had heard that people often talked under questioning. It was an open secret that horrible things went on in the Tower.

'What misconduct?' she asked.

'That you did have congress before your marriage with a Mr Manox and with one Dereham, who is now employed in your household.' There was an edge to Audley's voice which implied that that in itself was suspicious. Did they believe that she and Francis had intended to resurrect their relationship? She would have no problem clearing herself of that charge!

All would be well, if she could establish her innocence so easily – and if they believed her. And if no one implicated Tom.

There was an old saying: least said, soonest mended. All her instincts were urging her to deny everything. 'I have always been a faithful wife to the King,' she declared. As far as giving her body entirely to another went, it was true. 'What happened before my marriage can have no bearing on that.'

The lords stood there, silent. Audley cleared his throat. 'Madam, the outer doors to your lodgings will be locked, but you may keep your keys to each room.' With that, he nodded at the others and they all left, the guards closing the door behind them, leaving her entirely alone.

She sank to the floor, all her optimism gone, and began wailing in terror and remorse. What had she done? She had been an utter fool to let her heart and her baser needs take her where they would. It was the not knowing what they had against her that frightened her so much.

But there was one thing that frightened her more. What could they do to her? More to the point, what would Henry do to her? Awful memories of the bloody fate of Lady Salisbury came to mind . . . that bungling executioner . . . the unimaginable agony. And Anne Boleyn, kneeling in the straw, waiting for the executioner's sword to descend . . . But they had committed treason. Misconduct before marriage *was not treason*.

She could not bear to think about Henry. He had held her in his arms only the night before last; he had thanked God publicly for her, calling her his jewel of womanhood. She could not get that out of her mind. Would it count in the scales against her, or in her favour? If all they ever found out was that she had had premarital affairs, would he find it in his heart to forgive her? But her conscience was pricking her sorely; she knew herself guilty of more than that.

Still she could not get the images of Lady Salisbury and Queen Anne out of her mind. The thought of their terrible fates made her feel faint with fear and she leaned forward, keening in anguish, hugging herself. But there was no one to hear, no one to comfort her.

At length, the storm of weeping dried up and Katheryn climbed shakily to her feet. She must be positive; she must be brave. They could not put her to death for what she had done before marriage, and it was clear that they knew nothing of what had happened afterwards, or they would have charged her with it.

Jane had been there when she was arrested, yet they had not come for her. She must take heart from that. Jane did not know about her past, but she must be quaking in her shoes, for she was guilty of aiding and abetting crimes the Council did not know about; and, of all people, she had good reason to comprehend the peril in which she and her mistress stood.

The return of Katheryn's ladies cheered her a little. Nothing had been taken from her apart from her freedom, and her canopy of estate was still in place. Henry could not mean her too much ill if he let her keep state as queen. But, when she tried to talk to her women about what had happened, she met with a wall of silence.

'We have been instructed not to discuss that with you, Madam,' Lady Rutland said stiffly.

They were wary of her. Some could not hide their disapproval. Of course, none of them wanted to be associated with a fallen queen. But she had not fallen yet!

The only person prepared to defy the Council's order was Jane, who insisted on attending Katheryn to the privy. Once the door was closed, she whispered, 'We were told that you have been arrested for misconduct before marriage. Is that all?'

Katheryn looked into her eyes. They were haunted, and no wonder. 'Yes, thank God. Have you heard anything of Tom?'

'Nothing, except that he went hawking yesterday,' Jane said. 'I would have gone to find him, but we were made to wait together in the hall and there were guards there. Everyone was staring at us. I dare not seek him out now, lest I am being watched.'

Katheryn was crestfallen. 'No, you could not risk it. Let us pray that no one suspects he means anything to me.' She was trembling in agitation. It was imperative that she impress on Jane the need to hold her tongue. 'If the matter doesn't come out, there is nothing to fear. *I* will never confess it and, if you love me, you will deny it utterly and in no way disclose it. I warn you, they may speak in a fair manner to you

371

and use all kinds of ways to make you talk, but remember, if you confess, you will undo both yourself and others.'

'I will never confess it, even if I am torn apart with wild horses,' Jane promised.

'We must thank God that you have not yet been questioned,' Katheryn said. 'We should take heart from that, for it shows that they know nothing about what has passed between us and Tom. Just hold your own if they question you. And be very afraid of the consequences if you do talk!'

'You think I don't know what they would do to us if we were discovered – and to Mr Culpeper?' Jane retorted shrilly. 'You silly girl, don't you think I go in fear already? Would I really sign my own death warrant?' Katheryn recoiled; she had never seen her friend so agitated. Jane's eyes were wild, her hands shaking. Given the circumstances, you could forgive her discourtesy.

'We must not be alone in here for any longer,' Katheryn said. 'Are you and the others allowed out?'

'Yes, but we have to state to the guards our business.'

'Then please find some pretext to look for Tom. Find out if he still walks free.' That would prove that she was not in danger – yet.

'I'm not going near him!' Jane was adamant.

'No, of course. That would be wise.'

It was strange, but she had no desire to see Tom – only to know that he was still at liberty. When Jane came back later and assured her that he was, the sense of relief lasted for a few hours, and then she had to ask her to go out and check again – and again. Jane bore this patiently at first, but her nerves were frayed too.

'That's the fourth time you've asked me!' she snapped, late that evening. 'The others will be wondering why I keep having to attend you to the privy – and I'm running out of excuses to give the guards for why I am going out.'

'But it's in your interests too to find out if Tom still goes free,' Katheryn pointed out.

'I'm not sure I can stand the suspense of trying to find out for much longer,' Jane said, her face crumpling. 'I keep telling myself that it's only a matter of time . . .' She broke down, sobbing. 'I can't stop thinking about my husband. It took three blows of the axe . . .' Her voice tailed off. 'It could be me suffering that dreadful death. It might be God's punishment for laying evidence against him.'

Katheryn stared as the normally self-assured Jane Rochford disintegrated in front of her eyes, clawing her neck and mouthing wordless cries. She felt like screaming herself, for Jane's words had struck fright into her anew. 'Peace be!' she hissed. 'You don't want anyone to hear you or see you like this. They will suspect something.'

Jane just stared at her, her eyes round with fear.

On legs that felt as if they would not carry her, Katheryn walked out of the privy and into her bedchamber. She had put off going to bed, fearing to be alone with her thoughts and the terrors that night brought, but her maids were yawning, and it was now past one. She wished Jane hadn't said that dreadful thing about Lord Rochford; she could not get it off her mind. It was the last thing she wanted to take to bed with her.

She suffered them to undress her and put her between the sheets, but forbade them to blow out all the candles. She did not want to be in the dark. For all she knew, she might soon be in eternal darkness. Stop it! she admonished herself. All is not yet lost. Think positive thoughts. They can't punish you for what went before. She had been saying that to herself all day. She wished she could believe it.

She lay there in torment, sleep eluding her. What was happening beyond the guarded door to her lodgings? That was the worst, not knowing how much the Council knew, or who had talked. Was Tom still at liberty? Had he heard of her arrest? And Henry – he was under this very roof. For all she knew, he too might be lying in bed weeping like her, coming to terms with the fact that she was not the person he had thought she was. But she had been told to keep quiet about her past! Uncle Norfolk had enjoined it, and the Duchess. Oh, how she wished she could see Henry and explain everything. She was sure he would understand.

As she lay wakeful, her resolve strengthened. She *would* see him! She would contrive it somehow. And, with that comforting thought, she finally managed to fall asleep.

* * *

The next morning, she woke early, seized with a sense of dread. The events of the previous day came rushing back to her and all she wanted to do was bury herself under the bedclothes and not come out. But she must; she had to concoct a plan.

She had eaten nothing the evening before; she had been too distressed and the thought of food had made her feel sick. But, seeing that she looked so wan in the mirror, she forced herself to eat some breakfast, then pinched her cheeks to put some colour into them. If she was to see Henry, she must look her best.

He would be going to the Chapel Royal for Vespers this evening, if he kept to his usual habit. Of course, he might be too grief-stricken or angry to show himself in public, but she must take that chance.

Her ladies were surprised when she told them to dress her in her tawny damask gown with the deep jewelled biliment. It was one Henry loved, and Master Holbein had painted her in it. She could have wept to think of those days now, but she must not dwell on that. Elizabeth Seymour brushed her hair until it shone. Soon, she was ready. All she had to do was wait.

The hours seemed endless. She sat there with her ladies, none of them saying very much. Isabel held her hand, looking as if she was about to burst into tears. Katheryn could not have borne to play or listen to music lest it call to mind happier days. She picked at her embroidery and made a mess of it. For much of the time, she sat staring into space, going over and over events and trying to think of any way the Council might hear of her affair with Tom.

The sky grew dark. Dusk came early in these November days and soon the candles were all lit.

It was time.

'I want some air,' she said. 'I feel faint.'

'Someone open a window,' Lady Rutland ordered.

'No,' Katheryn moaned, 'I must go into the garden.' She lurched towards the main door of her apartments and banged hard on it. A key turned in the lock and the door opened. A guard peered at her.

'Help!' she gasped. 'I must have some air! I'm going to faint.' And she half collapsed against him.

'Get help!' he told the other guard, putting an arm around her to steady her. As his fellow hurried off, Katheryn twisted her body out of the man's grasp and flew down the gallery in the direction of the Chapel Royal. She could hear the guard's feet pounding on the floorboards behind her and his cries of 'Come back! Stop!' Fortunately, the gallery was deserted. Everyone was at Vespers. The doors to the chapel closets were open – it was as if God was with her!

Her plan was working out as she had prayed it would. At that very moment, Henry walked out of the chapel attended by some of his gentlemen. The first thing she noticed was how haggard and old he looked.

'Your Grace!' she cried. 'Sir!'

The men stopped in their tracks. Henry turned his head in her direction, then looked away, his expression set like stone. And then the guard caught up with her and grabbed her from behind. She screamed. 'Henry! Listen to me! I beg of you!'

As she struggled in the man's arms, she saw Henry hesitate. Then he turned his back on her and walked off in the other direction, his gentlemen following.

'Henry!' she screamed. 'Henry, help me!'

The other guard had now arrived on the scene and he and his fellow dragged her back to her apartments. She was like a mad thing, screaming and howling, wild with fear, knowing that Henry had abandoned her and that all was lost. When, finally, they bundled her back into her privy chamber, she was still struggling, still shrieking. Her women ran to her and bore her off to her bedchamber, where they made her lie down. She gave in, keening and whimpering like an animal in pain.

'He has forsaken me!' she cried, when at last she could speak. 'I don't want to die!'

'Who said anything about dying?' asked Lady Rutland, briskly. 'Calm yourself, Madam! This is doing you no good, no good at all.'

'But he walked away! I was crying out to him, and he walked away.' She kept reliving the moment, over and over again, in her head. 'He will do to me what he did to Queen Anne!'

'That's nonsense,' Jane said sharply. Katheryn could hear the fear in her voice. 'You haven't done anything worse than pretend to be virtuous when you weren't.'

'We are not supposed to be discussing it,' Lady Rutland reproved her.

'We can hardly ignore her Grace when she is in such a state!' Jane retorted. 'And I speak truth.'

'Who knows what the truth is?' Lady Rutland muttered, which made Katheryn start wailing again.

'Hush, now,' Lady Rutland said, more kindly now. 'Stop this! You must try to rest, Madam.'

Isabel tried too. 'Come on, Katheryn. Pull yourself together. You aren't helping yourself.'

Katheryn was beyond good advice. She lay there moaning and sobbing, her body convulsed with fear. She had lost Henry's love, the one thing she had counted on, and, without his protection, she herself was lost. There was no help for her.

She spent the next two days mired in grief and terror, veering from one to the other. The ladies were in despair. They did all they could to rouse her from her misery and calm her when she became hysterical, but to little avail. She would not eat, she could not sleep and she would not change her clothes. She lay wakeful, feeling as if she was trapped in a nightmare.

At one point, she heard a lot of voices and bustle in the courtyard below her rooms. Then everything went quiet. Lost in her fears, she thought no more of it, but later she heard one of the ladies saying that the palace seemed so quiet now that the King had left for London. So he had gone – and left her to her fate. That provoked a fresh spate of weeping.

Chapter 30

1541

On the third day, there was a knock at the door, quite early in the morning, and Isabel entered. It was the first time they had been alone together since her arrest.

'Katheryn, rouse yourself,' she said. 'We have just been informed that Archbishop Cranmer is coming to see you.'

'Archbishop Cranmer?' Hope dawned anew. Could it be that Henry was thinking in terms of ending their marriage rather than proceeding against her? Divorce rather than death? Maybe this was not the end after all. Why else would Cranmer be coming?

She got out of bed. 'Ugh, I stink.'

'Let's get those clothes off,' Isabel said, unlacing her. 'That under-smock can go in to soak.'

Soon, Katheryn was washed and dressed, her damp hair drying loose. Isabel had insisted that she wear a modest black gown with a stand-up collar, with very few jewels. 'You do not wish to look the part of a scarlet woman,' she said.

Katheryn peered in her mirror. She looked quite demure – and very pale.

At ten o'clock, she was sitting in her privy chamber, trying to concentrate on her embroidery, when the door opened to reveal not just Archbishop Cranmer, but Lord Chancellor Audley, her uncle of Sussex, Bishop Gardiner, whose eyes remained averted from her, and her uncle of Norfolk, who glared at her as if she was beneath contempt. How unfair! she thought bitterly. He had known about her past – and made her keep it secret.

Her heart sank. Had they come to bully her into agreeing to be divorced? Well, they could spare themselves the trouble. She would agree to anything if it saved her life.

She eyed the lords warily. Cranmer was no friend to her. He was hot for church reform, and – it was bruited – a secret Protestant. He had never approved of her marriage, for it had brought the Catholics into power at court, and he would no doubt welcome this opportunity of getting rid of her and ousting his reformist opponents. And Gardiner and Norfolk were clearly angry with her for offending the King; they would be worrying about their own political futures.

The Archbishop looked vexed. 'Well, Madam, this is a sorry state of affairs. You know, of course, that you are charged with grievous misconduct before your marriage to the King.'

She nodded.

'What does your Grace say to the charge?'

'I deny it,' she declared.

Norfolk gave her a calculating stare in which she detected a trace of admiration. Maybe he thought that all was not lost. Maybe she was doing the right thing by refuting everything.

'You deny it?' Audley echoed, frowning.

'I do. I know there are malicious persons who seek to do me harm and think to profit by it. Whatever you have been told, it is all lies.'

'But we have the sworn depositions of witnesses.'

'Then they are foresworn!'

'Think carefully on what you say, Madam,' Cranmer warned. 'We will give you a little time to reflect. I will return later.'

Another endless, agonising day. She spent it in anguished speculation as to whom had laid evidence against her. She was still convinced that Francis had had a hand in this, and that maybe some of her women had talked. They were all here in attendance on her, and she scrutinised their faces, one by one, looking for some sign, some furtiveness, some inability to meet her eye, anything that might give the culprit away. It was useless. Most were on their guard with her. Only Isabel was showing her kindness. Jane was keeping her distance.

At dusk, Cranmer returned, accompanied only by Sir John Dudley, her Master of Horse, whom she had never liked, for he had a cold, abrupt manner. But he was here apparently only to take notes, for he sat at the table and set out writing materials, saying nothing.

At the sight of Cranmer, Katheryn burst into tears, letting out all her pent-up fears and emotions. She could not stop and sank to her knees on the floor, wailing. The Archbishop looked most distressed.

'Madam, calm yourself, please!' he begged, but she was beyond responding. He looked around helplessly. 'I pray you, my ladies, come and help!' he said. 'The Queen is in much lamentation and heaviness. I never saw creature so distraught, and it would arouse pity in any man's heart to look upon her.'

Isabel hurried over. 'Come now, Katheryn, the Archbishop is here to talk to you. At last, you have an opportunity to defend yourself.'

But Katheryn was still howling, unable to control herself.

'It is impossible to speak rationally with her in this state,' Cranmer said. 'I tell you, I do fear for her sanity. I will leave her to calm down and return later.'

When he had gone, Isabel knelt beside Katheryn. 'Child, you must calm yourself, do you hear me? My lord of Canterbury is coming back later, and you must compose yourself to talk to him. This is very important. Katheryn, do you hear me?'

But Katheryn barely heeded her. All rational thought had left her; she was convinced that Cranmer's visit boded ill and she remained in a frenzy, rushing around the room in terror, trying to get out. None of the efforts of Isabel and her other women had any effect. At length, she subsided onto the floor, hugging her knees to her chest, sobbing and retching. And that was how the Archbishop found her on his return after supper.

'My daughter,' he said gently, dropping to his knees beside her, 'I am come to find out the truth and to offer you comfort, for his Grace is a most benign and merciful prince. He has promised you mercy if you will confess your faults.'

Mercy! Henry had promised her mercy. He had not abandoned her entirely.

The frenzy left her. She raised her tear-stained face and held up her hands. 'Oh, my lord, I give most humble thanks to his Majesty, for he has showed me more grace and mercy than I thought myself fit to sue for, or could have hoped for.' She was crying quietly now, overcome by Henry's kindness, which was indeed far, far more than she would have expected in the circumstances. Then, with the fresh realisation that she had forfeited his love and ruined her own life, she began howling again, shuddering in distress.

Cranmer grew brisk. 'Now, Madam, no more of this nonsense! There is no need for it. What is upsetting you so? The King has promised you mercy. Is that not good news?'

'Yes,' she sobbed.

'Listen, child, all I want you to do is open your heart to me. Tell me why you are crying.'

As she sat huddled there, trying to control herself, he held out his hand and helped her to rise and sit in her chair by the fire, himself taking the one opposite. 'Now,' he said, 'why are you in such a miserable state?'

'Alas, my lord, that I am alive!' she cried. 'Fear of death grieved me never so much as the remembrance of the King's goodness does now, for when I recall how gracious and loving a prince I had, I cannot but sorrow. And this sudden mercy, more than I could have looked for, being so unworthy, makes my offences appear to me more heinous than they did before. And. the more I consider the greatness of his Grace's mercy, the more I sorrow in my heart that I should have so misconducted myself against his Majesty.' And she began weeping again.

Cranmer tried in vain to comfort her, but she paid him no heed. It was some time before she calmed down.

'That's better,' the Archbishop smiled. 'Now, all we are going to do is talk.'

At that moment, the clock struck six and Katheryn wept afresh, remembering that it was at that time each evening that Master Heneage would bring her news of Henry if he was unable to join her, and often a loving message. When she told Cranmer this, he just smiled sadly.

She rested her head on the back of the chair. She had no more tears left and felt quite ill. Her nose was blocked and her handkerchief sodden.

'Now, are you ready to tell me the truth behind the accusations made against you?' the Archbishop asked.

'Yes, but who made those accusations?' she replied.

'I am not at liberty to tell you, but it would be wise to make a statement. Sir John here will write down what you say. First, there must be a preamble. Sir John, write the following: "Being examined by my lord of Canterbury, I, Katheryn, Queen of England, shall here answer faithfully and truly, as I shall make answer at the last Day of Judgement, and by the promise that I made in baptism and the sacrament I received upon All Hallows' Day last past." I trust you understand that, Madam?'

'Yes, my lord.'

'Good. You are now under oath. I want to ask you about your relationship with Francis Dereham. Did you bed with him before you married the King?'

She felt herself grow hot. 'Yes,' she said in a small voice. 'But it was long before I met his Grace.'

Cranmer made no comment. 'It seems that there was a precontract between you and Dereham that might invalidate your marriage to the King.'

So Francis had talked! He had ruined her! And yet it seemed that Cranmer was more concerned about that wretched precontract than about her bedding with Francis. Maybe this *was* all about ending her marriage.

More composed now, she chose her words carefully. 'I admit that Mr Dereham moved me many times to consent to marry him, but, as far as I remember, I never granted him more than I have already confessed. He did speak about a promise to wed, but I thought it to have been no contract.'

'Nor would it be if carnal copulation had not followed,' Cranmer told her, looking severe. 'But it did follow the making of such a promise, did it not? You had sworn, by your faith and troth, that you would have no other husband but Dereham!'

'No, I am sure I never promised that,' she insisted, fearful that confessing the truth would do her no good.

Cranmer looked vexed. 'Did you ever say to Dereham, "I promise you I do love you with all my heart"?'

'I do not remember that I ever said those words,' she answered, aware that she probably had.

'What tokens and gifts did you give to Dereham, and he to you?'

'I gave him a band and sleeves for a shirt. They were made by a lady in Lambeth. I never gave him any other present save those he took from me and kept against my wishes.' She was certainly not going to mention the money he had extorted from her.

Cranmer felt in his leather scrip and drew out a ring. 'This was found among Dereham's possessions.'

It was her mother's ring, the ruby ring she had given Francis, thinking that theirs would be a love to last for ever. 'It is none of mine,' she lied, feeling as if she was betraying her mother. Oh, God, if they had the ring, they had Francis!

'What presents did Dereham give you, Madam?' Cranmer asked.

'Mainly lovers' tokens. He knew of a little woman in London with a crooked back, who was skilled in making all sorts of flowers of silk. She made a French fennel for me, and he gave me heartsease of silk for a New Year's gift, although my lady of Norfolk gave it back to him. He bought me sarcenet to make a quilted cap, and I delivered it to a little fellow in my lady's house to embroider – as I remember, his name was Rose – to make whatever pattern he thought best.'

'Did you ask for it to be embroidered with friar's knots?'

'I did not ask Mr Rose to make it with friar's knots, as he can testify, if he be a true man, but he did embroider the cap with them.' It was important to show that she had not cared about Francis that much.

'But when Dereham saw the cap, he exclaimed, "What, wife, here be friar's knots for Francis!" did he not?' Cranmer probed. 'It seems to me that his familiar use of the word "wife" was strongly indicative of a precontract between you.'

'No, my lord, it was just Mr Dereham being presumptuous,' Katheryn insisted.

'Did you exchange any other gifts?'

'No, not to my remembrance, saving that, this summer, around the beginning of the progress, he gave me ten pounds in gold. I took it for a bribe, for he wanted a post in my household.'

'Is it true that he lodged a hundred pounds with you when he left the household at Lambeth?'

'Yes. It was most of his savings. He said that, if he did not return, I was to consider the money as my own.'

Cranmer leaned back and smiled. 'That, Madam, argues an established relationship. It is the part of a wife to look after her husband's money.'

'I but did it as a favour, not as his wife, I do assure you,' she declared.

The Archbishop turned to Sir John. 'Pray bring the Queen's confession here. Madam, will you read over what you have stated so far and agree that everything is correct?' He handed her the document.

'Yes, that is correct,' she said, after a time.

Outside, the clock chimed seven.

'It grows late and you need to rest, Madam,' Cranmer said. 'I will return tomorrow and we shall continue. Remember, if you will acknowledge your transgressions, even though your life has been forfeited by the law, the King has determined to extend to you his most gracious mercy.'

His words so shocked her – how could her life be forfeit? – that she barely heard him say that she had but to petition Henry in writing, admitting her offences and begging for forgiveness.

Her life was forfeit . . . Her life was forfeit. She could not get the words out of her head. When Cranmer and Dudley left, she fell to weeping again. She felt so alone, so helpless – and she knew so very little about the law.

The ladies all stood up and looked at her searchingly as she stumbled into the bedchamber an hour later. But she dared not confide in them. They had been told not to discuss anything with her, and it had occurred to her that they might have been set to spy on her. Anyway, what would any of them know about legal matters?

Isabel might, though. Isabel was married to Sir Edward Baynton, who knew everything, and she was very well informed herself.

'I'm going to have an early night,' Katheryn said. 'I feel wrung out.'

No one spoke; they just went about their tasks silently.

As her women finished undressing her, she bade Isabel brush her hair and murmured in her ear, 'Come back as soon as you can, as you love me!'

Isabel behaved as if she had not heard, but later, when all was quiet, she lifted the latch quietly and tiptoed into the bedchamber. At once, Katheryn was sitting up, peering around the bed curtains. 'You came! Thank God!'

'Yes, Katheryn. What is it?'

'I have to talk to someone.' Katheryn was near to tears again. 'Archbishop Cranmer said today that my life is forfeit.'

'Oh, my God!' Isabel gasped. 'Are they going to proceed against you?'

Katheryn shook her head. 'I don't know. I pray not. My lord of Canterbury said that if I confess my faults, the King will show me mercy. In truth, I do not know what I have done wrong, save not tell the King I loved others before I even knew him. So how can my life be forfeit? I could not think of anyone else to ask.'

'In truth, I do not know,' Isabel confessed, looking distressed. 'What did the Archbishop ask you?'

'He kept asking what went on before my marriage. Was it a crime not to tell the King about my past life?'

Isabel looked dubious. 'Not that I've heard of.'

'He kept asking if I was precontracted to another before I wed the King. How can my life be forfeit for that?'

Isabel hesitated. 'If you had been precontracted to someone else, your marriage to the King would be invalid. What if you had borne him a child? Its paternity, and its legitimacy, would be in question. That might be said to be impugning the succession, which is treason. It's the only explanation I can think of.'

'The problem is, I don't know if I *was* precontracted.'

'Did you ever make a mutual promise to marry Dereham?' Isabel asked.

Katheryn remembered Francis making her promise to wed him and calling her his wife, and herself calling him 'husband'. 'Yes, but I didn't know it was binding.'

Isabel flushed. 'And – forgive me, but I must ask – did you bed with him after?'

'Yes,' Katheryn admitted.

Isabel shook her head, as if despairing. 'Then I fear it sounds as if you were precontracted. A promise to wed followed by a bedding is as good and binding as a marriage.'

'So, by marrying the King, I could have impugned the succession and committed treason?'

'Possibly, though I am no lawyer.'

'But it makes sense,' Katheryn said. 'Therefore, I will keep denying it. It's only my word against Francis's.'

'I dare not advise you,' Isabel said. 'There is too much at stake, and I should not be discussing this with you anyway. But it might be best to tell the truth and throw yourself on the King's mercy. Say you were young and naive and did not know the import of what you were doing, and that you married his Grace in good faith.'

'I did! I did! It's the truth.'

'Then tell it. I am sure it's the right thing to do.'

'But, Isabel . . .' Katheryn's voice tailed off. Yes, she had been young and naive, but she had just this instant thought of a better way to save herself and win sympathy. It would mean lying, but Francis hadn't cared about the consequences for her when he betrayed her.

'What is it, Kitty?' Isabel asked gently.

'There's something I haven't told anyone,' Katheryn said. 'About what Francis did . . . He forced me to bed with him; he did not do it with my consent and will. He was violent to me.'

Isabel stared at her. 'He raped you?'

Katheryn nodded, as tears welled in her eyes. It was as if it had really happened.

'Archbishop Cranmer must be told of this,' Isabel declared. 'I will go and find Edward.'

* * *

When Cranmer returned the next morning, Katheryn had had second thoughts about accusing Francis of rape, but dared not go back on what she had said because she hated to think what Isabel would say – and she really was convinced that it would be her salvation. She felt so dreadful about lying about such a serious matter that she was crying almost as hysterically as she had the day before.

'What's this?' the Archbishop chided her. 'Have I not told you that the King will be merciful if you confess your faults?'

'Yes,' she sobbed, wondering what they might do to Francis if they believed her. What *was* the penalty for rape?

'Now, Madam,' Cranmer said, taking a chair and signalling to Sir John Dudley to write everything down.

He stared at her as she gulped the words out in fits and starts.

'You are telling us that Dereham forced you and used violence?'

'Yes,' she said, sniffing.

'Did you ever call him "husband"?'

'Yes.' The tears had stopped now.

'And he called you "wife"?'

'Yes. There was talk in my lady of Norfolk's house that we two should marry, and some of his enemies were envious.'

'Mr Manox, perhaps?'

'Yes. He and I had loved each other before I knew Mr Dereham.'

'This was a carnal relationship?'

'No. I was a maid and very young. He was my music master. He used flattery and fair persuasions to make me suffer him to touch the secret parts of my body, which I should not have permitted, nor he required.'

'So he was envious of Dereham?'

'Yes, which was why Dereham desired me to give him leave to call me "wife", and many times I called him "husband". And he used many times to kiss me, but he did that all the time to other girls in the house. One time, when he kissed me often, some who were watching us said they thought he would never have enough of kissing me. And he answered, "Who shall stop me from kissing my own wife?" Then they said it would come to pass that Dereham would have me.'

Cranmer nodded. His face gave nothing away. 'Are you certain that you and Dereham did not promise each other to wed?'

'No, we did not.'

'Think carefully. Bigamy renders the second marriage invalid; it is not a felony, but a spiritual offence and would be dealt with by the church courts; they alone have the authority to pronounce on the validity of a marriage. Concealing the existence of a precontract might in this case be construed as misprision of treason, because it endangers the royal succession; for that, the penalty is imprisonment. Now, think again!'

'We were not promised,' she declared.

Cranmer looked sceptical, but he let it pass. 'Now, I regret that I must touch on delicate matters. The matter of carnal knowledge. What can you tell me about your relations with Dereham?'

Katheryn felt herself reddening. She had not thought to be asked about that again, and she was uncomfortably aware of the objectionable Sir John listening to her every word. She took a deep breath. 'I confess that many times he lay with me, sometimes in his doublet and hose, and two or three times naked, but not so naked that he had nothing on, for he had always, at the least, his doublet and, as I remember, his hose also; but I mean naked, when his hose were put down.'

'I am told that there were disports in the gentlewomen's chamber at night.'

'Yes. Many times, Dereham and others would bring wine, strawberries, apples and other things to make good cheer, after my lady was gone to bed.'

'Did he ever stay after the dormitory was locked at night?'

'That is utterly untrue.' Another lie.

'Did you ever steal the keys from the Duchess?'

'No, I never did, nor desired anyone to steal them to let in Dereham; but, for many reasons, the doors were opened, sometimes overnight, and sometimes early in the morning, at my request and at the request of others. And sometimes Dereham came in early in the morning and behaved very lewdly, but never at my request or with my consent.'

Cranmer frowned. 'Yet we have a deposition that my lady of Norfolk had the keys of the gentlewomen's chamber brought to her own chamber at night, and that you would come in and steal them.'

Who had told him that?

'It is not true,' she insisted.

'What happened when your relationship with Dereham ended?'

'I remember that, after I knew I was going to court, he said to me that he would not stay long at Lambeth when I was gone. And I said he might do as he pleased. I don't remember what else we said.'

'Did you say it grieved you as much as it did him to be parted?'

'No, I never said that.'

'Did you weep on parting and tell him he would never live to say you had swerved?'

'None of that is true. Everyone who knew me knew how glad I was to be going to court.'

Cranmer interrupted his questioning to send for some ale for them both. They sat there, saying nothing, until it was brought. Then, as Katheryn gratefully sipped hers, he resumed.

'I understand that Dereham went to Ireland. Did you keep in contact with him after his return?'

'No. As far as I can remember, he sought me out and asked me if I was to be married, for he had heard a rumour of it and was jealous. I asked him why he should trouble me about that, for it was none of his business and he knew I would not have him; and, if he had heard such a rumour, he'd heard more than I had.' She'd deliberately avoided mentioning Tom and was praying that she would not be quizzed further on this, but Cranmer did not pursue that line of questioning. She was almost certain now that he knew nothing about her affair with Tom.

'You say that Dereham raped you, yet you gave him gifts and called him "husband" and you were close to him for some time. Madam, that does not sound like the actions of a woman who has been violently forced to have carnal relations.'

Katheryn felt bad again about the lie. 'I was scared of him, of what he might do. I knew he had a violent temper. I played along to keep him sweet.'

'And when you ended your association, he made no protest or showed no violence?'

'No. But things had been cooling between us for a while. After the Duchess found us together, we lacked opportunities for meeting in private.'

Cranmer nodded. 'I think that is all for now,' he said. 'Sir John, bring me the statement.'

He looked it over, then gave it to Katheryn to read.

'Will you sign it?' he requested. She did so and gave it back.

'I will now confer with my fellows on the Council,' he told her.

When he and Dudley had left, she sighed with relief. This really was all about her and Francis. It had nothing to do with Tom. She was beginning to believe that she was safe. She reminded herself that the King had shown mercy to Margaret Douglas and Thomas Howard, and he had not executed Lord Lisle. He might divorce her, he might no longer love her, but he might well spare her worse punishment. Anything would be better than this nightmare. After these last terrible days, she would quite welcome becoming a private person again. She would be happy to leave court and live out her days in obscurity.

The following morning, the Archbishop returned with some of the lords of the Council.

'Your Grace, we are here to help you draft a plea for forgiveness to send to the King,' he told her. That was heartening news, for, if they were ready to assist her in this, they could not mean her any harm.

At their dictation, she wrote, slowly and laboriously, Cranmer correcting her spelling.

I, your Grace's most sorrowful subject and the most vile wretch in the world, unworthy to recommend myself to your most excellent Majesty, do make my most humble submission and confession of my faults. And while I know your Majesty has no cause to grant me mercy, yet, out of your accustomed mercy, which has been extended to other undeserving men, I most humbly, on my hands and knees, desire one particle to be

389

extended to me, even though I am most unworthy to be called your wife or subject. No words can express my sorrow; nevertheless, I trust your most benign nature will consider my youth, my ignorance, my frailness and my humble confession of my faults; and so I refer myself wholly to your Grace's pity and mercy.

Now, the whole truth being declared to your Majesty, I most humbly beseech you to consider the subtle persuasions of young men and the ignorance and frailness of young women. I was so desirous to be taken into your Grace's favour, and so blinded with the desire of worldly glory, that I did not consider how great a fault it was to conceal my former faults from your Majesty, considering that I intended always to be faithful and true to your Majesty. Nevertheless, the sorrow of my offences was ever before my eyes, when I considered the infinite goodness of your Majesty towards me. Now I refer the judgement of all my offences, with my life and death, wholly to your most benign and merciful Grace, to be considered only by your infinite goodness, pity, compassion and mercy, without which I acknowledge myself worthy of extreme punishment.

She took comfort in the fact that the councillors knew how best to approach Henry and that this abject plea was the most likely means of stirring his heart to pity.

Soon after the lords had left to take her confession to the King, the guards admitted Sir Thomas Seymour. Katheryn had never liked him much. He was Queen Jane's brother, uncle to the Prince and younger brother to the ardently reformist Earl of Hertford; he was also conceited, bombastic and unpredictable. Many ladies found him attractive, but Katheryn was wary of him.

There was no trace of his air of devil-may-care today. He bowed and addressed her soberly. 'Your Grace, I am here to take an inventory of your jewels. Where might I find them?'

'Fetch them, please,' Katheryn instructed Lady Rutland, who brought the casket from the bedchamber. Katheryn's eyes filled when

Sir Thomas opened it and all the gorgeous contents spilled out on the table; she was remembering how Henry had showered her with them on the morning of her uprising, gifts of love for an adored wife. How she had enjoyed wearing them, the beautiful, precious, sparkling things. And now she was adored no more and, of a certainty, they were to be taken from her.

His list drawn up, Sir Thomas returned the jewels to the box and asked Lady Rutland to put it away.

'Good day, your Grace,' he said, bowing again, and left Katheryn wondering why he had not taken them with him. Was Henry considering letting her keep at least some of them?

Chapter 31

1541

That afternoon, Jane came back from one of her forays into the court looking distraught. 'I could not find Mr Culpeper anywhere,' she whispered, as she bent down by Katheryn's chair to pick up her embroidery tambour. 'And no one would tell me where he was.'

Katheryn went cold; her skin was erupting in goose bumps. This was the news she had dreaded. She felt sick. They knew. They knew! And from Jane's face she could see that her friend had drawn the same conclusion.

'Say nothing, remember!' she hissed in Jane's ear.

She could not sew. She kept dropping stitches. She was taut with anxiety, awaiting a knock on the door, sure that they would come for her any minute. Misconduct before marriage was one thing; infidelity afterwards quite another. It was treason. It was why Queen Anne had died.

She caught her breath on a sob. Her ladies looked up, but, with a huge effort, she composed herself and bent her head to her task.

Lust had brought her to this. Lust, and the unbridled frailty of tender youth, had made her swerve from the path of virtue and reason and led her to indulge in those illicit affairs. But she had been so young, and few had exhorted her to guard her chastity and reputation. She had been ill prepared to resist her own wanton appetites. She had thought only of carnal delight, never of the consequences. How blind she had been! Why, oh, why, had she not kept to the straight and narrow path of honest wifehood? *Oh, Tom; we were both too feeble to deny our lusts!*

On and on went her tortuous thoughts, giving her no peace. If only, if only . . . But it was too late for regrets now. All she could do was wait and pray.

Jane looked as drawn and fearful as Katheryn felt. Katheryn knew, without being told, that Jane's thoughts were all for Tom. Without any means of knowing if he was still at liberty, they must both endure the suspense of wondering if he had been arrested. And that, Katheryn realised, was the main reason she kept thinking about him. Had she loved him so little? It all seemed like a dream now.

When Margaret Douglas burst into her bedchamber the next morning, Katheryn was alarmed to see that her face was streaked with tears.

'What is it?' she cried, leaping out of bed, fearing the worst.

Margaret broke down afresh. 'Charles has been banished from court. Our love has been discovered. And I am to remain here with you and may not leave these rooms.'

The other women had crowded in behind her and were looking on in sympathy. Katheryn put her arms around Margaret, then they were both crying, sobbing on each other's shoulders. Was there no end to the misery?

'What will become of him?' Margaret wept.

'He is resourceful; he will survive,' Katheryn comforted her. 'He may not be banished for long.'

'It was made very plain to me that I was never to see him again,' Margaret said. 'I do not know how I will live without him. Oh, I am so unlucky in love! I will die an old maid.'

Katheryn relinquished her. 'I will pray for you.' Empty words! She could not even pray for herself. She could not be still for long enough, so racked was she with anxiety.

But poor Charles. He had done so well at court, risen so high. Uncle Norfolk must be most vexed with him – as if he had not enough to anger him with her own disgrace! She was under no illusions. He would lift no finger to help either of them.

* * *

393

The days dragged on. Nothing happened, for which she fervently thanked God, telling and there was no news. Had the King rejected her petition? She kept telling herself that no news was good news.

Somehow, she filled the hours. She had never stitched so much embroidery. Where once she had done nothing but dance, she could not now bear to have music, for she felt so fragile that it must surely break her. Music evoked joy or sadness; it brought back memories or lifted the soul. She could not take any of that now. She was merely existing, trying not to think too much. When her musicians knocked at her door, she told her women to tell them that that it was not the time for dancing.

Isolated in her rooms, she thought she would go mad. She had no idea what was happening in the world outside, or whether her offence was still being investigated. Her attendants, even Isabel, could not, or would not, tell her anything. But surely she must have news soon of what her future was to be? Henry would not allow this situation to continue indefinitely. She thought she would go crazy with the waiting and the not knowing.

Hampton Court was eerily quiet without the bustle of the court. The only people Katheryn could see when she looked out of her windows were guards stationed below. She did not even know if Archbishop Cranmer and the other councillors were still here. Her ladies, who sometimes ventured out into the deserted palace, said they saw no sign of them.

Why all this delay? she asked herself. Were they still trying to uncover evidence against her? Or had others talked? If only, if only she could speak to Henry. She was sure he would forgive her; they might even be reconciled. Yet she did not even know where Henry was, and she knew from experience that love could die quite suddenly.

She received a jolt when, on a Friday afternoon, nine days into her confinement, the door to her chamber was flung open by the guards and Sir Thomas Wriothesley walked in. She did not know him well, but discerned a certain ruthlessness in his manner. He was not gentle with her as Cranmer had been.

'Your Grace, I am here to speak to you about a matter that has come to light concerning Thomas Culpeper,' he began. Immediately, she began to tremble. This was the one thing she had dreaded. She dared not look at Jane, who had retreated with the rest of her women to the far end of the room.

'What do you mean, Sir Thomas?' she asked.

'I mean, Madam, that it appears that you have not mentioned in your confession any communications between yourself and Mr Culpeper.'

Katheryn willed her heart to stop pounding and clenched her hands to still them.

'I have no idea what you refer to,' she said. 'There have been no communications between me and Mr Culpeper.'

Wriothesley gave her a long, hard stare. 'Really?'

'Really! I have confessed all my offences. I do not know what else I can tell you.'

'I see,' he replied. 'I will report your answer to the Council.' And, to her surprise, he left, making the sketchiest of bows.

Katheryn rose, went through to her bedchamber and waited. As she had anticipated, Jane joined her there, looking panic-stricken.

'I heard him mention Mr Culpeper!' she whispered.

'He did.' Katheryn related the conversation. 'But I denied everything. I said I did not know what he was talking about. If they ask you, you must say the same, for both our sakes.'

Jane began crying. 'Oh, God, they know! It is only a matter of time now.'

Katheryn drew in her breath, appalled. She feared it was true. Once again, she found herself fighting down hysteria.

Late that evening, Archbishop Cranmer arrived. Katheryn was feeling very fragile by then and was terrified lest he begin questioning her about Tom, but it turned out that he had come about an entirely different matter.

'Madam, the King's pleasure is that your Grace removes to the house of Syon, where you will remain until further notice. You will be kept close under house arrest and be allowed to maintain the state of a queen, but moderately, without any cloth of estate, as your conduct has deserved. You will depart on Monday.'

Katheryn did not know whether to laugh or cry. At least she was not being taken to the Tower, which was a huge relief and indicated that she was not considered to be guilty of serious crimes. She remembered passing the silent, abandoned pile of Syon Abbey that time she had been on the river with Henry, and how creepy it had looked. But she could cope with that. Anything was better than going to the Tower. She knew that, in its heyday, Syon had been famous as a place of piety and learning and much patronised by royalty. It seemed an odd choice for a place of confinement; it was as if Henry had chosen the next best thing to immuring her in a nunnery.

'You will be allowed to take a moderate number of servants,' Cranmer was saying. 'Your chamberlain, Sir Edward Baynton, will have the government of your household, and you shall have four gentlewomen and two chamberers of your choice, so long as my Lady Baynton is one of them. Your almoner shall also go with you.'

'I am deeply grateful for his Majesty's consideration,' Katheryn said humbly. 'I shall be pleased to have my sister, Lady Baynton, with me. May I also take Lady Rochford? And Mrs Leigh and Mrs Mewtas?' She could do with the kindly common sense of Elizabeth Leigh, and Jane Mewtas was a quiet, restful soul. Katheryn did not want any of those ladies or gentlewomen who were married to men of the reformist persuasion and might gloat at her downfall; already, she had noticed a change in their attitude towards her.

'That will be acceptable.' Cranmer wrote the names in a little book. 'And for chamberers?'

She did not want Kat Tilney or Meg Morton, or Mrs Luffkyn.

'Mrs Restwold and Mrs Frideswide,' she suggested.

'Not Mrs Restwold,' said Cranmer.

'Why?'

'I may not tell you.'

So Alice had talked! There was a surprise.

'Very well, Mrs Luffkyn, then.' Katheryn did not like her, yet she would have to do. 'But what of the rest of my servants?'

'They are to be dismissed and shall also depart on Monday. Some will be transferred to the service of my lord Prince and the Lady Mary.

Lady Margaret Douglas is going to my lord of Norfolk's house at Kenninghall, with my lady of Richmond. The maids-of-honour will return to their families.'

Katheryn's heart had plummeted. The trappings of queenship were to be diminished; most of her household were to be dismissed. It would be divorce, she knew it – divorce and disgrace, possibly a long confinement at Syon.

'Can I take any personal possessions with me?' she asked nervously.

Cranmer consulted his notebook. 'His Grace has ordered that you must take with you clothes of sober design, unadorned with precious stones or pearls.' Nothing a queen might wear, then. 'You are allowed six French hoods with edges of goldsmith's work, but there must be no gemstones or pearls in them; likewise, you may have six pairs of sleeves, six gowns and six kirtles of satin damask and velvet, but none with stones and pearls. You may take personal items, such as sewing materials and the jewels you had before your marriage, but not the books the King gave you. They will remain in the royal library. Provision will be made for food, wine, beer and other necessities at Syon. I trust that is all clear, Madam?'

'Yes, my lord. I should be grateful if you could inform Sir Edward Baynton of these requirements.'

'Of course. Now I must leave your Grace. I bid you good night.'

This, she hoped, would be an end of it. As long as she was still living and breathing, she could endure a long sojourn at Syon. There were worse places.

It was not an end to it. The next day, the Archbishop returned, this time with the Lord Chancellor, her uncles of Norfolk and Sussex and Bishop Gardiner.

'We have come to examine your Grace touching Culpeper,' Cranmer said, striking fear into Katheryn. 'We understand that there was talk that you and he would marry before you wed the King. Did you plan to marry?'

What happened before with Tom could not hurt her, surely? After all, they had done nothing to be ashamed of. 'He did wish to marry me, and I was thinking about it,' she told them, believing it the safest thing to say.

'How did you come to renew the affair?' Gardiner asked.

'Renew the affair? I don't understand,' she lied.

'Don't play games with us!' Uncle Norfolk snapped. 'We know you were meeting him in secret on the progress.'

She must not faint, for everything depended on what she said now. Desperately, she searched in her mind for the right words. It dawned on her that to save herself, she must incriminate Jane and shift the blame on to her. 'It was not an affair, more a favour to Lady Rochford,' she said, hating herself. 'Many times, she urged me to speak with Mr Culpeper. She kept saying he bore me goodwill and favour, and that he desired nothing else but to speak with me; but I felt she was constraining me to love him, although I had the impression that it was she who loved him, and I wasn't really sure what she wanted from me. I told her to bother me no further with such light matters, but she would not desist. Only when she assured me that he desired nothing else from me, and said she would swear upon a holy book that he meant nothing but honesty, did I grant that he should speak with me.' She realised, with a shiver of horror, that she had probably got Jane into serious trouble, for she had effectively implied that Jane had tried to lure her into committing treason. She prayed that no harm would come to her friend through her loose tongue. She was already struggling under a burden of guilt. Oh, why had she not kept her mouth shut, or come up with some other explanation?

She was hoping that the lords would react, so that she could judge how likely it was that Jane would be punished, but Norfolk gave nothing away. 'And did you speak with him?'

'We talked in a little gallery at the stairhead at Lincoln when it was late at night, about ten or eleven o'clock.'

'How long did you talk?' Cranmer asked.

'For an hour or more. Another time, we met in my bedchamber at Pontefract, with Lady Rochford present, and another time in her chamber at York. That was all.'

The lords were watching her closely, grim-faced and giving no indication as to whether they believed her or not.

'Were you ever alone with Culpeper?' Sussex asked.

'Never. Lady Rochford was always there.'

'Did you give Culpeper a velvet cap and a ring?'

'Yes. Lady Rochford suggested it would be a mark of favour to give him gifts.'

'Did you ever call him your "little sweet fool"?' Gardiner made it sound like foul language.

'Yes, once, in jest.'

'And did you send him bracelets?'

'Yes, at Lady Rochford's bidding; she had chosen them.'

'We must ask you,' Cranmer said, 'if you and Culpeper had carnal knowledge of each other.'

That was easily answered. 'Never, upon my oath,' she declared firmly.

'Did he ever touch you in any way?'

'Nothing but my hand.' How easily the lie slipped from her tongue. But it would be death to tell them the truth.

At a nod from Cranmer, the councillors rose with a great scraping of chairs and left her alone.

Like a ghost, she drifted into her bedchamber and lay down. Had they believed her? Or would they come back, pressing for more information?

It was not over, by no means. She had thought that, after her confession, they would not enquire further; but now, who knew what they might discover? Something told her that Henry would not brook infidelity in a queen a second time, and that his love would soon turn to hatred if he discovered that she had betrayed him. At the thought, she became hysterical again, and her ladies struggled in vain to calm her. She wailed and wept, crying like a madwoman, thrashing about on her bed.

'I will kill myself and spare the executioner the trouble!' she screamed, barely aware of their shocked faces. When they brought food, she refused to eat or drink.

'I will starve myself to death, and then I shall be free of this misery,' she sobbed. 'They will kill me anyway if the suspicion of adultery is proved, so why should I give them the pleasure?'

Later, when the storm had passed and she had finally calmed down, she roused herself. Isabel, who was sitting by her bed, had fallen asleep. Katheryn felt guilty for causing her and the others so much grief. Yet there was no escaping her fear; it hung over her like a dark cloud. It was as if she was doing and seeing everything for the last time, for there might not be a future for her. She feared she would never take pleasure in anything again. At her core was her terror of what they might do to her. She could not get the image of the block out of her head, nor stop imagining herself kneeling there, waiting for the blow to fall. Would it hurt? Would she suffer like Lady Salisbury? Or would it be over so quickly that she would not feel it? All the same, losing your head was a dreadful thing to contemplate.

Stop it! she admonished herself, remembering that she was going to Syon, not the Tower. If imprisonment was all she had to suffer, she would be very happy indeed and endure it patiently. At least Isabel would be with her.

She must eat! She sat up and swung her legs over the side of the bed. Isabel woke up. 'Katheryn, you're awake! Are you feeling better?'

'Yes, I was going to order something to eat.'

Isabel got to her feet, rubbing her eyes. 'I'll do that. What do you fancy?'

'Some cold cuts and bread, and a little ale.'

The meal was duly delivered and placed in front of Katheryn. 'Where's my knife?' she asked.

'I will cut your meat for you,' Isabel said. 'Your knives are locked away. You threatened to kill yourself.'

'I did not mean it!' Katheryn assured her. But Isabel would not relent.

'I know you're not supposed to tell me,' Katheryn said, as she ate, 'but do you know what is going on? Is there anything I should know? I am desperate, being kept in the dark.'

Isabel shook her head. 'I don't know anything.'

Katheryn knew she was lying. Isabel might be concealing something awful from her. Why, she might even know if she was to live or die!

'Are you sure?' she asked.

'Katheryn, I am not in the confidence of the Council and Edward tells me nothing. He says it is better that way. But I can assure you that I have not heard anything that suggests you are in peril.'

That, at least, was something. 'You would tell me, wouldn't you?'

Isabel nodded and took her hand. 'I doubt if I could keep it to myself.'

That Sunday, as Katheryn and her ladies were preparing to leave Hampton Court, Sir Thomas Wriothesley was announced. He bowed to her, then called upon all her ladies and gentlemen to attend him in the Great Watching Chamber. As they filed out, she wondered if she would ever see them again.

They were not gone long. When they returned, most of them resumed packing their possessions. Katheryn caught Jane Rochford's eye and Jane followed her into the prayer closet.

'What did he say?' Katheryn asked.

'It's all right,' Jane said. 'He declared the offences you had committed in misusing your body with certain persons before you married the King, then he discharged all your household, apart from those who are to accompany you to Syon, and commanded the people who are leaving to repair to their homes.'

Katheryn had known this was going to happen, yet still she felt upset, but she maintained her composure as, one by one, those who had been dismissed came to bid her farewell and kiss her hand. Some wished her good luck; others looked relieved to be going. She too would be glad to leave these sumptuous rooms, which were now associated with so much misery.

Soon, there were just her six chosen women left. She watched as they selected and folded into travelling chests the clothes now deemed appropriate for her. She had to leave her gorgeous court dresses and jewelled hoods behind, which caused her more pangs. Worst of all was the moment when Sir Thomas Seymour came to take away her jewels.

She could not help remembering Henry pouring them into her lap. Oh, how she longed to see him just one more time, if only to say that she was sorry, so deeply sorry for hurting him and not being honest. She would give her all for the chance to have her time again. How differently she would have behaved!

Chapter 32

1541

Very early on Monday morning, under guard, Katheryn and her small household left Hampton Court for Syon. Her departure was discreetly managed. Wearing a plain black gown and cloak, she was conducted along a privy gallery to the landing stage, where she boarded a covered barge. In the cabin, the curtains had been pulled together. The eight-mile journey seemed endless; no one felt like talking, and she could not stop worrying about what her new accommodation would be like. Would she be confined to one of the nuns' cells?

The barge was pulling in now; she could hear orders being shouted to the oarsmen. The door to the cabin was opened.

'Time to disembark, Madam,' the barge master said, not looking at her.

The first thing Katheryn saw as she alighted at a jetty by the riverbank was the enormous abbey church, as large as a cathedral, dominating the rural skyline. Turning back, waiting for her ladies, she could see Richmond Palace across the river, and wondered if the Lady Anna of Cleves was in residence. How she envied Anna, who had no idea of how lucky she was to have escaped marriage to the King with no hurt and a generous settlement.

They walked towards the church and the surrounding abbey buildings, guards flanking Katheryn on either side.

'The abbey belonged to the Bridgettines,' Sir Edward told her, making conversation. 'It was founded by King Henry V and named after the hill of Zion in the Holy Land. The Bridgettines were a mixed order, strictly enclosed.' As I will be, Katheryn thought, with a sense of dread. She understood now why Henry had sent her here.

'Syon was a very wealthy abbey,' Sir Edward continued. 'It owned all the land roundabouts. There are acres of orchards and gardens.'

'Will I be able to walk in the gardens?' Katheryn asked.

Edward frowned. 'I have received no instructions about that, but I will ask.'

They passed through a great gatehouse and across a deserted outer courtyard, then under an archway into an inner court, which had been the nuns' cloister and adjoined the church.

'The church is locked, as is the chapter house,' Sir Edward explained. 'That building over there was the library, which was famous in its day. It's empty now, of course. All the books were carried away.' The whole place had an air of desolation about it. Crisp fallen leaves littered the cloister garth, which Katheryn knew would have been a place of burial for the nuns.

There were doors set into the brick walls around the cloister.

'These are our apartments,' Sir Edward announced, producing a set of keys and unlocking one of the doors. Katheryn noticed that there were crosses on the paving stones on either side of it. It occurred to her that they might be graves. She shuddered. She would rather not have had such reminders of mortality so near her windows.

The guards stood back to let them enter before closing the door behind them and taking up their positions outside.

There were only four rooms. All the floors were tiled in green, black, brown, yellow and blue. The dining chamber had stone walls hung with threadbare tapestry and was furnished with a plain wooden table, benches and a cupboard. The next room was clearly intended to serve as Katheryn's chamber. At one end was an upholstered chair, but no canopy of estate, as the King had ordered. There was a dining table here too; Edward explained that she was to dine apart from himself and her other servants. Beyond was her bedchamber, containing an old oak bed covered with a rubbed green velvet counterpane, and pallet beds for her women. On the other side of the dining chamber, a door led to a bedchamber for Edward and Isabel.

'Your almoner, the Bishop of Rochester, will visit at your request,' Edward told Katheryn. 'I am to inform you that your servants might be augmented or diminished at the Council's discretion. We will wait on you till the King's further pleasure is made known to us.'

So a long imprisonment was by no means a certainty, Katheryn realised despairingly, as she walked back to her bedchamber to help supervise the unpacking. But at least she had fared better than Anne Boleyn. She was not in the Tower – yet. There was still room for hope. Wasn't this punishment enough, being confined in this dreary, cramped place, deprived of most of the trappings of queenship and consigned to a tedious seclusion that looked to offer no distractions? And with no idea of what was to happen to her, nor any hope of finding out, unless Isabel could help her.

She sat on the bed trying not to cry. What would she do with herself here?

Jane was sobbing. 'To think I have come to this!' she wept, as the others stared at her. 'And none of it is my fault! I come of good parentage, but I was brought up in the court, unbridled, and left to follow my lust and filthy pleasure!'

Katheryn went over and put her arms around her. 'What do you mean?'

'I could have had my pick of anyone,' Jane sniffed. 'I had lovers enough, to my shame. But I had to marry George Boleyn. To say we were unhappy would be an understatement. When George abused me, I looked elsewhere. I had no respect for virtue; I did not dread God. And when my beauty began to be spent, I grew bitter. It was I, I who accused George and Anne of incest! I sent them to the scaffold!' She was becoming hysterical. Her own plight all but forgotten, Katheryn exchanged appalled glances with Isabel, Elizabeth Leigh and Mrs Mewtas. Then Jane started laughing. 'And I did it to be rid of him!' she cackled. 'I had no grounds for saying it.'

Katheryn froze. Was Jane losing her mind? If she could be so indiscreet as to confess that she had lied to send her husband and his sister to a cruel death, what else might she blurt out? It was going to be bad enough lodging here, without that fear hanging over her.

'I think we're all a little overwrought, my dear,' Isabel said briskly to Jane. 'Now, let's have no more of this wild talk. You lie down over there and we'll finish putting everything away.'

Still snivelling, Jane obeyed. Within minutes, she was asleep.

'She hasn't slept for nights on end,' Elizabeth revealed. 'I heard her up and about, pacing up and down.'

'She has taken this business so much to heart,' Isabel said.

If only you knew, Katheryn thought.

Lying on the lumpy mattress in an unfamiliar room, Katheryn could not sleep. Thank goodness her women were protective of her, but what if Jane said something compromising in front of Edward? He would be bound to report it – and then what?

It would be ironic if, having escaped discovery all this time, Jane betrayed them all.

She wished she knew what had happened to Tom. She was glad she had told him about her affairs with Francis and Harry. She guessed that she was now notorious for her naughtiness, but Tom had understood; he had forgiven her the follies of her youth. And that was all they had been! She didn't deserve such opprobrium.

She prayed that he had destroyed her letters, few though they had been. In vain, she kept trying to remember what she had written in them. She knew she had signed one 'Yours as long as life endures, Katheryn.' She trembled to think that someone might find that. But Tom would have been sensible; he would have got rid of it.

She doubted if she had any friends left. People would be hastening to dissociate themselves from her, Francis and Harry most of all. The Duchess, like the Duke, would have abandoned her. There was no one to speak in her favour. Who would dare? Maybe she was best away from it all, here at Syon.

It was dawn before her mind ceased tormenting her and she slept. And then Isabel came to wake her and help her dress. Drab room, drab gown. It was as if a pall lay over her.

Sir Edward came into Katheryn's bedchamber as she sat at the table, staring into space, wondering what to do with herself. He glanced at her ladies, who had formed a sewing circle at the other end of the table, and cleared his throat. 'My Lady Rochford, you are summoned to Whitehall. The Council wishes to question you.'

Katheryn froze. She dared not look at Jane, but she heard her laugh, a laugh that quickly escalated into uncontrolled hysteria. With the help of the guards, Edward hauled her out. They could see her through the window, struggling against the fast grips of the men – and then the laughter faded, and she was gone.

The others looked dumbstruck. If Katheryn had not been sitting already, she would have fallen to the floor. Jane's outburst was tantamount to an admission of guilt. This was the end. There was no hope now.

Jane did not return. No one knew what had become of her – at least, so they said. Desperate, Katheryn pumped Isabel for news, but Isabel insisted she had heard nothing. Katheryn suspected the worst: that Jane had talked and was now in the Tower. Soon, she was sure, they would come for her too.

She was existing in a state of anguished tension. What of Tom? Had they taken him as well? She thought she would go mad not knowing. At every sound, every footfall, she jumped with fright, and once, when she heard voices outside the window, she became hysterical. But it was only the local baker, bringing bread.

In the third week of November, Sir Edward came to her, his face grave. 'Madam, I am instructed to inform you that proclamation has been made that, as you have forfeited your honour, you shall be proceeded against by law, and are henceforth no longer to be called queen.'

'Proceeded against?' she cried, wild with fear. 'Will they put me on trial?'

'I do not know,' he told her. 'I have received no further orders.'

She wailed piteously at that. Would this horrible waiting never end? If she knew what awaited her at the end of it, she could prepare herself, but the future was just a terrifying blank. Hope was dying in her, overcome by a sense of dread. Would Henry show mercy to her? It was all she had to cling to.

* * *

December came in, overcast and chilly, and still she was cast in gloom, huddling over the meagre fire in her room, wrapped in a shawl. And that was how Archbishop Cranmer found her when Sir Edward flung open the door. She sprang to her feet. This must be news at last – but what kind of news? She began to tremble.

'There is no need to look so frightened, Madam,' Cranmer said. 'I am only here to ask you some questions.'

'By all means, my lord.' Her voice came out as a croak. 'Pray be seated.'

He pulled a stool up to the hearth and sat there in his fur-lined gown, putting some papers in order.

'Shall we begin?'

She nodded.

'Did you ever send for my lady of Norfolk to come to court and bring Dereham with her?'

She was surprised to be asked about Francis. She had expected to be questioned about Tom. 'No,' she said.

'The Dowager Duchess removed some writings from Dereham's coffer at Lambeth. Do you know what was in them?'

Still Francis.

'No. We never exchanged any writings.'

'Were you aware that my lady had suspicions of your misconduct with Dereham at the time?'

Where was this going? 'I think she knew about us.'

'Did she ever find you and Dereham in each other's arms, kissing?'

'Yes, and she beat us for it.' Katheryn was beginning to think that the Duchess had come under censure for not telling the King the truth about her step-granddaughter.

'Did the Duchess know that you used to banquet and feast with young men in the maidens' chamber?'

'I don't think so.'

'She never rebuked you for doing so?'

'No. As I said, I don't think she was aware of it.'

'Did she ever witness any other familiarity between you and Dereham?'

'She knew that we were close. She used to joke about it.'

'So she didn't mislike it?'

'No.'

'Did she ever rebuke or strike you for light behaviour with Manox?'

'Yes. She caught us together too.'

Cranmer sighed. 'Did she know the extent of your light and wanton behaviour with Dereham?'

'No, I don't believe so.'

'When the King first favoured you, did she give you new apparel?'

'She had given it to me when first I went to court.'

Cranmer narrowed his eyes. 'But did she give you more when the King showed an interest?'

'Yes.'

'And this was to entice the King to love you?'

'Yes.' Katheryn hated admitting that, because Henry would be sure to hear it, and he would think that her motives had been entirely mercenary and be hurt all over again.

'When she knew of the King's favour, what advice did she give you?'

'She told me to be pleasant, amenable and virtuous.'

'Did anyone else in the Duchess's household witness the familiarity between you and Dereham?'

Katheryn felt herself blushing at the memory of what she had done with Francis in full sight of others. 'Some of the women in the gentle-women's chamber did,' she said.

Mercifully, the Archbishop asked her no more about that. Having consulted one of his papers, he looked up. 'Do you know if Dereham sued the Duchess to get him into your service?'

'I think he did.'

'Did she ask you to take him?'

'Yes, she did.'

'Did the Duchess know of the precontract between you?'

Katheryn bridled. 'There was no precontract.'

Cranmer said nothing. He put his papers back in his scrip, rose and bowed slightly. 'Thank you, Madam,' he said. 'I bid you good day.'

She was bewildered. All those questions, and he had not mentioned

Tom once. Hope soared in her. She could not die for what had happened before her marriage, surely?

She caught the Archbishop's hand as he passed her. 'What is to happen to me?' she asked. 'I beg of you, tell me!'

He looked down on her with an expression that was hard to read. 'Alas, Madam, I cannot say. That is a matter for the King to determine.'

She dropped his hand, defeated. So the interminable waiting was to go on . . . and on. At least she now had hope to cling to. But if this was just about her life before her marriage, why had Jane been taken for questioning and never come back? Maybe, she consoled herself, they were just asking her about what had happened between Katheryn and Tom before Katheryn had married the King.

It was a miserable Christmas. They made what cheer they could with a few evergreens plucked from the wilderness that had been Syon's gardens; Sir Edward had allowed Katheryn to go with her women for this seasonal task, although he bade the guards keep close to her. It had been good to be out in the crisp, fresh air and she'd managed to prolong the search until the early winter dusk fell.

They had a goose for Christmas dinner and sat around the fire afterwards, trying to make merry, but Katheryn could not forget the shadow that lay over her, and knew that the others were aware of it too. It had occurred to her, in a bad moment, that she might not be here next Christmas, and she could not get the horrible thought out of her mind. Nor could she forget the innocent Christmases of her childhood or the lavish Yuletide celebrations at court, where she had been at the centre of the festivities. A year ago, she had not been in love with Tom or betrayed the King's trust. How she wished she could turn the clock back! She was glad when Twelfth Night was over, and life resumed the dreary pattern of recent weeks.

Chapter 33

1542

Emerging from her bedchamber one January morning, Katheryn heard voices coming from the dining room, the door being ajar.

'What did he say?' That was Isabel.

'He said that his Grace meant to condemn the Queen and Lady Rochford to perpetual prison,' Edward said. Then the door was pulled shut.

Katheryn's heart skipped a beat. It was bad news, and the mention of Jane was ominous, but it was not the worst she had expected. She could bear it, if her life was spared; and Henry might relent later. She did not blame him for dealing severely with her now; she deserved it, God knew. But, oh, she so wanted to live, even if it meant being confined here at Syon, never again to know freedom or love or the joy of children.

Edward's words seemed to be borne out when, in the middle of the month, Katheryn ventured out for the daily walk around the cloister she was now permitted and found herself more closely guarded than before. Was this a good omen? Had her long imprisonment begun?

At the end of January, Cranmer came again, accompanied this time by the Duke of Suffolk, the Earl of Southampton and the Bishop of Westminster. Katheryn could tell by their faces that they had some heavy news to impart and felt her legs begin to buckle beneath her. Falling to her chair, she waited, heart thumping, to hear her fate, feeling like an animal in a trap.

Cranmer cleared his throat. 'Madam, his Majesty has directed

Parliament to deal with your offences and a Bill of Attainder has been drawn up against you and other persons.'

Again, Katheryn had that dreadful faint feeling. Was this the legal process that would imprison her for life?

Suffolk spoke. 'Parliament will debate and consider your Grace's offences, thus sparing you – and his Majesty – the shame of a trial in open court. The Bill will receive three readings and, after it has been passed on the third, it becomes law as an Act of Parliament. Do you understand?'

'Yes,' she nodded.

'We are here,' Cranmer said, 'because it concerns us all not to proceed too hastily with the Bill of Attainder, which has been read only once. You are no mean or private person, but a public and illustrious one; therefore, your case ought to be judged in a manner that leaves no room for suspicion that there was some secret quarrel between you and the King. His Majesty does not want people saying that you had no opportunity to clear yourself. So we are come partly to help calm your womanish fears and to advise you that, if you can say anything in your defence, you should do so. It would be most acceptable to your most loving husband if you could clear yourself in this way.'

She brightened at that. It sounded as if Henry was offering her a lifeline. Maybe he had repented of his harshness and was hoping she would give him some pretext to forgive her.

'Madam, we urge you to declare to us now whatever you think might benefit your case,' the Bishop said.

'First,' Cranmer intervened, before she had a moment to gather her thoughts, 'we must read to you the Bill of Attainder, so that you may know what offences are imputed to you. Are you ready to hear it?'

Something in his voice warned her that she would not like what she was going to hear, but she nodded and sat straight in her chair, gripping the arms.

Cranmer unravelled a scroll. 'The Bill states that you, Katheryn Howard, have been proved to have been not of pure and honest living before your marriage to the King; and the fact that you have since taken into your service Francis Dereham, the person with whom you shared

412

that vicious life before, and have employed as chamberer Katherine Tilney, a woman who was privy to your naughty life before, is proof of your will to return to your old abominable life.'

'But I didn't—'

Cranmer held up his hand. 'Pray let me finish, Madam. Also, you have conspired with Lady Rochford to bring your vicious and abominable purpose to pass with Thomas Culpeper, late of the King's Privy Chamber . . .'

Late? What had happened to him? Panic flooded through her. *They knew! Had Jane confessed? Or had Tom himself betrayed them all?*

'. . . and you have met Culpeper in a secret and vile place, at eleven o'clock at night, and remained there with him until three in the morning, with only that bawd, Lady Rochford, present. For these treasons, Culpeper and Dereham have been convicted and executed.'

'No!' she screamed. 'No!' Never had she dreamed of anything as brutal as this.

'They were executed in December, Madam,' Southampton said, watching her closely. 'You did love them, it is clear.'

She could not speak. She was rocking to and fro in her misery, utterly horrified. Tom was dead. And Francis. She caught Isabel looking at her with eyes full of compassion. She did not seem shocked. *She had known.*

'How did they die?' she whispered, dreading the answer.

'As traitors, Madam,' Southampton said coldly, 'although the King was gracious enough to commute Culpeper's sentence to beheading.'

That was terrible enough, but she could not bear to think of what Francis must have suffered. 'Dereham was innocent,' she wept. 'He was my lover only before my marriage—'

'And intended to be after,' Suffolk interrupted. 'He said so himself. Intending treason is as good as committing it, under the law.'

She could not deny it. Francis had made plain to her his intentions. And look where it had brought him.

'You, Madam, and Lady Rochford now stand indicted,' Cranmer continued, impervious to Katheryn's distress and her sobs. 'And the Dowager Duchess of Norfolk and Katherine, Countess of Bridgewater, are indicted of misprision of treason for concealing your treasons; likewise, Lord and Lady William Howard, Edward Waldegrave, Katherine Tilney, Alice Restwold, Joan Bulmer, Robert Damport, Malyn Tilney, Margaret Bennet and William Ashby have all been convicted of misprision, and all shall forfeit their goods to the King and be imprisoned for life.'

Katheryn sat open-mouthed as the full extent of her folly was revealed to her. She had had no idea that all this had been going on; she could not take it in. All these weeks of her confinement, the Council had been busy gathering evidence and moving in on most of those who had been associated with her and known of her misconduct. Those questions about the Dowager Duchess should have given her a clue as to what was happening.

'My lords,' she asked, 'what is "misprision of treason"?'

'It means concealing an act of treason,' Cranmer told her. 'Now, Madam, the Bill of Attainder has yet to pass its second and third readings. You will be informed of the outcome. We will leave you to consider whether you wish to make a declaration. We bid you good day.'

As soon as the door had closed behind the councillors, Isabel came over and folded Katheryn in her arms. 'Oh, my sister, my poor sister! How awful to find out like that. If I had known how they would break it to you, I would have disobeyed the King's order not to tell you anything of the proceedings against you and the rest. Can you ever forgive me for my silence?'

Katheryn squeezed her tightly. 'Of course. You are not to blame for any of this. It is all my own fault. You have shown me great kindness in my adversity, and I am so grateful. But – oh, God, I cannot believe that Tom is dead, and Francis. Do you know if they died well?'

'Edward was there,' Isabel revealed. 'You remember that day he said he had to go to court?'

'But that was weeks ago!' All this time, and she had not known.

'He felt he ought to be present,' Isabel recalled. 'Dereham and Culpeper were drawn on hurdles from the Tower to Tyburn. Culpeper

414

asked the people to pray for him, then he knelt down and had his head cut off, very cleanly. And then . . . Dereham died a more cruel death. You know what happens to traitors.'

She did. She envisaged the life being choked out of Francis, then his being revived, only to be butchered to death; he would have been in unimaginable, prolonged agony before merciful oblivion claimed him. She felt sick to think of it.

'Is there anything else I should know?' she asked, searching Isabel's face.

'No, upon my honour,' Isabel declared. 'We all await Parliament's verdict.'

'Most of those accused have been imprisoned,' Katheryn said, 'so there is hope for me yet.' She shuddered as she realised that she was probably deluding herself, for, in the eyes of the Council, and probably the King, and Parliament, she was as guilty, if not more, than the men who had died on her account. As the realisation hit her, she could not speak and swayed on her feet.

'Katheryn?' asked Isabel, taking her hand. 'What is it?'

'They will do to me as they did to Tom and Francis, for mine is the greater offence,' she whispered. 'I will be put to death, and I have deserved it. I shall make no declaration, nor ask for any favour, except that the execution shall be secret and not under the eyes of the world.'

Isabel looked shocked. 'You are running ahead of yourself,' she said. 'Parliament has not yet spoken. Edward was told, at court, that the King intended to imprison you for life. You must hold to that. Promise me you will! Do not torment yourself with morbid thoughts.'

'In my position,' Katheryn told her, 'I can think of little else.'

She would not let go or lose control. There would be no more hysterics. If she was to get through the next days, or weeks, she must be positive. She must remember that she was a daughter of the Howards and must behave as one. Her cousin Anne had faced death bravely, and she must do likewise. Besides, it probably wouldn't be death for her. Please God, Henry would show mercy.

She put on a cheerful face and the best of her gowns and hoods, taking care with her appearance. A look in her mirror told her that she was as pretty as ever, even if she had put on weight in these weeks of idleness. She tried to assume her most imperious regal manner and behaved as if she were queening it over a palace and not these dismal rooms at Syon. Her household indulged her; it was as if they realised that she was doing her best to be brave.

It was a week into February, and still there was no news. Katheryn thought she might go mad with anxiety. It was hard to maintain her composure when her very life hung in the balance.

When she heard footsteps in the cloister, she stifled a scream and held her breath to see who would be announced. It was Sir John Gage, the Comptroller of the King's household, a man in his early sixties who had been most pleasant to her when she was queen. Her heart was filled with dread at the sight of him, for he was also the Constable of the Tower.

He bowed. 'Madam, I am here to break up your household. Your servants are to be dismissed, but you may keep Lady Baynton.'

'Am I to go to the Tower?' Katheryn cried, shrinking in fear.

'No, Madam. I am given to understand that no final decision has yet been made as to what your future is to be, but I am told that the matter will be cleared up in two or three days, and it will be known what will become of you.'

None of this augured well. Thinking that it must betoken the worst, she watched her servants packing their things and Isabel saying a loving farewell to Edward. Katheryn had to turn away, so deeply did it upset her to witness the love between them, and to know that they had a future to look forward to. And yet, surely, if Henry meant to have her executed, he would have sent her to the Tower today. Truly, she did not know what to think, and she was aware that her carapace of bravery was wearing thin. She could not take much more.

It was Thursday, the ninth day of February, and bitterly cold. Wrapped in their cloaks, Katheryn and Isabel sat by the fire playing cards.

Katheryn kept losing because she could not concentrate. The tension in the room was palpable.

Footsteps again! And then a rapping on the door. They heard the guards opening it and men's voices. One was Cranmer's.

He came in, accompanied by some of his fellow privy councillors and others whom he introduced as members of Parliament. Katheryn could hardly breathe. In a few moments, she would know her fate.

'Madam, the Bill of Attainder has received the royal assent and become law. You and Lady Rochford have been attainted by both Houses of Parliament for high treason and you are sentenced to death and the confiscation of your property.'

Death! The worst that could befall her. She could not believe that this was happening. If she had not been seated, she would have collapsed on the floor. This was the reckoning; this was God's punishment for her wickedness.

Isabel, weeping uncontrollably, was blindly reaching out a hand to her, but she had no strength to take it.

She forced herself to listen to the Archbishop, although what could anything else he said matter now?

'His Majesty,' he was telling her, 'wishes to proceed with all moderation and justice in your case, and has sent us to you to propose that, if you wish, you may defend yourself in Parliament.'

What good would that do? Parliament had already condemned her, and there was nothing she could say in her defence. But she had often thought about what she would say if this awful day ever came. She was prepared.

'My lords . . .' she began, haltingly at first. 'I thank his Majesty, but I will not avail myself of his gracious offer to defend myself in Parliament. I submit myself entirely to his mercy, for I admit that I have deserved death. I acknowledge the great crime of which I have been guilty against the most high God, a kind prince and the whole English nation. I beg you, my lords, implore his Majesty not to impute my crimes to my family, but that he will extend his unbounded mercy and benevolence to all my brothers, that they might not suffer for my faults.'

'We will convey your pleas to his Majesty,' Cranmer assured her. 'Is there anything else?'

She took a moment to collect her thoughts. 'My only care is to make a good death and leave a good opinion in people's minds. All I ask is that the execution be carried out in private, and not in the face of the people.'

Cranmer nodded. 'I think we can safely promise that, Madam.'

'And could I beseech his Majesty to let me leave some of my clothes to those maidservants who have been with me since my marriage, as I have nothing now to recompense them as they deserve.'

'We will convey your requests,' Cranmer said.

She hesitated. 'Do you know the date set for my execution?'

'No, Madam. We will take your answer back to his Majesty, who will decide what is to happen to you.'

'Am I not to go to the Tower?' she faltered.

'We have no instructions to that effect,' he replied. 'We must leave now, to catch the tide. May God bless you, my child.' And he made the sign of the Cross over her. It nearly broke her, for he had never done that in all their meetings before.

When the lords had gone, Katheryn knelt by her bed, trying to pray, aware that she must start saying goodbye to the world and all the fabric of her life. There was little hope for her now, and she must place her trust in God and start preparing for the end, although how she was going to begin to do that she had no idea. Isabel knelt beside her, her head in her hands, her body shaking with the force of her pleas to the Almighty to spare her sister. 'She is so young!' she wept.

In all the anxiety of the past weeks, Katheryn's birthday had been forgotten, even by herself. She was twenty-one now. It was too young to die.

On Friday afternoon, Isabel went out to gather more firewood, for the store they had been left was proving pitifully inadequate. But she was soon back, hurrying along the cloister, clutching her cloak around her. Moments later, she burst into the room.

'Madam! A barge carrying the Duke of Suffolk and the earls of Southampton and Sussex has just moored at the jetty. They will be here at any moment.' They looked at each other, both knowing what this might mean, and then Isabel threw her arms around Katheryn and held her close. 'My darling girl, have courage!'

Katheryn wanted nothing more than to stay safe in her sister's embrace for ever, but disentangled herself when the door opened.

'Madam,' Suffolk said briskly, with an air of wishing to be anywhere else, 'we are come with orders to convey you to the Tower of London.'

Katheryn's knees almost buckled, but she managed to stay standing and preserve her dignity. She could not speak.

'Fetch her things,' Suffolk ordered Isabel. They stood in silence waiting for her. Katheryn felt like screaming, but reminded herself that, even when all hope was lost, a daughter of the Howards must not lose control.

Isabel came back and, with shaking hands, draped Katheryn's cloak over her shoulders and gave her her gloves. With the guards walking on either side, the lords led Katheryn through the cloister and the outer court, and out of Syon. It was drizzling as they continued down the path to the jetty, where three barges were waiting; the first was manned by four sailors, while the two to the rear were packed with liveried retainers and more armed guards. At the sight, Katheryn baulked, knowing where they would take her and what awaited her there. This was real; it was happening. She was going to die. Henry really did mean to have her executed. Until now, she had only half believed it, had placed more hope than she should on his showing mercy.

All her calm deserted her; Howard or not, she was shaking with fear. 'No,' she said, halting. 'No, I'm not going!'

'Madam, it is the King's order,' Suffolk said. 'We must all obey.'

'No!' she shrieked. 'They're going to kill me! I won't go!' And she turned and began running back towards the silent abbey. The guards caught up with her, of course, and she struggled as they gripped her arms. 'Let me go! Let me go!' she screamed.

Sussex was shaking his head, looking desperate. 'Madam, this will not help you. You must come with us.'

'No!' she wailed, beside herself with fear. She sank to her knees on the grass, but the guards hauled her up.

'Come on, Mistress, no nonsense!' one said gruffly.

'Let me talk to her,' Isabel was pleading.

'Get in the barge!' Suffolk snapped.

'No!' Katheryn shrieked again, and then the lords themselves laid rough hands on her and bundled her, crying and resisting, into the first boat. She tried to get out and the little vessel rocked perilously, but they blocked her way and manhandled her into the cabin, pushing her down on the padded bench. Three women were seated there already, Lady Dudley, Lady Denny and Lady Wriothesley, women she had not chosen to serve her at Syon and would rather not have had around her at this time. They were staring at her with dismay, and some sympathy, but she was too distressed to speak to them.

'Stay there!' Southampton commanded, leaning forward and closing the curtains. 'Lady Baynton, see that she does not get out until we reach the Tower. And keep the curtains closed. We'll be in the barges behind.'

Leaving guards stationed at the cabin door, the councillors departed. Katheryn was moaning in misery and fear, and her black velvet dress was damp from where she had knelt on the grass. Isabel put her arms around her and held her tightly.

The sailors steered the barge out into the river and then they were on their way to London. Katheryn lay back listlessly on the pillows, peering through the corner of the window at many well-remembered scenes and buildings, her eyes devouring them for what she knew would be the last time. She could not quite comprehend the enormity of her situation. Not that long ago, she had been enjoying pleasure trips with Henry along this very stretch of the Thames. She could not bear to think of it now. When they passed Lambeth and the Duchess's house, the scene of her carefree youth – and her great folly – she had to avert her eyes.

By the time they reached London, the raging turmoil in her head and the motion of the boat were making her ill. She feared she would be sick. 'I must have some air,' she gasped, clawing at the curtain.

'No, Madam!' Lady Dudley cried.

'I must have air or I will throw up!' Katheryn insisted, and, drawing the curtain, she opened the window and leaned out. They were passing under London Bridge and she could see its tower on the south bank. Then she looked again, horrified, riveted, for there, on long spikes, were two heads. They were black and somewhat decayed, but she knew them at once: Tom and Francis.

She burst into a passion of weeping and would not be comforted. The sight had chilled her to the bone and brought home to her how terrible was the fate of those who offended the King. 'My head will be up there too!' she howled.

'No, never,' Isabel soothed. 'Queen Anne's head was not displayed.' But that was small comfort.

Chapter 34

1542

It was nearly dark when they arrived at the Tower. They alighted at the stairs that led up to the Court Gate in the Byward Tower, Southampton and Suffolk going first, then Katheryn herself, barely able to drag herself up the steps. At the top, Sir John Gage was waiting for her. He bowed low and received her with as much ceremony as if she was still queen.

'I will escort you to your lodgings, Madam,' he said, and led her and the lords and ladies through the outer ward of the Tower to an archway below what he told her was the Garden Tower, because it stood next to his garden. At the other end of it, they turned left and Katheryn saw in front of her a fine new half-timbered house.

'This is my own lodging, Madam,' Sir John informed her. 'You will stay here. I regret that I cannot accommodate you in the Queen's apartments in the palace over there, as they are occupied by those prisoners who have been sentenced to perpetual imprisonment.' And all because of me, Katheryn thought dismally. Then another, chilling thought struck her: she was not going to be in the Tower for long enough to justify moving those prisoners out. Again, she began trembling, nervously looking across the green to her right for any sign of a scaffold, but there was none. When will it be? she wondered. *When?*

Two guards standing by the entrance opened the door to the Constable's house, and Sir John himself led the way up the stairs, showing Katheryn into a small chamber with few furnishings – a bed, a chest and a chair – but made bright with hangings and rugs. There were chambers along the corridor for her ladies and a pallet bed in her room. One of the ladies was to be with her at all times, Sir John said. The ever-present guards had already taken up their places outside her door.

'I will have supper brought up to you,' he told her.

'I couldn't eat,' Katheryn replied. She still felt nauseous.

'Try to, Madam,' he advised. 'I will send it anyway.'

As Isabel busied herself folding away Katheryn's few garments, Katheryn sat on the bed, feeling as if she was made of glass and might break at any moment. A servant arrived with a tray of food – roast beef, a dish of peas, a slice of pigeon pie and a mug of ale – but she only toyed with it. What good was food to her now?

Soon after supper, the King's confessor, Dr Longland, the Bishop of Lincoln, arrived.

'My child,' he said kindly, with that air of calm assurance that had made him such a favourite with Henry, 'I am come to hear your confession and offer you spiritual comfort.'

It was a faint hope, but, maybe, if she told the strict truth now and made an abject confession of her transgressions, Henry might relent and grant her a reprieve. 'It will be a comfort to me to unburden myself,' she said. 'I have found it hard to pray these last two days. Fear prevents me . . . I have lost sight of our dear Lord.'

'That is understandable,' said Dr Longland, putting on his stole. 'But He is ever present and He has not lost sight of you; He is with you now. He will not fail you, but will lift you up when you are cast down.'

She wept at his words, but his quiet conviction spoke to something within her. The faith of her childhood was strong in her, and now she saw that it might well sustain her when she most needed it.

Drying her eyes, she knelt. 'I confess that I misconducted myself in my former life before the King married me,' she declared, 'but I stand absolutely to my denial that I committed adultery. My reverend lord, in the name of God and His Holy angels, and on the salvation of my soul, I swear that I am innocent of the act for which I stand condemned. I never defiled my sovereign's bed!' It was true: she had never let Tom take her as a man takes his wife. 'As for the faults and follies of my youth, I do not seek to excuse them. God will be my judge and, in His mercy, He will pardon me, for which I pray you pray with me to His Son, my Saviour Christ.'

The Bishop placed his hand on her head and granted her absolution.

Then they knelt together and prayed, and she wept again when she remembered what lay in store for her.

'Hold fast to your courage, my child,' the Bishop said. 'You are in a state of grace now, armoured against all spiritual peril. Remember, you are not alone.' He spoke so firmly, and with such conviction, that she did feel a little comforted.

As he made to leave, she tugged at his sleeve. 'You have my permission to divulge what I said in confession to his Majesty,' she said. 'I want him to know that I did not betray him as he thinks.'

The Bishop nodded, made the sign of the Cross over her and departed.

I am not alone. I am not alone. She kept repeating the words to reassure herself.

It was hard to sleep, what with her ever-present fear, the strange surroundings and being unable to forget that she was in the Tower under sentence of death. Tomorrow, at any moment, they might come for her . . .

In the morning, when Sir John Gage arrived to bid her good day and ask how she had slept, she jumped up in fear. This waiting, this not knowing, was dreadful.

She could contain herself no longer. 'Sir John, when will it be?' she blurted out.

'Madam, I have not received any instructions as yet. Be assured that you will be given time to prepare yourself.'

Time – it was the most precious thing, and it was running out for her. Would she ever be prepared? Never! She wanted to live. She wanted to feel the sun of another summer, the breezes of April, even the winds of March. Another month, another week, even another day would be a glorious boon. But she might have only hours left.

She lay down and sobbed, crying out in fear and grief, bringing Isabel and the other ladies hastening to her bedside.

'I don't want to die!' she screamed. 'I didn't do what they said I did!'

'Katheryn, stop tormenting yourself!' Isabel cried. 'Try to be brave.'

But Katheryn was feeling anything but brave. The small comfort of the night before had evaporated, leaving only terror. If she screamed loudly enough, someone would surely do something to help her! So she went on shrieking like a madwoman.

She barely heard the running footsteps.

'What's this?' It was Sir John's voice. He sounded alarmed.

'She is very distressed,' Isabel said.

'Who wouldn't be?' he muttered.

'Can't you inform the Council how she is?'

'I can.' He sounded reluctant. 'The King will not want her making a spectacle of herself when . . .' His voice tailed off. Katheryn howled even louder.

'She needs time to compose herself,' Isabel urged.

'Indeed. It will be easier for everyone. I am still awaiting orders, but I will send a message to the Council now, urging that there be a deferment for three or four days, to give her time to come to terms with the sentence and make peace with her conscience.'

He left then, and Katheryn rallied a little. Perhaps, when Henry learned how much anguish she was suffering, he might take pity on her.

Clinging to that hope, she ceased wailing and lay there quietly, with Isabel sitting beside her, holding her hand. She could not still her teeming thoughts. How had she come to this? How had the carefree girl become a weeping woman clad in black, facing an untimely death? Fortune was so cruel, so wayward and so unstable! How quickly her wheel could turn. It was Fortune who had made her a queen, when she had been flourishing in her youth and beauty. She remembered how Henry had once said that nature had made her fit to shine equal with the stars. Oh, he had been good to her! He had loved her so. Why could she not have contented herself with that? She had reigned in joy and pleasure, wanting for nothing that his love could not procure for her, so highly beloved, far beyond the rest. She had been blessed and not known it.

What good was beauty without grace? It was a brittle gift, fuelling only lust; and lust had done for her. What good was even a blazing beauty when it could lead to such mischief?

But she had been in her tender youth, too frail to resist her wanton appetites, too greedy for carnal delights. How blind the young can be! She had not known what danger lay in Cupid's fire. And she would pay a heavy price for her shameless pleasures. She would get no pompous funeral, no trains of mourners clad in black. She could only hope that some good souls might perchance think kindly on her, and pray that her soul would merit better than her body had deserved.

She spent much of the rest of Saturday and most of Sunday in prayer. *I am not alone. I will not be alone.* She kept repeating these assurances over and over again.

There seemed to be a lot of coming and going in the house. She was aware that Sir John was very busy. When he came to see her, as he did three times each day, he looked harassed.

Her room overlooked Tower Green, whence, all day long, came the sound of hammering. She knew what they were building and could not bring herself to look out of the latticed window. She would see the scaffold all too soon.

It was getting on for evening when Sir John Gage entered her chamber. She knew before he spoke what he had come to tell her.

'Madam, you must dispose your soul and prepare for death, for you are to be beheaded at nine o'clock in the morning.'

She had no words to answer him. She merely bowed her head. A strange calm was settling on her. Now that she knew the worst, she could face it.

'Dr Mallet, your confessor, will be here later this evening so that you can unburden your conscience to him and receive the last rites.' Sir John cleared his throat, looking pained. 'I am instructed to tell you that you will die by the axe.'

Not a sword for her then, unlike her cousin Anne. She thought of the Howard motto, *Sola virtus invictus*: 'Bravery alone is invincible'. The courage she thought had deserted her now came to her aid. She would make a good death, for the honour of her house. She would give her kin no further cause to be ashamed of her. She would get through these last, short hours without becoming hysterical again, so that men would say that she had died bravely. It would be quick, and over in an instant.

Sir John was watching her nervously, no doubt expecting her to start screaming again. But she drew herself up like the queen she had been. 'I submit myself to the King's justice,' she said, realising that there would be no reprieve and that she must have hurt Henry very deeply for him not to have extended his mercy to her. 'I have one request. I desire that the block be brought to me, that I might learn how I should place my head on it.'

Sir John looked surprised, but he nodded. 'It shall be done,' he said.

The block was brought, a low, heavy wooden object with a semicircle carved out of it to accommodate the chin. The wood was smooth, with no grooves or cuts in it. Had it been new-made for her? She knelt, as Isabel watched, appalled, and bent over it. It was very low. But she would not be uncomfortable for long. She practised kneeling gracefully and leaning forward until she was satisfied that she would make a good show of herself.

'That's enough, please,' Isabel said, plainly distressed.

'I have discovered that it is better to confront your fears,' Katheryn told her.

The block was taken away and they sat there together, holding hands, until Dr Mallet arrived.

To her surprise, she did sleep. Isabel had lain down with her and held her in her arms all through the night. When Katheryn awoke, it was dark. The clock had just chimed six and dawn would soon be breaking. She would see daylight one last time before the end. Three hours to go.

It was cold. Isabel, stumbling out of bed to throw on a robe and make up the fire, said there was frost on the ground. With shaking fingers, she helped Katheryn dress in her black velvet gown with a warm grey kirtle beneath it. She plaited her long hair and bound it up high under a coif, on top of which she placed a French hood. Katheryn stood there unheeding, focusing on her prayers. *I am not alone.*

Meat, bread and ale were brought, but neither of them could eat anything. Isabel kept glancing out of the window, but Katheryn would not look. They waited . . . and waited. Surely, Katheryn thought, she should be making the most of these last, precious minutes. But there was nothing she wanted to do. It was as if she had moved on from worldly things. In an hour, probably less, she would be in Heaven, and earthly concerns would not matter any more.

'I want to thank you for all your kindness,' she said.

Isabel was clearly fighting off tears. 'It was the least I could do.'

'Will you give our sisters my love? And Charles and Henry and George?'

'I will, I promise.'

'Tell them I am sorry, from my heart, for letting the family down.'

The door opened. Katheryn's heart juddered. Sir John stood there, flanked by the guards, who had their halberds raised.

'It is time, Madam. It is nearly nine.' He pressed into her hand a purse of coins. 'This is the executioner's fee; you must give it to him.'

Isabel threw her arms around Katheryn and they clung to each other briefly in a last embrace.

God gave Katheryn the strength to walk out of the Lieutenant's Lodging. Sir John lent her his arm, and she leaned on him as they crossed Tower Green, escorted by a detachment of yeomen warders. Ahead of them, in front of the House of Ordnance, a crowd of people had gathered. As she neared them, Katheryn recognised most of the King's Council, although when she looked for her uncle of Norfolk and the Duke of Suffolk, she could not see them. Her cousin Surrey was there, but he would not meet her eye.

The crowd parted to clear a path to the scaffold. It was three or four feet high and hung with black cloth. As she approached it, she could see the block standing on a bed of straw and the headsman wearing his mask and apron. By the time she got to the steps, she was trembling so much that she could hardly stand.

Sir John had told her that it was customary to make a speech, and that she should do so, provided she did not speak ill of the King or question his justice. Standing there, looking down on the sea of expectant faces, she was struck dumb and feared she had forgotten what she meant to say. Her heart was racing wildly and she felt dizzy with fear, but she had to make a good end.

I am not alone.

Suddenly, she found her voice, although it sounded weak and husky. 'I die having faith in the blood of Christ,' she began. 'I desire all Christian people to have regard to my worthy and just punishment for my offences against God, heinously, from my youth, in breaking all His commandments, and also offending against the King's Royal Majesty very dangerously; wherefore, being justly condemned by the laws of the realm and Parliament to die, I require you, good people, to profit by my example, amend your ungodly lives and gladly obey the King in all things, for whose preservation I do heartily pray, and I will you all to do so. And now I commend my soul to God and call upon Him to have mercy on me.'

The moment was upon her. She turned to the headsman and gave him the purse of coins. He surprised her by kneeling and begging her forgiveness for what he must do.

'I forgive you,' she whispered. 'Pray hasten with your office.'

Isabel came forward and removed her gown and hood, leaving her standing there shivering in her kirtle and coif. She then tied on a blindfold and Katheryn knew a leap of panic as she realised she had looked her last upon the world. Every instinct was urging her to flee, but she knew it would avail her nothing. There was no escape for her.

She fell to her knees before the block and braced herself for the blow, her flesh shrinking.

'God have mercy on my soul,' she prayed aloud. 'Good people, I beg you pray for me! God have mercy—'

Author's Note

On 22 December 1541, as Katheryn languished at Syon, Lord William Howard, his wife, Margred Gamage, Katherine Tilney, Alice Restwold, Joan Bulmer, Ann Howard (wife of Katheryn's brother Henry), Robert Damport, Malyn Tilney, Margaret Bennet, Edward Waldegrave and William Ashby were found guilty of misprision of treason and sentenced to forfeit all their possessions to the Crown and perpetual imprisonment. Lady Rochford was attainted with Katheryn and executed the same day. Agnes Tilney, Dowager Duchess of Norfolk, and her daughter, Katherine Howard, Countess of Bridgewater, were attainted for misprision of treason and sentenced to perpetual imprisonment, with confiscation of all their property. The Act of Attainder condemning all four women was remarkable for one clause, which declared it treason in future for any woman to marry the King without disclosing if her life had been unchaste beforehand.

Lady William Howard and eight others, mostly women, received pardons on the last day of February 1542; but Lord William and the Dowager Duchess of Norfolk were kept in prison until 5 May, when the Duchess too, received a pardon. Lord William was released at the end of August.

I am deeply grateful to the wonderful publishing teams at Headline in the UK and Ballentine in the USA for their support and creative contributions to this book, and to my commissioning editors, Mari Evans and Susanna Porter. Flora Rees, as ever, has been a brilliant editor; working with her has been a joy. Huge thanks also to Frankie Edwards, my lovely editor, Caitlin Raynor, for brilliant, fun publicity, to Jo Liddiard, for amazing marketing, Siobhan Hooper, for the gorgeous design of the jacket, Becky Bader, Frances Doyle and Chris

Keith-Wright for fantastic sales support, Hannah Cawse for audio, and not forgetting the assistance of Katie Sunley and Emily Patience. At Ballentine, I owe a great debt of gratitude to Emily Hartley, Melanie DeNardo, Kim Hovey and the rest of the dynamic team.

Julian Alexander my literary agent, has, as usual, been wonderfully supportive of me during the writing of this book, and I am warmly grateful.

Love and thanks go, as always, to my rock when I'm in a hard place, my husband Rankin.

Numerous sources, most of them contemporary to the Tudor period, have informed this novel, or rather, the revised and expanded biography on which it is based, the original version of which was published in my book, *The Six Wives of Henry VIII*, in 1991. I am indebted in particular to Dr Nicola Tallis, for sending me a copy of her unpublished DPhil thesis, *All the Queen's Jewels, 1445–1548*. While the novel is based chiefly on original sources, I should like to acknowledge the works by Katheryn Howard's biographers, Lacey Baldwin Smith, Josephine Wilkinson, David Loades, Gareth Russell and Joanna Denny. Marilyn Roberts's website, *Trouble in Paradise* (www.queens-haven. co.uk), proved most useful.

The part titles are taken from George Cavendish's verses about Katheryn Howard in his book, *Metrical Visions*, written in the 1550s and comprising a series of tragic poems reflecting on the bloody fates of those who had perished on the scaffold under Henry VIII.

Katheryn Howard was born either at Lambeth or Lady Hall in Essex. As Justice of the Peace for Surrey, her father, Lord Edmund Howard, had a house in Church Street (now part of Lambeth Bridge Road) in Lambeth, one of two properties given him by his father, probably when he married. The other was in Epping Forest. In 1538, in desperate need of funds, Edmund alienated to his brother, the Duke of Norfolk, a messuage (a house with outbuildings and land) called Lady Hall (or Ladyhall) in the Howard manor of Moreton, Essex, which had passed down in the family from the first Duke of Norfolk. The manor of

Lady Hall was later divided into those of Nether Hall and Over Hall. In 1708, Lady Hall was the manor house of Over Hall, and was also called Over Hall or Upper Hall, by which name it is now known. In 1818, it was described as standing in a field a short distance from Moreton parish church. The house that survives today is a late-sixteenth-century T-shaped timber-framed and tiled building, situated on the site of Lord Edmund's house. There could not have been much land attached to Lady Hall, for, in 1532, Edmund told Thomas Cromwell, 'I have no lands.'

Katheryn's date of birth is disputed. All contemporary writers are agreed that she was very young when she married the King in 1540. She was certainly born before April 1527, when, in a letter to Cardinal Wolsey, her father stated that he had ten children, 'my children, and my wife's'. As the date of Lord Edmund's marriage is not known, it is not possible to estimate a date of birth for their eldest son, Charles, but Charles and his brothers, Henry and George, were born before 12 June 1524, when they were mentioned in the will of John Leigh, their mother's stepfather. Katheryn and her sister Mary are not mentioned in this will, although Katheryn is named in the will of John Leigh's wife, Isabella, made on 11 April 1527, suggesting that Mary was not yet born. Some have inferred from the wills that Katheryn was not yet born in 1524, and that she was born in or around 1525.

In July 1540, Richard Hilles, a London merchant, described Katheryn as 'a very little girl', which some have taken to refer to her age as well as her diminutive stature. The 'Spanish Chronicle' (see below) called her 'a mere child' and 'so young'. The French ambassador, Charles de Marillac, who knew Katheryn personally, stated in 1541 that her relationship with her kinsman, Francis Dereham (pronounced Derham, as it is spelt phonetically in the sources), lasted from when she was thirteen until she was eighteen. As it ended around January or February 1539, this would place her date of birth around 1520–1, a date many historians accept. If that was the case, it might be concluded that Katheryn was excluded from John Leigh's will of 1524 because she was a girl. According to Marillac, she would have been thirteen in 1533–4, yet her liaison with her music teacher, Henry Manox, cannot have begun before 1536, when he entered the Dowager Duchess's service. Marillac was therefore wrong in this respect. But he was probably on firmer ground in stating that she was eighteen when her affair with Dereham ended early in 1539.

A birth date of 1520–1 correlates with the age given on Hans Holbein's portrait of an unnamed young woman 'in her twenty-first year' (according to the Latin inscription), probably painted around 1535–40. The subject bears some resemblance to a young lady who appears in two Holbein miniatures, in the Royal Collection and the Buccleuch Collection, and can be identified on good grounds as Katheryn. Her cloth-of-gold bodice, rich jewels and fur sleeves show her to have been a lady of high rank, and she is wearing an ouche and necklace that appear in portraits of Jane Seymour and Katharine Parr, and which were clearly in the jewel collection handed down from consort to consort. Furthermore, her hood with its biliment of goldsmith's work can be identified with one in the inventory of Katheryn's jewels.

Holbein's original portrait of the unnamed woman hangs in the Toledo Museum of Fine Arts, Ohio, and there are copies in the National Portrait Gallery, in a private collection, and at Hever Castle. Again, the rich clothing and jewellery proclaim that the lady depicted was of high rank. The brooch on her breast depicting Lot and his family guided away from Sodom by the angel was designed by Holbein, whose original drawing of it survives. The jewel at her waist shows God the Father flanked by angels. The jewels have been tentatively identified with items in Katheryn Howard's inventory, and the sleeves with items in an inventory of Whitehall Palace taken in 1542, although the latter could have belonged to the King or anyone else, not necessarily Katheryn, and descriptions of the jewels do not tally exactly with those in the portrait.

The portraits in Toledo and the National Portrait Gallery were once in the possession of the Cromwell family, so the sitter was probably a member of that family. The likeliest candidate is Elizabeth Seymour, sister of Queen Jane Seymour; she married Thomas Cromwell's son, Gregory, in August 1537. Securing such a desirable bride for his son would have been reason enough for Thomas Cromwell to commission both jewel and portrait from Holbein and would account for there being more than one copy of the portrait. Elizabeth Seymour's birth date is unrecorded, but she was younger than her sister Jane, who was born around 1508; if this is her marriage portrait, then she was born around 1517.

If this portrait is discounted as evidence of Katheryn's date of birth, we must look at the other evidence, the best of which is probably Marillac's statement that she was eighteen in early 1539, suggesting that she was born around 1520–1. Therefore, she was nineteen when Henry married her, and twenty-one when she died.

I know Lambeth quite well. I was christened in St Mary's Church by Lambeth Palace and, during my childhood, we lived in St Thomas's Mansions, now demolished, by Westminster Bridge, facing County Hall. I walked over Lambeth Bridge daily to my school off Horseferry Road. It was easy for me to imagine Katheryn's life at Lambeth.

In the novel, Katheryn refers to the Dowager Duchess of Norfolk as her 'grandam'. It derives from the French *grande dame* and is an archaic word for 'grandmother', but it also means a female ancestor or old woman, so it seemed appropriate for a step-grandmother.

After Katheryn's music master, Henry Manox, was dismissed in disgrace from the Dowager Duchess of Norfolk's household, he is stated to have become tutor to the children of Lord Bayment, who lived nearby in Lambeth. Yet there is no record of a Lord Bayment, or even of a Lord Beaumont, in the peerage of that time.

Batrichsy is the old spelling of Battersea.

The details of Katheryn's relationships with Henry Manox, Francis Dereham and Thomas Culpeper come from the depositions of witnesses at the time of her fall. I wove those testimonies into a chronological thread that gave me my narrative for these sections of the book. I have modernised speech where Tudor English looks out of place in a modern text. Apart from fictionalising the historical record, I have invented very little.

Marillac stated in 1541 that Katheryn's relationship with Francis

Dereham lasted for five years, but he was probably misinformed. Katheryn herself claimed that the affair lasted for three to four months, from around October 1538 to January 1539. Yet she lied elsewhere in her testimony (for example, in regard to the Duchess's keys), and no doubt felt it prudent to play down the length – and seriousness – of the affair. Her statement that she slept with Dereham for more than a hundred nights suggests it lasted longer, as does his bringing strawberries, which would have been well out of season, to their trysts.

For a long time, historians writing about Katheryn Howard relied heavily on the colourful account of her in the anonymous mid-sixteenth-century *Chronicle of King Henry VIII*, or the 'Spanish Chronicle', as it is commonly known, which covers the period 1537 to 1549 and was mostly written prior to 1550. We know that the author was an associate of the Imperial ambassador, Eustache Chapuys, but not a close one. Internal evidence in the chronicle suggests that he lived at St Katharine's by the Tower. His work is full of glaring inaccuracies; there are barely any dates in it, and the chronology is confused, so that Katheryn Howard becomes Henry VIII's fourth wife and Anna of Cleves his fifth. He was an eyewitness to certain events, in which respect his work is valuable, but it is clear that much of it is based on unreliable hearsay or gossip.

The Spanish chronicler spins a garbled tale about Katheryn's affair with Culpeper, telescoping events and getting the facts hopelessly wrong. He is the source for a speech she allegedly gave on the scaffold, in which she stated, 'I die a queen, but I would rather die the wife of Culpeper.' But this differs significantly from eyewitness reports of Katheryn's execution. Although I have made creative use of one or two extracts from the Spanish Chronicle, I have otherwise avoided it as a source.

There is good evidence that Katheryn and Culpeper were in love before Henry VIII resolved to marry her. Culpeper's plea to Katheryn to tell Henry that they planned to marry comes from the 'Spanish Chronicle'. His illness after her marriage is documented in more reliable sources.

It appears that Culpeper committed rape and murder. On 10 May 1542, when Culpeper's infamy was notorious, Richard Hilles, a London merchant with radical religious views who had fled abroad to the safety of Strasbourg, expressed outrage in a letter to the German reformer Henry Bullinger that 'one of the parties who was first hanged, and afterwards beheaded and quartered, for adultery with the Queen was one of the King's chamberlains, and two years before, or less, had violated the wife of a certain park-keeper on a woody thicket while, horrid to relate, three or four of his most profligate attendants were holding her. For this act of wickedness, he was, notwithstanding, pardoned by the King, after he had been delivered into custody by the villagers on account of this crime and, likewise, a murder, which he had committed in his resistance to them, when they first endeavoured to apprehend him.'

We don't know where these crimes took place, for there is no corroborating evidence, but they can be dated to 1539 or 1540. The guilty man is not named, and it has been suggested that Culpeper's brother and namesake, who served Thomas Cromwell, was the culprit, but Hilles was clear that it was a servant of the King who was executed for adultery with Katheryn Howard. He was incorrect in the details: Culpeper was not hanged, drawn and quartered, but merely beheaded, and he was not a chamberlain of the King, but a gentleman of the Privy Chamber; living abroad, however, Hilles might be forgiven for confusing the offices and the manner of his dying. Thus, the man guilty of rape was almost certainly Culpeper. It may be significant that both his parents excluded him from their wills, which were drawn up after the likely date of the crimes. Was it because they were sufficiently appalled at their son's behaviour to disinherit him? Or did they feel that the King's bounty was provision enough for him?

Henry VIII's government took a dim view of rape and murder. In 1540, an Act had been passed depriving those guilty of such crimes of the right to seek sanctuary. Murder and rape were usually excluded from general royal pardons granted by Henry, except for one in 1540, in which rape was not on the list of exclusions. Possibly Culpeper benefited from this general pardon, despite the fact that murder was excluded. In his case, murder may have been represented as manslaughter; after 1533, juries were able to acquit anyone who had killed someone who had tried to murder or rob them.

The practice of the monarch granting individual pardons accelerated in Tudor times; such pardons did not exclude crimes such as murder and rape. If Henry did pardon Culpeper, the bedfellow whom he greatly favoured, he was apparently content to harbour in his service a rapist and murderer who might often come into contact with his Queen. Possibly, as in the novel, Culpeper persuaded Henry that his offences had been misrepresented.

Given that Culpeper became so notorious, it is surprising that no other source mentions this pardon for rape and murder. If Hilles had heard of it, others must too, and we might expect to find ambassadors' reports of it. It may be that Hilles was reporting gossip that had become exaggerated in the repeated telling, and that the offence was not as serious as he made it sound.

There can be little doubt that Dereham did enter into a precontract with Katheryn, although the scene in which he makes her give her promise is fictional. A precontract was a promise to wed and it was as binding as a marriage; only an ecclesiastical court could break it. Dereham stated he had asked Katherine if he might have leave to call her 'wife', and she agreed, promising to call him 'husband', and they had fallen into the habit of using these terms, and did so before witnesses. This, and the fact that they were having sex, was sufficient to constitute a marriage.

At the time of her fall, Katheryn was too naive to realise that, by admitting to a precontract, she could have saved her life, for, if she had never been the King's legal wife, she could not be accused of adultery, only bigamy, with the second marriage being rendered invalid. Bigamy was seen as a spiritual offence and could be dealt with by the ecclesiastical courts, who had the authority to pronounce on the validity of a marriage; it did not become a felony until 1604. It could have been argued that concealing the existence of a precontract constituted, in Katheryn's case, misprision of treason, because it endangered the royal succession, but for that, the penalty was only imprisonment. The reformist Council was aware of this and, after Cranmer's initial interrogation, deliberately avoided giving Katheryn the chance to admit to a precontract.

* * *

The sound of ghostly chanting in the historic church at Fotheringhay has been reported on several occasions. Katheryn's odd feelings in front of the fireplace in the great hall of Fotheringhay Castle are indeed portentous, because Mary, Queen of Scots, would be beheaded on a scaffold on that spot forty-six years hence.

There is no historical basis for the poignant tale of Katheryn evading her guards. A long-established legend tells how, in disordered white garments, wild with fear, she ran to intercept the King, bent on pleading for mercy, when he attended Mass in the Chapel Royal, but was caught as she reached the royal pew, and dragged back screaming to her apartments. Her ghost has allegedly re-enacted the scene in the so-called Haunted Gallery at Hampton Court, from which the entrance to the holy day closets and the royal pew leads off. The gallery is right by the site of the new Queen's Lodgings built for Anne Boleyn and refurbished for Jane Seymour, which Katheryn occupied, and where she was held prisoner. A recent investigation suggests that the ghost story was a fabrication by an occupant of a grace-and-favour apartment who wanted a pretext to leave it for a better one.

Before her execution, Katheryn was almost certainly held in the Lieutenant's Lodging in the Tower of London. So many people had been arrested on her account that, weeks before her arrival, the Constable had informed the Council that 'there are not rooms to lodge them all severally in the Tower, unless the King's and Queen's lodgings be taken'. He begged 'that the King will send hither his double key or permit them to alter the locks, or else signify whether the great personages may be committed to the Tower and the rest to other custodies until rooms may be prepared for them'. The Council instructed that 'the King's and Queen's lodgings in the Tower are to be used. The King does not remember that he has any double key and is content that the locks be altered'.

Even with the royal lodgings being used, not all the prisoners could be accommodated in the Tower, and some had to be sent to other London prisons. Katheryn therefore could not have lodged in the old

Queen's apartments in the royal palace, since they were full, and she was not going to be in the Tower for long enough to justify moving the occupants out. Sir John Gage was ordered 'to take the Queen to his own lodging', the half-timbered Lieutenant's Lodging, newly rebuilt in 1540. One source says she was assigned a small chamber with hangings and rugs, barely furnished.

When writing the novel, I could not use most of the vast amount of research I did on Katheryn's fall because she was kept very much in the dark as to the investigations into her misconduct. I had to determine what she would have been told or managed to find out. But I used the detailed material from the depositions of witnesses and those accused with her to construct the story of her earlier years. In the novel, Katheryn never finds out who first laid information against her. In fact, it was John Lascelles, who went to Archbishop Cranmer in the autumn of 1541, after his sister Mary told him about the immoral life Katheryn had led.

A lot of people believe that Francis Dereham unfairly suffered a traitor's death, merely because he had slept with Katheryn before she married the King. That is a misconception. The Council was convinced that his joining her household when she was queen 'was to an ill intent. He traitorously imagined and procured that he should be retained in the service of the Queen to the intent that they might continue their wicked courses'. It was the intention that was treasonous. Under the Treason Act of 1534, anyone who did 'maliciously wish, will or desire by words or writing, or by craft imagine, invent, practise, or attempt any bodily harm to be done or committed to the King's most royal person, the Queen's or the heirs apparent' was guilty of treason. The word 'maliciously' implied evil intent, and it appears throughout the Act.

It was the same Act that brought Culpeper to the block. Although he stated that he and Katheryn 'had not passed beyond words' – and her evidence corroborated that – fatally, 'he confessed his intention to do so'. Manox escaped punishment because he had married and shown no further interest in Katheryn.

We do not know for certain if Henry VIII originally intended to keep Katheryn in prison for life. In January 1542, an Italian diplomat, Giovanni Stanchini, reported from Fontainebleau in France to Cardinal Farnese 'that the King meant to condemn the Queen and an aunt of hers who helped her, to perpetual prison'. We do not know how Stanchini came by this information, or what happened (if anything) to change the King's mind about the Queen's fate.

A theme I was unable to develop in the novel, because it was written entirely from Katheryn's viewpoint, was the possibility that Henry VIII did not want her to die. He had loved her so much, and his grief went so deep, that he may have baulked or wavered about having her executed. He was lenient in his treatment of her: he did not send her to the Tower while her offences were investigated, but to the dissolved abbey of Syon. He did not immediately deprive her of the status of queen, which he did only after her affair with Culpeper came to light. It was said that 'he would bear the blow more patiently and compassionately and would show more patience and mercy than many might think – a good deal more tenderly even than [Katheryn's] own relations wished'. He was unusually merciful in commuting Culpeper's sentence – this was a privilege customarily extended only to peers of the realm. He kept six of the jewels Katheryn had worn; they had perhaps been her favourites.

But the reformist radicals who dominated the Council and had brought down the Howards at a stroke were not about to collude in their restoration. Under the pretext of sparing Henry pain, they took charge of the investigation with zealous, unremitting thoroughness and a studied determination to find evidence of adultery. The Council carried out the investigation on its own, with the King sanctioning further action as necessary. Having raged against Katheryn in Council, then broken down in tears, Henry removed himself from the investigation, 'with no company but musicians and ministers of pastime'. In his grief, he refused to deal with business, which allowed his councillors a free hand. He did not order that Katheryn be tried in court, but referred the matter to Parliament.

In a speech to Parliament, Lord Chancellor Audley 'aggravated the Queen's misdeeds to the utmost', as did everyone else involved in the investigation of her offences. The councillors' insistence on not publicly mentioning the precontract with Dereham, 'which might serve for her defence', shows how determined the reformist faction were to bring down the Queen. An annulment was not enough, for there remained the risk that Henry's anger and grief would abate to the point where he was ready to forgive his erstwhile darling.

In Parliament, the Lord Chancellor expressed Henry's concern that Katheryn 'had not liberty to clear herself'. After she was condemned, 'the King, wishing to proceed more humanely, and more according to forms of law, sent to her certain councillors and others of the said Parliament, to propose to her to come to the Parliament chamber to defend herself', which was unusual in the attainder process. 'It would be most acceptable to her most loving consort if the Queen could clear herself in this way.' Clearly, the lords were aware that the King was hoping she would do so.

Giovanni Stanchini had heard that Henry 'meant to condemn the Queen to perpetual prison'. The Imperial ambassador, Eustache Chapuys, wondered: 'Perhaps, if the King does not mean to marry again, he may show mercy to her or, if he find that he can divorce her on the plea of adultery, he may take another thus.' The unreliable 'Spanish Chronicle' (perhaps not so unreliable in this case) stated: 'The King would have liked to save the Queen and behead Culpepper, but all his Council said, "Your Majesty should know that she deserves to die, as she betrayed you in thought and, if she had had an opportunity, would have betrayed you in deed." So the King ordered that they should both die.'

At the time of Katheryn's fall, Henry would not hear of taking another wife, possibly because he could not come to terms with her loss. He was unlikely, at his age and in his state of health, to find again the kind of love he had enjoyed with her; all he now had to look forward to were encroaching illness, old age and death. Understandably, his councillors might well have feared that he would relent and take her back.

Petitioning Henry not to 'vex himself with the Queen's offence' and to give the royal assent to the Bill of Attainder by letters patent under his great seal, so that the Lord Chancellor could expedite matters in the

King's name, reflects a determination on the part of the councillors that their master should have little opportunity to relent, and that the Queen must die, 'specially because the King could not marry again while she lives'. The lords were already begging and urging him to marry again, doubtless hoping he would take a reformist bride, which he in fact would do in 1543, when he married his sixth wife, Katharine Parr.

The lords had their way. Katheryn died, and the King lifted no finger to save her.

Katheryn's reflections on her offences and her youth, and those of Jane Rochford, are based on verses in George Cavendish's *Metrical Visions*. Cavendish had been gentleman usher to Cardinal Wolsey and evidently maintained close links with the court, having been personally acquainted with some of the people who feature in his poems. It is fitting to end with his epitaph on Katheryn Howard:

> By proof of me, none can deny
> That beauty and lust, enemies to chastity,
> Have been the twain that hath decayed me
> And hath brought me to this end untoward,
> Sometime a queen, and now [a] headless Howard.
> Yet pray ye to God, although that I have swerved,
> That my soul may have better than my body deserved.

Dramatis Personae

(In order of appearance or first mention. Names in italics are fictional.)

Katheryn Howard, daughter of Lord Edmund Howard and Joyce Culpeper.

Joyce Culpeper, Katheryn's mother, daughter of Sir Richard Culpeper, by his wife, Isabel Worsley.

Lord Edmund Howard, Katheryn's father, son of Thomas Howard, 2nd Duke of Norfolk, by his first wife, Elizabeth Tilney.

Isabel Leigh, Katheryn's half-sister, daughter of Joyce Culpeper and her first husband, Ralph Leigh; lady-in-waiting to Anna of Cleves and Katheryn Howard.

Mary Howard, Katheryn's younger sister.

Charles Howard, Katheryn's oldest brother.

Henry Howard, Katheryn's second-oldest brother.

George Howard, Katheryn's third-oldest brother.

John Leigh, Katheryn's oldest half-brother.

Katheryn's nurse at Lady Hall.

Margaret Cotton, sister of Jocasta Culpeper and aunt of Katheryn Howard.

Thomas Howard, 3rd Duke of Norfolk, older brother of Lord Edmund Howard and uncle of Katheryn.

William Cotton, husband of Margaret Culpeper and uncle of Katheryn.

Thomas, John, Joan and Anne Cotton, Katheryn's cousins.

Sir Richard Culpeper, father of Joyce Culpeper and Katheryn's grand-father.

Edward I, King of England (1239–1307).

Thomas Culpeper, gentleman of Henry VIII's Privy Chamber, Katheryn's distant cousin.

Henry VIII, King of England.

Dorothy Troyes, second wife of Lord Edmund Howard and Katheryn's stepmother.

Mary Tudor, sister of Henry VIII and queen of Louis XIII of France.

Katherine of Aragon, Queen of England, first wife of Henry VIII.

Anne Boleyn, maid-of-honour to Katherine of Aragon and, later, queen of England and second wife of Henry VIII.

The Princess Mary (later the Lady Mary), daughter of Henry VIII and Katherine of Aragon.

Cardinal Thomas Wolsey, Henry VIII's chief minister.

The chaplain at Oxon Hoath.

Margaret Mundy, third wife of Lord Edmund Howard and Katheryn's stepmother; lady-in-waiting to Katheryn Howard.

Margaret Leigh, Lady Arundell, Katheryn's half-sister; lady-in-waiting to Anna of Cleves and Katheryn Howard.

Joyce Leigh, Katheryn's half-sister.

Thomas Cranmer, Archbishop of Canterbury.

Sir Edward Baynton, a courtier, later chamberlain to Queen Anna of Cleves, and husband of Isabel Leigh.

Thomas Arundell, a courtier, husband of Margaret Leigh.

Thomas Cromwell, later Henry VIII's Principal Secretary, chief minister and Earl of Essex.

Agnes Tilney, Dowager Duchess of Norfolk, second wife and widow of Thomas Howard, 2nd Duke of Norfolk, and Katheryn's step-grandmother.

Anne of York, daughter of King Edward IV and first wife of Thomas Howard, 3rd Duke of Norfolk.

Elizabeth Stafford, second wife of Thomas Howard, 3rd Duke of Norfolk.

Lord William Howard, son of Thomas Howard, 2nd Duke of Norfolk, and Agnes Tilney.

Richard III, King of England (1452–1485).

Henry VII, King of England (1457–1509).

John Skelton, poet laureate.

Henry Howard, Earl of Surrey, son and heir of Thomas Howard, 3rd Duke of Norfolk.

Mary Howard, daughter of Thomas Howard, 3rd Duke of Norfolk, and widow of Henry Fitzroy, Duke of Richmond, bastard son of

Henry VIII; lady-in-waiting to Anna of Cleves and Katheryn Howard.

Bess Holland, mistress of Thomas Howard, 3rd Duke of Norfolk.

Mother Emmet, mistress of the maids in the Dowager Duchess of Norfolk's household.

Malyn Chamber, wife of Sir Philip Tilney and a dependent of the Dowager Duchess.

Joan Acworth, Mrs Bulmer, one of the Dowager Duchess's gentlewomen.

Sir Philip Tilney, kinsman of the Dowager Duchess, later usher of Henry VIIII's Privy Chamber.

Dorothy Berwick, one of the Dowager Duchess's gentlewomen.

Dorothy (Dotty) Baskerville, one of the Dowager Duchess's chamberers.

Katherine (Kat) Tilney, niece of the Dowager Duchess; later one of Katheryn Howard's chamberers.

Master Chamber, Katheryn's tutor.

Katheryn's dancing master.

Martin Luther, founder of the Protestant religion.

Margaret Bennet, one of the Dowager Duchess's gentlewomen.

Margaret (Meg) Morton, one of the Dowager Duchess's gentlewomen; later one of Katheryn Howard's chamberers.

Margery, one of the Dowager Duchess's chamberers.

Alice Wilkes, one of the Dowager Duchess's gentlewomen, later the wife of Anthony Restwold; later one of Katheryn Howard's chamberers.

Edward Waldegrave, one of the Dowager Duchess's gentlemen.

Robert Damport, one of the Dowager Duchess's gentlemen.

William Ashby, one of the Dowager Duchess's gentlemen.

Richard Faver, groom of the Dowager Duchess's chamber.

John Bennet, gentleman and groom of the Dowager Duchess's chamber.

Andrew Maunsay, the Dowager Duchess's usher.

Mary Lascelles, one of the Dowager Duchess's gentlewomen, later the wife of John Hall.

Agnes Howard, infant daughter of Lord William Howard.

Dorothy (Dolly) Dawby, one of the Dowager Duchess's chamberers.

Mr Dunn, yeoman of the Dowager Duchess's cellar.

The Princess Elizabeth (later the Lady Elizabeth), daughter of Henry VIII and Anne Boleyn.

Joan of Arc, French peasant girl heroine (d.1431).

The porter at the Dowager Duchess's inn.

'Mrs Isabel' (Izzie), one of the Dowager Duchess's chamberers.

Jane Seymour, Queen of England, third wife of Henry VIII.

Henry (Harry) Manox, Katheryn's music master.

Mr Barnes, Katheryn's singing master.

Lord Thomas Howard, younger son of Thomas Howard, 2nd Duke of Norfolk, and Agnes Tilney.

Lady Margaret Douglas, niece of Henry VIII and daughter of his sister Margaret Tudor, Queen of Scots, by her second husband, Archibald Douglas, Earl of Angus.

Edward, Prince of Wales, son of Henry VIII and Jane Seymour.

Dorothy Howard, Countess of Derby, daughter of Thomas Howard, 2nd Duke of Norfolk, and Agnes Tilney.

Anne Howard, Countess of Oxford, daughter of Thomas Howard, 2nd Duke of Norfolk, and Agnes Tilney.

Katherine Howard, Countess of Bridgewater, daughter of Thomas Howard, 2nd Duke of Norfolk, and Agnes Tilney.

Elizabeth Howard, Countess of Wiltshire, mother of Anne Boleyn.

Margred Gamage, Lady William Howard, wife of Lord William Howard and lady-in-waiting to Anna of Cleves and Katheryn Howard.

Thomas Boleyn, Earl of Wiltshire, father of Anne Boleyn.

Arthur Plantagenet, Viscount Lisle, Lord Deputy of Calais and uncle of Henry VIII.

Henry Baynton, son of Sir Edward Baynton and Isabel Leigh.

Cardinal Reginald Pole, cousin of Henry VIII.

Margaret Pole, Countess of Salisbury, cousin of Henry VIII and mother of Cardinal Reginald Pole.

Pope Paul III.

Harry Manox's father (whose name is unknown).

Lord Bayment, a neighbour of the Dowager Duchess at Lambeth.

Francis Dereham, gentleman usher and cousin of the Dowager Duchess.

Margaret Tilney, grandmother of Francis Dereham.

Isabel Paynell, mother of Francis Dereham.

John Dereham, father of Francis Dereham.

Sir Thomas Dereham, older brother of Francis Dereham.

A silk woman in London.

A sewing woman in Lambeth.

Mr Rose, the Dowager Duchess's embroiderer.

Elizabeth Somerset, Lady Brereton.

William Bulmer, husband of Joan Bulmer (Acworth).

Mr Hastings, a mysterious gentleman.

Mrs Manox, wife to Harry Manox.

Anna of Cleves, Queen of England, fourth wife of Henry VIII.

Mary Norris, daughter of Sir Henry Norris, and Katheryn's cousin, maid-of-honour to Anna of Cleves.

Katherine Carey, daughter of Henry VIII and Mary Boleyn, niece of Anne Boleyn, and cousin of Katheryn Howard, maid-of-honour to Anna of Cleves.

Sir Thomas Manners, Earl of Rutland, chamberlain of Anna of Cleves' household.

The Dowager Duchess's tailor.

The Dowager Duchess's milliner.

The Dowager Duchess's jeweller.

Sir Thomas Heneage, Groom of the Stool and chief gentleman of Henry VIII's Privy Chamber.

Mrs Stonor, Mother of the Maids in Anna of Cleves' household.

Anne Bassett, maid-of-honour to Anna of Cleves and Katheryn Howard.

Dorothy (Dora) Bray, maid-of-honour to Anna of Cleves.

Katherine Bassett, sister of Anne Bassett.

Honor Grenville, Lady Lisle, wife of Arthur Plantagenet, Viscount Lisle, and mother of Anne and Katherine Bassett.

Lady Lucy Somerset, daughter of Henry Somerset, 2nd Earl of Worcester, and maid-of-honour to Anna of Cleves and Katheryn Howard.

Margaret Beaufort, Countess of Richmond and Derby, grandmother of Henry VIII.

Ursula Stourton, maid-of-honour to Anna of Cleves.

Margaret Garnish, maid-of-honour to Anna of Cleves.

Margaret Coupledike, maid-of-honour to Anna of Cleves.

Damascin Stradling, maid-of-honour to Anna of Cleves.

Mrs Frideswide, one of Anna of Cleves' chamberers; later one of Katheryn Howard's chamberers.

Mrs Luffkyn, one of Anna of Cleves' chamberers; later one of Katheryn

Howard's chamberers.

Katherine Willoughby, Duchess of Suffolk, lady-in-waiting to Anna of Cleves and Katheryn Howard.

Mary Arundell, Countess of Sussex, lady-in-waiting to Anna of Cleves and Katheryn Howard.

Eleanor Paston, Countess of Rutland, lady-in-waiting to Anna of Cleves and Katheryn Howard.

Elizabeth Blount, Lady Clinton, former mistress of Henry VIII and lady-in-waiting to Anna of Cleves.

Henry Fitzroy, Duke of Richmond, bastard son of Henry VIII.

Jane Parker, Lady Rochford, widow of George Boleyn, Viscount Rochford, and lady-in-waiting to Anna of Cleves and Katheryn Howard.

George Boleyn, Viscount Rochford, brother of Anne Boleyn.

Catherine St John, Lady Edgcumbe, lady-in-waiting to Anna of Cleves.

Anne Parr, Mrs Herbert, lady-in-waiting to Anna of Cleves.

Elizabeth Seymour, sister of Jane Seymour and wife of Thomas Cromwell's son, Gregory; lady-in-waiting to Anna of Cleves.

Hans Holbein, King's painter to Henry VIII.

Alice Gage, Lady Browne.

Charles Brandon, Duke of Suffolk.

Susanna Gilman, Flemish painter, chief gentlewoman to Anna of Cleves.

Mother Lowe, Mother of the Maids to Anna of Cleves.

Frances Brandon, Marchioness of Dorset, daughter of Charles Brandon, Duke of Suffolk and Henry VIII's sister Mary Tudor.

Sir William Holles, Lord Mayor of London.

Will Somers, Henry VIII's fool.

Thomas Paston, gentleman of Henry VIII's Privy Chamber.

The wife of a park-keeper.

Stephen Gardiner, Bishop of Winchester.

Sir John Dudley.

The Bassanos of Venice, Anna of Cleves' musicians.

Francis, son of Antoine, Duke of Lorraine.

Charles de Marillac, French embassador at the court of Henry VIII.

Sir George Seaford, a friend of the Dowager Duchess.

John, Lord Russell, Privy Councillor and Member of Parliament.

Sir Anthony Wingfield, Vice Chamberlain of Henry VIII's household.

Edmund Bonner, Bishop of London, Henry VIII's chaplain.

Sir Thomas More, former Lord Chancellor of England.

John Fisher, Bishop of Rochester.

Sir Alexander Culpeper, father of Thomas Culpeper.

Robert Barnes, a Lutheran heretic.

Bess Harvey, maid-of-honour to Katheryn Howard.

Elizabeth FitzGerald, maid-of-honour to Katheryn Howard.

Jane Cheney, Lady Wriothesley, niece of Bishop Gardiner and lady-in-waiting to Katheryn Howard.

Mrs Josselyn, Katheryn's dressmaker.

Robert Ratcliffe, Earl of Sussex, Katheryn's uncle.

Frances de Vere, wife of Henry Howard, Earl of Surrey.

Ann, wife of Henry Howard; Katheryn's sister-in-law.

Edmund Trafford, husband of Katheryn's sister Mary.

Thomas Chaucer, son of the poet Geoffrey Chaucer.

Alice Chaucer, Duchess of Suffolk, Thomas Chaucer's daughter.

Edmund de la Pole, Duke of Suffolk, attainted traitor.

A priest of Windsor.

Edward IV, King of England (1442–1483), grandfather of Henry VIII.

Elizabeth Wydeville, queen of Edward IV, grandmother of Henry VIII.

Maud Green, Lady Parr, mother of Anne Parr.

Thomas, Henry VIII's juggler.

Sir William Butts, Henry VIII's physician.

Richard Jones, High Master of St Paul's School, London.

William Fitzwilliam, Earl of Southampton, Lord Privy Seal.

Sir Anthony Browne, Master of Horse.

Sir Anthony Kingston, Privy Councillor.

Eustache Chapuys, Imperial ambassador at the court of Henry VIII.

Master of the King's Hawks.

Two maids of the Lady Mary.

Anne Stanhope, Countess of Hertford, wife of Edward Seymour, Earl of Hertford, brother of Queen Jane Seymour.

Thomas, Lord Audley, Lord Chancellor of England.

William, Lord Sandys, Captain of Guisnes.

John Longland, Bishop of Lincoln, Henry VIII's confessor.

Master Scutt, Katheryn's tailor.

Sir Thomas Wyatt, poet and diplomat.

Sir John Wallop, diplomat.

Sir William Rochel, Lord Mayor of London.

Bess Darrell, mistress of Sir Thomas Wyatt.

Elizabeth Brooke, wife of Sir Thomas Wyatt.

Elizabeth Darcy, wife of John Leigh; Katheryn's half-sister-in-law and one of her gentlewomen.

Henry Webb, Katheryn's usher.

Mr Morris, Katheryn's page.

Katherine Astley, nurse to the Lady Elizabeth.

James V, King of Scots (1512–1542), son of Margaret Tudor and nephew of Henry VIII.

Robert Holgate, Bishop of Llandaff, Lord President of the North.

Sir John Gage, Constable of the Tower of London and Comptroller of Henry VIII's household.

A blundering executioner.

Edward Seymour, Earl of Hertford, brother of Jane Seymour.

Sir Ralph Sadler, joint Principal Secretary to Henry VIII.

Sir Robert Tyrwhitt, High Sheriff for Lincolnshire.

John Taylor, Dean of Lincoln.

John, Lord Hastings.

Richard Pate, Archdeacon of Lincoln.

The Recorder of Lincoln.

Vincent Grantham, Mayor of Lincoln.

Katherine Swynford, mistress then wife of John of Gaunt, Duke of Lancaster, mother of the Beauforts and Henry VIII's ancestress.

Edward Stanley, 3rd Earl of Derby.

Thomas, Lord Burgh.

Agnes Tyrwhitt, Lady Burgh.

John Huttoft, Katheryn's secretary.

Master Cotes of Lambeth, haberdasher Lambeth.

Richard II, King of England (1367–1400).

William, Lord Parr, brother of Anne Parr.

Mr Dane, one of Henry VIII's ushers.

Mr Johns, Katheryn's gentleman usher.

Edmund Knyvet, Serjeant Porter.

Edward Lee, Archbishop of York.

Sir Robert Constable, one of the leaders of the Pilgrimage of Grace.

Edward V, King of England (1470–1483?) and Richard, Duke of York, sons of Edward IV: 'the Princes in the Tower'.

Dr John Chamber, physician to Henry VIII.

Sir Thomas Seymour, brother of Jane Seymour.

Sir Thomas Wriothesley, joint Principal Secretary to Henry VIII.

Jane Astley (or Ashley), Mrs Mewtas, lady-in-waiting to Katheryn Howard.

A barge master.

Henry V, King of England (1386–1422).

Nicholas Heath, Bishop of Rochester, Katheryn's almoner.

Thomas Thirlby, Bishop of Westminster.

Jane Guildford, Lady Dudley, wife of Sir John Dudley.

Joan Champernowne, Lady Denny.

Dr Mallet, Katheryn's confessor.

An executioner.

Timeline

1491
- Birth of Henry VIII

1509
- Accession of Henry VIII
- Marriage and coronation of Henry VIII and Katherine of Aragon

1510/15
- Marriage of Lord Edmund Howard and Joyce Culpeper, Katheryn's parents

1513
- Battle of Flodden

1516
- Birth of the Princess Mary, daughter of Henry VIII and Katherine of Aragon

1520/1
- Probable birthdate of Katheryn Howard

1524
- Death of Katheryn's grandfather, Thomas Howard, 2nd Duke of Norfolk

1528
- Death of Joyce Culpeper

1528?
- Marriage of Lord Edmund Howard and Dorothy Troyes

1530
- Death of Dorothy Troyes
- Marriage of Margaret Leigh and Thomas Arundell

1531
- Lord Edmund Howard appointed comptroller of Calais. Katheryn Howard sent to live in the large household of her step-grandmother,

Agnes Tilney, Dowager Duchess of Norfolk

1533

- Marriage of Henry VIII and Anne Boleyn (January)
- Birth of the Princess Elizabeth, daughter of Henry VIII and Anne Boleyn

1534

- Parliament passes the Act of Supremacy, making Henry VIII Supreme Head of the Church of England, and the Act of Succession, naming the children of Queen Anne the King's lawful heirs

1536

- Death of Katherine of Aragon
- Execution of Anne Boleyn
- Marriage of Henry VIII and Jane Seymour
- Parliament passes a new Act of Succession settling the succession on Jane's children by the King

1537

- Birth of Prince Edward, son of Henry VIII and Jane Seymour
- Death of Jane Seymour (24 October)

1537/8

- Katheryn Howard's affair with Henry Manox

1538

- Henry VIII excommunicated by the Pope (December)

1538/9

- Katheryn Howard's affair with Francis Dereham

1539

- Henry VIII opens negotiations for a marriage with Anna of Cleve (January)
- Henry VIII signs the marriage treaty (4 October)
- Katheryn Howard appointed a maid-of-honour to Anna of Cleve
- Anna sails to England (27 December)

1540

- Official reception of Anna of Cleve at Blackheath (3 January)
- Marriage of Henry VIII and Anna of Cleve (6 January)
- Thomas Culpeper begins courting Katheryn Howard (spring)
- Henry VIII begins courting Katheryn Howard (April)

- The Privy Council begins looking for grounds for an annulment (May)
- Thomas Cromwell arrested (10 June)
- Cromwell attainted in Parliament (29 June)
- Parliament begins debating the validity of Anna's marriage (6 July)
- Anna's marriage formally annulled by Act of Parliament (12 July)
- Execution of Cromwell (28 July)
- Marriage of Henry VIII and Katheryn Howard (28 July)
- Katheryn Howard proclaimed queen (8 August)
- Rumours that the King would take back Anna first emerge (October)
- Henry VIII and Katheryn Howard away on progress (August to October)

1541
- Anna of Cleve visits Henry VIII and Katheryn Howard at Hampton Court
- Thomas Culpeper resumes his courtship of Katheryn Howard (spring)
- State entry of Katheryn Howard to London (19 March)
- Katheryn Howard believed to be pregnant (March to April)
- Execution of Margaret Pole, Countess of Salisbury (27 May)
- Henry VIII and Katheryn Howard depart on progress to the north (30 June)
- Henry VIII and Katheryn Howard arrive at Lincoln (9 August)
- Katheryn Howard appoints Francis Dereham usher of her chamber (27 August)
- Henry VIII and Katheryn Howard arrive at York (18 September)
- Henry VIII and Katheryn Howard return to Windsor (26 October)
- Katheryn Howard placed under house arrest at Hampton Court (2 November)
- Francis Dereham arrested (before 6 November)
- Katheryn Howard's household discharged (13 November)
- Katheryn Howard sent to Syon Abbey (14 November)
- Thomas Culpeper imprisoned in the Tower (around 14 November)
- Lady Rochford imprisoned in the Tower (by 19 November)
- Dereham and Culpeper tried and condemned to death at the Guildhall (1 December)
- Dereham and Culpeper executed at Tyburn (10 December)

- Several persons implicated in Katheryn's offences condemned to imprisonment for misprision of treason (22 December)

1542

- Bill of Attainder against Katheryn Howard drawn up by Parliament (21 January)
- Royal assent given to the Act of Attainder condemning Katheryn Howard and Lady Rochford to death (9 February)
- Katheryn Howard conveyed to the Tower (10 February)
- Executions of Katheryn Howard and Lady Rochford (13 February)

Reading Group Questions

- *The Tainted Queen* opens and closes with death. After Katheryn's own mother dies, she frequently loses new mother figures, either through death or separation. Do you feel this has an impact on Katheryn's life and the choices she makes? How does this lack of a concerned, responsible adult's guidance lead to her craving attention whenever it is offered?

- *Katheryn would not join in the bedtime romps – but she could partake of the good cheer and companionship. Who was she to betray her friends? Having found Paradise, she was not about to leave it.* The laxity of the young women's life at Lambeth is startling, yet it is all drawn from contemporary first-person accounts. Do you feel it was inevitable that fun-loving, naive Katheryn would be drawn into the hedonism of the dorter? How did this affect your preconceptions of a certain rank of women in Tudor society?

- How did you react to the constant manipulation Katheryn faces from the men in her life – whether through the hopeless self-pity of her father; the ruthless expedience of her uncle, who clearly has not learned the lesson of his previous attempt to force a queen on Henry; the increasingly nasty obsession of Francis Dereham; or the questionable intentions of Tom Culpepper? With these examples around her, was it surprising to see her respect and love grow for Henry, who treats her as a gift from Heaven?

- *'It is a marvel to me that, in my old days, after so many troubles of mind caused by my marriages, I have obtained such a perfect jewel of woman-hood.'* As Henry says to Katheryn, he has 'married both for policy and for love. Love is the more important.' Katheryn understands early on how complicated Henry's character is and, while she uses his affection to achieve her own ambition, she does so with a genuine affection for him. The reader of course knows that this marriage too is doomed to end in disaster, so how does Alison manage to maintain such a compelling story line, showing Katheryn and Henry's growing relationship so sympathetically?

- Katheryn embraces her new role as queen with verve and joy, and has always had a sense of entitlement to power as a Howard – that was clearly drummed into her from a young age. At the same time, she is fearful, deep down, of her deepest secrets being revealed, and attempts to contain the knowledge of people around her. How does this affect her behaviour and relationships with others? Was she right to keep her old 'friends' close by?

- *It was folly for the Queen of England to behave so rashly. Her cousin, Queen Anne, seemed to be much in her thoughts these days. Yet she loved Tom so much . . .* Katheryn is often aware of the 'right' thing to do, then does the opposite. Writing the love letter to Tom, for example, which survives today, seems incredibly risky. Did you empathise with Katheryn's belief that her desire for Tom is irrepressible, and that Henry genuinely loves her too much to punish her cruelly, especially as they did not physically commit adultery? Or was she simply deeply foolish not to realise that the unpredictable, highly sensitive King would see any betrayal as a personal wound?

- Jane Rochford has lurked in the background of most of the Six Tudor Queens series, but here she becomes a key character, and her role in Katheryn's downfall is a real curiosity. Alison has used contemporary sources to tease out Jane's connection to Tom Culpeper and Katheryn herself, yet Jane's motivation remains shadowy and intense. What do you think led Jane to encourage their relationship when she had seen first-hand the dangers this type of betrayal could bring? Do you feel any pity for her, at the end?

- Did you find that Isabel's kindness is the direct opposite to Jane's malign and underhand influence? Her love and care for her half-sister throughout her life, even to the last page, makes her one of the few positive role models Katheryn can look to. For all the simplicity to her ambitions and pleasures in life, Katheryn can be insightful about other people, and recognises the contrast between them, so why does she turn from Isabel to Jane when under pressure to misbehave? And which of their two characters did you find most interesting and compelling?

- Katheryn's harridan grandam is a wonderful figure of powerful (if lazy) Tudor matriarchy; the royal children are briefly but memorably brought into the story; and we get to meet Henry's jester Will Somers along with many other historical figures. Which of these, or of Alison's other supporting characters, did you find most engaging? If you have read the other titles in the Six Tudor Queens series, who did you particularly look out for from the previous books, and why?

- *'No!' she shrieked. 'They're going to kill me! I won't go!' And she turned and began running back towards the silent abbey.* As the end approaches, Katheryn reacts with an instinctive fear that fits perfectly with the personality Alison Weir has crafted, before discovering her own courage. It is heart-breaking to witness – Katheryn's zest for living is so joyful, her flaws terribly human and her end pure tragedy. She retains a strange kind of innocence throughout the book, and yet so many lives in addition to hers are destroyed by the end of her story. Seeing the entire tale through her eyes only, what did you learn about Katheryn? Does Alison's portrayal give you a new insight and understanding of the young queen now remembered mainly for adultery and an early death?

- Alison Weir works a huge amount of careful research into the background of *The Tainted Queen*. How does she create the atmosphere behind the narrative with so strong a sense of authenticity and vibrancy, bringing to life the Tudor court, its political machinations and the world Katheryn inhabits? What most stood out for you among the many impressions of manor, castle, court and country, and what has changed in the course of the Six Tudor Queens series?